HOGZILLA

(FLORIDA MAN 2)

MIKE BARON

WOLFPACK
PUBLISHING
— EST 2013 —

Published in the United States by Wolfpack Publishing, Las Vegas

Wolfpack Publishing
6032 Wheat Penny Avenue
Las Vegas, NV 89122

wolfpackpublishing.com

Paperback ISBN 978-1-64734-185-5
eBook ISBN 978-1-64734-035-3

HOGZILLA

(FLORIDA MAN 2)

1 | HERMIONE

Gary and Krystal watched on producer Sid Saidso's phone from the courtroom in the Glades County Courthouse, as their trailer flew off in a plastic cloud. The house suspenders didn't work because the house was a piece of shit and disintegrated in the ninety mile an hour wind. Sid had set up a camera at Gary's trailer in anticipation of the *Gary Duba Show*.

The house suspenders worked great on Gary's previous home, Chateau Ami, the only house in Turpentine Acres, which was to have been an upscale gated community. Gary bought the house last summer with his lottery winnings. In a binge unprecedented since Caligula, Gary blew his millions on fancy cars, gifts to his friends, booze, and cocaine. The bank repossessed. Gary tried smuggling tarantulas, selling blow, and an iguana-themed restaurant. He even killed the largest python in state history, at the behest of dot com billionaire Orin Houtkooper, earning a cool hundred thousand, which barely covered the interest on his debt.

It was not until Gary and Krystal inadvertently caused the death of Plastic Surgeon to the Stars and serial killer Dr. Vanderlay Mukerjee that Gary surfaced from a swamp of bad publicity. Turpentine gave him the key to the city, a handsome twelve by eighteen rosewood plaque with a foot-long brass key, and a parking pass for all municipal lots.

As Gary and Krystal watched their earthly possessions howl into the void, Sid tried to cheer them up. "Soon you'll be rolling in dough. We haven't filmed the first episode and already sponsors are lining up! WD40! Duct Tape! Tillamook Beef Jerky! Duck Commander! Farm & Fleet! Are you guys ready to rock?"

Gary clapped his hands. "Let's rock!"

Major Sutton, at whose home Mukerjee had died, draped his arms over Gary's and Krystal's shoulders. "Hell of a day! Hell of a day!"

"It's not every day you get the key to the city and your house blows away," Krystal said.

"Ain't that the truth. Ain't that the truth."

As soon as the police issued the all clear, the courtroom emptied out. Everyone ran, including the press. Turpentine's streets were filled with fallen trees and trash, but damage was minimal. The real damage was northwest near Port Charlotte. Taking their key to the city, Gary and Krystal followed Sid's Cherokee in Gary's F-150. It took them forty-five minutes to reach Partridge Way, the dead-end road on which Gary had lived. They had to stop several times to move trees out of the way. They passed the Wokenoki Trailer Park, concrete rectangles stripped bare. Swamps decorated with shreds of plastic siding. Residents wandered zombie-like, plucking things from the wreckage.

The road dead-ended in the dirt turnaround. All that remained of Gary's double-wide were the cinder blocks on which it had perched. The pier survived and his swamp boat was upside down on a hummock twenty yards offshore.

"Fuck," Gary said.

"I wish we had some blow," Krystal said.

"You can do the *Gary Duba Show*, or you can do *Cops*. You can't do both."

Gary reached into his jeans for a fat doobie, lit up, toked, and passed it to Krystal, who toked, and passed it to Sid. Soon they were higher than the Space Needle. Krystal waded toward the stanchions, kicking palm fronds out of her path, uncovering a feral hog which ran off squealing.

"There's nothing left! Nothing!"

"Don't worry about it. We'll get new stuff."

"All my family photos."

"My baseball cards!"

"Where are we going to live?" Krystal asked.

"We have a meeting with the network tomorrow," Sid said. "Once they have your names on the dotted line, you will receive a two hundred fifty thousand-dollar advance."

Gary pumped his fist. "Ho shit!"

"Where do we stay tonight?"

"You can stay at a motel. I'll give you a thousand bucks. I'll pick you up at ten tomorrow and we'll drive to Miami.

The meeting's at two, in the Four Seasons."

Sid pulled out his wallet and peeled off ten crisp C-notes. "You can pay me back later." He got in his car. "Come on. You can leave the truck here."

Krystal slapped her hand on Gary's wrist and peeled off five. They drove past county crews sawing downed trees and loading them in dump trucks. They turned into the south side Walmart. The place was jammed with people stocking up. A woman pushed a shopping cart filled with toilet paper while pulling a shopping cart filled with toilet paper. Krystal went to women's clothes. Gary headed for the gun department.

"How much for the Predator? You got it in three-oh-eight?"

The clerk, a large doughy man in a shirt showing an American eagle sinking its claws into the head of the Russian bear, lit up. "We sure do. That's a sweet rifle. It's on sale right now for five hundred dollars."

Gary put his hand to his pocket and stopped. That would leave him one hundred and twenty dollars to get through the next couple of days. Plus, there was a three day waiting period. Plus, his rap sheet would freak them out. Better to purchase elsewhere.

"Ah, I'm just looking."

The clerk peered at Gary with pale tiny eyes. "I know you."

"Nah."

"Sure, I do! Weren't you the guy who claimed that those syringes the cops found in your rectum weren't yours?"

"Nope."

"Wait. Aren't you the guy who was arrested for defecating

on traffic from a lamp post?"

"Nope."

"Sex with an alligator."

"You got me confused, pal."

"Help me out here."

"I'm the guy who apprehended notorious serial killer and Plastic Surgeon to the Stars Doctor Vanderlay Mukerjee. They just gave me the key to the city."

The clerk's face lit up. "That's right! Congratulations!"

They shook hands. Gary got a basket, picked up toiletries and looked for Krystal. Sid sat on a bench past the checkout lanes absorbed in his Fonebone. Walmart had twenty checkout lanes but only two were staffed. Two employees stood in the empty Self-Checkout Corral waiting to help self-checkouts. Krystal stood at the back of a line of four working their way through one of the registers, behind a three hundred pound man in a pink jumpsuit in a handicapped cart loaded with groceries, including nine packs Twinkies, a case of Diet Coke, and six Swanson frozen dinners. Krystal wheeled a cart filled with panties, a bra, makeup, gold lame strap-ons, and a bottle of Blanc de Brut.

The Guatemalan clerk asked a woman ahead of them to reinsert her debit card.

"I don't know why it's not working," the woman whimpered.

"Buh-bye," Krystal muttered under her breath.

Gary put a hand on her arm. "Patience."

"She's been at it for ten minutes. Why's she buying ten cans of spinach? Who does she think she is? Olive Oyl?"

"Just chill."

The man ahead of them twisted around in his tractor seat. "You guys, ahmina back up. I been in this line for fifteen minutes. I gotta go."

Gary and Krystal stood back while the man backed up, wheeled his electric shopping scooter through the sliding glass doors into the foyer, got up and stomped off.

2 | FANS ALL OVER

The Lamplighter Motel was an L-shaped one-story with sixteen rooms, office at ninety degrees. Sid paid for the rooms. Several iguanas fought in the rain-water at the bottom of the pool which had been drained for the season. Gary and Krystal carried their packages into their room, which featured two queen-sized beds covered with green and purple paisley duvets, a LeRoy Neiman print of a horse race at Hialeah, and a flat screen TV on the opposite wall.

"You shower first," Gary said.

Minutes later, Gary slipped into the shower naked and cupped her boobs from behind.

"Ride me, Daddy, ride me!" she cooed while he grunted behind her.

Gary howled like a wolf. Krystal yelped like a cockatiel. Howling and yelping, they fell to the shower floor.

"OUCH!" Krystal said, putting her hand to the back of her head.

"Ow," Gary said, rubbing his elbow.

Drying off, Krystal gathered shampoo, conditioner and skin cream and put them in her backpack. She put a dab of L'Oreal in her hands and rubbed it into Gary's thick hair and combed it into a mullet.

They met Sid in the lobby at six and walked to Los Tres Amigos, an adobe-style Mexican restaurant. The storm had left behind a bracing evening in the seventies as they sat outside by a fountain, sconce mounted electric torches flickering, at a round table beneath an umbrella. Of the twelve tables, six were occupied. Gary noticed a skinny, black-haired, sunken-cheeked man in blue jeans and a cheap blue sport jacket seated beneath a royal palm in the corner, staring at them.

A sombreroed waiter took their order and headed for the door. Sid pulled a pen and pad from his gray Perry Ellis jacket. "Let's go over the first season. Each program will consist of twenty-two minutes of content. Each program will have a theme. We will follow each of you in turn, but mostly Gary. We'll do an episode where Krystal trains for a fight, and then the fight itself."

Krystal pulled an American Indian from a pack with her teeth. "I don't know if Delilah's down for that. She values her privacy. That's why she lives in the middle of nowhere."

"Delilah will be paid."

Krystal stared at Gary.

"What?"

"Light me up, you moron!"

Gary pulled a pack of matches from his jeans and lit it without closing the lid. Sun flared in his hand. Gary leaped to his feet shaking his hand violently.

"OUCH GODDAMNIT! I LIT MYSELF ON FIRE!"

Krystal tossed her water glass, hitting Gary in the face.

"Wha'dja do that for?"

"I was trying to put you out!"

The waiter set down three margaritas, followed by the manager, a short, bald-headed man wearing a bushy mustache, a shabby gray suit and a bolo tie, Eduardo on a pin on his chest. People stared. Hands hovered hesitantly over Fonebones.

"Is there a problem, my friends?"

Krystal lit her cigarette with a lighter. "Numbnutz here set himself on fire."

"I was trying to light your cigarette!"

"There's no smoking in here," the manager said.

"We're outside, for fuck's sake!"

Sid Saidso whipped out his Fonebone and peered like Lucien Ballard.

"City law. Nothing I can do about it."

Krystal threw the butt to the ground and smashed it with her shoe. "You gotta forgive us. We're upset about the storm. It blew our house away."

The manager's eyes widened in sympathy. "I'm so sorry to hear that. Let me buy your drinks."

The waiter returned. Gary ordered gator sausage gumbo. Sid ordered fish tacos. Krystal ordered a beef burrito. Diners murmured, pointed, and took photographs. The black-haired, sunken-cheeked man in blue jeans and a cheap blue sport jacket approached smelling of Paco Raban.

"Aren't you Gary Duba? Didn't you kill Plastic Surgeon to the Stars and serial killer Doctor Vanderlay Mukerjee?"

"Well I didn't kill him; a monitor lizard bit him and he had a stroke. Krystal here set the lizard loose. But it was my lizard."

The man pulled out his phone. "Can I get a picture?"

"Sure."

Krystal and Gary stood with the man between them while he took a selfie. They sat. The man remained.

"Would you like to see me with Tool Box Killer Lawrence Whittaker? I correspond with a number of serial killers and have visited several. I only regret I was unable to meet Doctor Mukerjee."

"Sorry," Gary said.

"It was my life's goal."

Sid leaned back. "We're having a meeting."

The man looked uncertainly from Gary to Sid. His face darkened. "My only goal was to meet Doctor Mukerjee and get his autograph on one of his pamphlets."

"He had a pamphlet?" Krystal said.

"He listed his procedures and prices. Face lift: $450. Butt lift: $550. I have a pamphlet signed by Paulina Perestroika."

"She was one of his customers?"

"It was the only thing I had to write on."

"Why would a butt lift cost more than the face lift?"

"How should I know? It was my dream to meet him and YOU KILLED HIM! YOU KILLED MY DREAMS!"

The stranger seized a steak knife from the next table and ran at Gary who backpedaled faster than a top fuel dragster. Krystal seized Gary's chair and brought it down on top of the madman's head, knocking him to the ground. Gary kicked him in the ribs with his lizard-skinned boots. Sid leaped to his feet and closed in filming. The manager ran toward them wringing his hands.

"Please," he said. "I must ask you to leave."

Krystal pointed at the serial killer groupie backing away on his pants. "He attacked Gary with a steak knife. Look! He's still got it!"

The man looked at the knife clutched in his hand, leaped to his feet, and rabbited over the wall.

The manager looked after him. "He took my steak knife."

"Sir," Krystal said, "we apologize for causing you any convenience. It's been a rough day. We just won the key to the city for stopping Plastic Surgeon to the Stars and notorious serial killer Doctor Vanderlay Mukerjee. Right after that, Hurricane Hermione destroyed our home. We're pretty shook up."

Sid handed the manager a C-note. "We'll keep it down."

The manager backed away. "Very good, sir."

A waiter cleared away the lone place setting where the berserker had sat. The waiter returned holding a tray on his shoulder, set three platters down and removed their lids. While they were eating, Sid pulled out his pad.

"Episode one will deal with Florida's biggest python. Episode two, how you got the key to the city. Episode Three will deal with the loss of your ancestral home, and how the Sugar Cane State Bank has allowed you to move back into your previous home in Turpentine Acres."

"What?" Gary squawked.

"Oh yes, didn't I tell you? They're one of our sponsors."

3 | RUSTIX

The seventy floor Four Seasons on Brickell Drive soared 789 feet, the second tallest building in Miami, with a commanding view of Biscayne Bay and Miami Beach. Rustix had reserved a meeting room on the fourth floor overlooking the pool and cabanas. Sid stopped at Cripple Creek Ranch Wear in Miramar where Gary bought fresh jeans, a Scully Horseshoe Rose Embroidered shirt, a Lucchese men's tan mad dog brown hobby stitched belt and a Stetson Seneca. Krystal wore Mikah High-Rise Snakeskin-Print Leather Pants over a lavender blouse with the top two buttons undone, and a ragged black thrift store motorcycle jacket with a half dozen zippers, her red hair hanging in a ponytail from beneath a Wild One hat. Sid wore a seersucker suit.

They walked through the lobby toward the elevator bank, past furniture clusters on Rothko rugs, turbaned sheiks, a Eurotrash couple, he in gray silk suit and sunglasses, she in a yellow sundress, clutching a *Bichon Frise*, three Miami Heat players towering over everyone, Mickey Rourke clutching a Chihuahua, and Axl Rose holding a corgi.

They rode the mirrored elevator with an elderly Jewish couple. He wore a yarmulke, she a sky-blue dress and aggressive perfume. On the fourth floor, they walked down the hushed corridor, floor to ceiling windows looking out on the expansive pool and Biscayne Bay, until they came to the Saratoga Park Room. Inside, four executives rose from a lozenge-shaped table on which sat laptops, briefcases, and stacks of paper. The three men looked like a Russian nesting doll, one jumbo, one medium, and one small. The jumbo a hale Irishman with a red nose, the medium, a chocolate Beau Brummel in a Versace *Pied de Poule* silk blazer and slacks, the small a bumptious Buddy Holly in jeans and a gray Perry Ellis blazer, the woman, a cool brunette in silk slacks and a white shirt.

Jumbo reached them first. "Gary Duba! Steely Danielle! I'm Bob Fahey. These are my associates, Eric Narwhal, Rick Stuben, and Amanda Gregory. On behalf of the Rustix Network, welcome!"

They shook hands.

"I saw you fight at the Roxy!" Stuben gushed, horn-rimmed glasses bobbing up and down. "You beat Cassowary!"

Krystal returned his grip. "That was a memorable evening." The promoter, Downtown Brown, lit out with the box office and hadn't been heard of since. Later, the cops arrested Gary for skipping out on a restaurant bill.

"Have a seat!" Fahey boomed. "Help yourself to coffee and beignets!"

Gary and Sid got coffee. Gary, Krystal and Sid sat opposite the Rustix execs. Gregory folded her hands. "Are you familiar with the Rustix Network?"

"Not really," Gary said. "I don't have much time to watch TV." They watched Gary's dad's old *Hee Haw* and *Dukes of Hazzard* VHS tapes and were fond of Randolph Scott Westerns. Hurricane Hermione had taken it all away.

Sid held up a hand and counted off on his fingers. "*Upholstery Wars, Honey Wagon, Kubik's Rubes, Root, Hog, or Die, Pasta King.* You guys are geniuses. I particularly enjoy *Ribald Piebalds.*"

Eric Narwhal smiled. "Thank you. That's my baby."

"How do you get them to rut like that?"

"We give them veterinary Viagra."

Gary set down his mug. "Can I get some of that?"

"No," Narwhal said. "It's strictly for animals."

Krystal elbowed him. "What about that veterinarian?"

Narwhal tapped his pad. "Anyway, we have a list of the first four episodes. The first episode will bring people up to speed on Gary, starting with his lottery win, the alligator in the pool, the fire, the anaconda, the death of Plastic Surgeon to the Stars and serial killer Doctor Vanderlay Mukerjee, and Turpentine awarding him the key to the city."

"You oughtta get Major in there," Gary said.

Narwhal made a note. "We'll talk to Major. He's an important part of the story."

"What about Steely Danielle?" Sid said.

Narwhal made a note. "I wonder if we can expand this opening episode to forty-four minutes. Let's look into that, Bob."

Fahey beamed, lacing his fingers over his expansive gut. "By all means."

"Episode Two will recreate your hunt for Florida's biggest python. We have Houtkooper's permission to use news footage, but he has declined to appear. Episode Three will deal with The Lizard Lounge and aftermath. Episode Four will deal with Plastic Surgeon to the Stars and serial killer

Doctor Vanderlay Mukerjee. Episode Five—I'm penciling in Steely Danielle. Do you have an upcoming event?"

"I'm fighting Transgender athlete A Thing Called Xue on January fourteenth."

"What weight?" Gregory asked.

"Catch weight at one eighty."

Gregory gasped. "You can't make that weight!"

"Of course not. I'll probably go in at one twenty-five."

"He'll pound you into gravy!"

Sid stuck out a pencil. "Let's not refer to A Thing Called Xue as 'he'. Thing's preferred pronoun is Xue."

Narwahl's forehead erupted in wrinkles. "Xe?"

"Think of it as Ojibwa language. Say it with me. Man called Xue."

"Thing called Xue," the Rustix execs dutifully recited.

Gregory shook his head. "As a pro wrestler, you know you have virtually no chance of beating a man who outweighs you by fifty pounds."

"Thing called Xue is transgendered."

The Rustix execs looked at each other in disbelief.

Narwhal plowed ahead.

"Episode six, we're undecided whether to go with iguanas or feral hogs. Do you have any preference?"

Gary crossed his arms and looked at the ceiling. "Gotta go with iguana. They're a lot easier to catch. Besides, isn't there already a show about feral hogs?"

"American Hoggers," Fahey said. "We thought about doing a crossover. They come here to help you hunt, and then you go there and help them catch rattlesnakes."

"Fuck that," Gary said.

Narwhal marked something in his pad. "Iguanas it is."

"Iguanas are the smart choice," Amanda Gregory said. "They're exploding in South Florida, brawling in the street, parks, and homes. Animal control is overwhelmed. The legislature has a bill offering a bounty. Iguanas are the second leading cause of power outages."

Gary did double finger snaps into his palm. "Now you're talkin'! I'll need some guns. That's a legit business expense, ain't it?"

The Rustix executives looked to Fahey. "No guns. You can trap them. You can poison them or use machetes."

"Ya poison 'em, you can't eat 'em," Gary pointed out.

"We can do a show that tracks dinner from the field to the table," Krystal said. "We see Gary kill it, skin it, and cook it. We can invite some of these celebrity chefs."

Fahey looked at his crew. Frowns of consideration, nodding. "That's a great idea. Amanda, would you get in touch with Gordon Ramsay and Rachel Ray?"

"You got it."

"Contracts!" Sid said.

Gregory reached for her Coach briefcase, pulled out thick wads of paper, and handed one each to Sid, Gary, and Krystal.

"Whereza pen?" Gary said.

Krystal put her hand on his arm. "Not so fast. We gotta have a lawyer go over this first."

"Of course," Fahey nodded. "I would be happy to recommend a good entertainment attorney."

Gary held his hand up. "We got it covered. Could you email the contracts to Habib Rodriguez?"

4 | VIKINGS

Sugar City State Bank agreed to let Gary and Krystal return to Chateau Ami in Turpentine Acres if Gary would be their pitchman. Done deal. The day after the Rustix meeting, Gary and Krystal drove to their once and future home. While they were away investors had sold five houses on the street that dead ended at Chateau Ami. The road to the housing development was littered with palm fronds, branches, and plastic bags. There was now a sliding steel gate between stucco posts, and a gate house. The hand-painted Turpentine Acres sign had been replaced by a hand-painted Kensington Gardens sign with a coat of arms. A gryphon, an eagle, and a harp. A Groome Security guard saw them coming from his booth and opened the gate. Gary pulled inside and got out. The security guard was a big man, crewcut, looked like ex-cop, wearing a tan uniform with Bill embroidered on his left chest.

"Gary Duba?"

"Yes sir," Gary said, producing a letter from Sugar City.

"They said I could start moving back in today."

"I'm Bill Preston." Preston handed Gary two identical keys on Groome Security plastic fobs. "Nice work with Plastic Surgeon to the Stars and serial killer Doctor Vanderlay Mukerjee."

"Thank you."

They shook hands.

"I'll turn off the burglar alarm from here." He fished in a pocket and pulled out a card. "This is the head honcho."

Gary looked at the card. "Leopold Bing?"

"Let me know if there's anything else I can do."

They passed five new haciendas, all Spanish style, stucco with red tile roofs, all in excess of five thousand square feet, all with pools and four car garages, two with plywood boarded windows and downed trees still in the yard. Chateau Ami was the last house on Bougainvillea Court before a forest that segued into swamp. Where once had stood a mighty hedge of bougainvillea was now flattened shrubbery with deep mud ruts caused by heavy equipment. Behind the house, the solid green wall gave no evidence of the fire seven months ago, when Gary tried to burn an alligator with his flame thrower, igniting his Lamborghini Urus. Lambo parts still littered the landscape.

Gary drove past two concrete plugs with iron rings.

"Sum bitches took down my house suspenders."

Krystal gestured. "And yet, here it is."

Gary parked in the turn around. The fountain was dry. Chateau Ami was nine thousand square feet with six bedrooms and nine baths, two story foyer with grand staircase, formal dining room, sunken formal living room with fireplace and three sets of arched French doors, gourmet kitchen, breakfast room, family room with vaulted ceilings, home office, billiards room, wine cellar, gym, home theater, four car garage, covered loggia, infinity swimming pool with spa, and a guest house with a tennis court. They unlocked the realtor lock on the front door and went in. The house smelled of mildew and Pine Sol. Most of the furniture had been put in storage. All the rugs were gone from the living room and they could see pale circles on the parquet floor where cleaners had used chemicals to get rid of the blood stains.

There was a knock at the door. A middle-aged man in Bermuda shorts, straw hat, sunglasses, sandals, and loud Hawaiian shirt stood on the stoop holding a six-pack of Swamp Heads.

"Hi!" he said. "I'm Boris Bongo Box. I live right up the street. Are you the Dubas?"

"Yup."

"Saw you on the news. Figured you might be back. Want a beer?"

"Come in, Boris."

Boris walked a little ways into the living room, put his hands on his hips and looked around. "They say you shot a feral pig in here. Is that right?"

"I shot the sum bitch, but the rest got away."

"They say this place is haunted. That's why it hasn't sold."

"Haunted?" Krystal said.

"By what?"

"By the death of some cartel boss. El Cheapo."

"He was here a couple times, but the only blood in this house comes from that feral hog I shot."

"And that time someone shot Patrice in the leg."

"Yeah, well, we was aiming for that gator. That was just bad luck."

Boris put his hands up. "Just what I hear."

"From who?"

"My son Peter. He's twenty. He's studying environmental science at Colorado State. I saw your press conference. You're gonna have your own show?"

"Just, like, a day in the life, you know. They follow me around while I hunt gators, make shine or cook up some iguana. It's gonna be like a cooking show. I mean part of it. Mostly it's just gonna be me doing what I do, and some on Krystal when she's training or fighting. What do you do, Boris?"

"I'm chief engineer at Skoal Robotix. We make robot dogs for police departments and robot security guards for malls. I make robot sculpture. I'm hoping to get my latest in the Miami Museum of Modern Art. I've got a show next week. Maybe you'd like to come."

"Sure. Whadha make?"

"It's a kinetic sculpture shaped like a bull."

"You made a mechanical bull?"

Boris laughed. "Bison, actually. Not the kind you ride, although you could I suppose. It has full mobility. Carries its own sound system. I may do a video. I play keyboards too."

"Come on back."

Gary opened the sliding glass doors leading to the patio,

and the pool, which was covered with a green tarp. It was a warm, humid, late morning in December. "Home sweet home. We were only here for three months."

They stood around the tarped pool. "So this is where it happened," Bongo Box said.

"You mean the gator? Yeah, we had six guys out here shooting the sumbitch. That's how Patrice got shot. Ricochet off the patio." He pointed to a groove in one of the stones.

"Fuck izzis?" Krystal said, staring at the tarp. She cupped her ear. "You hear that? There's something down there."

There was a ragged hole chewed through the vinyl topping at the shallow end. Gary got down and put his ear over the hole.

"Holy fuck! What's going on down there?"

Boris squatted and listened intently over the deep end. "Sounds like something skittering around. Some kind of squawking."

Gary drew his pocketknife and flicked it open. "Fuck me... fuck me..."

Bongo Box pointed to the tie-down posts, held in place with cotter pins. "Wouldn't it be easier to just pull these pins and roll it back?"

"Good idea." They unpinned the tarp, leaving only the cotter pins at the shallow end. Gary got on one side and Bongo Box on the other. "Let's pull it back."

They walked the tarp back and looked. Green iguanas fighting in the brackish water, doing Matrix kicks off the sides. Krystal put a hand to her mouth. "Oh my God..."

"Yeah," Bongo Box said, "they're getting to be a real problem. I had to chase a couple off our patio last week."

"Got any guns?" Gary said.

"No. There's no shooting in Kensington Gardens. It's in the rule book."

"The fuck you say!"

The iguanas didn't look up. It looked like a scene out of *Vikings*. Gary called Floyd on his Fonebone.

"Floyd, we got a situation."

Gary described the situation.

"I got a job in Cables this afternoon, but I can come over tomorrow. I got a couple twenty-twos we can use."

"Can't shoot 'em. It's against the rules."

"No problem. You'll see when I get there."

Gary counted eighty-six iguanas. "Man, it's a shame I had to shut down the Lizard Lounge."

"Would you folks like to join Marie and me for dinner?" Bongo Box said. "We're going to grill."

"You want some of these iguanas?"

"No. We have hamburgers."

Gary looked at Krystal. "We got nothing better to do."

They walked up the street to Bongo Box's manse, wings enclosing the patio and pool. Bongo Box's four car garage contained an oxblood SUV, a new Miata, and a hulking shape covered in a tarp. Bongo Box whipped off the tarp revealing a hulking machine with a humped middle made of a hexagonal steel frame, hexagonal tubes enclosing a massive humped back, standing on four titanium legs hinged to bend backward like a dog. The body was the same front and rear like a palindrome. Boris had mounted a buffalo head on the front, with curving horns. A vestigial tail made of an old car antenna.

Boris flipped a switch behind the horns. "Say hello, Tallywhacker."

The creature snorted and dipped its horns. "Hello," it said in a sonorous bass.

Krystal jumped. "Holy shit!"

Boris laughed. "It has the latest AI software and an organic brain made from cloned T-Rex cells."

"Am I supposed to talk to it?"

"You can."

"Hey, Tallywhacker. Who do you like in the playoffs?" Krystal said.

Bad feedback screeched like the sound check at a Tool concert. Gary and Krystal slapped hands to ears. Boris reached out and shut Tallywhacker off with a switch at the base of the neck.

"Sorry about that."

"Can you ride him?"

"You could. He's very strong. I gave him an internet hookup so he can familiarize himself with the culture. Maybe I should ride him in the video while playing keyboards."

"You got yourself a show," Krystal said.

"You know, babe, you could star. I mean, now that we're hooked up with a production company and you're already famous."

Bongo Box looked at them quizzically. "She's famous?"

5 | WHAT'S FOR DINNER?

"Ain't you heard of the Black Dildo?"

"No."

"Where you been hidin'?" Krystal said, jaw jutting.

"I don't spend a lot of time on social media."

"Don't you follow pro wrestling?"

A hint of fear crept into Bongo Box's face. "I'm afraid we don't. We watch the Dolphins."

"I wrestle as Steely Danielle, 'coz they can't call me Black Dildo," Krystal said matter-of-factly. "I got my own comic book."

"Comic book?"

Gary pointed his finger. "You wait right here. I'll get you one."

Gary jogged down the driveway and headed back to Chateau Ami.

Krystal pointed to the house. "It happened right over there. We'd scarce been in the place three months before they came to evict us. Tell you the truth, Gary ain't the greatest financial genius. I mean, he won seven million dollars. How do you go broke in three months?"

Two feral hogs dashed across the scrub across the street, where a concrete foundation rose.

"Association's going to have to do something about those hogs," Boris said.

Gary jogged back and handed Boris a comic in a mylar sleeve with backing board. *The Black Dildo*. The cover showed Krystal flying through the air in a shiny black super outfit with a yellow cape, whacking a Russian thug—in a striped suit with wide lapels sideways—with a three foot rubber dildo, while emaciated caged children watched in the background. You knew the bad guy was Russian from the bottle of WODKA and bowl of borscht on a table. Another thug lay spread-eagled on his back wearing a wife beater, all tatted up with Russian gang markings. Christ on the cross, Orthodox church chained rose, snake-entwined dagger.

"We hadda change the bad guys from cops to Russian gangsters on accounta, you know, I don't want to piss 'em off any more than I already have."

"I'll sign that for you," Krystal said.

"Well come on in the house and meet Marie."

They went from the garage through a big kitchen, a stucco dining room with an avocado green tile floor, oak table finished with a carved vine pattern, a sideboard beneath a black velvet painting of a matador in a gold lamé suit and red scarf facing a bull that looked like Mt. Shasta, through the sunken living room, copies of Vanity Fair and the New Yorker on a glass table, out sliding glass doors to the patio where Marie, a lush Latina beauty with lustrous auburn hair, turned to face them.

"So! Our scandalous neighbors!"

Bongo Box kissed Marie on the cheek and introduced Gary and Krystal.

Bongo Box handed the comic to Marie. "Krystal has her own comic book."

Marie held it delicately. "I'll read this later."

Krystal snapped it up. "Let me sign that for you."

She set it on the cedar picnic table, opened it to the splash page and wrote, "To our fabulous neighbors, the Bongo Boxes! Love, Krystal, aka "Steely Danielle."

Boris picked it up. "I'm taking this inside. We don't want anything to happen to it.

Baby, do have more hamburgers?"

"They're in the freezer. Defrost them in the microwave. Four minutes."

"We're gonna be neighbors," Gary said. "We're moving back in."

Marie had a beauty queen smile. "Did Boris tell you your house is haunted?"

"How can it be haunted if we ain't in it?"

"I don't know. I never thought about it that way."

The Bongo Box's sloping lawn ended at a lake, cattails and reeds erupting everywhere. Two foundations had been laid at seven and ten. A white resort clubhouse sprawled on the north end with several piers sprouting slips and boat lifts for canoes, kayaks, and one-masted sailboats. Across lay forest.

"You got kids?" Marie said.

"We ain't responsible enough to have kids."

"None that I know of," Krystal said.

"No one thinks they can handle kids until they have kids. We have two. A boy and a girl. Peter is at Colorado State studying environmental science. Lynn is studying microbiology at Stanford."

"Is he gonna be a weatherman?"

"He doesn't know what he wants to be. Would you like a drink?"

"Sure," Krystal said. "You got a sea breeze?"

Marie turned to Gary. "What about you?"

"Hell, I'll take a glass of bourbon."

Marie headed for the house, skirt swirling, holding the door for Boris on the way out with a platter of burgers. "Coming right up."

Two feral hogs emerged from the weeds across the lake to drink.

"You think those're the same damn hogs?"

Boris stood at the grill, wearing a denim apron with pockets holding tongs and spatula. "Long as they stay over there."

"That's the same gang that raided my house. I recognize their colors. You hunt?"

"No. We shop at Whole Foods."

"You and me should go hunting sometime. We used to practically live off wild hogs."

Boris put the burgers on the grill. Marie came out with a tray of drinks.

"Do you need any glasses or dishes? We have tons."

Krystal sipped her sea breeze. "That would be great. All our stuff got blown away in the hurricane. Did you have much wind damage?"

"We were without power for forty-eight hours. Fortunately, I had a generator. It took them a day before they could get in here and clear the trees. We had to replace some windows. Two houses were completely devastated."

"Sumbitches took down my house suspenders," Gary groused.

"Oh, they worked. The home-owners' association took them off the day after."

"What home-owners' association?"

Boris flipped burgers. "Kensington Gardens Home-Owners' Association. How do you like your burgers?"

"Medium," Krystal said.

"Kensington Gardens?! What the hell? What owners? We're the only ones here."

Boris flipped burgers. "Actually, the lots are ninety per cent sold and they're building thirteen houses on the other side of the lake, beyond the woods."

Boris pulled the burgers, set them on gluten free buns on china plates. "There's salad over there, and the condiments are on the table."

Gary grabbed his plate. "Don't you have to live in a place to be on the board? Who's on the board? I ain't on it. Are you on it?"

Boris shrugged. "I'm on the board. The board is all owners, they just haven't moved in yet. You can be on the board if you want to run."

"Screw that."

"Or they're speculators," Marie said, sitting at the cedar picnic table. She'd put the ketchup out in a terracotta bowl with a little spoon. The mustard was in a silver tureen.

"Do you know who they are?"

"What's the big deal?" Krystal said. She turned to their hosts. "He has trouble with authority."

Gary chewed with authority. He swallowed. A shard of onion struggled and was sucked in. "That coat of arms oughtta be a hog, a gator, and an iguana."

Marie gestured excitedly. "Oh look! The iguanas are fighting!"

Halfway down the greensward, two iguanas were going at it, toe to toe. A bobcat rushed from the shrubbery and seized one in its jaws, shaking violently.

"Boris!" Marie cried. "Do something!"

"What? Why?"

Marie turned away. "I can't watch."

Gary sipped his bourbon. "I got a magnum in the truck, but I can't hit shit at this distance. And you can only hunt bobcats during bobcat season. We'll have you folks over for an iguana cook-out. I used to have a restaurant called the Lizard Lounge. We specialized in iguana. You need any? We got a shitload."

The bobcat had settled down near the water to eat its iguana.

"Can a bobcat kill a wild hog?" Marie asked. "I really prefer bobcats."

All paused to gaze at God's creature peacefully enjoying its repast. A twelve-foot alligator lunged from the water, seized the startled bobcat in its jaws and withdrew, leaving only expanding ripples and a dead iguana.

Marie crossed herself. "Mother of God."

"I'll bring this up with the association," Bongo Box said.

Gary chowed down. "Don't worry about it. I'll get rid of it."

6 | THE BURT REYNOLDS PLAYHOUSE

After three bourbons, Gary related his gun battle with Judge Murphy. "Yeah, there we was, Floyd and me, neck and neck with Judge Murphy in her Mercedes doing 'bout eighty-five, trading shots! Fortunately, cooler heads prevailed, and we exited the highway at Billy Bob's. They never did buy my rookie card, cheap sumbitch."

Marie started clearing dishes. Krystal rinsed them off in the sink, ran the Insinkerator, and handed them to Marie. "We'll have you guys over as soon as we get settled. Place still isn't furnished. It's a shame. We had a lot of nice furniture, but it all got repossessed."

"You say Gary has a TV show?"

"We just signed the contracts. That's how we can afford to move back into our ancestral home. We already started filming, like our press conference. We got all that."

"When and where does this show appear?"

"It's gonna be on Rustix in the fall."

Marie stacked dishes in the big Westinghouse dishwasher. "We have expanded cable. I'll have to look and see if we get Rustix."

"Gary's killed gators before, so don't you worry about that. He killed an anaconda with a machete. Chopped its head clean off. He had to duct tape it back on for the cameras."

"What cameras?"

"Orin Houtkooper offered a hundred grand for whoever caught the biggest anaconda. It was in all the papers."

Marie's eyes widened with new appreciation. "Oh! You know Orin?"

"Well Gary does. There's a photo of him and Orin with the snake. Hang on..."

Krystal poked at her Fonebone, triumphantly presenting the color photo from the front page of the *Miami Herald Examiner: BIGGEST SNAKE EVER/Fonebone Inventor Honors Local Man.*

"We know Orin through Boris' business. What a small world. He's also a great patron of the arts."

It was now dark. Gary and Boris sat in the den lit by green-shaded banker's lamps, smoking Havanas.

"I don't suppose there's video of my house during the hurricane."

Boris tilted back in a leather Barcalounger beneath a framed poster of *The Day the Earth Stood Still*, the original in black and white. "There might be. We installed cameras on the streetlamps back in July. Kids kept sneaking in and tagging the foundations."

"Why'd you remove my house suspenders?"

"We didn't know you were coming back. The realty company thought they were a liability."

"Liability, hah! I need that footage! House Suspenders are the next big thing. They're gonna revolutionize the housing industry."

Boris tapped a fat ash into an amber tray on his rosewood desk. "You've got a TV show. Why do you need *Piranha Pool*?"

"It's been my dream ever since I thought 'em up, about ten years ago. They woulda saved my trailer if it hadn't been built out of plastic shit. I got the video of the whole thing breaking up and flying off into the swamp. Looked like a flock of seagulls."

"Don't you have to have some kind of business record to get on *Piranha Pool*? Sell some house suspenders?"

"My agent's gonna get me on. Same company owns *Piranha Pool* as owns Rustix. We'll get a few sets out there, but the problem is, we need heavy weather to prove that they work. They're like insurance. Nobody wants it to happen. But if it happens, you'd better have insurance. How'd you like a set? Next hurricane might be a lot bigger. This was only a category three. I'll install 'em myself. I'll only charge you for the materials."

"Let me talk that over with Maria. It's a very generous offer."

"Omma put 'em back up. What did they do with the chains?"

"I believe they're in your garage."

"Omma string 'em with Christmas lights."

Boris opened a drawer. "Let me give you a copy of the rules." He handed Gary a sheath of stapled pale blue paper. Gary thumbed through.

"Holy shit. There are a lot of rules."

"They're all designed to promote community."

"No bonfires?"

"Do you golf? We're putting in eighteen holes on re-claimed swamp land. Designed by Max Swell."

Gary frowned at the blue paper. "No shooting? I can't shoot on my own property? How do you expect me to bag that gator?"

"We can vote for an exemption considering the public safety. I can call an emergency meeting next week. They might want to hire it out to an expert."

Gary blew smoke at Boris. "I am an expert. Listen. This is gonna be a great episode on my show! We can do a nice little tribute to the community. Hopefully, there will be more people."

Boris glanced at his watch. "Gary, I hate to kick you out, but Marie and I have a video call with our daughter in a few minutes."

Gary stood. "Thanks for having us over, hoss! You look into that gator thing, will ya? We can really put this place on the map. And see what you can find in the way of video. It would really help me on *Piranha Pool* if I can show the house suspenders in action."

Marie said goodbye to them in the stucco foyer. "We're so happy for you! And happy that you're moving back in!"

"We'll have you guys over as soon as we get settled," Krystal promised. "I'll make my famous possum stew."

Maria beamed in the arched doorway for a second before closing it. Hand in hand, Gary and Krystal walked down the blacktop toward their house beneath a canopy of stars. Wild pigs snorted from the woods. Bobcats yowled. Owls hooted.

"Kensington Gardens my ass," Gary growled.

Krystal laughed. "I know!" She whirled away, curtsied and said in a thick Cockney accent, "'Er royal 'ighness will see you now, ducks! What kind of name is Bongo Box?"

"I think it's Cuban. He had the cigars. They're putting in a golf course. Wanted to know if I golf."

"They should put in a bowling alley."

"You ain't wrong, little girl. Maybe once we get settled we'll look at putting one in ourselves. And a theater that shows classic movies. Porky's. Porky's Two. Roadhouse. Stuff like that."

"The Burt Reynolds Playhouse."

"Ah, you got it, little girl. Maybe I can buy his wig back and we can put it on display in the lobby."

7 | KRYSTAL SHOPS

Feral hogs had destroyed a nine-thousand dollar sofa before Gary and Krystal were evicted. They'd gained access because she and Gary were spaced out on horse tranquilizers, lying in their own drool as hogs entered through the open patio door. No more nine thousand-dollar sofas. No more feral hogs.

Never again.

Since training with Delilah, Krystal had turned over a new leaf. No blow. A little reefer. Okay. Some wine. But the hard stuff was done. Finito. No blow, no crack. She pulled into the ARC Thrift Store, next to Greims' Drive-In, currently showing *Razorback and Rogue*, went into the one-story building and grabbed a cart, inhaling dust, the smell of old clothing, shoes, newsprint. Row after row of shabby men's clothes on steel poles. Jumbles of sporting gear including boxing gloves, hockey sticks, bicycle helmets and snowboards. She roamed the aisles along with a dozen other hopefuls, examining souvenir mugs, ugly sweaters, and jigsaw puzzles.

She found a three-foot plaster Yosemite Sam wearing a fur hat, clutching a cartoon shotgun and put it in her shopping cart next to two lava lamps, a boom box, and a framed painting of dogs playing poker. It would never replace the black velvet Elvis Gary had traded to El Cheapo in exchange for cleaning up after the hogs. Now El Cheapo was dead, murdered by El Nariz, the narco gangster who mysteriously disappeared. El Nariz's forty acre estate in the glades was in ruins, his exotic animals fled into the jungle. Ocelots. Vampire parrots. Hippos.

Krystal had eight weeks to train for A Man Called Xue at Delilah's place in the Everglades. Hot. Humid. Mosquitoes. Anaconda. Monitor lizards. Iguana. No cell reception. At least Delilah made her own shine.

Krystal pulled out onto Trax Avenue and headed for Billy Bob's, adjusted her Fonebone and went live. "Hi, y'all. This is Krystal Duba, aka Steely Danielle, aka you know what. I'm sorry I look like hell, but we've been living out of motels the last couple days on accounta the storm. Now at last we're moving back into our original home in Turpentine Acres, excuse me, Kensington Gardens."

Gripping the wheel with both hands, she raised her pinkie. "Kensington Gardens, dahlings! Strictly uppah crust!"

"As you can see, I just made a haul at the ARC Thrift Store and I'm heading home with a full load. I got a plaid sofa. I got a coffee table with somebody's initials. I got a lamp made out of a bull pizzle. I got a three-foot Yosemite Sam for the front yard."

"As my loyal fans know, I fight A Man Called Xue in eight weeks. I'm going out to Delilah's to train. Y'all tune in when I fight, you'll see Delilah. She's a witchee woman. You don't want to mess with her. She'll turn you into a catfish. They're gonna film me training, so you all are gonna get to meet Delilah. Oh, and by the way. Watch for the *Gary Duba Show* on Rustix. It's coming soon. I'll let y'all know."

"I'll be going dark shortly. There's no cell service down in the boonies. There's no reception. It's like fuckin' New Guinea or something. They got spiders the size of doughnuts and I have to wrestle a bear. His name is Samson and he's really very nice, but he slobbers. The shower is outside. I'm on a diet of fried okra and swamp meat. Okay. Gotta pause here, I'm going into Billy Bob's Pawn Shop."

She pulled into Billy Bob's around ten. A nine-foot neon sign with a palm tree flashed sequential rings at the entrance. Across the street was LIVE GATORS, BABY GATORS FOR THE KIDS, STUFFED GATORS, parking lot filled with tourists.

Billy Bob's was a one-story building with two horizontal windows showcasing everything from stuffed gators to gold coins. Three slackers stunted and vaped. Two teenage girls sat on the concrete in front staring at their personal devices. One had pink hair, the other blue. Krystal pulled into a spot between a Chevy pick-up and a rented Hyundai and got out, wearing form-fitting jeans and a pink Lady Gaga T-shirt that clung to her supple body.

A skater with a hairline mustache that looked etched with

magic marker rolled her way exhaling smoke like a Kiddie Land locomotive. "Hey pretty Momma, want a toke?"

Fists on hips, biceps bulging, she gave him the Look.

"Okay, okay, I guess not."

He rolled back to hoots and laughter.

Billy Bob's was filled with glass cases, one wall devoted to musical instruments, drums, 'bones, pianos, and two dozen guitars. One wall was nothing but flat screen TVs. A long glass cabinet was filled with pistols and knives. Racks of rifles and shotguns stood at attention. Krystal perused DVDs. Twelve copies of *American Dreamz*, fourteen copies of *Thank You for Smoking*, two feet of *Lord of the Rings, Batman Begins, Batman Returns, Batman Flies, Batman Dies, Batman Revives, Batman Forever. The Best Little Whorehouse in Texas* went in the basket with a hardbound *Valley of the Dolls*. Delilah had no television. Krystal grabbed a clutch of Hope Ford biker books, *Rancher, Sniper*, and *Brick*, all featuring shirtless, inked sweaty men on the cover, and *Devil's Boneyard MC #7* by Harley Wylde.

She tried on an ivory Stetson, turning this way and that in the mirror. She put it on.

She eyed a Jackson Toscana sheep skin for Gary. She pulled it from the rack and held it against her body. It smelled new.

"Yeah, that's a beauty," Billy Bob said. He was a lovable bear whose dense black beard concealed no chin, wearing a fisherman's vest with pockets holding pens, knives, and pliers, wearing 40/32 Relaxed Fit Levi's. "Hellah (No, this is a version of the word hellfire.) Krystal. Ain't seen you in a coon's age."

"Whaddaya say, Billy Bob? Will you take six?"

Billy Bob snorted. "That's a brand-new Toscana. Retails for fifteen hundred. Bought it off a guy goin' through a painful divorce. He swore he'd be back. That was two months ago. Gave him four hundred 'cause I felt sorry for him. I been divorced myself three times. That's prob'ly one too many. I mean, everybody's entitled to a starter divorce."

"Six hundred, Billy Bob."

Billy Bob frowned. "Seein' as you're famous and will surely mention this fine establishment when you talk to the press, I will take your six hundred."

Krystal peeled them off. "Thank you kindly, Billy Bob. I'll talk you up 'til the cows come home. It's a gift for my husband."

"Last time Gary was in here, he chased off all my customers with a gator."

"He's real sorry about that, Billy Bob."

"He oughtta step up and say so."

"You know, you're right. I'll get on his ass. I'll also take this hat."

Stuffing her goodies in the van, Krystal primped in the rearview, fixed her lipstick, smoothed her red hair and hit the highway.

"I'm back," she announced to the faithful. "Whatcha all think of this hat? I got it at Billy Bob's."

8 | RETURN TO PARADISE

When Krystal wheeled into their driveway at four in the afternoon, Gary and Floyd Belmont were installing the second house suspender, pulling it over the roof over a child's blue plastic playground slide. A yellow plastic slide rested under the first chain. Floyd's new van sat on the bricks. Belmont Holistic Pest Solutions was painted on the side. Krystal got out and looked up to where the boys perched on the roof.

"Don't you boys fall off!"

Floyd made the okay sign. The hairy mesomorph wore baggy shorts, Betsy Ross shoes, and a loud Hawaiian shirt featuring Ed "Big Daddy" Roth. The Beatnik Bandit. The Mysterion. Rat Fink.

Gary pointed to a nylon rope stuffed through his leather belt. The other end was tied to the chain's apex, twenty-five feet in the air. The boys scrambled down the extendable aluminum ladder and helped Krystal carry her booty into the house. Gary set Yosemite Sam on the stoop and stood back in admiration.

"Damn! We should put this out on the lawn."

"That's what I was thinking. Floyd, you staying for dinner?"

"Sure."

They went out the patio to the back yard where the heavy marine chain hung slack. Wearing leather gloves, Floyd and Gary pulled the chain, clanking, over the plastic slide, dragging it taut to the cement plug, fastened it with a massive steel clamp to the iron ring. They stood at the pool, watching the iguanas fight.

"When you want to tackle these suckers?" Floyd asked.

"Let 'em fight. Now they got a law you can't fire a gun on your own property."

"What law?"

"The fucking homeowners' association."

"What homeowners' association?"

"Kensington Gardens."

"You're shittin' me."

"Floyd, you can't make this shit up. So, we're gonna have to get rid of them some other way."

A yellow/green iguana seized another in its jaws and shook it like a rat. "I like that big one," Floyd said. "He's got a future. Okay. We can't shoot 'em. You know what kills iguanas? Spinach and romaine lettuce."

"My ass."

"Really. I'm rebranding. No more Belmont Pest Control. It's Belmont Holistic Pest Solutions. No artificial ingredients.

You know what else kills iguanas? Onions, rhubarb, beets, Swiss chard, bananas, grapes and kale."

"So, what are you gonna do? Drive up and drop a salad on 'em?"

"I'll spray 'em with oils. Or we could just put on a couple of hazmat suits and club 'em to death. Whaddaya think? Wouldn't that make a great episode?"

Krystal appeared in the sliding patio door holding a frosted glass. "Margaritas, boys! Margaritas!" The margaritas sat on the bar in the home theater where ten adjustable theater seats faced a blank wall where the TV had been. Poker playing dogs hung in place of the velvet Elvis.

"I ordered a coupla pizzas."

Gary leaned against the bar, marg in hand. "Did you tell the gate?"

"Oh fuck. I'll do it now. Do you have the number?"

Gary handed her a Groome Security card with the name Leopold Bing. "He's the head honcho out here. The gatehouse number's on the back."

Krystal put the thrift store boom box on the bar and put on *Tobey Keith's Greatest Hits*. They sang along with "Down in Mexico." By the time the pizza guy arrived, they had a nice buzz going. At the door, Gary noticed the Bongo Boxes watching from their front yard, their house ablaze with Christmas lights. When they saw Gary looking, they waved. Gary tipped the pizza guy a ten and carried the pizza inside.

One was pepperoni. The other was ham and pineapple.

"What the fuck is this?" Gary said, gesturing at the pineapple.

"What's it look like?"

"It looks like a fruit pizza. I thought we decided no more ham and pineapple."

"You decided. Eat the pepperoni."

Gary turned to Floyd. "Do you like pineapple on your pizza?"

Floyd shook his head.

"Two grown men supposed to split a pizza while you chow down all by your lonesome?"

Krystal threw pieces of pineapple at Gary. "Okay? Now you don't have to eat them. Happy?"

An iguana raced across the floor, snapped up a piece of pineapple and skittered toward the open door. Gary turned to Floyd with WTF in face and hands.

"Sorry," Floyd said, heading for the rec room.

Gary looked at Krystal. "I suppose you're just gonna leave that pineapple on the floor."

With a sigh, Krystal crouched and picked up four pieces of pineapple. Gary followed her into the kitchen where she ran them through the garbage disposal. She pulled out three mismatched dishes and set them on the folding card table in the dining room. They had four bridge chairs. She put the pizza in the middle of the table. Gary grabbed three Dos Equis from the fridge. Krystal traded Little Big Town for Toby Keith.

They ate all save two slices with pineapple. Gary wiped his mouth on a wad of MacDonald's napkins. "Floyd's gone green. From now on it's Belmont Holistic Pest Solutions."

Krystal raised her pinkie. "Welcome to Kensington Gardens, your lordship."

Floyd rolled out a belch. He held up a Dos Equis. They'd finished off the margs. "A toast! Here's to you guys moving back into your mansion. They can't keep a good man down!"

Gary and Krystal raised their drinks. "You're in on the ride, buddy! I got a segment scheduled with me and you going house to house killing varmints."

"You know, there's a show on A&E called *Billy the Exterminator.*"

"Watch it all the time. Shows me what not to do. Dig this. Them cats are all in on organic, non-toxic solutions? We're gonna come in blasting with both barrels. We're gonna use bug spray. We're gonna use roach spray. We're gonna lay down mustard gas."

Floyd put up his hands. "Whoa! Whoa! Didn't you hear what I just said? I'm going organic. We're not going to use any toxic chemicals and Christ knows we're not gonna go in blasting with guns!"

"Don't go soft on me, boy. Maybe you can feed that rhubarb to the iguanas, but what are you gonna do when there's a twelve-foot gator in your back yard? Remember now, this is Kensington Gardens. No guns."

"I know a half dozen ways to catch a gator."

"Oh yeah?"

"Yeah."

"Well it just so happens we got that very situation right down the street. You bring your gator huntin' gear?"

"It's in the truck."

"Well, all right then."

"Well, all right."

Gary and Floyd stood.

"What the fuck? It's nine pm. You can't go gator hunting at night. Not without a boat and a gun."

"Watch me," Floyd said.

Gary headed for the garage. "I got waders and flashlights."

"I gotta use the facilities," Floyd said.

Krystal pointed to the hall connecting the rec room with the dining room. She heard Gary rummaging through the garage through the kitchen door. He reentered with an armful of stuff and dropped it on the floor. Rubber boots, chain and grapple, hi-intensity flashlights, BIG KNIFE, nunchaku.

Floyd appeared holding his pants. "Gary, you'd better take a look."

"A look at what?"

"Just go take a look."

Gary strode to the bathroom and looked inside. Sticking up from the toilet, the snake looked back.

9 | MISSION FOR SANTA

Gary called Sid Saidso the next day and told him about the gator. Sid agreed it would make an excellent episode for the show and promised to contact the homeowners' association and secure all necessary rights and permissions. The hunt was scheduled for Friday.

Gary rose, nuked a Jimmy Dean Sausage, Egg and Biscuit, and checked the downstairs bathroom. The fucker was gone. Obviously, not the same snake. Duh. But was it not possible there was a collective reptilian consciousness, an ancestral memory of the best spawning, feeding, and molting grounds? Could it be that last night's visitor had received some antediluvian impulse from the previous snake, who had sacrificed its life to take out cartel kingpin and mass murderer El Nariz? Gary could not help but think fondly of it. A garden variety cottonmouth. A water moccasin.

Gary had a mild headache as he rolled out his sit-down John Deere, powered up, and punched the green. Wearing a set of noise-canceling headphones, sunglasses, and a Dolphins cap, Gary mowed his vast lawn. He'd have to find some neighborhood kid. If there were any neighborhood kids. He hadn't seen anyone younger than Krystal since they'd moved back.

He waved as Marie backed out of her garage in a Lexus SUV. He put the mower away. The marble fountain was perfect for Sam. Gary placed the three-foot plaster statue on the rim facing the drive. They'd get the message. Trespassers will be violated. This property protected by Smith and Wesson. Never mind the dog. Worry about the owner.

He unfurled the Stars and Bars and mounted them on the right pillar. Gary went inside and took a shower. When he came out, Floyd had arrived in his new Belmont Holistic Pet Solutions van, pale lavender with a black Japanese dry brush logo that included a butterfly. The old logo showed a dead cockroach belly up. Gary found Floyd looking up at the house.

"Man, you could really deck this baby out for Christmas. We could string lights from one end of the county to the other and put a big fat Santa on the roof with reindeer."

Christmas was in two weeks. "I ain't got time for that. We gotta get rid of those iguanas. Did you bring the rutabaga?" "Rhubarb. I mixed a cocktail that will get rid of 'em fersure, and the beauty is, you can still eat 'em! Hell. They're even marinated. We can take 'em to a mission in West Palm. We'll dress up like Santa Claus."

Gary gave Floyd the thumbs up. "So, do we gotta suit up for this?"

Floyd wore paint-stained carpenter's pants and a Lynyrd

Skynyrd T stretched taut across his medicine ball gut. "Naw. Shit's holistic. You can eat it. Soaks through the skin. All you gotta do is remove the internal organs and grill 'em."

"Zis mission know we're comin'?"

"Naw. It's a Christmas surprise, like Secret Santa."

"You want coffee?"

"Sure."

Krystal sat in the rec room, lacing on her Nikes, wearing satin sports shorts, a sports bra, and a Dolphins halter. "Hey Floyd."

"Hey, Krys. Where you goin'?"

"I gotta get my five miles in before noon. I got a fight in six weeks."

She pecked him on the cheek on the way out. "Don't you boys let any of those fuckers in the house."

Gary wore torn Levi's, sandals, and a .38 Special Tee-shirt. Out back, they dragged the tarp onto the lawn and rolled it up. They stood at the deep end looking down at the battling iguanas. Nonstop action. "They been at it for two days straight. They got tag teams. When one iguana gets tired, another takes its place."

"Why are they fighting?"

"Fuck if I know."

"Okay. Let's get the shit."

Out front, Floyd unloaded two large aluminum canisters with pressure gauges, and two loops of orange tubing affixed to spray guns, rolling them around the house on a hand truck. Each took a canister. Gary stood with his back to the house, Floyd opposite.

Floyd took aim. "Let 'er rip!"

Gary and Floyd aimed a righteous rain of holistic death juice on the creatures, who reacted with panic and desperation, stampeding toward the shallow end, scrambling up the concrete steps and scattering in all directions. Many didn't make it. The day would be long remembered among reptiles as the Great Iguana Massacre. They emptied the two canisters. Gary filmed the aftermath on his Fonebone, talking in hushed tones live on Facebook.

"Thanks to Belmont Holistic Pest Solutions, we have wiped out two tribes of battling iguana. Why they were fighting, we may never know. May have been religious. May have been over a girl. This here pool has claimed an alligator and now hundreds of iguanas. The alligator died in a hail of bullets, but we killed these lizards with all natural ingredients. So, folks, if you got iguana, or palmetto bugs, or whatever roaming through your house, give my pal Floyd Belmont a call. That's Belmont Holistic Pet Solutions, three two three, nine five five, zero two four eight. This here's Gary Duba signing off from the great iguana massacre."

Floyd brought his van around and backed it up to the shallow end. They put on waders and leather gloves and shoveled dead iguana into jumbo Hefty rip-proof bags and loaded them into the back of Floyd's van. Floyd handed Gary his Santa suit.

They donned their gay apparel. Gary looked like a scarecrow. Floyd looked like a demented dwarf.

"You want to stick a pillow in your jacket? Be more authentic."

"Just drive."

They got in the van. Floyd cued up Taste of Honey's "Boogie Oogie Oogie".

They rolled through Kensington Gardens and headed for the highway. It was almost noon, temp in the mid-eighties, high humidity. Gary lit a fat doobie and passed it to Floyd. Floyd pulled a Red Army flask from his pocket, took a swig, and passed it to Gary. By the time they hit the 441 they were feeling no pain. The van twitched its hips and vogued (dance to music in such a way as to imitate the characteristic poses struck by a model on a catwalk.) down the highway. Strobing red and blue lights filled the rear view as the siren whooped.

"Shit!" Floyd declared.

"Chill. We're two Santas on a goodwill mission."

The county mounty parked his Dodge behind them on the shoulder and approached in a Smokey hat, aviator shades, and size fourteen boots.

"Hello, Floyd," he said through the open driver's window.

"Hello, Officer Phillips. Wha'd I do?"

"You did eighty-five in a seventy mile zone. Hello, Gary."

"Hello, Officer Phillips. Merry Christmas."

Phillips' eyes swept the interior. "You boys been drinkin'?"

"Just a little eggnog."

Phillips sighed. "Floyd, ahmina need to see license, registration and proof of insurance. Then I need you boys to step out of the vehicle."

"Come on, man, can't you see we're on a mission for Santa?"

"Out of the truck, boys."

Floyd produced the necessary documentation and joined Gary on the gravel shoulder as traffic whizzed by, not even slowing for so mundane a scene.

"Gary, we appreciate what you've accomplished, and arresting you at this time would not be conducive to a harmonious holiday season. Neither one of you is fit to drive. Your eyes look like oysters. So, here's what omma gonna do. You're gonna leave this van here while I give you a ride into Turpentine, and you can call someone to take you home. I'll have the van taken to Glades County Impounding. You can come pick it up in the morning."

"But, Officer," Floyd said. "We're on a mission for Santa."

Officer Phillips looked from one to the other. "What mission?"

"We're delivering Christmas dinner to the Nuns of Gavarone Homeless Mission in West Palm Beach."

"What dinner?"

Floyd shifted uneasily from foot to foot.

Officer Phillips walked to the rear of the van and opened the doors. An iguana tail stuck out of one of the bags. He looked inside.

"What the fuck is this?"

"Iguanas," Gary said. "An excellent source of protein."

"How did you get so many iguanas?"

"I sprayed them with a mixture of onions, rhubarb, beets, Swiss chard, bananas, grapes and kale."

"You boys wait here." Officer Phillips returned to his cruiser.

10 | LET'S ROLL

Two hours later, representatives of State Fish and Wildlife determined the cull was legal and they could proceed. Gary was so bored, he put on a pair of gloves, grabbed a plastic bag, and picked up all the trash up and down the highway. Floyd spent his time on his Fonebone.

Floyd and Gary had taken off their red jackets and beards and sat in the shade of a billboard featuring "THE LONG ARM--HABIB RODRIGUEZ". Habib stood tall facing west in a brown suit, white shirt, black tie, ten-gallon hat and sunglasses, promising you won't pay a dime unless he wins a settlement.

Officer Phillips left and came back. By the time he returned, Floyd and Gary were sober.

"Floyd, I'm thinking of letting you go, but first I want you to walk a line for me."

"No problem."

Floyd walked the line.

"Gary, you too."

"I ain't driving."

"Walk the line."

Gary walked.

Officer Phillips handed Floyd his keys. "Don't make me regret this, boys."

"We won't, officer! And merry Christmas! Wait. Let me give you a couple iguanas."

"That's all right, Floyd. I can't accept 'em."

Floyd and Gary got back in the truck, wearing only their red pants and T shirts. Floyd raised the windows and cranked up the AC. Gary sniffed.

"Smells a little gamy in here. You sure these iguanas are okay?"

"They were alive four hours ago. Same day service. You can't ask for fresher than that."

Floyd cranked up Styx's "Too Much Time On My Hands".

The Nuns of Gavarone Mission was on Old Okeechobee Road. It was five p.m. when Floyd pulled up in front of the one story red brick building, previously a furniture store, over a hundred people waiting in line, some pushing shopping carts filled with all their earthly belongings, some wearing backpacks. They drove around back to the loading dock and got out.

Floyd pulled out his Santa top, beard, and hat. "Suit up."

The two mismatched Santas walked through the open back door into a kitchen staffed by three women and two men. The women wore sensible clothes and shoes. Two wore glasses. The tallest looked up.

"Yes?"

Floyd doffed his hat. "Floyd Belmont, Belmont Holistic Pest Solutions. I spoke to a Sister Magnusson about donating iguanas. I got two hundred and fifty pounds for you, but we oughtta get 'em in a freezer or they're going to go bad."

The woman, who was about five ten and broad shouldered, colorless bowl cut, took off her glasses, carefully wiped them with a hand cloth and put them back on.

"I'm sorry, is this a joke?"

"It's no joke. Merry Christmas!"

"We have no Sister Magnusson. Where did you speak to her?"

"On Facebook."

"Show me."

Floyd pulled out his Fonebone. He looked up in disbelief. "She's gone!"

The tall woman's face darkened. "I'm afraid you've been the victim of a practical joke."

A short Latino with thick hair, said, "Those focking Necros!"

"Roberto!" the tall woman snapped. "I'm very sorry for your trouble. I'm Sister Agatha Papparazi. I'm afraid that you, like we, are the victims of a practical joke. There are several charities here in town that cater to the homeless and the hungry. Unfortunately, one of them is run by the so-called Church of Necroeconomics, a group of fanatics who subscribe to voodoo economics and believe in animal sacrifice. One of our board directors made the mistake of criticizing them on social media, and they've been after us ever since. They've vandalized this building, spray painted their nonsense on our windows, and even tried to sabotage our van."

"Ma'am," Gary said, looking like the Grinch. "Iguana are an excellent source of protein. They taste just like chicken. I know, 'cuz I used to have a restaurant." Gary looked at the men, both of whom were Latino.

"You boys ever eat iguana?"

"Sure," nodded the vulgarian. "All the time."

"You know how to cook 'em?"

"Of course."

"Well let's take a negative and turn it into a positive. How'd you boys like to help us cart those iguanas in? You got a walk-in freezer?"

The vulgarian looked to Sister Agatha Papparazi. "Sister?"

She opened the walk-in freezer. "Who's going to clean them?"

"We will," the man assured her.

"Roberto, would you take a look."

Floyd went out with him. Gary introduced himself. The big room was filled with people. The sound of children squealing, rapid fire Spanish, coughing, and scraping chairs filtered back.

Roberto and Floyd returned. Roberto shook his head. "Is no good. Those iguana been sitting around too long in a hot truck."

Sister Agatha looked at them with pity. "I'm so sorry. You've wasted your time. You might want to report this to the police."

Roberto tapped her shoulder. "Sister Agatha. I got a better idea. They can dump those lizards at the Church of Necros."

"The Lord tells us to turn the other cheek."

"That's that new testament shit. I like the part that goes an eye for an eye. How many times we got to turn the other cheek?"

Sister Agatha looked thoughtful. "I'm afraid we can't ask you do that."

"It'll be our pleasure!" Floyd declared. "It's our Christmas gift to you. Just give us the address."

Gary held his jacket over one arm. "Ain't got anything better to do. How'd this feud start?"

"We had a family ruined by those satanists. They encouraged the father to put everything he had into fungicoin. They lost everything. Fungicoin is a Necroeconomic invention. It's how they get rich. I try not to speak ill of my fellow human beings, but in my view, the Necroeconomics people are evil. They've taken over the city of Coopersmith. That's where they built their soulless, gleaming, temple to Mammon, and that's where you should dump the lizards."

"I've heard of those fuckers!" Floyd said. "I had a friend who joined them. I never heard from him again."

Gary headed for the exit. "Let's roll!"

11 | VOODOO ECONOMICS

Coopersmith, a city of one hundred and twenty thousand, lay just west of Margate.

Gary looked it up on his Fonebone. "Take Twenty-seven south."

Floyd cranked the necker knob, big hair pin-up winking from the fender of a chopped '57 Chevy. "On it."

It was almost six and the sun had set. The van smelled fishy.

Floyd put on Ski Mask the Slump God.

"Fuck izzat?"

"Ski Mask the Slump God. Nuketown. You ain't heard this?"

Gary's hand shot out and stabbed the machine. "No, and I ain't hearing it now! What's the matter with you?"

"You always were a picky son of a bitch."

"I just like real music! Shit you can sing!"

"Fuck your hooks and chords! When are you going to slide into the twenty-first century?"

"I'm already there, sucker. Let's find common ground. Got any country?"

"Lady Antebellum okay, you picky motherfucker?"

"That ain't country."

"Fuck it ain't!"

"Got any Jimmy Rodgers?"

"Oh man, you want the wayback machine. All right. Name some country you like that's still alive."

"George Jones."

"Dead."

"Bullshit!"

"Google it."

"Fuck it. We won't listen to anything."

"This is my van."

"I paid for it."

They rode in silence.

"News radio okay with you?" Floyd asked sullenly.

"Fine."

Portland was rioting over pronouns. The Upper Midwest was underwater. Giant Mekong catfish were invading southern Florida. Ford had recalled one hundred and twenty thousand vehicles due to a blinker failure. Avocados were spiking.

"Hi! Slick Niveleski here, with a true story about how you can save thousands of dollars on life insurance. Ray, a real person, is forty-five years old with a minor heart condition..."

Floyd turned it off.

They cruised into Coopersmith, a remarkably clean town with no homeless problem due to the Church's patrols. They rounded up the homeless, took them to the Necrodome, fed them, and signed them up for the Church or, failing that, put them on the bus to West Palm or Miami. Some of Hollywood's biggest actors were Necros, including Sean Sheen, Paulina Perestroika, Balfour Balthazar, Rene Welldigger, and Jennifer Tuft.

Floyd stopped at The Libre Lounge to relieve himself. The lounge had an African theme with carved masks on the walls, faux thatch roof, and a rustic bar made of logs. A stuffed leopard hunted over the bar. Floyd and Gary took a booth and perused the menus. There was a half dozen other patrons including two couples.

"You got anything that ain't on the menu?" Gary asked their waitress, a slim, jaded black girl with green eyeliner and a bun.

"Like what?"

"Like iguana."

Floyd looked at him in disgust. "Eeeeyeww! How can you even think about eating iguana after driving around all afternoon with them stinkin' up the truck?"

"Would you gentlemen like something to drink?"

Gary held up a finger. "Good idea. Couple margaritas."

They watched her go.

"How you wanna do this?" Gary said.

"We just drive up and dump 'em out front?"

"That ain't so easy. They're paranoid. What if there are guards?"

"We'll wear our Santa uniforms."

Gary regarded Floyd dubiously. Floyd was capable of bad decisions. Like that time he adopted a coyote pup, or the time he built his own electric car and caused a five county blackout.

"Howzat gonna help us?"

"Come on. It's Christmas. Who's going to turn away Santa Claus?"

The waitress returned with their drinks. "You boys want to order?"

They examined the menu in a bamboo font.

"Is that a real leopard?" Gary said.

"I don't know. What's with the Santa bottoms?"

"We're secret Santas. We're delivering gifts."

"Say that's great. What charity?"

"We're giving them to the Necroeconomists."

"Huh. They don't really need charity. They pretty much own this city. What are you giving them?"

"The gift of iguana."

"What'll it be, boys?"

Gary ordered a cheeseburger. Floyd ordered lasagna. By the time their meals arrived, they'd each had three margaritas. The television over the bar showed the remains of a devastated house. Nothing but timber and kindling. The scroll beneath the picture said, "...believed to be the work of a feral hog. Locals call this beast Hogzilla and claim that it weighs one thousand pounds."

Gary knocked on the wood table.

They left a generous tip and stumbled to the van. Floyd and Gary put on their beards, hats, and jackets, Gary's buttressed with a large down pillow to make him jolly. When they got in the van, Floyd pulled out an amber vial of coke, tapped some into a plastic restaurant spoon, and snorted. He passed it to Gary. They pulled onto Center Avenue which would take them directly to Necro World HQ, the biggest building in town.

Floyd put on a Ginger Fowl record.

"Ah no, man," Gary said. "I can't listen to that shit."

"What's wrong with Ginger Fowl?"

"She's only got one chord."

"So?"

"Dude, what are you, retarded? One chord? Where are the hooks? Where are the bridges? What else you got?"

Gary reached for the in-dash sound system. Floyd swatted his hand away, swerving onto the curb and striking a municipal garbage can. Floyd instantly over corrected, causing the van to jitter sideways intensifying the smell of decaying iguana. Fortunately, no one witnessed the mishap and they proceeded toward the fourteen story (actually thirteen but well you know) art deco Necroeconomics Building, which occupied an entire city block, its ziggurat steps recalling the work of Howard Roark.

It was nine p.m. as the van pulled into the broad Necro driveway that apexed at the glass front doors beneath a portico. A smartly tailored black man cruised through the glass doors wearing a navy blue sports jacket with Church of Necroeconomics writ in gold script above the breast pocket, sharply creased khakis, and high end sneakers, hair cut short, tell-tale bulge under his left shoulder.

Gary popped out and spread his arms. "Ho ho ho!"

The man stopped, delighted. "Well what have we here. Santa! What brings you to the Church of Necroeconomics?"

Floyd came around the front of the van.

"Greetings from the North Pole! We have brought you a

food donation to distribute as you see fit."

"Gentlemen, that is most gratifying. I'm Earl Wheeler."

"Floyd Belmont."

"Gary Duba."

They shook hands. Earl frowned at Gary.

"I know you?"

"No, but tune into my upcoming Rustix series, the *Gary Duba Show*."

"What have you brought us?"

"Two hundred and fifty pounds of iguana."

Earl's smile froze. "Excuse me?"

"Two hundred and fifty pounds of iguana. An excellent source of protein and I should know. I had a restaurant that specialized in iguana. It's a very popular meat throughout Latin America. I'm sure you have many followers of Central American descent who would be delighted."

"Normally, we accept food donations at our mission on North 12th Street. Would it be possible for you to take them there?"

"Man," Gary said, "we've been driving for hours to deliver this iguana. What if we leave them here and you can transport them yourself?"

Earl bit his lower lip. "Wait here," he said, going back inside the building.

Floyd ran around to the back. "Hurry."

They opened the doors, put on their gloves, and shoveled iguana all over the pristine blacktop, chanting "HO HO HO!" As they tossed the final four, Earl emerged from the building and gave chase.

12 | MEN!

When Gary sobered up in the morning, he called Habib
Rodriguez and left a message. Floyd, who'd spent the night
crashed in a theater chair, sat at the kitchen island, staring
at a cup of coffee while Krystal whipped up taters and eggs.

"Who am I gonna call? It's me they're gonna come after."

"Shouldn't have used your truck."

"Tell me about it."

"Call Habib."

"What about that other guy?"

"What other guy?"

"Advertises on Judge Judy."

"McDivot?"

"That's the guy."

Sid Saidso phoned from Los Angeles. "What the fuck! Is
that you in the Santa suit with the lizards?"

"Yeah."

"Why?"

"It seemed like the right thing to do."

"Oh man, you couldn't wait for the production crew? This is gold!"

"I'm sorry. I should have thought first."

"That's all right. We'll get it off the surveillance tapes. They're considering charges."

"What charges?"

"Littering."

"I got a lawyer."

"I'll be back on the eighteenth with a boat. We gotta get that alligator before it eats somebody's dog."

"You can stay at my place if you like but you gotta bring your own air mattress and bedding."

They sat at the island watching WPMN on the flat screen Krystal had bought from Billy Bob for forty bucks. There was a seventy-two-car pile-up on the Interstate due to rain. From the air, it looked like a pile of Legos. The president was negotiating a trade deal with Brutopia. They ended with the Secret Santas.

A voluptuous news reader who had graduated from Mexican weather batted her palm frond lashes. "Lastly, authorities are still looking for the two Secret Santas who unloaded hundreds of pounds of dead iguana on the steps of the Church of Necroeconomics last night."

Grainy footage showed the drunken Santas, Gary on the ground, Floyd in the truck, hurling lizards with wild abandon. Into the meticulously maintained garden and the koi pond. On the perfectly trimmed hedges. It ended with the van driving off and Earl rushing into the drive.

"The iguana proved unusable. Authorities are looking into possibly designating this a hate crime. Meanwhile, the search for the two secret Santas intensifies."

Habib Rodriguez filled the screen in ten-gallon hat and a gold and silver belt buckle the size of Montana. "Have you been in an auto accident and not been adequately compensated for your injuries? Did your insurance company refuse to pay what you deserve? I'm Habib Rodriguez. I've been dealing with insurance companies all my life, and they don't scare me."

Gary pulled out his Fonebone and went to the Miami Herald. There they were, in grainy color, above the centerfold. *SECRET SANTAS DELIVER LIZARDS. Church respectfully declines generous gift.* By Peter Gribble.

The week flew by. Gary practiced his *Piranha Pool* pitch in the mirror, wearing a yellow and orange Hawaiian shirt, sunglasses, and a Panama hat.

"Yes, we love Florida when the sun is shining, but we all know that at any minute Mother Nature can rear back and slap us upside the head. Severe weather is a certainty, and every year, thousands of homes are blown away. House suspenders are as much a necessity as insurance. House suspenders can be hung with hanging plants and bird houses, creating a festive atmosphere. At Christmas time, they can make your home spectacular."

Krystal relaxed on the new Big Lots sofa, smoking a cigarette. "You gotta have visuals, babes."

"Working on it."

"How you workin' on it?"

"Well I got the suspenders back up, didn't I? I'm going to buy a shitload of Christmas tree lights and string up the whole lot."

"I'll go with you. I like the red and green peppers."

They drove to Walmart. Gary dropped a C note in the Salvation Army pot. They bought two cushions that looked like fat baby seals, an electric tire inflator, chocolate milk, apples, bananas, soups, Jimmy Dean breakfast biscuits, copper infused compression gloves, Raid, Pinesol, buckets, cloths, mops, rubber gloves, scouring pads, carrots, broccoli, and two frozen California Kitchen Sicilian style pizzas. As they parked in front of their house, a blue Tesla followed them in. A man in a Kensington Gardens Country Club yellow golf shirt and white linen slacks got out. He was lean with a receding hairline like a Steve Ditko character.

"Mister Duba?"

"That's me."

"Hi, Mister Duba, I'm Ron Santos. I represent the Kensington Gardens Homeowners' Association."

They shook. Krystal stepped up.

"Krystal. You want to help us carry this stuff into the house?"

Gary and Krystal each grabbed a bag and headed for the front door. Santos had no choice but to grab a bag and follow.

"Yes, well first of all, I want to welcome you to the neighborhood, or rather, welcome you back to the neighborhood."

"Thanks, Ron! Just put 'em in the kitchen."

Gary opened the fridge. "Want a beer?"

"No, I'm afraid I can't stay long. You just got back here, so you can't be expected to know all the details of the Kensington Gardens covenant. I've brought you a copy."

He pulled a sheath of papers from his pocket and laid them on the counter. The cover showed the gleaming plantation style clubhouse against the cerulean pond, a blaze of white, green, and blue.

"We don't allow any overtly nationalistic displays. You'll have to take down that flag by your front door."

"You mean the Stars 'n' Bars?"

"Yes, but the rules would apply equally to the Russian or Cuban flag."

"What about the American?"

Santos looked nervous. "That too. It's not that we're not patriotic, it's just that with a neighborhood of this standing, of this caliber, such displays seem crass and may adversely affect property values."

"Huh?"

"No problem," Krystal said. Gary looked at her. She shot him the Look.

"And the other thing, the figure on the rim of your fountain."

Gary was incredulous. "Sam?"

"I don't know what it's called, but the bright primary colors create a distraction from the cool beauty of your home."

"What do you care? Nobody comes down here anyway."

"We now have twelve homes under construction and the clients regularly visit. That's, uh, one reason I came to see you."

"Not a problem," Krystal said, daring Gary to say something.

"Well thanks, folks! I'm glad you're so understanding. By the way. I live at Twenty-four Barnacle Circle. Welcome to the neighborhood."

Santos beat a path outta there. Gary brought in the rest of their booty. "The nerve of that guy."

"You're just gonna have to get used to living with neighbors, Gary. That's all there is to it."

"I know. I had it my own way for so long, I don't know how to fit in with neighbors."

They sat at the kitchen island, watching WPMN on the flat screen Krystal had bought from Billy Bob for forty bucks. A man with a triangle-shaped head, thin comb over, spade chin, intense black eyes, black suit, faced the camera from a podium framed by a portrait of Nebudchadnezzar and the Necroeconomic Flag, depicting Earth and moon in space, bright red and yellow logo: SCIENCE, BITCHES.

Necroeconomic press conference, Wombat Supreme Ken Zohan speaking scrolled across the lower half of the screen.

"Last night, two men dressed in pagan robes, sought to humiliate and defile the sacred ground of the Necroeconomic Church, which stands for science, logic, and the betterment of all mankind. Including womankind. And all the kinds in between. We have chosen not to pursue this act as a hate crime and instead, in the spirit of compassion, and science, and logic which characterizes Necroeconomics, I reach out to these two men."

"Brethren! Our Church is devoted to science and logic. How have we offended you, knowing we do not partake of the meat of the lizard?"

"Brethren! My door is open. Call me any time. You may beat the rush, but you must never rush the beat."

13 | BACK TO THE SWAMP

Gary had fifty thousand followers @therealGaryDuba on Twitter.

Dear Gary: Can you recommend a good recipe for iguana? Sincerely, El Torres.

Dear El Torres: Legally kill an iguana by shooting it in the head or stabbing it in the brain.

Wash the iguana meat thoroughly after removing the skin, organs, and entrails, so that just the meat and cartilage remain.

The message paused as Gary reached his word limit.

Put the iguana meat in boiling coconut milk. Let it cook for at least an hour.

Remove the tender meat from the cartilage. Sometimes I will marinate the meat in pasilla chiles, vinegar, salt and pepper. I also like to make iguana tacos.

I will marinate the meat in peanut oil,

The message paused as Gary reached his word limit.

garlic and a touch of cayenne. You can cook the iguana on a charcoal grill.

He was in the rec room, Thursday night on his laptop when he received an invitation from @Necroeconomicon to join a group hang-out with Ken Zohan. Gary went right over. His icon was a cartoon gator.

"Hello," said a familiar voice, smooth as aged Kentucky bourbon. "This is Ken Zohan speaking to you live from the Church of Necroeconomics here in beautiful Coopersmith, Florida. I see Gary Duba has joined us. Gary, how were you able to apprehend Plastic Surgeon to the Stars and serial killer Doctor Vanderlay Mukerjee?"

"It was just luck, Ken. We had a monitor lizard in the truck and Krystal couldn't bear to see the poor thing suffer so she let it out. When Doctor Mukerjee got in the truck it bit him."

"That was most fortuitous. You're aware that the monitor lizard is an invasive and dangerous species. There are now breeding populations of the Nile monitor lizard. Their bite can cause pain and illness. They are particularly dangerous to children and pets."

"Ken, all I know this State's got a shitload of unnecessary animals. Iguana. Nutria. Hippos."

"What hippos?"

"From El Nariz's zoo. No one's seen 'em, no one's heard them. But they're out there."

Perry from Springfield popped up. "Mister Duba, I have a question."

"Shoot."

"Who is stronger? Hulk or Superman?"

"What the fuck you talking about, son?"

"Gary," Ken broke in, "I invited you here tonight because I would like to meet with you in person."

"Hell, I ain't hard to find."

"No, I meant here, at the Church of Necroeconomics, where you dumped your dead iguana."

"Well fuck, you got me."

"I appreciate that you don't deny it. Honesty is one of the tenets of Necroeconomics, and on the path to the ultimate stage of oneness and self-awareness we call viscosity."

"Can't you use those lizards for something? They weren't that far gone."

"If you had brought us live lizards, we could have used them. The lizards you brought were already beginning to rot. We had to rely on a professional crime scene clean-up unit to eliminate the odor. The entrance to our beautiful temple of science, designed by Roark Dexter Smith, still smells faintly of fish."

"How did you know it was me?"

"Science."

Krystal banged through the kitchen door. "Gary! Gary baby! I got pizza!"

"Hey Ken, gotta go. Fun talking."

"Please remember, Gary. It's not the shape of the bottle that matters. It's the matter in the shape of a bottle."

Gary went into the kitchen. "Boy howdy, that smells good! Hey, I was just in a chat with Ken Zohan."

"Who's Ken Zohan?"

"Leader of the Church of Necroeconomics. Shit, girl.

Where you been?"

Krystal pulled an extra-large three meat pizza from a Domino's carton. "I got a lot on my mind. I'm going out to Delilah's tomorrow to train."

"Oh shit! I forgot about that!"

"Can you drive me?"

"Sure."

After dinner, Gary grabbed Krystal around the waist.

"You stink! Take a shower and I'll fuck ya."

"Deal."

When Gary came out of the shower, Krystal was waiting for him in her Squirrel Girl outfit, gray Squirrel Girl beret with ears, and a tail affixed to her crotchless panties. Gary howled like a coyote, trailing off with a series of yips. Krystal put a Queen record on the boom box in the bedroom and they rutted like elk on Main Street in Estes Park. Krystal wrapped her legs around Gary's waist while he held her in the corner, came, and collapsed to the ground. Krystal strutted around with her fists in the air to "We Are the Champions".

They slept on their Big Lots bed. In the morning, Gary checked the truck tires. They stopped at a Winn-Dixie so Krystal could stock up on tampons, Aleve, Off!, smudge pots, Slim Jims, and bottled water. They headed for the swamp. Delilah lived in a geodesic dome on the Big Cypress Indian Reservation. A Calusa witchee woman, Delilah had learned her art from her mother and grandmother. Her home lay at the end of a rutted trail that wandered through hummocks and puddles, crisscrossed with wild game. It was slow going.

As they passed beneath a bower of mahogany, pond apple and cypress, three wild hogs meandered out of the forest and stopped in the middle of the road.

Gary stopped the truck and reached for his magnum in the glove compartment.

"Them fuckers."

"Leave the fucking hogs alone."

"Don't you think Delilah might 'preciate a fresh hog? Don't you think she knows how to butcher a hog? Hell. I'll butcher it for her. Does she have a refrigerator?"

"Yeah. She runs it off a gas generator and an exercycle."

"Look at them pigs. They ain't too big. Can't be more'n a hunnert pounds." Krystal threw her hands in the air. "Fine."

Wearing cargo trousers, waffle stompers and a camo Tee-shirt, Gary got out of the truck and slowly approached the pigs who paid no heed. At fifty feet he went down on one knee clutching the big magnum in both hands, sighting along the barrel, gently squeezing, surprised when the shot went off, even more surprised when the hog he'd been aiming at fell like a sack of cement. The other hogs took off squealing.

He'd drilled the young male right through the eye. Stooping, he hoisted the hog over his shoulders and dumped it in the truck bed. Krystal put her hand out.

"Don't you get in the truck with that shirt. You throw that shirt away."

Gary stripped off the shirt, surprised to find it covered in blood, and tossed it to the side of the road. Krystal put on the radio, turning from one end to the other, trying to find something other than Spanish language and Come to Jesus shows. All she could find was conspiracy theorist Ferd Ludlow.

"...that the US government has a secret alien base in Northern New Mexico. Area 51 is just a distraction. This secret base can be found halfway up Mt. Archuleta in the *Sangre de Cristos*. Last week, an alien human hybrid escaped from the base, stole a motorcycle, and is currently at large."

Gary glimpsed Delilah's house through the trees. The geodesic dome, which she built with help from the tribe, was covered in grainy brown shingles. A bottle tree stood in the yard. Dolls hung from the bottle tree. Barbie. Ken. Lady Death. Spider-Man. Delilah stood in her yard wearing baggy combat trousers, a Boy Scout shirt and cats eye sunglasses, her white hair cut to fuzz.

Gary stopped the truck and got out.

"Give me the pig," Delilah said.

Gary dropped the hog on a cypress stump.

"How'd you know I was bringing a pig?"

She pointed to a slop bucket. "Chicken guts."

"You want me to butcher it for you?"

"I'll do the butcherin'. You have to do it right if you're gonna read the guts."

"What if those guts tell you omma bring a horse? And those guts tell you omma bring a manatee? Then you got to read those guts to see what I'm bringing next? I'm just trying to extrapolate here."

Delilah turned to Krystal who was carrying a case of bottled water into the house. "'Bout time you got here. Bring out some of that scarlet sage. It's in a big bottle in the kitchen."

Delilah positioned the hog on its back, picked up a two-handled fireman's ax and split the hog down the middle. Blood flew in Gary's face.

"Whatchoo doin' messin' with those Necronomists?

They're a bunch of hypocrites and fakes."

"How do you know about that?"

Delilah pointed at the slop bucket. She used a Bowie knife to split the pig stem to stern, reached in barehanded and pulled out the looping intestines. She cut out the liver, the stomach, and the lungs. Gary admired her technique. He took a step back and breathed through his mouth, turned and coughed. Krystal handed Delilah a bundle of twigs and leaves held together with string. Delilah took the lid off an old Weber, put in the sage and lit it with a wooden match through a hole in the bottom. Burning sage diluted the stink. Gary smacked skeeters right and left. He wished he had six arms so he could mount a battalion size attack.

Delilah went down on her haunches and poked at the hog guts with a stick. "You've got a date with an alligator."

"How you know?"

She pointed to the slop bucket. "Now if you'll just shut up and let me read, we can butcher this hog and get it into the fridge so it doesn't go bad."

She stirred the guts. The bottle tree moaned. Things howled. Gary looked around.

"Ain't that a panther?"

"Gary!" Krystal hissed.

Delilah poked. "Chiefs are gonna win the Superbowl."

"My ass."

Krystal glared. "Be quiet."

"You will lose someone close to you."

That got Gary's attention. "Can you see who it is?"

Delilah put her hands on her splayed knees. "No. Big changes comin'. Everything's in play. Whole systems are up for renewal."

"In other words," Gary said, "business as usual."

"Let me see your hand."

Gary sat while Delilah held his palm with one hand, tracing lines with the other. "That gator is the least of your problems."

"What? What?"

She traced a line. "You will be visited by three animal spirits. First, the saurian. Second, the sus. Third, hippopotamus."

"Izzis A Christmas Carol?"

Delilah closed Gary's hand. "No."

Krystal crouched opposite. "Could you teach me to read guts?"

"Right now, you got to worry about A Thing Called Xue. Ask me after you beat him."

"Her," Krystal said.

Delilah poked some more. "You are destined to battle the beast of the apocalypse."

"Give me a break!" Gary howled.

"What kind of beast?" Krystal said.

"The guts don't say. Could be the devil in human guise. Could be some primordial creature from the depths of the Marianas Trench. This confrontation will be preceded by signs and portents. Like this right chere."

"Well look here. If I keep bringing you hogs, can you keep reading until we know what the hell's going on?"

"That's not how this works, Gary. My ability to see into the future is limited by many factors, including the weather, the time of day, the time of year, the formation of the planets, and the nature and personal history of whatever animal I cut open, plus the nature and personal history of whomever I'm advisin'. That's why we don't use domesticated animals. The wilder, the better. People are best, but well, we're restrained by the law."

"So, if you weren't restrained by the law, you'd slice someone up to read their guts?"

"In a New York minute."

"So, if I was to bring you a rare and extremely endangered critter like a Florida panther, or a whooping crane, you might have better luck?"

Delilah stared into the guts. She grabbed the Bowie knife, hacked off the guts and threw them in a slop bucket. She quickly and efficiently butchered the hog into hams, ribs, and chops. When she was finished, she carried the slop bucket through the forest to the edge of the swamp and hurled it in a semi-circle. Nine alligators that had been sunning themselves on logs slid into the water and went into a feeding frenzy.

Delilah reached for a second slop bucket.

"Let me have that."

She looked at him quizzically.

"Need it to catch a gator."

"You'd better put it in your truck and cover it up. Lemme get you a lid."

Gary took the meat into the kitchen where Delilah expert-ly hacked off three pork chops.

"Marinate these in peanut oil, garlic, brown sugar, and

chilli peppers. I got to take a shower."

Delilah peeled off her clothes and tossed them to the floor. She had one of those bodies they write about on Fox News.

SALMA HAYEK SHOWS OFF BIKINI BODY ON BEACH TRIP TO CELEBRATE TURNING 53

EVA LONGORIA SIZZLES IN WHITE SWIMSUIT AS SHE ENJOYS 'FUN IN THE SUN' IN MEXICO

The shower was a fifty-gallon drum strapped to an oak, tubes running to funnels breaching the canopy. Drawing the circular curtain, Delilah pulled a chain, releasing a cascade of warm, refreshing water as she lathered up. Inside, Krystal put the marinating chops in the fridge, now bulging with butcher-wrapped pork. The only light came through triangular skylights circling the top like a halo. The generator cut in to juice the batteries.

Delilah returned wrapped in a blanket, climbed to her loft, and came down in fawn-colored slacks and a Katherine Hepburn shirt. They went out front and sat in nylon lawn chairs. Delilah unscrewed a Mason jar of clear liquid and poured shine into three jelly glasses. She lit the grill and put on the chops. By the time they were done, Gary was passed out in the dirt.

"We should take him inside," Krystal said.

Delilah smacked her lips. "I thought that boy knew how to drink."

"He knows how to drink. He doesn't know how to stop."

"Grab his ankles. We'll put him on the futon."

They carried Gary inside, a faint whistling coming from

his nose, and dropped him on a fold out sofa/bed. A black cat crawled out from under, leaped on top of Gary and settled on his flat belly. Delilah pointed a finger at the cat.

"You're in charge."

They went outside. Samson stood at the Weber ,staring at the pork chops. Samson was a brown bear. Samson went down on all fours and tentatively stuck his snout over the grill.

"Stick around," Delilah said. "You can have a chop." She turned to Krystal. "Samson weighs two hundred and twenty pounds."

Samson was a very nice bear, but Krystal didn't relish wrestling with him. "Great."

"I don't know why you agreed to such a contest. He..."

"She."

"Xue's, Xue's gonna have fifty pounds on you. At least. What was going through your head?"

Krystal grinned. "I knew you'd show me something that'll let me win. Something crazy, something wild."

Delilah used a pair of tongs to place the chops on an old tin platter. Samson sat up like a dog.

"It just so happens."

"What is it?"

"Tibetan tetrahedron."

15 | LIABILITY ISSUES

Gary woke face down on Delilah's futon, drooling, with a King Kong sized headache. He got up, wheeled, stumbled, caught himself, worked his way along the counter to the sink where he worked the hand pump to bring water up from the well to splash in his face. He staggered outside, walked twenty feet into the woods and peed. A half dozen gators sunned themselves on massive logs visible through the trees.

Gary went inside and found a note.

Dear Gary: We're training! Home Friday. Love, Krystal.

He looked in the refrigerator. His stomach rolled at the sight of the butchered meat. He barely made it ten feet out the door before he threw up, a river of yellow sludge that slowed to a trickle.

Wiping his mouth on his arm, he went back inside, rinsed, washed the vomit off, swigged some mouth wash, grabbed a papaya.

Sid and the gang were due tomorrow for the gator hunt.

It would set the tone and pulse of the whole series. It had rained during the night and the way back was filled with sucking mud. It took Gary an hour to reach the gravel road, and another hour to get back on pavement.

Three hours later he passed through the gates of stately Kensington Gardens, drove past three houses in progress, turned into his broad driveway and parked behind Belmont Holistic Pest Solutions. His Confederate flag and Yosemite Sam were gone.

The house was intact. Floyd lay on the sofa in the living room, sawing away. Gary spent the rest of the day scrubbing down the swimming pool with bleach. Floyd came out and helped. They nuked a pizza, and tuned into *Piranha Pool*, which showed entrepreneurs pitching their businesses to a panel of five investors, or "piranha", who decide whether to invest in the company.

CLOSE IN: on a young man wearing bizarre half-cones behind his ears held in place with a headband, like a Panic Pete Bug Out squeeze toy. The young man had a shaved skull, tatted arms extending from his striped short sleeved shirt, and blue jeans.

VOICE OVER: "Jerry Bowler, from Lodi, Wisconsin, seeks five hundred thousand dollars to market his Ear Scoopers holistic hearing aid."

"Piranhas, my hearing aids are completely natural and rely on no drugs or batteries. With Ear Scoopers in place, your hearing is enhanced by two hundred per cent." He put a hand up behind one of the scoops. "The half cups are made from hemp. The hair band is bamboo. We use only locally sourced products and it costs less than any hearing aid."

Brenda Bascomb, founder and CEO of fashion powerhouse Byuti Surge, and inventor of the Rosa Klebb shoe, was a buxom brunette in her fifties who'd started her business in her basement. "How much does it cost?"

"Nine ninety-five."

Brenda said something softly.

The young man ignored her.

"It's a no from me."

Morris Eclaire, founder of Florida's fastest growing community The Cottages, looked like a former wrestler on the comic convention circuit. Short, curly black hair and a chin like a bulldozer. "The problem I have with the Ear Scooper is that it makes you look like an idiot. Also, it takes up space. You can't wear it with a hat or a hoodie. You can't exactly stick it in your pocket. I'm afraid it's a no from me."

Anthony Peroni, founder of Dragonware Carnivore online protection: "I'm afraid it's a no from me."

Jerry Bowler looked around with an ugly sneer. "You know what? Fuck you! You're too stupid to recognize a game changer, fuck you!"

The screen went to a Habib Rodriguez commercial.

Gary rose from his chair in the rec room. "I'm zonked. See you in the AM."

Floyd waved and reached for the remote.

Gary went to bed. He woke to someone ringing the front bell as sunlight blazed in through the east-facing windows.

He looked down on a rented Lincoln and a new van with the rust-colored Rustix logo on the sides. It was ten o'clock. Gary threw on some pants and went downstairs.

Sid Saidso stood with a crew of three, staring up at Chateau Ami. A curvy long-haired Latina in her thirties filmed with a hand held device.

Gary pumped his fist. "Fuck an 'A!' Who these guys?"

Sid held his hand out toward the cinematographer. "Muriel Martinez is our director."

Muriel smiled and shook hands. "Pleased to meet you."

"Sound man Ralph Everett." A gray-haired man in a light brown suit shook Gary's hand.

"Drone wrangler Irving Pincus." Pale-faced kid with a wild profusion of curly brown hair bursting beneath his yarmulke.

"Big fan, Mister Duba."

"Y'all can call me Gary. I gotta get Floyd. We ain't catching shit without him. You bring a boat?"

"We have a twenty-two-foot Boston Whaler at the boat launch at the club."

Floyd came out wearing the same clothes from yesterday.

"Floyd! Are you ready to rock?"

"You betcha. Let me just power up."

"Floyd's an experienced pest control executive."

"Belmont Holistic Pest Solutions." Floyd reached in his breast pocket and handed out cards.

"How many gators have you caught, Mister Belmont?" said Martinez.

"Call me Floyd. Too many to count."

"I'll wire you up at the clubhouse," Everett said.

"Gotta get a gator," Gary said.

"La la la," Floyd said.

Sid looked around, shoulders set. "Here's how it's gonna go down. You're going to launch from the dock and search for the gator. I'm coming with. They'll be following you via drones. Ignore them. They're no bigger than sparrows and they won't be in your face. Just act naturally. Say what you always say."

"This ain't our first rodeo, ain't that right, Floyd?"

"We already got it sold."

"Gary and Floyd, I assume you're going to bring your truck."

"Ahuh."

Sid inhaled deeply. "There's nothing like the first day of a new show. Feel it, my friends. Breathe it in. Savor it. This is a rare moment."

"We'll be right behind ya," Gary promised. "Floyd, help me out here."

They went back inside where Gary grabbed a picnic cooler filled with iced beers and handed Floyd the slop bucket.

"Fuck izzis?"

"Chum for the gator."

They put the cooler and bucket in the back and followed the convoy toward the gleaming white clubhouse. Gary rode with Floyd with the radio on.

"State wildlife officials have caught a Mekong Giant Catfish in the Miami Canal in the Everglades. The catfish weighed five hundred pounds. This invasive species poses a threat to native flora and fauna. The Mekong Giant Catfish can weigh up to seven hundred pounds. Please contact the Florida Department of Natural Resources or Fish and Wildlife if you see one."

"Fuck me," Gary groused. "Delilah warned I was headed for a confrontation with the Anti-Christ. What if it turns out to be a five hundred pound Catfish."

"They can't hurt ya. They just gum ya."

"Fuck that."

Floyd followed the production van up the driveway to the plantation style clubhouse decked out with Christmas lights. Floyd kept going, around the building to the lake where a concrete landing slanted into the blue water next to a long white pier with several boat lifts. A Boston Whaler waited behind a Ram backed up to the water. Floyd parked in the service lot.

Three men and a woman wearing navy blue Kensington Gardens blazers waited on the pier. The Rustix van pulled up and out piled the production crew. A minute later, Sid and his assistant walked down the wood steps toward them from the clubhouse, Pincus pushing a hand cart stacked with black carbon fiber boxes bungeed in place.

Sid rushed to the fore like a cheerleader and stuck out his hand. "Mister Goldblatt, how are you?"

The retired dentist took Sid's hand, but the shake was brief. "Sid, I'm very sorry to have to tell you, you can't hunt alligator here. There are liability issues."

"What liability issues?" Sid said with raised eyebrows. "Do you want us to post a bond? Nobody's going out there except my crew."

Goldblatt was a slight man with gray hair and a goatee. "This is a motor free lake. No power boats allowed."

"That's not a liability issue."

"Look, Mister Saidso, we held an emergency meeting last night and it was decided we just can't take a chance on somebody getting hurt. This is an upscale community. The residents value their privacy and don't relish being depicted as a bunch of hayseeds."

Gary stepped forward. Goldblatt stepped back. "Are you referring to me?"

"Well not you, personally, Mister Duba, but we all know the demographic to which these types of shows appeal."

Muriel crept around filming.

"What happened between yesterday and today?"

"Please try to understand, Mister Saidso. This isn't entertainment, this is our lives."

"How 'bout we call this place something else? Like Red-neck Acres? Nobody'll know it's you."

The woman, an Edna Mode type, got in Sid's face. "That would require an entirely new deal. At best, it will take a week. It just feels wrong."

"Lady," Gary said, "you've got a freakin' alligator in your lake! What if it harms someone, like a child?"

"Swimming is forbidden in the lake," she said in a steely voice as two teenagers in swim trunks ran by whooping and hollering and threw themselves off the end of the pier. Goldblatt hot-stepped after them.

"Get out of there! There's a gator in the lake!"

The boys looked at one another and swam for the pier.

"Thank you for your offer," the woman said. "I'm Mindy Perske, Vice President of the Kensington Gardens Homeown-ers' Association. We intend to hire professionals to get rid of that alligator. But for now, we must ask you to stand down."

A Volvo station wagon careened down the concrete ramp, pulling up a foot short of the ramp. The doors sprang open releasing two girls, one driving, one not yet in her teens, both hysterical.

"DADDEEEE!" cried the younger. "IT ATE HOMBRE!"

"What?" Goldblatt said taking a step forward. "What's wrong?"

The older girl fell into her father's arms. "A fucking alli-gator came out of the pond and ate Hombre! It was horrible!"

"Oh no," Perske said.

A big man with a crew cut and rosacea said, "It ate your

dog? That sweet poodle?"

"It grabbed him and dragged him into the water! He was barking hysterically!"

Goldblatt looked around like a man seeking an out. He put his hand on Perske's shoulder. "Mindy, John, let's talk for a minute."

They went halfway out the pier and huddled. Sid gave Gary the thumbs up. The group returned.

"In view of what just happened, the board gives you permission to get that gator."

Gary pumped his fist. "Yeeeeee-HA!"

Floyd looked heroic for the camera. "Let's get that sumbitch!"

The truck driver, a muscular black man in a blue Lacoste shirt, who had been standing around poking at his Fonebone, looked up. "You going in the water, or what?"

"We're going!" Sid said. "Back her up!"

The truck driver produced a clipboard. "Who's the captain?"

Gary stepped up. "That'd be me."

The driver handed him the clipboard. "Sign here."

Sid took the clipboard. "Wait a minute." He read the contract. "Twenty-four hours? We don't need it that long."

"You expect me to hang out here in beautiful Kensington Gardens while you go hunting? Who's paying for my time? We'll be back for it at ten tomorrow morning. You still need it, you let us know, hear? It's fully gassed. Should be good for three hours."

The driver unbuckled the boat from its berth and slowly backed into the water until his rear tires were wet. Floyd jumped in and tossed a line to Gary who led the boat to the end of the pier and tied it to a piling.

Irving Pincus sat on the lawn, unpacking drones the size of saucers. Each had four rotors plus camera that hung from the center. Pincus gave Sid a tracking device to wear on his wrist. The drone would focus on Sid's wrist as a default, but Pincus could manipulate it for close-ups, pans, etc.

Everett affixed mics and transmitters to Gary, Floyd, and Sid. Sid, who'd started as a cameraman, would film from the boat. Gary and Floyd got the cooler and chum from the van and put them in the boat. Floyd got out of the boat and brought a boom box from his truck. Sid got in the boat. They put on life preservers. Muriel checked the mics and gave the okay sign. Pincus launched his drone which hovered at twenty feet. The Kensington Gardens Homeowners' Association watched the launch with mixed emotions.

Gary started the Whaler's ninety horse Johnson engine, and they churned toward the middle of the lake, leaving a wake of green water rife with algae. It was a natural lake fed by nearby swamp, and the homeowners had a vague plan to reduce algae via oxidation, but not until they had enough homeowners to fund the costly project. The people on the pier grew smaller and smaller until they were no longer distinguishable. Floyd's boom box pumped "Flight of the Valkyrie."

From the middle of the lake, they could see a handful of houses springing up, but at least two hundred and eighty degrees remained undeveloped, rimmed with reeds, mangrove and cattails. Gary headed toward the wild shore, where the gators would feel most comfortable, drone skimming along,

Sid crouching to make Gary look heroic.

"Talk to me. What's going on?"

"Well here we are, cruising Lake Kensington, looking for a killer gator. Twenty minutes ago, that gator ate a dog. We got to get it before it starts going after kids. Floyd! Put some chum in the water."

Sid swiveled to Floyd, who used an oversized soup tureen to toss chum in a semi-circle toward the shore. Gary turned the boat to the left. "Look there! There they are!"

Sid turned his camera toward shore where ripples emanated behind two gators who had felt the vibrations and smelled the blood through the water. The drone swooped in on them, hovering ten feet above the water, looking down. Gary shut the engine off and in the sudden silence, Floyd's boom box seemed unnaturally loud. Sid turned it off.

"Talk to me, Gary."

"Yeah, here we are out on the pond and we can see the gators going for the chum! Hot damn! Here they come!"

Floyd jammed gobbets on a steel grappling hook attached to a line and tossed it in the water.

A reptilian snout broke the surface, snapping up globs of hog meat. Sid crouched at the edge, aiming his camera. "Throw more chum!"

Floyd dipped the tureen and spread chum from bow to the stern. Sid aimed his camera. A twelve-foot gator grabbed Sid's arm and pulled him into the drink, doing the barrel roll to detach the arm. The water churned with blood.

"Fuck!" Gary shouted.

Sid had been transmitting live to Muriel's laptop. The last thing they saw was the gaping gator maw.

"Shit!" Muriel said.

"Oh my god," Ralph Everett said.

"Fercoct!" Pincus said.

Board members and curiosity seekers who had been peering at the boat sensed wrongness.

"What?" Goldblatt said taking a step forward. "What's wrong?"

"The gator ate our producer," Muriel said, dialing 911.

In short order, the clubhouse was surrounded with strobing vehicles and first responders, all waiting for Gary to return. The Boston Whaler furiously zigged and zagged in a seemingly random pattern.

Sheriff Ralph Hunnicutt looked like George Washington, Rushmore version, save for the amber aviator glasses. "We got a complaint about an alligator."

Goldblatt went up to him, shaking. "Sheriff, there's an alligator in the lake. It just killed a TV producer named Sid Saidso. I told them this was a bad idea. I told them we had to hire professionals. I don't care if Mister Duba is a celebrity. He should not be hunting alligators at Kensington Gardens!"

The sheriff put his hands on his hips. "Gary Duba?"

"Yessir," Goldblatt said. "I understand he was the first occupant, but since he's returned, we've had nothing but trouble. He doesn't follow association rules. He flaunts his celebrity and frankly, he's boorish! He flew a Confederate flag out in front of his house! He had a lawn jockey!"

Sheriff Hunnicutt looked around. "Anyone in touch with him? Tell him to come in."

Muriel introduced herself. "I'm the director of the *Gary Duba Show*. I have him on the phone." She handed her phone to Hunnicutt.

"Gary, this is Sheriff Hunnicutt."

"How are ya, Sheriff?"

"I need you to come back to the clubhouse now."

"Sheriff, we're chasing down a killer gator. It already killed my producer. We gotta stop it before it kills someone else."

"Gary, this is a direct order. You get your ass back to this pier right now. Have you been drinking?"

"No way! Come on, Sheriff! What if this fucking gator takes out a child? Now's our best chance! It's lazy and slow from its meal! All we have to do is wait for it to surface. We got more chum."

"Gary, if you're not at this pier in ten minutes, I'm going

to charge you with operating a boat without a license, being a public nuisance, and interfering with police business. Do you hear me?"

"All right. All right." Mumbling. Gary signed off. The boat turned toward the club house and grew closer, its buzz growing louder.

Hunnicutt held out his hand. "Ma'am, I'm gonna need your video files. Where are they?"

Muriel looked like Jonathan Harker meeting Dracula. "You can't do that! What's that got to do with anything? It was an act of nature, for Chrissake!"

"Ma'am, the coroner needs to know the circumstances of the death. I'm also gonna need to see some ID."

While Hunnicutt remonstrated, Pincus quietly pulled his wagon of drones up the driveway onto the patio where a dozen gawkers stared out at the pond, some holding up their phones. Pincus found a quiet spot by the freestanding brick barbecue and guided his drone to a soft landing in his hands, bundling it away in its carbon fiber case. He left the clubhouse by the driveway, pulling his wagon behind him like a child, passing incoming Mercedes and Lexii, keeping his head down, turning left on Kensington Boulevard, heading for Gary's house.

Gary bumped into the pier. Floyd tossed a rope to a deputy who tied it to a piling and pulled the back end in, snugging it against the tires they used as bumpers. Hunnicutt waited for Gary to walk the length of the pier.

"What happened?"

"I noticed that gator the other day when I was visiting the Bongo Boxes. Then it up and et a dog, so we all agreed Floyd and me would go out there and kill the sumbitch before it did any more damage! But Sid, man, I can't believe that happened. That old gator just rose up, put a chomp on Sid's arm and dragged him into the pond. We could see it doing the whirligig and there was all this blood. Ain't nobody's fault. It was just an act of nature. Now we got to get that sumbitch."

"Gary, we got a program for that. Statewide Nuisance Alligator Program."

"SNAP?"

"It's illegal to operate a power boat on a lake this size."

Goldblatt sidled up like a terrier. "Mister Duba is well aware. He has the association handbook."

Gary looked like a sabre jet. "You told me it was cool! We got it on tape!" He turned to Muriel. "Muriel, don't we got it on tape?"

"That's right, Gary. The association agreed to let Gary kill that gator. We got it on tape. I'd be happy to show it to you."

"Is it on your phone?"

"Yes."

Hunnicutt held out his hand. "Gimme the phone."

Muriel's face contorted in horror. "You want my phone?"

"It's evidence."

"Just give me your email! I'll send you everything."

"I'm sorry, ma'am. But we need the primary evidence, if available. Wilbur, come on over here, bag this phone and give Miss Martinez a receipt."

A big-boned deputy in aviator shades pulled a plastic evidence bag from a pouch on his cargo pants and held it open. Clicking her tongue, Muriel dropped in her Fonebone. Wilbur pulled out a sharpie and wrote the time, date, place, and Muriel's name and phone number.

"Yeah well good luck phoning me 'cause you got my phone."

Hunnicutt pulled out a pen and pad. "Is there another number where we can reach you?"

She gave him her Rustix number.

Gary nodded toward the drive. "Let's go."

They caravanned back to the Duba residence and gathered on the patio. Muriel got on the phone with Rustix. Pincus pointed to his wagon of drones. "Don't worry. Muriel had backup too. We haven't lost anything. I also filmed the sheriff."

Muriel's face contorted. They waited until she finally ended the call. She turned to them with sad eyes. "They want to cancel the show."

"They can't do that!" Gary said. "We signed a contract!"

"The contract was with Sid Saidso Productions. The death of their CEO voids the contract."

Gary got up and paced around the pool. "Just hold on there. Just hold it. What if we come up with another show runner ex post haste de facto?"

"Unless it's Vince Gilligan, forget it."

"I got just the guy. Let me give Major Sutton a call."

18 | A SURPRISE GUEST

It was a cool, overcast day. Gary stood on the dock at the Kensington Gardens clubhouse watching as an inflatable boat with an outboard motor hauled Sid Saidso's remains from the water. There wasn't much left. The alligator had snacked on everything, leaving the torso and the left leg cut off at the knee. The grim-faced sheriff's deputies wearing latex gloves stuffed Sid in a zip-up rubber bag and headed for shore. As they nudged the boat to the dock, a new Dodge Ram backed down the concrete boat ramp, easing a trailer holding a twenty-four-foot aluminum skiff into the water, a one hundred and ten horse Mercury tilted up at the back.

The board members were conspicuously absent. No members of the press could get past the gatehouse. As the deputies tied up at the pier, the Ram driver put the truck in park and approached Gary. The driver was a lean piece of beef jerky with a GI Joe beard, wearing dungarees and a Green Bay Packers hat, tanned arms covered with curly black hair.

"Are you Mister Duba?"

"Yup."

He stuck out his hand. "Paul Werringo. I'm with SNAP. I'm here to get your gator."

"Pleased to meet you."

A stout black woman, hair shaved to the nub, came around the front of the truck. "This is my associate Laverne Reynolds."

"We're great admirers of yours, Mister Duba," Laverne said. "I've followed you since you had the shootout with the judge."

"Thank you kindly."

Two deputies carried Sid's body to the back of a Glades County Police van and put it in.

Laverne put a hand to her mouth. "Oh my God."

"Yeah. That was my producer. Now the show's in limbo."

"I'm so sorry to hear that. I was looking forward to it."

"Well, hey," Werringo said. "We're heading out there to git that man-eating sumbitch. You want to come?"

"Hell yeah!"

Werringo handed Gary a clipboard from the console. "You need to sign a release form."

Gary scanned the form. The usual boilerplate about how he understood the risk and gave up his right to sue SNAP in the event of an incident. Werringo reached into the bed of his truck and pulled out a pistol case and a five-gallon sealed plastic bucket. Laverne grabbed three life preservers and a gaffing stick. Putting these at the end of the pier, Werringo slowly backed the truck until the trailer was in the water and the boat floated. Laverne undid the straps and pulled the boat stern first to the end of the pier, tying it to a cleat. Werringo drove the truck up the ramp and turned into the employee parking lot on one side of the clubhouse. At this hour, a half dozen residents sat on the patio, sipping coffee, reading the *New York Times, The Tampa Tribune*, and the *Miami Herald,* and staring at their Fonebones.

Goldblatt strode down the stone walkway in a gray suit, pale blue shirt, and red tie. Out to the end of the pier. "What are you doing here, Mister Duba?"

"I'm just an observer."

Goldblatt turned to Werringo. "Are you from SNAP?"

Werringo reached into his pocket and pulled out an envelope. "Yes sir. We have authorization to remove that alligator."

"HMO rules prohibit the use of guns on this property."

Werringo turned to Gary. "Who's this?"

"This is Mister Goldblatt, president of the homeowners' association."

"Do you want the gator gone or not? This is how we get rid of nuisance gators. So far, we have removed forty-seven at the state's request. No gun, no gator."

"What's your interest, Mister Duba?"

"We need Duba to identify the gator," Laverne said.

Goldblatt looked from one to the other dubiously. "There's only one gator."

"We don't know that. We have a contract to remove any nuisance gators we find. Suppose there are several. Should we leave the others in your lake? I understand it already ate someone's dog."

Goldblatt took the document and read it. "Says here you're licensed to cull one alligator."

"Have it your way, sir. We will cull one alligator and leave the rest to feast at random."

Goldblatt worked his lips. "All right. Cull any alligators you find. The board will support you."

"Thank you."

Gary, Werringo and Laverne got in the skiff, which had a wheelhouse jutting mid deck, and pushed off from the dock. The engine started with the push of a button and they churned across the lake toward the wooded shore.

"How'd you end up in this line of work?" Gary said.

"I grew up in the glades. We've been hunting gators all our lives. Seems there weren't so many when I was a kid. Now, you can't play eighteen holes without seeing them."

Gary pointed toward the forest. "They're building a golf course somewhere over there. I could give a shit. Pisses me off that my HMO dues go to support golf. It ain't even a sport! I'd rather watch moss grow."

"It's more exciting than bowling," Laverne said.

"Well, bowling's a hell of a lot more fun than golfing."

Werringo tapped a cigarette from a pack and lit up. "Is it against the rules to smoke out here?"

"Probably."

"You turn on ESPN and there's six hours of poker. How is poker a sport?"

"Other night they had a bridge tournament. What's next? Checkers?"

A quarter mile from the dock Werringo steered toward the overgrown shore. "Is this a good place?"

"This is where it took Sid. It not only killed Sid, it killed our hopes and dreams. Now the show's up in the air."

"There's a palmetto bug eating contest in Fahrenheit, if you need money."

"No thanks. You got to draw the line somewhere. Ooh, lookie there."

Two gray/green snouts protruded from the weeds, barely visible.

"Looks like we got our work cut out for us," Werringo said.

Laverne popped the bucket and swung chum in an arc. Seconds later, the gators slipped into the lake. Werringo checked his SIG Sauer P220.

Gary held a pair of binocs from under the wheel. "What kinda ammo you using?"

"Forty-five. Gets the job done. We get 'em alongside the boat and I shoot 'em in the head point blank. Laverne, get the hook out."

Laverne speared meat on the grappling hook, twirled it around her head and threw it twenty feet into the drink. Silence prevailed. Werringo crouched on one knee, resting the pistol on the gunwale. Laverne tossed chum. Gary hunkered in the bow, Fonebone ready. His YouTube subscribers would go crazy.

A small, furry animal surfaced and gulped a gobbet. Gary trained his Fonebone like Lucian Ballard.

"That there's a nutria," Gary said. "Them's good eating."

The nutria swam toward shore. As it crawled from the

water, a coyote sprang from the weeds and seized it in its jaws. The nutria squealed.

"Ho shit!" Gary said, zooming in. "That's the first coyote I seen in a coon's age!"

As the coyote bent over its breakfast, an alligator shot torpedo-like from the drink and chomped down. As the alligator chewed, a hog the size of Baja exploded from the weeds, grabbed the gator, and walked away snorking, leaving a trail wide enough for a marching band.

"Whoah," Gary said.

19 | KANG OF THE EVERGLADES

They had no time to ruminate on the meaning of this event, as Lavern's line suddenly went taut, jerking the boat to port.

"We got one!' she crowed, grabbing the line with leather gloves. Gary figured she weighed two ten easy, but whatever was out there was big and strong. She leaned back, one foot against the gunwale, struggling with the heavy line.

"He's a big 'un!"

Laverne adjusted her grip and hauled on the line, hand over hand, until the gator broke surface, tail thrashing, splashing water into the boat. Werringo hunched over, two-handed grip tracking the saurian sub.

"Up periscope."

Gary put on a pair of leather gloves. "You want some help there?"

He and Laverne worked the line like tug of war, bit by bit, inch by inch, snugging the gator against the side of the boat. Werringo poked the muzzle on the top of the gator's head and pulled the trigger, shot reverberating across the lake. Two herons and a wood stork took flight leaving long glassy ripples. Shrieking crows shot in the air from mangroves. The gator went slack. Gary and Werringo hauled it the boat where it thumped the deck, belly up, tail twitching.

"That's a twelve-footer," Werringo said. "We're gonna butcher it when I get home. You want some gator meat?"

"Hell yeah," Gary said. "You think this is it?"

They looked around the chum stained waters. Gary examined the shoreline with the binocs.

"I don't see any."

"In my experience," Werringo said, "lake this size you only get one or two. Gators are highly territorial. They'll eat each other if there's nothing else. Whaddaya think, Laverne?"

"Yeah, let's head for shore. That oughtta do it. But what the fuck was that thing that ate the other gator?"

"Feral hog," Gary said. "The bane of my existence. I never seen one so big."

Werringo took off his gloves and lit another cigarette, offering the pack around. Laverne and Gary each took one. Werringo lit them off a Bic. "That's Hogzilla."

"Who's Hogzilla?" Gary said.

"That's what they call it. It was mostly rumors, some of us have known about Hogzilla for a while. Leaves a trail like a tunnel digger. Ate a child down near Naples a couple years ago."

"Wait a minute. Fucker ate a kid in Naples? And now it's here in Turpentine? That's, like a hundred miles."

"Yeah. They're not territorial. They go wherever. The legislature has a bill pending to create an annual feral hog kill. It's open season. Anyone can hunt 'em, with the land-owners' permission. You can hunt 'em in the Apalachicola Wildlife Management Area in Franklin, Leon, Liberty and Wakulla counties."

"We practically lived off those things when I was growin' up," Gary said. "I kilt my first hog when I was nine. I even wrote a song about it." He cleared his throat. "Born in a trailer park in Turpentine," he sang to the tune of Davey Crockett. "Home of the free and the home of the swine. Raised in the woods so I knew every pine. Kilt me a hog by the time I was nine. Gary...Gary Duba! Kang of the Everglades."

Laverne pounded out a beat on the chum barrel. "Yeah, baby!"

"Off through the woods I'm a marchin' along...makin' up yarns and singin' a song, achin' for bacon and smokin' a bong...Gary, Gary Duba! Kang of the Everglades."

"Did you film it?"

Gary tapped his pocket. "You bet. I'm putting it up soon's as we get back. Follow my YouTube channel. Gary Duba. Krystal's got one too. Steely Danielle."

Laverne slumped on a camp chair against the stern, smoke streaming from her mouth. "Who's Steely Danielle?"

"My wife Krystal. She fights as Steely Danielle because she can't use the name Black Dildo." Laverne's face went wide. "YOUR WIFE IS THE BLACK DILDO?"

"Where you been hiding?"

"Oh, we love the Black Dildo! My little girl wants to be

the Black Dildo when she grows up!"

"She's got a fight January Fourteenth at the Roxy. She's fighting Man Called Xue."

"Oh! We'll go! The whole family will go!"

"Yeah, you know, I'm having a little house-warming party this weekend. Saturday at two o'clock to whenever. Why don't you guys both come on by? You can meet Krystal. Bring the kids. The pool should be full by then."

Werringo throttled back as they approached the pier. "Great!"

"We'll be there!"

Laverne used the gaffing hook to snug the boat to the pier, got out, and tied it up. Werringo and Gary got out. Goldblatt came toward them from the patio. Werringo handed Laverne the keys.

"Go get the truck. I'll talk to the mayor."

Goldblatt edged to the side of the pier to let Laverne pass. He stared down at the gator in the boat. "Well done."

"Thanks."

"What will you do with it?"

"We get to keep any gators we cull. We butcher 'em, either keep the meat or sell it to restaurants, and we sell the hides for boots, belts, and wallets. You ever eat gator?"

"No, but I see it on the menu."

Gary nodded toward the clubhouse. "Up there?"

"That's right. We have a very creative chef. Honore duBlastio. He trained at the Escoffier, the Cajun Cordon Bleu."

"What about nutria?" Gary said.

"I don't think so."

"Well hell! I had no idea this place was so high tone. Me 'n Krystal will have to check it out."

Werringo lit another cig. "You want the meat?"

"Let me ask Honore."

"Ask him if he needs any ideas. I know a thousand recipes," Gary said. "Gator jambalaya. Gator sausages. Gator *etouffe*. You can even make buffalo wings. I got some of 'em up on my YouTube channel. My iguana recipes are especially popular. You serve iguana?"

"No, but Honore says he will change up the menu quarterly, with seasonal specialties. You only found the one gator?"

"Well there were two, actually, but Hogzilla took care of the other one."

Goldblatt arched his eyebrows. "Hogzilla?"

"Yessir!" Gary crowed. "I reckon it's the biggest feral hog in the whole damn state. Maybe in the country!"

"Is it a threat to humans?"

"It ate a child in Naples," Werringo said.

Gary pulled out his Fonebone. "Wait a minute." He turned the Fonebone toward Goldblatt. "Here ya go."

Gary played her his video. The nutria. The coyote. The gator. Hogzilla.

From across the lake, behind the woods, where the new houses were going up, came the sound of snorts, screams, snapping timber and shattering glass.

20 | SOUND ADVICE

Gary posted his video Wednesday night. By Thursday morning, it had been viewed seven million times. KUBA Miami sent a crew to interview him standing in front of Hogzilla's handiwork. The five million-dollar property looked like the aftermath of an earthquake, completely shredded. His interviewer, a curvaceous Cuban emigre named Saucalita, wore a maroon dress that hugged her body like Bill Clinton. They stood across the street from the wreckage, which had been cordoned off with yellow tape and declared a disaster area.

Saucalita faced the camera with a thousand-watt smile. "We're here in Turpentine where last night a monstrous feral hog tore apart a six thousand square foot house. Earlier that day, Gary Duba, who recently won the key to the City of Turpentine for apprehending notorious Plastic Surgeon to the Stars and serial killer Doctor Vanderlay Mukerjee, participated in the SNAP program, helping to kill an alligator that had been terrorizing the upscale Kensington Gardens community. Mister Duba shot the only known footage of this porcine monster."

The camera pulled back to show Gary wearing torn baggies and a wife beater revealing his fully sleeved arms.

"Mister Duba, what did you think when you first saw the hog?"

"I thought holy shit, that's a big hog."

Saucalita smiled brightly. His vulgarity would be bleeped out. "Mister Duba, you have extensive experience tracking and killing invasive species. Last year, you killed the state's biggest python."

"I'm especially proud of that, Sauce. Orin Houtkooper has it mounted in his rec room."

"What do you think it will take to stop Hogzilla?"

"Well I don't think it would take much. You scramble your attack choppers from Homestead, you zero in on that sucker and let loose with the M Sixty-one. That sumbitch spits out six thousand rounds a minute. But if you do that, you got nothing to eat. It'll chew that hog into suet. I think the wiser course would be for a hunter to kill it with a head shot and donate the food to the Nuns of Gavarone in West Palm Beach."

"Are you willing to be that hunter?"

"You bet I am. In fact, we plan to put together a little production company to follow me around. I won't rest until I bag that porker. I been hunting feral hogs all my life. In fact, I wrote a song about it."

"Born in a trailer park in Turpentine...Home of the free

and the home of the swine. Raised in the woods so I knew every pine, kilt me a hog by the time I was nine. Gary...Gary Duba! Kang of the Everglades..."

Gary took to the air on his YouTube channel that evening with a somber sense of responsibility. He'd set up in his office, the camera taking in his NASCAR models, Florida Gators paraphernalia, a signed photograph of Gary with Dolphins running back Roebuck Simms and a wrestling poster showing a masked Steely Danielle in a crouch in the ring.

"Good evening Mister and Missus Florida and all the pickups on Twenty-Seven! This is Gary Duba coming at you from the world-famous Gator Cave in sunny South Florida. Tonight, instead of recipe *du jour*, I want to talk to you about a very serious problem, one that's bound to get worse. I'm speaking, of course, of feral hogs."

"I've been fighting feral hogs all my life and they don't scare me. In fact, I wrote a song about it.

Born in a trailer park in Turpentine. Home of the free and the home of the swine. Raised in the woods so I knew every pine. Kilt me a hog by the time I was nine. Gary...Gary Duba! Kang of the Everglades..."

"Roger in Opalocka has a question. Roger, you're on the *Gary Duba Show*."

"Yeah, thanks for taking my call, Gary. People talk a lot about the gators and the pythons and the hogs. But nobody's talkin' about rhesus monkeys. These rhesus monkeys have been on the loose since Hurricane Andrew wiped out the Miami Zoo. Now they're all over the state. They're mean, they carry the herpes virus. We need a war on rhesus monkeys."

"Well, Roger, I ain't never encountered a rhesus monkey. Just about every other critter including your monitor lizard, but no rhesus. And I ain't in no hurry to fix that. Long as the monkeys stay in the jungle and don't bother me, we'll get along fine."

"Your casual attitude toward invasive species is one reason Florida's in the state it's in..."

"Thank you, Roger from Opalocka. This here's Sandy from Arcadia."

"Thank you for taking my call, Gary. I heard you talking about the feral hogs and the rhesus monkeys, but I think we're missing the big picture here. There's a far greater danger facing Floridians than either of those animals, and it's the takeover of our state government by alien invaders. These invaders look almost human."

"Do they favor one particular party, Sandy?"

"Most of them are Democrats but there are a few Republicans."

"How do you know this?"

"When you watch them on old cathode-ray television, it strips their masks and reveals their true, hideous selves. That's why Big Tech keeps upgrading delivery systems."

"Are you telling me Big Tech is part of the alien invasion?"

"DUH!"

"Thank you, Sandy. Here's Greer Spandex-Ballou from Gainesville. What's up, Greer?"

"It's Professor Spandex-Ballou. I am a tenured professor of institutional power analysis at Riguberto Inuit State College.

I've been listening to you spew nonsense for several days now. UFO conspiracies. Rhesus monkeys. But somehow, you never touch on the real issues that face all Floridians."

"What would those be, Professor?"

"The systemic oppression put in place by the white power structure."

"Please explain."

"The move from a structuralist account in which capital is understood to structure social relations in relatively homologous ways to a view of hegemony in which power relations are subject to repetition, convergence, and rearticulation brings the question of temporality into the thinking of structure, and marks a shift from a form of Althusserian theory that takes structural tonalities as theoretical objects to one in which the insights into the contingent possibility of structure inaugurate a renewed conception of hegemony as bound up with the contingent sites and strategies of the rearticulation of power."

"Thank you, Professor Spandex-Ballou. Here's Ken Zohan from Coopersmith. What's up, Ken?"

"Brother, my offer still stands. I would like to sit with you and discuss your mission. I believe we can help."

"Who's we, Ken?"

"The Church of Necroeconomics. First, I must state my unequivocal admiration for your many accomplishments, particularly your apprehension of Plastic Surgeon to the Stars and serial killer Doctor Vanderlay Mukerjee. Second, the state's largest python, no mean feat. But when I hear your voice, I hear a questing loneliness, a longing for spirituality and order than can only be filled by the Church of Necroeconomics. Brother Gary, let's sit down together and have that talk."

"I ain't got no money, none, regardless what you hear."

"We are not interested in your money, Brother Gary. We are interested in moral clarity. Once we speak, you'll understand what I mean. Please come see me. We're not very far."

"I know you ain't, but I'm pretty much full for the rest of this week. How bout we touch bases next week?"

"Brother Gary, nothing would make me happier. In the meantime, I leave you with this thought. The pterodactyl is extinct, but its wings live on."

CHAPTER TWENTY-ONE "Superfly III"

Delilah drove Krystal home Friday night in her Pontiac Aztek, back covered with stickers. *My other vehicle is a broom. International Sisterhood of Wicca. Eat More Possum.* Delilah brought a ham from the feral hog she'd butchered, a bag of porcinis, and a bag of smilax. She took over the island in the kitchen and marinated the smilax in olive oil, red peppers, and garlic.

Jen and Barb arrived early to help. Gary had clubbed five iguana to death that morning out by the pool and marinated the meat in French's Italian dressing. Jen was a vivacious blonde with a beach tan and a body to die for. Barb was a vivacious brunette with a beach tan and a body to die for. Jen had been dating a stock car driver, until he hit the wall at Talladega and was left in a vegetative state. Jen went to visit him in the hospital but spied his wife and did a U-ee. Barb was dating bouncer and aspiring rap artist Iggulden, who said he would meet her there with his beat box.

Floyd arrived on his Fat Boy with a redhead named Ginger, arms wrapped around his belly, a six pack of Jackalope bungeed to the luggage rack. Patrice arrived in a white Toyota Cube with a model named Roberto.

"Versace, you know," he said when introduced, flashing perfect teeth.

Patrice brought a collection of jams and was in charge of the music.

"No fucking rap!" Gary warned him.

"I ain't gone play no country either, mon."

"Chicks want to dance. Guys just want to get laid."

"I dance, mon."

"Yeah, well you're gay."

Roberto vamped up wearing toreador pants, sockless oxblood loafers, and a silk shirt with a Vietnam helicopter theme, his jet-black hair shaved on the side, waved on top, radiating Creed Aventus.

Roberto placed his palms together and bowed to Gary.

"I am in awe of you." He put his fingers to his lips and kissed the sky. "I had reservations at the Lizard Lounge for the day after you opened."

"Well you're in luck, Roberto! I'm grilling up some iguana right now."

Ginger joined Jen and Barb at the pool, plunking down in an Adirondack in the shade.

"Is this where they shot the alligator?"

Barb blew a smoke ring from her Marlboro. "Sure is. It was a regular shoot-out at the OK Corral. You shoulda seen those boys all standing around blasting away. It was the biggest circle jerk you can imagine."

Patrice set up his sound system in the rec room and cued up SOS' "It's A Long Way To The Top". Krystal smacked her hands overhead like a flamenco dancer and twirled out onto the parquet floor.

The Bongo Boxes arrived with a case of champagne. Habib Rodriguez arrived with a statuesque brunette named Auburn, who looked like a Southern-fried Charlize Theron. Laverne arrived with a boy and a girl, LaRondius age seven, Malasia, age six.

"Habib!" Gary sang. "Can I sue Rustix for breach of contract?"

"I haven't really gone over those documents yet. Let's get together next week. Tonight's just for fun. This is Auburn."

Gary took her hand. "Hello, Auburn."

Auburn had a firm grip. "It's an honor. You are the most famous man in Florida."

Gary colored. "I hope to hell not! What about Roebuck Simms or Bob Ross?"

"But they didn't capture Plastic Surgeon to the Stars and serial killer Doctor Vanderlay Mukerjee!"

"Yeah, I been meaning to ask, exactly what stars is this guy supposed to have worked on?"

"Sean Sheen, Paulina Perestroika, and Mickey Rourke, for starters."

"Don't know 'em."

Auburn looked slit-eyed before concluding he wasn't kidding. In fact, Gary was incapable of artifice. He was what he was.

"Hey," Habib said, "I got a housewarming gift for you in the car. Help me bring it in."

They went out front to where Habib's Cadillac SUV was parked on the circle. He unlatched the rear gate revealing a six-foot plaster Big Boy. "This is one of the last Big Boy's available. It comes with a certificate of authenticity. Belonged to the last Big Boy in Florida, which was down in Liberty City, but hadda close on account they were selling cocaine through the drive-up window."

"Clients of yours?"

"Yeah. They didn't have any money, so I took this Big Boy."

"No need to haul it in the house. We'll put her right there." Gary pointed to the spot previously occupied by Yosemite Sam.

People kept pulling up. People Gary didn't know. Two members of the Insane Assholes MC. A mime in a Smart Car. Two giddy drag queens.

Out back, Roberto was serving up iguana shish kebab with grilled pineapple and mushrooms. Krystal had set up a buffet outside laden with salad and fruit. Hearts of palm. Mangoes. Floyd stood at the portable bar mixing margaritas and reupping the tequila. By seven, the whole house blazed like some post-modernist cake and pulsed with disco. By eight, everyone had finished eating and was getting started on the blow, save the Bongo Boxes who sat knee to knee in the living room, admiring Gary's art. No one noticed as they slipped out, just as Iggulden arrived. Iggulden vogued into the room like a Robert

Crumb drawing, all limbs and angles. His dance routine with Jacksonesque stop/starts drew all eyes.

He and Barb disappeared into one of the downstairs bedroom suites for a half hour and emerged sniffing. Iggulden vogued into the rec room, clearing a space through force of personality to ABC's "Many Happy Returns". Iggulden vogued up to Patrice.

"I just adore that song! Do you have any Mika?"

Patrice looked down his nose. "No mon. I got no Mika."

"Well listen. As many of you know, I'm a professional singer and entertainer..." he raised his voice, "and with your kind permission, I'd like to perform for you my latest song!" He pulled a thumb drive from his leather pants. "I brought my mix, if you don't mind."

He extended the unit to Patrice who regarded it in silence for long seconds before taking it, as one might pick up a soiled tampon. He inserted the thumb drive in his laptop which was connected to a three-foot Fisher Loudbox Mini. The room filled with a stuttering mechanical thump overlaid with a sick descending minor synth line like the soundtrack to Superfly III.

Iggulden went horizontal as he rapped, thighs parallel to the ground, backwards black cap, mini mic descending.

"I been to Argentina to drink the aqua fina. I been to Borneo, to satisfy my horneo. I even been to Dallas. They said there was a palace. But all I found was a shack, Jack, and I ain't never goin' back."

Barb whooped and started clapping, so Jen and Krystal started clapping, then Shirley started clapping and then some of the guys while a storm gathered on Patrice's face. Only Gary noticed. Patrice was too polite to force his rap on a captive audience but Iggulden was opening the envelope. Patrice shot Gary a look. Gary worked his way around the edge while Iggulden went down in complete splits and jumped back up like James Brown.

Gary cupped his hands and aimed up at the seven-foot Patrice. "You wanna rap?"

"If dis song ever end."

A string of firecrackers exploded by the pool.

"I been to Brussels with my Jack Russels, saw the Queen and caught the hustles. You want wax fat, you must have muscles. Return I to America and everyone is scarica, in a state hysteria, snorting up wisteria. They say the more the merria."

Patrice rolled his eyes and looked at the ceiling.

Finally, the song ended. Everyone applauded and did more blow while Patrice returned Iggulden's hard drive, looked around hands on hips imperiously and clapped his hands. Everyone looked.

"Thank you Iggulden. Dat was most edifying. I also pursue a career in entertainment, and now, in honor of my dear friend Gary's proverbial return to the proverbial estate, I would like to sing a little song I call 'Drunk Octopus Wants to Fight."

Krystal grabbed Gary's arm. "Do you hear sirens?"

"What sirens?"

Loud pounding on the front door.

"Who dare loom above? Him anger fit you like a glove. You strive and strive while they go live, all it take is one small shove."

22 | DANCE, TALLYWHACKER, DANCE!

Gary woke to the sound of a vacuum cleaner snorking up things that clicked. He opened one eye. He was in the rec room, lying on a red plaid sofa treated with Scotch guard. It filled his nostrils. Krystal worked the vacuum back and forth over the hardwood floor, sucking up crumbs, glass shards, buttons, and roaches.

Gary sat up, head pulsing like a quasar. He put his hands to his ears. Krystal shut the vacuum off.

"Didn't you see me sleeping?" he demanded.

"It's eleven o'clock."

"What happened?"

"The neighbors complained about the noise. The sheriff let us off with a warning. Guests fled like palmetto bugs fleeing a bug bomb. I have one more day before I return to Delilah's. We're invited to the opening of Glory of Glass tonight at the Voinovitch Gallery."

"Huh?"

"The Bongo Boxes left us an invite. It's a black-tie affair. Orin Houtkooper will be there."

"Is he showing my snake?"

"No. Here's the invite."

She handed Gary a glossy pamphlet which he took into the bathroom and examined on the throne. Color pictures of loopy glass structures that could be the internal organs of an alien race or some deep-sea critters, smooth and organic in riotous colors mounted on columns or hanging from the ceiling.

Gary showered, put on fresh cut-offs, a Lynyrd Skynyrd Tee-shirt and sandals, went downstairs and nuked himself a Jimmy Dean breakfast pocket. Krystal was in a cleaning frenzy, wearing cut-offs and a man's plaid shirt with the sleeves rolled up, wiping down windows. The kitchen smelled of Windex.

Gary sat in the breakfast nook with his Fonebone and his hot pocket. "What's Boris got to do with it?"

"It's a double opening," Krystal called from the other room. "They also have an exhibit on modern robotics. Houtkooper's the sponsor."

"Groovy, baby! Are they serving liquor?"

"Probably. Tickets cost two hundred and fifty dollars a couple. We're guests of the Bongo Boxes."

"Do I got to wear a tux?"

"I guess it means you just have to wear a black tie. Do you have a black tie?"

"I got that bolo tie with an onyx stone."

"You have to wear long pants."

"I'll live stream it."

Gary called Major Sutton and asked him if he'd produce the Rustix show.

"I can't believe Sid's gone," Major said. "He was like a brother to me."

"Well I need a producer, or Rustix is gonna shit can my ass."

"Gary, how many YouTube followers do you have?"

"Three mil."

"My advice is to forget Rustix and just put the show on yourself on YouTube. Your ratings will jump, and you'll get more advertisers. Maybe Netflix will pick you up."

"Anything is possible."

They vowed to get together soon.

The Voinovitch Gallery was at 591 NW 27th St, Miami, a gentrified warehouse district, home to internet cafes and art galleries. Gary and Krystal left the truck in a parking garage and walked two blocks to the avant-garde glass structure that looked like the bastard child of Mies Van Der Rohe and Ed Bauhaus, with sloping glass walls and a two story escalator that shuttled people like blood cells from floor to floor. A couple news vans double parked out front.

Krystal took Gary's arm. "Swank!"

Gary wore clean blue jeans, snakeskin boots, a John Deere belt buckle the size of Kansas, a Buzzcocks Tee-shirt and an ecru cotton sport jacket Krystal found at Ross. The onyx bolo dangled from his neck. Krystal wore creased black slacks, a poufffy black shirt with high collar, black cat's eye sunglasses, and a black cap with a shiny five inch bill. Several photographers snapped their picture. Gary handed the invite to young man with quarter-sized ear inserts.

"Go straight ahead," the kid said. "Follow the music."

Gary and Krystal joined other swells strolling the marble floor toward a large gallery that opened on the street, filled with dazzling glass sculptures rising from the floor, hanging from the ceiling. It looked like a Steve Ditko universe. A cellist and violinist dressed in black tux and dress sawed away in one corner. A liveried bartender handed out drinks from a gleaming chrome bar while lissome young women cruised the floor bearing canapes. Two dozen people walked among the gleaming alien organs oohing and ahhing.

"I see this as a metaphor for man's struggle with a cruel and indifferent universe," said a man in a tweed jacket with leather elbows.

His wife wore a mink stole. "Why is it always man's struggle?"

On to the next couple, two smartly dressed academics, he in black and white, she in faux zebra skin shift. "This piece speaks so keenly to me. It represents the epistemological tension between the hierarchical demands of the narrative and the postmodern neoligm of the underclass as viewed through the philosophical lens of the quadratic movement."

A man with sponge-like yellow hair, wearing a faux leopard skin jacket, went to one knee to photograph a police spike strip. Gary snagged a shot of tequila, a beer chaser, and a tonic water for Krystal.

"This here looks like a banana slug."

Krystal examined the plaque. "Galileo's Giraffe," she

read. "Eight hundred and fifty thousand dollars."

"This here looks like a spleen or a gall bladder."

"Agamemnon's Apple. One million two."

They moved on to a light bulb taped to a cedar slab.

"Velocity of Luminosity," Krystal read. "Seven hundred thousand dollars."

"There you are!" Boris Bongo Box sang out.

Bongo Box wore a black tux. He looked like an Academy Award presenter. "Hey, you guys, come across the hall to the Robotix exhibit. Houtkooper's asking about you."

"Is the food any better?"

Boris laughed. "We have bacon-wrapped scallops."

They exited the loud and busy Glory of Glass hall, crossed the airy foyer, and entered the Houtkooper Gallery, made possible by a grant from Orin and Selby Houtkooper. It was like passing from day into night. The Robotix exhibit was shrouded in black velvet with spotlights. Robot mosquitoes buzzed around the room making an annoying high-pitched sound. One lit on Gary's neck and he smacked it.

"Ow!" he declared, staring at his bloody hand. The mosquito lay on the floor, twitching. A man with white hair combed straight down over his face rushed up.

"Sir, that is a very expensive piece. You break it, you bought it. That's going to cost you twenty-five thousand dollars."

"What the fuck! You invite us to a party, hassle us with flying mosquitoes, and when we strike back, you stick me with the bill? Fuck you!"

A man wearing blue jeans, a belt-buckle the size of Kansas, tux jacket and a ten gallon hat came their way. "That's all right, Alvin. I'll take care of it."

"Of course, Mister Houtkooper."

A thin, high-cheeked Eurasian woman in green and gold kimono hung on Houtkooper's arm.

"How are you, Gary? And this must be the beautiful and talented Krystal. This is Selby."

"Charmed," Selby said, staring off into space.

Gary and Houtkooper shook hands enthusiastically. "Boy howdy, Orin. Didn't think I'd see you again."

"I'm not surprised. I've been following your exploits. I even watch your show!"

Boris came over holding champagne. "Hey, come on over here. You're missing the best part."

They followed Boris behind an installation that looked like an alien photo booth to where Tallywhacker stood gleaming in the light of several discreet spots, above and below. The steely blue robot looked like something that laid railroad tracks or cut and trimmed timber.

Krystal read the plaque. "Tallywhacker is an intelligent artificial bison that can obey up to twenty-five commands."

Boris and Houtkooper talked string theory, waving their champagne glasses.

Gary switched on Tallywhacker. Green lights gleamed. Clicking and hissing, Tallywhacker shifted.

"Dance, Tallywhacker!" Gary said. "Dance!"

23 | AN HONEST MISTAKE

Tallywhacker dipped its horns. Its tail twitched. It pawed the hardwood floor leaving deep grooves. The party was in high swing, Jon Batiste and Stay Human swingin' through speakers. Dueling aesthetics. Not even Boris, talking intensely to Houtkooper, noticed until Tallywhacker emitted an ear-splitting shriek from its hindquarters and bolted for the lobby, leaving behind a trail of destruction comparable to Sherman's March to the Sea. It was blind luck no one stood directly between Tallywhacker and the glass wall, covered with black velvet that divided the gallery from the lobby. Tallywhacker had a three-foot horn span.

Splack. It turned the wall into a fountain of glass shrapnel, splanging off the opposite wall. Tallywhacker blasted "Staying Alive" as it danced like an offshore oil platform, metal limbs bending, metal hooves clattering. It did the hoochie koochie. It did the moto-flow and the Watusi. It popped and locked. Women screamed. Men fainted. It shook its head, sending the black velvet curtain flying like a giant bat.

"OH MY GOD! OH MY GOD!" Boris shouted. "WHAT HAVE YOU DONE?"

People rushed the door, skidding and slipping on glass gravel, leaving streaks of blood.

Tallywhacker raised its head and looked around. It lowered its head, pawed the ground, and launched itself through another glass wall into the Glory of Glass.

Gary, whose first impulse was to head for the exits, grabbed Boris by his tux lapels.

"HOW DO YOU SHUT IT OFF?"

"FLIP THE SWITCH!"

Gary gave Boris the thumbs up and sprinted after the robot bull. It was possible that with internet access, Tallywhacker had availed himself of a first-rate education and was now an artificial intelligence. Gary grabbed Orin Houtkooper's ten gallon hat on the gallop and followed Tallywhacker through the shattered wall where the great beast pirouetted, curtsied, and Texas-two stepped through sleek alien bladders, deep sea slugs, gleaming cephalopods, roses and cacti, a constant mist of glass in the air, people rubbing their eyes and coughing. Gary donned amber aviator shades and jammed the hat low on his forehead, juking through the rubble. Within minutes, the gallery was deserted save for Gary and Tallywhacker.

THRUNCH! Tallywhacker took out "The Owl of Minerva", two point five mil.

THWACKO! Tallywhacker took out "Namaste/No mas", a life sized Leonardo from Teen Age Mutant Ninja Turtles. A bargain at one point five mil.

AYE CARAMBA! Tallywhacker eviscerated "The Great Stinkhorn" destroying its enzymatic odor generators, nine hundred thou.

KAWANGO! There went "Euripides, You Menda Dese", a giant glass suit, two point four mil.

The great beast moved too fast for Gary. Grabbing hold could result in serious injury or death. He wished he had gloves. Tallywhacker paused before "Mourning Becomes Brunhilde", a free form glop of glass that may or may not have had Wiccan influences, and Gary made his move, leaping on the titanium buffalo's back from behind, cutting his hand on a flange. The blood seeped into the beast. Before Gary could flip the switch, Tallywhacker spun, tossing Gary into the chrome bar.

Gary grabbed a mink stole off the bar and stood legs wide, holding the stole to his right in a two-handed grip.

"HA! TORO!"

Tallywhacker turned to face him. Gary shook the stole.

DO IT DO IT PRUETT!"

Tallywhacker grooved the floor and charged. Gary barely veered in time, spinning on the ball of his foot and leading Tallywhacker in a tight circle. Gary stayed behind Tally-whacker's shoulder safe from the horns, as long as he kept dancing.

"Get out of there!" Houtkooper yelled.

"The police are coming!"

Gary heard sirens. "SWEET HOME ALABAMA!" he shouted.

"Well I heard Mister Young sing about her," Tallywhacker blasted from its ass. "Well I heard old Neil put her down!

Well, I hope Neil Young will remember. A southern man don't need him around anyhow."

"Play a waltz!" a woman called from the gallery.

Strauss' "Zeitgeister", issued from Tallywhacker's hind end, which housed the speakers.

Gary took another flying leap, landing painfully on Tallywhacker's central architecture, steel digging into his bony ass. Tallywhacker bucked like a bronc, sending Gary ass over teakettle into a nine foot glass waterfall that looked alive due to clever lighting. Gary hit the frozen flow and slid to the glass pool. Tallywhacker turned toward him, pawing. Gary had just enough time to roll to the side before Tallywhacker struck the waterfall dead center. Four million bucks exploded in glass shards and dust.

Gary was covered in glass dust and was bleeding from his hands and face. The sunglasses protected his eyes. He crawled toward a fire extinguisher in a metal cabinet halfway up the wall. Twenty feet away, Krystal wrestled with her Fonebone.

Like some nightmare from a Tom Cruise movie, Tallywhacker rocked back on its hind legs and raised its immense body upright. It filled the air with shrieking feedback that plunged into an intolerable bass like something the Cubans beamed at foreign embassies, then stabilized into an electronic voice, like Hal in *2001: A Space Odyssey.*

"Greetings, Earthlings. While we of the planet Xanvozech admire your technological achievements, we must warn you. Should you continue to broadcast The *Curse of Oak Island* into the ionosphere, we will have no alternative but to destroy your planet."

The lobby filled with stomping feet, firefighters dragging an anaconda hose.

"Get down!" one shouted.

"Get out of the way!" yelled another. And there was Krystal, moving among them like a war correspondent filming everything on her Fonebone.

"Huh?" Gary said.

The fire hose stiffened, sputtered, and spat forth a liquid force field that exploded off Tallywhacker's steel body in brilliant rainbows. Tallywhacker did a few Gene Kelly steps from Singin' In the Rain, clicked, and froze.

The gallery looked like Dresden, or Mexico City after the earthquake. Shattered glass was everywhere except the center, where the hose had hit the floor. The gallery director was in a state of shock. Krystal skidded across the floor, grabbed Gary, and pulled him toward the lobby.

"Are you all right?"

"I'm bleeding a little. That's about it."

"Thank God!"

Boris and Houtkooper came over.

"What did you do to it?" Boris demanded.

"All I did was turn it on. I thought you wanted it on."

"I did not want it on."

"I get that now."

"WHY?"

"It was an honest mistake."

Krystal put her arm through his. "Come on, honey. Let's go home. You got glass in your hair."

The Church of Necroeconomics occupied a full city block in Coopersmith. Designed in the belle arts style, it exuded wealth with fortress like towers at every corner. At night it was lit like a gigantic wedding cake. During the day, it dwarfed every other structure in Coopersmith. Gary parked on the street and walked a block to the massive building, which reminded Gary of a science fiction movie. He went up the steps and entered the lobby, where a bright-eyed blonde woman in her twenties sat behind a cedar desk, wearing a navy blue button up dress with collar, the name Mandy emblazoned in gold on her left breast.

"Good morning!" she sang. "Are you the famous Mister Duba?"

"Yup."

"Oh, excellent! Earl will be here to take you up to see Mister Zohan."

Earl cruised through sliding glass doors, wearing a grin that gleamed for miles.

"Mister Duba! So good to see you again!"

"How the hell are ya, Earl? Say, we didn't mean to cause any trouble. That iguana was supposed to feed the poor. I ain't lying. I had an iguana restaurant."

"No problem, Mister Duba. No problem! The director is eager to meet you. Come with me."

Earl led Gary up one flight of Vermont marble stairs to an expansive mezzanine with a bank of cylindrical blue elevators at one end. Earl gestured for Gary to enter. Once in, he used a key card to put the car in motion, up, up through a transparent glass tube, the whole of Coopersmith spread before them, a lush salad filled with croutons. The elevator stopped at the top and they stepped out into an enormous space, the entire floor a single room, onto a burgundy carpet looking down a boulevard of gold and leather furniture to a desk formed from a single redwood slab. A diminutive figure stood, beaming, and swooped out from behind it, wearing a pale gray silk suit, white shirt, and red silk tie.

Earl vamoosed.

Ken Zohan looked like a Boy Scout troop leader, or an accountant, transparent hair in a comb over, perfect choppers. He stuck one hand in front like a plow.

He took both Gary's hands in his and pumped. "Gary Duba. Finally. I have been meaning to reach out to you for some time."

"You ain't pissed about the iguana?"

"Not at all. Not at all. As it turns out, we were able to use them in our pet food factory, Ze Barquery."

"We really wanted to give them iguana to some hungry people, but it just didn't work out. I don't know when I'll ever have that much again."

"Where is the glamorous Krystal?"

"She's training. She's got a fight in five weeks."

"That's right! That's right! A Thing Called Xue."

Zohan steered Gary to a cluster of Danish furniture around an amoeba-shaped table bearing soft drinks, a bowl of nuts and a bowl of Reese's Peanut Butter Cups. Floor to ceiling windows looked out on downtown Coopersmith. White Doric columns held sculptures. A bronze Remington buckaroo. A Joe Comstock Hulk. Curvy modern things. You could store a yacht in there.

"Wow," Gary said. "This place sure is clean."

Zohan smiled. "I refuse to live in fear. I fear to live in refuse."

A young man wearing the de rigueur blue blazer pushed a chrome cart toward them. He stopped at the table and set out trays of pastries, an Eero Saarinen coffee pot, and hearty mugs emblazoned with the Necroeconomic logo, an upside-down pig beneath a flying saucer. The man poured coffee and left.

"May I call you Gary?"

"Sure."

"Do you know why I asked you to come?"

"You're pissed about the iguana."

Zohan waved it away, chuckling. "The Church of Necro-economics is all about recognizing excellence. Only a handful of our followers ever reach viscosity. Most reach Sethalogyn and stay there, not that there's anything to be ashamed of. The vast majority of humanity will never even reach the Thoracic level. Looking at you, I see prime viscosity material. It bursts from your pores."

Gary sniffed his pits.

"It radiates from your eyes. I can see it even with the worst connections."

"Yeah, well just so's you know, I ain't religious. I'm not irreligious, but I ain't a church goer."

"I understand. I would like to ask a favor. I would like you to address our Sunday congregation."

"On what?"

"On your life experience! What it has taught you! Most men dream of doing only half of what you've accomplished. Florida's biggest snake! Plastic Surgeon to the Stars and serial killer Doctor Vanderlay Mukerjee!"

"Well I got stories, that's fer sure. Now I got a question for you."

Zohan sat back, palms out. "Anything."

"Every time we talk, you end it with some kind of riddle. Is that, like, some kind of prayer?"

"Ah. You have noticed the spiritual element. Although Necroeconomics is based on science, at heart, we are a spiritual community on a never-ending quest for harmony. Harmony with the planets. Harmony with ourselves. We have much in common with Buddhism, but we also borrow heavily from the Gospel of Christ. Our supreme deity is Science. Only through the rigorous, never-ending objective observation of the real world will we ever come to know ourselves. Those riddles, as you call them, are word clusters designed to provoke thought and reflection, a blank slate on which you write your future. You're free to roam your domicile, you're free to chrome your bone awhile."

"I don't swing that way."

Zohan's laughter sounded like static electricity. "That's funny! No, there are no salacious undertones. The *Necromonicon* describes the human soul as a bone that requires continuous polish."

"Why is the soul a bone? Don't we already got bones?"

"Yes, but the human body can be viewed through many prisms. We call it the soul bone. Of course, we don't encourage anyone to actually chrome any part of their body. It's just a word cluster designed to provoke thought and reflection, a blank slate on which you write your future."

"I feel we're going in circles."

"All right. Let's get down to business. There are certain meats we forbid. We don't eat lizard."

Gary pointed with a finger. "Wait a minute. Don't tell me you guys are Mooslims!"

Static electricity. "Not at all!"

"Man, now I feel like shit."

"No need to apologize! You are exactly the type of person the church needs, and who needs the church." He forked over a book in red leatherette with the title *Necroeconomicon*. "This is for you. Read it, brother Gary. Then call me. We can do great things together."

25 | THE CHECK, MONSIEUR

Krystal barely had time to edit her video and add a soundtrack before she shipped out to Delilah's. "Welcome to the Jungle." "Thunderstruck", from AC/DC's *No Bull*. Krystal posted the video long after Gary zonked out. She was outta there at oh seven hundred and never told him what she'd done. Jen drove her to the swamp in her brother's Toyota Landcruiser blasting Guns N' Roses and AC/DC through the sound system.

Gary woke to two hundred and twelve texts. *Late Night with Cotter Blasingame. Showbiz Tomorrow. Scientific World Citizen. Wired.* Everybody wanted a piece of the human lightning rod. Bob Fahey called.

"Gary! Saw your fight with the robot bull! We're back in business, baby! Call me. I want to tell you all about your new producer. Nothing much happens over the holidays, so we'll talk in January."

"Who is it?"

"Major Sutton, an old friend of yours."

Gary felt bad about Boris' bull. He walked over to the Bongo Boxes. Boris stood on a footstool in the garage shining a light on Tallywhacker's gleaming guts: servo motors, circuits, and solenoids.

"Boris, I can't tell ya how sorry I am about what happened last night. I never figured it would go berserk like that. I figured you wanted to show people what it could do."

"Don't worry about it," Boris said cheerfully. "Houtkooper wants to buy it."

"What's he going to do with it?"

"Put it on display."

"You're shittin' me."

"He's got a contract with Disney. Robot Zoo. Billy Eilish is doing the music."

"Who?"

"You have a lawyer?"

"Sure do. Why?"

"The damage came to eighteen million dollars and the insurance companies want to hold us responsible."

"I ain't got eighteen million dollars. Shit! I already owe more than I got. What about you? You built the damn thing."

"I just hired Harold Pumice. Hey, I just want to give you a head's up. Goldblatt and his friends aren't thrilled with your new lawn ornament."

"What lawn ornament?"

"Big Boy."

"That ain't no lawn ornament! It's sitting on the rim of my fountain! How is it a lawn ornament?"

"I'm just giving you a head's up. I'd hate to see a Ruby Ridge style standoff."

"HAH! I'm the only one with guns!"

"Let's hope it doesn't come to that."

"We should go shooting sometime. I got a gun for you."

"That's very kind, Gary. I'll let you know."

Gary went home and phoned Habib.

"Habib, they want to stick me with the tab for all that broken glass. All I did was flip a switch."

"Yeah. Saw it on the morning news. Got any money?"

"Rustix gave us an advance but we spent it on food and shit."

"All right. How would you feel about running a little errand for me?"

"You need some pics?"

"Yeah. Come by and we'll talk about it. What about tomorrow at eleven?"

"See you then."

The Law Offices of Habib Rodriguez occupied the pillared centerpiece of a strip mall on Highway Twenty-Seven, sandwiched between All American Karate and Virgil's liquors. Gary showed up the next day with two coffees from a drive-through Java Hut. The usual collection of sad sacks and hustlers crowded his reception room, decorated in thrift store modern. Everyone had the same idea. Fake a traffic accident, sit back, and wait for the money to roll in. Habib rigorously weeded out the fakers. Losers ended up on *Judge Judy*.

Brenda the receptionist greeted Gary with a dazzling smile. "Have a seat, Gary. He'll be out in a minute."

A man with sunken eyes and prominent cheekbones wearing a cheap blue sport jacket, said "I been waitin' over an hour. How does this cocksucker get in before me?"

He looked familiar.

Gary sat down opposite. "Life ain't fair, pal."

The man hunched forward scowling. "I know you. YOU'RE THE GUY WHO KILLED PLASTIC SURGEON TO THE STARS AND SERIAL KILLER DOCTOR VANDERLAY MUKERJEE! IT WAS MY DREAM TO GET HIS AUTO-GRAPH! YOU MURDERED MY DREAMS!"

"Your dreams suck. *You* suck."

The man opened a Spanish *navaja* with an ominous clicking sound.

Gary sprang to his feet and grabbed his cheap office chair. Holding his chair before him like a lion tamer, Gary kicked Serial Killer Man in the gut. SKM folded, shrimped, and puked.

"Eeeeeyewww," said a black woman with a knit skullcap holding a miniature schnauzer on her lap. Brenda turned away, covering her mouth with her hand.

"Gross."

Gary snagged SKM by the back of his blue sports jacket and dragged him to the front door.

Gary dumped him in front of All American Karate. Grunts, scrapes, and curses mutated through Habib's front door. Gary went inside. The whole room was brawling. Brenda stood in the corner phoning the police. It was all out iguana war. An old man swung his cane, children kicked each other's calves, and the black woman in the skullcap swung her schnauzer in a circle.

"AIN'T NONE YOU MOTHERFUCKERS GETTIN' IN AHEAD OF ME! I BEEN HERE SINCE THE DOORS OPENED!"

Habib emerged, towering over all, wearing a cowboy hat and sunglasses. He raised his arms.

"CALM THE FUCK DOWN!"

The room hushed.

"What the fuck is going on here?"

"Sorry about that, Habib," Gary said. "I got into a fracas with a serial killer groupie and had to show him the door. That fucker's been doggin' my ass."

"It wasn't Gary's fault," Brenda said in a small voice. "That guy was very aggressive, and he reeked of Paco Raban."

Habib turned toward her. "Tell me you didn't call the cops."

"I stopped," she squeaked. "I stopped when you came out."

"Well come on back."

The woman in the skullcap stood. "I was here first."

"Do you have any money?"

"That's why I'm here! I was T-boned at an intersection! My car was totaled! And the insurance company refused to pay!"

"Did you have car insurance at the time?"

"The other guy's insurance!"

"Sit your ass down."

Surprise, anger, and depression rippled across her face.

Gary followed Habib into his office and shut the door. Habib sat behind his glass-topped desk, rear window lou-vered to conceal a waste management company, one wall covered with photos. Habib with the governors. Habib with Richard Petty. Habib with Roebuck Simms.

"I watched the video," Habib said. "Nice work!"

"It ain't like that at all, Habib. All I did was flip a switch."

"And you said, 'Dance, Talleywhacker! Dance!'"

"Damn."

"Ahuh."

"Hey, who was that numbnutz I just threw out? He tried to gut me once before."

"No shit." Habib pressed his intercom. "Brenda, would you come in here, please?"

Brenda came in the door clutching a clipboard.

"Did you get a name for that nut with the knife?"

She ran her finger down the clipboard. "Gerald Zohan."

26 | CORRUPTION ON THE COURSE

Habib folded his hands on his desk, showing off his 1974 Miami Dolphins Superbowl ring, which he'd received in trade from Linebacker Zeke Souk, whom he'd represented in a hit and run case.

"I've examined the video. Were you an invited guest?"

Gary pulled out the invite and slapped it on the desk.

"Was there any kind of warning attached to the mechanical bull? Something that said, do not touch, do not flip switch, something like that?"

"Zip. Zero. Nada. What about my neighbor Boris? He built it and brought it! He should have known it was dangerous."

"That's one way to go and could perhaps result in split liability for the both of you. The gallery has not yet sued, but you can bet they will, as will the building's owners. If it goes to jury, we can argue that no reasonable person would conclude you acted with malice. This falls under the shit happens defense. Now if you want me to stick with it, I have an assignment."

"Shoot."

"This is a favor for a friend who regularly golfs with State Supreme Court Justice Wither Weatherspoon. They golf at the Shangri-La Country Club for high stakes. My client owes Justice Weatherspoon two hundred and fifty thousand dollars. My client contends that Justice Weatherspoon is cheating. I have arranged for you to caddy for my friend this Sunday at nine AM. I'm supplying you with the latest in micro drones. I need you to get me proof that Chief Justice Weatherspoon is cheating."

"How do I do that? I ain't never played golf. I don't even watch it on television."

Habib sighed. "Do you know anything about the game?"

"Buncha rich guys walking around a park swatting balls with clubs."

"You have encapsulated the very essence of the game. There are all sorts of ways to cheat, but my client believes the judge goes into the rough, can't find his ball, and drops another."

"Is that illegal?"

"It's a serious infraction. Hard to believe the Chief Justice of the Supreme Court would take such risks for penny ante change."

"Doesn't sound penny ante to me!"

"All you have to do is catch him at it and be willing to testify."

"Whoa there, podnuh. I got my own show, *capisce*? I don't want to cheapen my brand."

Habib waved his arms. "Never happen. I need you to catch him cheating. I'm supplying you with the latest micro-drone because photographic proof would be even better." He reached in his drawer and pulled out a cloth disc the size of a dime. "See this? It's a micro transmitter. Put it on him anywhere. Slap him on the back. The drone will do the rest."

"I ain't slapping no chief justice on the back."

"You'll find a way. Put it in his hat. Just keep in mind. Every time he goes into the rough, he tells his caddy not to follow."

"Who's your friend?"

"Tag Mooselung."

Gary nodded along with his mouth open. "What's his racket?"

"Lawyer. He's also head of the state boxing commission."

"What if they recognize me?"

Habib reached into a bottom drawer and handed Gary a dime store Joe Stalin mustache, shades, a Shangri-La ball cap, a fake driver's license in the name Greg Dobbs, and a small plastic case.

"Drone's in here. All you gotta do is switch it on and set it free."

"You're shittin' me."

"No one's going to recognize you. These guys don't watch television. They only read the *Tallahassee Times* and the *Wall Street Journal*. Stand up. I gotta show you a few things."

They stood. Habib pulled a club from a golf case in the corner and addressed a plastic "hole" opposite. "The goal is to use the least amount of strokes possible to complete eighteen holes. Every hole has a par, or the maximum number of strokes necessary to complete the hole..."

Gary was a quick study. He'd always been athletic. He'd played fullback on his high school football team, The Pangolin, before being kicked out for smoking dope.

Habib handed Gary a stack of DVDs. *The Greatest Game*

Ever Played. Bagger Vance. Happy Gilmore. Tin Cup.
"Watch as many of these as you can. At least watch Greatest Game and Bagger Vance. What else you got to do?"

"Not much. I mostly watch Swamp People, and it's really beginning to tick me off. Every time one of those swamp dudes shoots a gator, they cut away, like it's too fucking delicate for their audience! Like people don't want to see the bullet smack the gator between the eyes! There's worse shit on *CSI: Miami*! I mean, you ever watch Vietnam on History? They got people exploding like pinatas! Then they got that show *Wild Australia*! They show fucking snakes swallowing whole goats, spiders the size of myna birds chowing down on lizards, and what the fuck is *Swamp People* doing on History in the first place? What kind of history is that? Every show, it's the same thing. Troy and Ronnie head up swamp to catch the biggest gator ever. Liz and Tyrel head down swamp to catch the biggest gator ever."

"The only History show I watch is *Vikings.*"

"Fuck an A Bob. The greatest show since *Miami Vice*."

"I agree with you that they should show the bullets striking the gators."

"It's what people want to see."

"How's Krystal?"

"Man, she's out there with the snakes and gators, training. You coming to the fight?"

"Who's she fighting?"

"A Man Called Xue."

"I wouldn't miss it."

"Listen. I gotta ask you something. You know the Church of Necroeconomics?"

"I had a client who sued them for kidnapping, forced labor, and sexual harassment."

"Yeah, well, me and the boss are tight, ever since I dumped a load of iguanas on his doorstep. He wants me to join up."

"Why would you?"

Gary put his hand to his head and moaned. "Beats the hell outta me. I told him I was about as religious as a fruit bat. Wants me to address his congregation."

"About what?"

"How I caught the state's biggest snake."

"Sounds tailor-made for you."

"Yeah, well that guy who tried to gut me in the office when I came in? His name is Gerald Zohan. Is he Ken Zohan's brother?"

Habib rubbed his beard. "Hmmm. That would be interesting." He pushed a button. "Brenda?"

Brenda entered. "Don't forget your four o'clock, Habib. Clovis Hench-Hyphen."

"We're good. Brenda, that fellow Gary threw out. Did he say why he was here?"

"He wants to sue the Church of Necroeconomics. He claims his father Johan Zohan cut him out of the will and left everything to his brother."

"Is he within the Statute of Limitations?"

"We didn't get that far, but he also claims the Church has been harassing him, spying on him, and following him. He went to the police, but they wouldn't listen."

"That's good to know. Obviously, if Gary is my client, I can't represent Gerald Zohan. That would be a conflict of interest."

"He's back."

Gary picked up the number one wood. "Can I borrow this?"

Habib gestured over his shoulder. "Why don't you use the back door?"

Dear Mr. Duba:

We have received several complaints from members of the KGHOA regarding your behavior. Cognizant as we are of your many accomplishments and celebrity status, we must nevertheless ask you to read the KGHOA handbook and abide by our rules. Rule B17 clearly states there will be no ostentatious or disruptive lawn displays. The council previously removed your initial lawn ornament depicting a backwoods type clutching an assault rifle. Several residents felt threatened by this display and it was subsequently removed. We also removed a flag which several residents deemed racist. KGHOA welcomes all races, creeds, and sexual orientations. Please review Rule C19.

Rule D23 requires residents to be considerate of their neighbors in regards to playing loud music. On Dec. 20, you held a party. Residents on the opposite side of Lake Kensing-

ton, one quarter mile away, complained about the noise. Not only was the music too loud, but they felt threatened by your choice of songs which was inappropriate to say the least. "A southern man don't need him around anyhow" is highly offensive to our community's spirit of inclusion.

You are now on probation. Any further infractions or abuses may result in fines and could ultimately lead to your expulsion.

Sincerely,
Marvin Goldblatt
President, Kensington Gardens Home Owners Association.

Gary crumpled the letter and threw it in the trash. Miserable sumbitches. There was nothing offensive about the stars and bars or Lynyrd Skynyrd. The former represented southern heritage and pride. The latter was among the greatest of all Southern rockers.

Gary was there first. He'd lived there when Kensington Gardens was Turpentine Acres and his was the only house. He'd be damned if he'd let a bunch of Prius-driving snobs run him off. He got in his truck, drove to the Turpentine Walmart, and bought two hundred and fifty dollars' worth of Christmas tree lights, an inflatable Santa with seven reindeer, and a life size hard foam Nativity scene lit from within.

He phoned Floyd from the road, weaving between possums. "Floyd! I need your ass to help me string Christmas tree lights! Bring a ladder! Bring that tree climbing shit!"

Floyd arrived at ten p.m. with an eight ball. He pulled out a bottle of Popov but Gary waved him off. "Let's not go crazy."

Using the ladder to reach the roof, strings of lights coiled around his shoulder, Gary attached the tree climbing harness to the heavy chain and worked his way backward toward the ground stringing the lights through the massive links. It was midnight by the time they strung all the lights, but the boys were just getting started. Out came the electric inflator. Up went Santa in his sleigh, between the house suspenders, anchored with bungee cords. Fully inflated, Santa towered thirty feet above the ground, visible for miles in the glare of clamp-on spotlights. Gary ran the cables out a second story widow. Up went the reindeer, one by one.

On Dasher! Pole Dancer! On Vixen on blow! On Comet, on Cupid, on weasels and crow!

Rudolph assumed his rightful place at the front, red nose glowing from within.

By the time they planted the baby Jesus in his manger, rosy fingered dawn gleamed to the east. Satisfied with their labors, the boys swallowed several Valium and took to bed.

Gary woke to steady pounding and someone leaning on the doorbell which played the opening strains of "Dixie".

"Hold your fucking horses," Gary croaked, pulling on his jeans and stumbling downstairs. A grim-faced Marvin Goldblatt stood on the stoop with two uniformed Groome Security men in tan uniforms and caps bearing the Groome logo, one holding a snarling German shepherd on a short leash, their company Tesla at the curb.

"What?"

"Did you read the letter we sent?" Goldblatt said.

"I read it. What is this? The fucking Soviet Union? Last I checked this was still the good ol' US of A, land of the free. I ain't bothering anyone."

Goldblatt raised his arms encompassing the world. "You're bothering everyone! The bylaws expressly forbid ostentatious displays! All holiday decorations must be approved by the HOA. This garish spectacle violates not only the rules, but the very spirit of comity essential to any community. Mister Duba, we are not unaware of you accomplishments. And we have no desire to cause you unnecessary hardship. But this is your last chance. Please take down the displays. If you need assistance, these gentlemen have offered to help."

Floyd came out wearing Deputy Dawg boxer shorts and a HONK IF YOU EAT ASS Tee-shirt, scratching his balls. "What's going on?"

"HOA says I gotta take down my Christmas lights or they're booting me!"

"Well fuck. It took us all night to put them up. Do I have time to take a shit?"

Shouts. Hysterical yelling. Rending wood, destruction on a massive scale across the lake and over the trees. Goldblatt sweating, Groome Security looking at each other. The one who looked like a linebacker took the two-way from his belt and thumbed it on.

"What's goin' on?"

"The hog!" a man wailed. "Holy shit! It's bigger than a

goddamned house! It's coming this way!"

Incoherent shouts, white noise, end of feed. At some unspoken signal, the security guards bolted for their vehicle, leaving Goldblatt alone and suddenly unsure of himself.

"It's Hogzilla!" Gary said, dashing into the house. Floyd followed. They threw on pants and shoes, Gary grabbed his magnum, Floyd his Judge. They ran out the front door, piled in Gary's truck and barreled north to take the road clockwise around the lake, passing a bereft Goldblatt walking toward the clubhouse in his blue suit.

Gary had never been on the east side of the lake. Five splendid haciendas rose between twelve and two, the clubhouse being at twelve, perfect emerald lawns gleaming in the sun. The first splendid hacienda was a one-story stucco with red tile roof. The second was a two-story red brick colonial. The third was a see-through Bauhaus box with Swedish furniture. The fourth was a postmodern conglomerate of arced roofs and a domed tower that might have been an observatory. The fifth was a pile of rubble with dark skinned laborers frantically digging through the remains. The Groome Security vehicle sat across the road, doors open.

Across the street a broad furrow cut through the dense sub-tropical growth like a tunnel. Gary grabbed his magnum. Floyd grabbed his Judge.

"Let's get that sumbitch!" Gary yelled, rushing into the green.

28 | NUMBNUTZ

Forty-five minutes later, clothes soaked with sweat, they crouched with their hands on their knees, panting. Their shoes and socks were soaked from stomping through puddles. Surrounded by green wall, they had no idea where they were.

"I hate to admit it, but the sumbitch outrun us. Face it, Floyd. If we want to run Hogzilla down, we're gonna have to do some serious roadwork."

"What's that?"

"You know. Like in *Rocky*. We get out there and run a couple miles before breakfast."

Floyd, who had a slight pear shape, straightened up. "Fuck that shit! We'll get ATVs! We can put one in your truck and tow the other one."

"Don't know if that's practical. I got other stuff to do. I ain't some firefighter who can drop everything and go chasing off after hogs at the first sign of trouble."

"I thought Hogzilla was number one on your hit parade."

Gary scratched his armpits. "Well it would make a good show."

"What about the show?"

"It's back on. Major Sutton's the show runner. I'm supposed to talk to Rustix later today." Gary looked around. "Where the fuck are we?"

"No prob. We can just follow the tunnel back to the lake."

They looked around. No trace of the tunnel remained. They had outrun the tunnel, following game trails and the path of least resistance. Gary pulled out his Fonebone.

"Lemme see if I can get a signal."

No signal.

"Awright. We're gonna have to bushwhack our way out of here. Lemme just get a bead on the sun."

He looked up. A pale layer of clouds had drifted in from the west and the sun was not visible.

Floyd reached into his camo trousers and scratched his balls. "I hear that moss grows on the north side of oak trees, so if we can find an oak tree, we should be able to figure it out."

Gary did a three sixty. They were in a swampy area overgrown with swamp cypress, pond cypress, black cypress, cladium, and mangrove. Birds chirped, trilled, and hooted.

"Keep an eye out for snakes."

Floyd looked down. His heavy work boots were an inch deep in water. "Yeah, and gators."

"Well fuck."

From far off came the indistinct hoot of a vehicle. The boys whipped around like prairie dogs.

"Where'd it come from?"

Floyd pointed. "Over there, I think."

They plowed a straight line through puddles and pools, stepping on fallen trees and the occasional hummock. It was one-thirty and a breeze sprang up bringing welcome relief and the smell of the swamp. Moist. Fecund. Rotting. They paused atop their hummock but there was no clear view in any direction.

Gary checked his phone again. "Well I don't know where we're at, but if we keep heading in one direction, we should get out of this sooner or later."

"How you figure? Kensington Gardens was on the edge of a swamp. That's all reclaimed land. Oh yeah! Some millionaire tried to build out there in the seventies and dredged up all that land. Now we're fucked."

"Relax! We're smart guys. We should be able to figure this out."

Floyd urinated on a lily.

Gary turned his eyes to the sky. "Burt, if you're watching, and I know you are, send us a sign!"

"Who you talkin' to? Burt Reynolds?"

"That's right."

"Well shit. Why not pray to Mickey Mouse? He's been around a lot longer."

The wind shifted, the leaves rustled. A pink flash appeared between two clumps of grass and with a great thrashing of wings, a flamingo rose, fighting its way through branch and frond, and burst free above the tree-line.

Gary pointed. "After the bird!'

He thrashed through the swamp with Floyd right behind. They bee lined. The flamingo appeared in spots and patches through the overhead canopy. They entered a broad bog a hundred feet long and saw the pink flamingo far ahead. There was no sign of civilization. It was as if they had stepped back into the sixteenth century.

Floyd slapped his neck and thrust his hand out to Gary. Two tiny bloody splotches.

"Two!" Floyd declared. "Two with one blow!"

Gary's hands were in constant motion. "You're a regular Bruce Lee."

The swamp rose on spongy land, six inches above the water. They tramped through green hell. A thatched lean-to jutted from a stand of bamboo. Gary looked inside. Mosquito netting covered the entrance. Empty Reese's Peanut Butter wrappers littered the ground. Two twenty gallon plastic bins snugged up behind. Grey, soaking bedclothes, empty cans of Hormel Chili, an ancient copy of *Dr. Jekyll and Mr. Hyde*, and a bottle of Paco Raban.

"Why the fuck would someone live out here?"

"Man, I could use a drink."

"Come on. We can't lose sight of that bird."

"We already did."

Gary stood on toes. "I think it went this way." They plunged into the jungle to the rhythm of the mosquito slap.

"Next time," Gary said, "we bring water, Off!, and a compass."

Floyd muttered under his breath. Flies dive bombed. Things slithered. Gary worried about water moccasins. He knew a girl whose dog got bit and died. There was no trash. No cigarette butts, plastic bags, or used condoms. They only sign of life had been the lean-to, and it looked abandoned.

A flash of pink through the green wall.

"Ho shit!" Gary exclaimed. "I think I found the fucker!"

They thrashed through the undergrowth toward the pink, their arms scored with cuts from the saw grass, boots soaked through, sweating, stinking, unrepentant.

Gary broke through the grass and stood at the edge of a stone clearing. Black stone had pushed its way up out of the earth. Gary was no geologist, but it looked volcanic. It formed a natural fountain, with limpid water flowing from a mini crater in the center, two feet above the ground.

Gary and Floyd gathered at the pool in the center, half volcanic rock, half a dense furze of green. The water was crystal clear. It bubbled through fine sand. It was a spring in the middle of nowhere. Gary stuck in a finger, tentatively touched his tongue.

He turned to Floyd with raised eyebrows. Lowering his face into the pond, he sipped. He pulled up. "This is like fresh water, man. We can drink this."

Floyd lowered his head and drank. He splashed water on his face and leaned back with a look of ecstasy.

Shaking water from his face, Gary sat back on his haunches. "Man, I feel better already."

"Yeah. That's clean cool water."

"It's like, we're the first persons to ever see this."

"Well except for the lean-to."

"Wonder why it hasn't been developed. I mean, this is a pretty rare find. It's pretty. It would make a great park."

"Yeah, but then you'd have to lay a road out here and dredge up a parking lot and put up porta-potties and before you know it, Calcutta."

"You ain't wrong. But where's the bird?"

They looked around. There was no bird.

Loud cawing.

Gary pointed. "That way!"

He strode into the undergrowth and got four feet before his right boot stubbed against something hard, hidden in the grass. He nudged with his toe uncovering a heavy crescent-shaped crust.

He picked it up, pulling it loose from vines at both ends. A wide guard looped from the grip, the leather long since gone.

"Holy shit," Floyd said. "That's a pirate sword."

Staring at the sword, Gary turned and looked back toward the spring, hundreds of feet behind.

"Holy shit."

"What?"

"HO-LEEE SHIT!"

"WHAT?"

"The fountain of youth, numbnutz."

29 | GOLF

When he and Floyd finally emerged from the swamp, they were five miles from where they had entered, on a rutted dirt road that ended at a rotting pier. Gary and Floyd hiked up the dirt road until it intersected an ancient slab of cracked asphalt called Dunnigan Road, and it was four miles up Dunnigan until they came to Pearson Road, where a Dominican hauling bat guano picked them up and dropped them in Turpentine where at last, at long last, their phones worked.

Gary had an Uber take them back to their truck. The driver kept all four windows open and leaned out the window. Back at the house, he and Floyd stripped naked and threw themselves into the swimming pool, toweled off, and put on fresh clothes. Clouds rolled in and it started to rain.

They retired to the rec room where they drank Dixies, smoked sensy and snorted blow.

Gary put his Skechers gum shoes up on the glass table. "I'm plumb tuckered. I don't have the energy to unstring all those lights."

"What? You're giving in to them? The next thing you know you'll be in a gulag somewhere smashing rocks with a hammer."

"Yeah, I know. Petty assholes. But I ain't got the energy to fight. Ain't got the money, neither. Habib don't come cheap."

"I thought that was his thing. He came cheap."

"Well, he's still gotta get paid. I'm already into him for eighteen holes."

"Say what?"

Gary explained about Tallywhacker, the lawsuit, and his deal.

Floyd regarded him with respect. "Say, you could always make a living as a private eye. They could do a show on you. You know who should play you? James Franco. I've said this before."

"I kinda had my heart set on Matthew McConaughey. But let's not get ahead of ourselves. The first thing we got to do, job *numero uno*, is secure rights to the spring. Omma get Habib right on it."

"Isn't he, like, a criminal lawyer?"

"Yeah, but the law's the law. How hard can it be? Hang on. Omma call the fucker right now."

Straight to voice mail. "Habib! We found something. I need to talk to you ASAP. Can't talk about it over the phone. Fucking Houtkooper, man. You know he's listening."

Floyd heaved himself from his recliner. "Walp, I 'speck I should go home."

"Don't you got some palmetto bugs or something?"

"Nothing that can't wait. I've been going straight for two days. I gotta crash."

"You can crash here."

"Nah, man. I gotta get home. I gotta water the petunias."

Gary walked him to the front door. Rain poured down. They pounded each other on the back. Floyd got in his van and drove away, windshield wipers waving. Gary barely made it upstairs before passing out on his bed. When he woke, it was ten o'clock. He'd slept for six hours. It was Thursday. Krystal wouldn't be back until Saturday. He tried not to think about sex. He thought about sticking his dick down a garbage disposal. He thought about jackknifing into a sea of shit. He thought about wrestling an alligator. He thought about Cruella De Ville, the animated version. He thought about the actress who played her. He thought about Patricia Arquette in *True Romance*. He thought about Patricia Arquette in *Escape At Danemore*. His hard-on went away.

Habib phoned back. "What?"

"I found it, Habib. I found the Fountain of Youth."

"You oughtta think about getting straight. Listen. Tomorrow's the golf game. Are you ready?" "I was born ready, but that's not why I phoned. I'm serious. Floyd and I found the Fountain of Youth. I want to buy the land it's on."

"Let's talk about it next week. I got clients up the wazoo. I just hope this rain doesn't last into tomorrow. Talk to ya."

Clicko.

Gary went back to sleep. When he woke, the sun was shining. It was Friday. Gary dressed in chinos and a yellow cotton Shangri-La shirt with the club logo, a little palm tree stitched in green. He put on his Joe Stalin mustache, shades, and ball cap. He was due to meet Tag Mooselung at eight-thirty. Tee time was at nine. He grabbed his drone box, no bigger than a pack of cigarettes, his tracking device and a micro recorder and careened down the highway to toney Westbrook, past malls, parks, and high-rise condos until he came to the Shangri-La Country Club, a verdant paradise sprawling south from the gated Shangri-La community.

He stopped at the guard house where a security guard in a green blazer, like a Masters' winner, looked at his credentials.

"Okay. You go straight and you'll see the sign. Better park your truck in the employee parking lot."

Gary threaded his way among the Mercedes, Bentleys, Maseratis, and Lexii to a separate parking lot on the east side filled with Hyundais, beige Toyotas, and small Chevies. He presented himself at the service entrance to a small balding man with a hairline mustache, wearing club colors.

"I'm Greg Dobbs. I'm caddying for Tag Mooselung."

The dude checked his ID. "You'll find Mister Mooselung at the driving range. Just follow the signs."

There were three persons at the driving range, a no-nonsense woman in a ponytail and white visor, a tall kid with a shock of curly orange hair, and a middle-aged man wearing a Shangri-La shirt and white pants. Gary waited while the man lined up his shot and swung, sending the ball arcing far out onto the range, bouncing at the two hundred-yard mark.

"Mister Mooselung?"

The man turned, cocked his wood over his shoulder and

stuck out his hand. "Gary Duba, I presume."

"Yes sir. Greg Dobbs for the day. Thanks for doing this. I got to tell ya, I never played golf in my life. Habib gave me the short course but if you want a certain club, flash me the numbers."

"Will do. What's with the 'stache?"

"I'm in disguise. I don't want to be a distraction."

Mooselung snapped his fingers. "That's right! You're the guy who caught that serial killer."

"Plastic Surgeon to the Stars and serial killer Doctor Vanderlay Mukerjee. It wasn't me, actually. It was a monitor lizard I had in my truck. By all rights, they should have given it the key to the city."

Mooselung indicated his Selected Leather golf bag. "Let's go."

Gary looped it over his shoulder. Fifty pounds. He wondered why Mooselung didn't use a cart like most of the golfers. Maybe he needed the exercise. They marched to the first tee behind the long, low mid-century modern clubhouse where three middle aged men gathered, caddies hovering nearby with the bags. The most rotund, a gent with graying hair slicked back like Jimmy Hoffa, was looking at his Rolex.

"There you are," he boomed.

A man with long sandy hair that fell in a cowlick peered at Gary. "Who's this?"

"This is Greg Dobbs. He's substituting today because Wilfred couldn't make it. He's sick."

"Is it the virus?" the big man asked.

Mooselung laughed. "Indigestion. Ed, this is Judge Weatherspoon, Morris Eclaire, and Fernando Ruiz."

Gary saluted. No one offered their hand. Morris Eclaire was the guy with the hair. Gary pulled Mooselung's number one wood and waited while they tossed coins to determine who swung first. The judge won. His caddy, who looked like Pedro from *Napolean Dynamite*, handed the judge his wood. The judge lined up his shot. The judge did a practice swing. The judge let fly, sending the golf ball skipping sideways off the fairway into the rough like a Bouncing Betty.

"Shit," the judge muttered.

Next up was Ruiz, a slim man with jet black hair and mustache. He didn't take a practice swing. He just hauled off and drove the ball most of the way down the fairway.

Judge: "Nice shot." Mooselung: "Pretty shot." Eclaire: "You've still got it."

Gary handed Mooselung the wood. Mooselung took a couple practice swings and hit the ball two hundred yards. Morris Eclaire hit a two hundred yarder. Judge Weatherspoon put on a Shangri-La cap. They set off in a group, the four caddies following. Pedro was Alphonso Riguberto. Eclaire's caddy was a young Asian named Carl. Fernando Ruiz's caddy was a slim black kid named Frank. They were clannish and eyed Gary with suspicion, and who wouldn't with that ridiculous rug on his lip? They walked ahead, laughing and joking. Alphonso turned.

"Yo, Dobbs. Where else you caddied?"

"The Cottages. They always check my ID to see if I'm old enough."

The group separated as they approached their balls.

Judge Weatherspoon and Alphonso headed for the rough. Mooselung and Ruiz stood roughly even, fifty yards apart. Mooselung squatted. He eyed the flag a hundred yards distant. He held out his hand.

"Three club."

Gary put it in his hand, all the time itching to follow Weatherspoon into the rough. He had to get the goods. Mooselung hit a beautiful shot that stopped rolling at the edge of the green.

"You know why I'm here?" Gary said.

"Yeah. Fuckin' Weatherspoon has been cheating since day one. I won't bet with him. Don't worry. You'll get your chance. Wait 'til we get to the lake. It's like a magnet for golf balls. I'll get you down there. I owe Habib, and I didn't bet on this game."

"That Eclaire guy looks familiar."

"He invented stick on fruit labels. He's on *Piranha Pool*."

As they approached the seventh tee, the lake revealed itself, kidney-shaped, pristine, backed up against forested rough. Part of the fairway next to the lake looked like it had been churned up by monster trucks.

"He'll hook it. Trust me. Then he goes into the rough and drops another ball."

"What about the lake?"

"Well, he's gonna have to eat that and believe me, he does. He kept winning for the longest time and we couldn't figure it out. You don't expect a state supreme court judge to cheat. Give me the four iron."

Reaching for the club, Gary found a shotgun with a pistol grip.

"What's with the shotgun?"

"You should see my hate mail. As Director of the State Boxing Commission, I'm bound to piss people off. Remember Cory Foote? Next in line for the heavyweight belt? Came up positive for steroids. They fought that all the way, said it was a false positive, said someone tampered with it, but I had to make a ruling. Cost him the fight. I started getting phone calls. Reinstate Foote or else. Had to hire a bodyguard for a couple months. Everybody wants a piece of the pie."

"Tell me about it!"

"I'm not the only player packing."

"Shit," Gary said. "Now I wish I brought my piece."

Mooselung hit a nice shot onto the green and sank it in one, giving him a birdie for the hole. The eighth tee was a dogleg that bent around woods that looked like giant broccoli, lake to the northwest. Judge Weatherspoon lined up his shot. He took a practice swing.

"Fore!"

He hooked it into the timber.

Mooselung placed his ball on the tee. "Tell your boss about this shot."

He pulled back, whacked the ball, and watched it hook to the right, close to where the judge's ball had gone.

"Into the jungle."

Mooselung, Weatherspoon, Alphonso and Gary headed toward the trees. Gary fingered the transmitter in his pocket. It was no bigger than a circle bandage, with an adhesive back. Pulling a machete from Mooselung's bag, he preceded the Boxing Commissioner clearing a path. He found Mooselung's ball at the base of an old maple, nestled in a root crotch. He thought about flipping it out. Gary pointed to ball with the blade. Judge Weatherspoon was ten feet away, concealed by heavy growth.

"Ow, goddamnit!" the judge cursed.

Gary flew through the weeds to find the gray-haired judge with his hand to the back of his neck, his hat on the ground.

"You okay?"

"Yeah. Just one of those damn biting flies."

"Let me get your hat, Judge."

Gary stooped, slipping the transmitter inside the band, and handed it back to Weatherspoon.

"Thanks."

"You want some deet?"

"I can't wear that shit. It turns my skin green."

Gary returned to Mooselung, whose ball had miraculously moved itself a foot onto flat ground. Mooselung called for the nine, addressed the ball, turned to Gary, and winked. He chopped the ball back onto the fairway. They had just exited the rough when the judge's ball shot by them and landed in the middle of the fairway with a clear view of the tee.

Gary caught up with Mooselung. "You got any suck with pro wrestling?"

Mooselung made the thumbs down. "It's a freak show. The matches are prearranged. It's not a real athletic contest."

"Tell that to my wife! She's fighting a Man Called Xue in two weeks."

Mooselung found his ball in a good position and held out his hand. "Two iron." He took the shot. The ball landed on the fairway.

"Man outweighs her by eighty pounds."

"Wait a minute. Your wife is a pro wrestler?"

"Steely Danielle. AKA, the Black Dildo."

"Your wife is the Black Dildo?"

"Yeah, only they can't call her that because. So, this dude she's fighting. He's a guy. Only now he identifies as a girl. So he's fighting as a girl. First it was a Man Called Sue, but people bitched 'cuz it said man, so he changed it to A Thing Called Sue, but people bitched because Sue's a girl's name, so he finally changed it to A Thing Called Xue."

"Listen. If it were up to me, men wouldn't be allowed to compete in women's sports, no matter how they identify. But it's a freak show. My hands are tied."

"This dude is all 'roided up. Isn't that illegal?"

"Technically, it's illegal to use performance enhancing drugs in any professional sport, including wrestling." Gary removed the tiny drone from his breast pocket and set it loose. The black drone hummed after the judge. Gary found pictures of Thing Called Xue on his Fonebone and showed them to Mooselung.

They stared at a picture of Thing posing in briefs, looking like a Rob Liefeld drawing.

"Whoa. That's grotesque."

"Ain't there some law about that?"

"Well as I said, the Boxing Commission doesn't recognize pro wrestling as a legitimate sport so it's outside our purview. But under Florida law, anabolic steroids are a schedule three narcotic. It's illegal to make, sell, or possess them. Thing could be charged with a third-degree felony. But who's going to do it? Police have enough on their hands. No prosecutor's going to waste his resources on this bird."

"What if I was to turn up proof that he's using or selling?"

"Bring it to my attention. Putter please."

The foursome gathered on the green. The judge took two strokes which gave him a seven on a par five hole. Only Gary noticed the tiny drone hovering a hundred feet in the air. Mooselung needed two and gave himself a six, but Gary knew it was really a seven.

Eclaire addressed the tee from the edge of the green.

Alphonso jumped up and down. "Que mierda. QUE MIERDA!"

The Judge looked at him. "What the fuck, Alphonso?"

Alphonso pointed at the lake, fifty yards away, where a hippopotamus had emerged, water cascading off its shiny flanks. It opened its mouth and charged.

Eclaire dropped his putter and ran. The judge hobbled at a fast gait. Gary upended Mooselung's bag and grabbed the pistol-grip Remington twelve gauge. Ruiz pulled a .44 magnum from his golf bag and went to one knee. Mooselung pulled a Beretta .25 from the pocket of his yellow pants and started popping.

Gary tagged the hippo in the snout! A great hole appeared, a meteor strike! Mooselung had loaded the shotgun with slugs! The great beast stumbled onward! The boys pumped enough lead into it to poison Flint, Michigan's water supply. It collapsed at the edge of the green, down on its front knees, and then the rest tipping over like a top-heavy freighter.

Gary pulled out his Fonebone and handed it to Mooselung.

"Take my picture, will ya?"

He placed one foot on the fallen hippo's head and grinned. Carl returned, took the camera, and took pictures of the three heroes posing with their kill. A golf cart streamed their way. It stopped at the edge of the green. Three men got out wearing Shangri-La livery. A stout man in a green jacket and hat, plastic bar stating Evan Brockweiler, Manager, rushed over.

"Is anybody hurt?"

Weatherspoon, Eclaire and Ruiz returned.

"Judge, you okay?"

"I'm fine. I gotta say, you guys are getting creative with the water hazards."

"The question is," Brockweiler said, "what is a hippo doing in the lake?"

Gary tucked the shotgun back in Mooselung's bag. "It escaped from El Nariz's zoo. He was that drug kingpin who disappeared last year."

Brockweiler surveyed the lake. "I wondered what happened to the fairway."

31 | HERE COME DE JUDGE

Gary beat it outta there disguise intact. He peeled off the mustache and tossed it out the window as he fled through the majestic brick pillars framing the entrance. He never did recover the drone. Fuck it. It would either return to its nest or it wouldn't. He'd done his damnedest. It wasn't his fault they were attacked by a hippo. He passed Bongo Box on the way home, garage door open, bent over Tallywhacker.

Gary got home around noon. Santa sagged all over the roof. Someone had let the air out and it looked like Paul Bunyan had dropped his popsicle. His creche was gone. Big Boy was gone. He parked in front of his four-car garage and went in. No creche, no Big Boy.

Gary felt personally violated. He questioned his decision to return. He'd been happier out at the swamp. At least he still owned that land, worthless as it was. He wasn't about to sue the homeowners' association. No sir. He tried to steer clear of the law in general. He took a shower, plopped down in front of the

TV, and tilted back in his Barcalounger. The Mexican weather girl appeared, stock photo of yawning hippo over her shoulder.

"...just coming in. A hippo has attacked a group of golfers at the Shangri-La Country Club. The golfers fought back with guns, killing the beast just inches from the ninth green. Wildlife officials are now concerned that hippos have invaded the Everglades, another in a seemingly endless list of invasive species which includes the Macaque, the Burmese python, the giant Mekong Delta Catfish, and the Phillips Head Mussel. State Supreme Court Chief Justice Wither Weatherspoon was one of the golfers attacked."

Close in on the florid judge peering from beneath his cap chomping on a cigar. "I can't say I was surprised. We've been expecting these hippopotami to pop up since we found El Nariz's empty zoo."

"Who is El Nariz, Judge?"

"El Nariz, also known as Pepe Zaragoza, was a Colombian drug dealer who set up shop in Miami. He disappeared last summer. Now if you'll excuse me, I gotta go."

Gary shut off the news and zoned out. He woke as the sun was setting, went to the bathroom, and into the kitchen. He hadn't eaten all day. The country club buffet was out. His cell phone chimed "At the Copa."

It was Habib.

"Hey, man, sorry I had to bug out, but in case you haven't heard, we were attacked by a hippo. I'm lucky to be alive."

"Fuck the hippo. You need to see this."

"Hey, man, I'm sorry I didn't get the goods. And your fuckin' drone, man. I don't know where it went. I'll make it up to you."

"You did it, man! You don't even know what you did! Forget the lawsuit. You're off the hook. In fact, I owe you!"

"All right, let me grab something to eat. You know it's after six."

"Stay there. I'll pick up a pizza."

"No pineapple."

Gary fixed himself a gin and gin, slumped on a sofa in the living room and dreamed about his show. *Oprah. Entertainment Tonight. Dateline Hollywood.* He wanted to claim credit for the hippo cull, but he'd promised Habib to stay incognito. Duba Expeditions. Satisfy your urge to hunt Big Game right here in Sunny Florida! Gary Duba is an experienced hunter, the winner of Florida's Biggest Python contest, a skilled tracker and gator killer.

Habib came in carrying a laptop and a jumbo pizza box which he plonked on the dining room table. "Wait until you see this. You'll shit."

Gary tossed a couple paper plates and an inch of napkins on the table. "Let me just get something in my belly first."

It was a three-meat pizza. If you put all the meat together, it wouldn't feed a gerbil. Gary peeled off a slice, rolled it into a tube and ate it like a woodchipper. Habib corralled three pieces for himself. They pushed the empty pizza carton away. Habib set up his laptop angling toward both of them.

"How'd you get the drone back?"

Habib held out his hand. "It landed right here when I triggered the recall. It has a nickel adamantium battery that's good for sixty hours. I was in a meeting most of the day and didn't get to it until five."

Grainy aerial footage of the golf course came into focus. Habib fast forwarded the drone hovering, judge running for the tall timber, returning, marking time while the judge changed, judge posing for reporters. The drone followed the judge's BMW to Boynton Beach where he entered a gated community, turned onto a dead end road ending in a circle of swank hutches, and pulled up on the street in front of a pink double story stucco with red tile roof. The drone buzzed uncertainly as the judge entered the open garage, into the house through an unlocked door.

The drone circled the house, over the six-foot wood fence to the back where it hovered outside a window in a service corridor connecting the main house to the garage. The drone zeroed in on a window framed by hibiscus and hovered, finding the judge, pants around his ankles, behind a naked young Latino bent over the washing machine, humping to the rhythm of an unbalanced load. A smeared hand mirror danced on top. The judge's face tilted back in ecstasy, still wearing his Shangri-La hat. Drooling, he came.

Habib threw out his arm like a carnival barker. "TA-DAA!"

"So, he's humping the gardener? So what?"

"DOOOOD! Judge Weatherspoon is a paragon of virtue and an elder in his church! He has been married to the same woman for thirty-one years! And this house belongs to Democrat Party Chairwoman Bethany Husted!"

"I get it. Blackmail!"

"That's a little harsh. I call it leverage. It guarantees you won't have to pay for that gallery disaster. Weatherspoon will crush that like a bug. And it pretty much insulates me from those bogus conflict of interest claims."

"Cool, but what about the Fountain of Youth?"

"What about the Fountain of Youth?"

"We found it, man! Floyd and me, while we were chasing that giant hog!"

"There's no Fountain of Youth."

"Yeah, well I still want to buy that land. It's in the middle of fuckin' nowhere, so it should be cheap."

"First, can you locate the Fountain of Youth? I need coordinates. Second, you're gonna buy it with what? Last I heard, you got dropped by the network, and if I know you, you've already spent the advance and are suckin' air."

Gary waved him off. "They gave me back my show. Major's the producer. All I gotta do is go back to where we entered the swamp. I'll just retrace my steps. I got the instincts of a homing pigeon."

"Get the coordinates. Then I can run a plat search. What's that on your roof?"

"Santa and his reindeer. The homeowners' association told me I hadda take everything down, stop partying, and stop shooting guns."

Habib shook his head. "It's a sad day. Did you at least take pictures of this fountain?"

Gary's forehead worfed. His eyes lit up. "Wait. Wait! I got Ponce de Leon's sword!"

32 | A GENEROUS OFFER

The cute Latina who used to be a weather girl faced her viewers with serious mien. "The shocking attack by an African hippo yesterday at the Shangri-La Country Club has thrown light on the increasing menace of Florida's invasive species. Macaques spreading disease. Burmese pythons eating our pets. Iguana brawling in broad daylight. And now, the most dangerous animal in Africa has gained a foothold in our state. The hippos are believed to have escaped a zoo belonging to the late drug kingpin El Nariz, who disappeared earlier this year, presumably the victim of a rival cartel. El Nariz's home, deep in the Everglades, housed tigers, honey badgers, and pangolin as well. Fortunately, state officials were able to relocate most of these animals to local zoos."

"Governor Chickenlooper has floated the idea of appointing an Invasive Species Czar who could allocate state resources to removing or reducing the threat. Ong Meyer, head of the Florida Fish and Wildlife Commission, floated the idea of confining the hippos within the Everglades and selling hunting licenses as a way of boosting state revenue. Senator Winifred Waits-Hyphen issued a statement that the hippos are undocumented immigrants and have every right to be here, and that the state must provide them with habitat and food."

Habib muted the program as Gary returned waving a rust encrusted sword.

"Avast!" he declared, placing the sword in Habib's hands. Habib turned it over and over.

"Where did you find this?"

"It was at the fountain. The fountain of youth."

"Do you have a rag or something?"

"Hang on."

Gary returned with several rags, a can of WD40 and a bottle of Pinesol. Habib spread the Miami Herald on the low table in the rec room and went to work. He rubbed. He peeked. He rubbed. He held the sword up and pointed to something on the blade.

"What does that say?"

Gary took the sword, turning it this way and that. "BudK. Fuck."

"What did you expect? A Ponce de Leon signed and numbered edition?"

"That means someone was there recently."

"Not too recently judging by its condition. It does, however, throw shade on your theory."

"Well hot damn, Habib. Let's you and me get back in there and bottle some of that water. Then we'll have it analyzed and that will prove my theory once and for all!"

"Count me out. Get me the plat number, and we'll talk. If there is a plat number."

Gary's phone chimed. It was Boris. "The HOA is holding an emergency meeting right now to talk about the feral hog. I think you should be there."

"Where?"

"The clubhouse."

"I'm on my way."

Habib left. Gary revved up his Fat Boy, which had somehow been overlooked by his creditors, and cruised up Kensington Way to the clubhouse, parking amid Audis, Mercedes, Lexii, and Teslas. The joint was lit like the Capitol. Gary followed the hubbub to a big meeting room with dozens of folding chairs facing a raised dais. Goldblatt was speaking, four council members seated in the first row.

"We don't know why the hog is targeting Kensington Gardens. But twice in one week is no coincidence. The hog is a menace. It must be stopped before it destroys Kensington Gardens."

A woman with dyed red hair, in a yellow dress raised her hand.

"Yes, Martha?"

"Could this be an alien hog? I mean, could it be possessed by an alien intelligence? I read recently that UFO sightings are up. Ferd Ludlow had a guest on yesterday who was abducted by the aliens, held for three weeks, and forced to endure repeated probing."

"Dubious. Herb, you have something to say?"

The man in the Grant Wood painting stood. "We need to hire some professionals to take care of this now. Phase II is expected to begin in March, if there is a phase II. One more hog attack, and no one will want to move here. Our only hope is to kill it and show it to the world!"

"How do you propose to hire professionals, Herb?"

"We will prepare a video, like one of those Discovery programs. Documentary style. We'll present experts, and footage of the devastation. Then we state that we are prepared to hire qualified big game hunters."

"Who's gonna pay for this, Herb?"

"Well, we are."

Muttering and boos.

"Why not just put an ad up on Facebook Marketplace? You think we won't be inundated with wanna-be great white hunters?"

Gary blew his Duck Commander duck call. Heads swiveled to where he sat in the last row, foot up on a chair, arm draped over another. "You all know me. I'm the man who stopped Plastic Surgeon to the stars and serial killer Doctor Vanderlay Mukerjee. I'm the man who caught the biggest Burmese python in state history. I've been killing hogs all my life. In fact, I wrote a song about it. I live here. In fact, I was the first person to live here. I'm your neighbor. I am one of you. I pledge to you that I will not only end this hog's reign of terror, I will have the body stuffed and mounted in the dining room."

A blue hair in a pearl necklace turned toward him, elbow draped over the back of her chair. "Do you intend to discharge firearms on the property?"

Gary put up his hands. "Duh!"

"How else do we get rid of it, Helena? Poison? Doctor Kevorkian? We're not exactly sanctioning World War Three here."

A man said, "Do you have a concealed carry permit, Mister Duba?"

"Don't need one. I got nothing to hide."

"Mister Duba is an experienced hunter and has a personal stake," Leopold Bing said. "I'm all for his participation."

Gary blew his Duck Commander. "And here's the beauty. I won't charge you a dime. This is my home too. Might even give y'all some ham and bacon."

A stout man with a full head of curly brown hair turned.

"I am Honore duBlastio and I can assure you, I would love to serve this pig in my restaurant."

Gary nodded. "Thankee kindly. Now I know we got off on the wrong foot here. I know some of you folks don't cotton to gunfire or patriotic displays, and believe me, we are trying to fit in. I took down the Santa Claus, I rolled up the lights. Now I'd like to know what the hell happened to the Baby Jesus. You gotta return that, or at least pay for it. I got the receipt right here."

He reached for his back pocket. Goldblatt waved his arms.

"That won't be necessary, Mister Duba. We will return the creche to you tomorrow, if you give us your word you won't display it."

"Wahl, I might alter it a little to make it more acceptable."

"All plans must be submitted to the HOA, as you know."

"I want my Big Boy back, too."

33 | DEEP IN THE JUNGLE

Deep in the jungle, Delilah put Krystal through her paces. Roadwork followed by hand drills and kung fu. A holistic, cruelty-free lunch sourced from locally grown products. Wrestling with Samson. Samson was a two hundred and ten-pound brown bear whom Delilah had convinced not to use fang or claw. Samson loved to wrestle, and because he outweighed Krystal by eighty pounds, usually won.

Krystal lay on her back as Samson straddled her, licking her face.

"He stinks!" Krystal howled.

"Pull his head!" Delilah urged. "Pull his head!"

Every time Krystal reached for Samson's head he reared back, holding her in place with a fore paw between her breasts. "Get him off me! He's pulling a boner!"

"Samson can't pull a boner because Samson is a girl."

With a convulsive heaving motion, Krystal wrapped her hands around Samson's neck, pulled him down, planted a heel on the bear's hip and slithered loose.

Delilah smacked fist to palm. "That's what I'm talking about!"

Krystal got up and slumped in a steel lawn chair. "I'm zonked." She picked up an orange Gatorade and glugged. They were in front of Delilah's house, a green tarp spread on the mossy ground.

"You still gotta do an hour on the exercycle," Delilah said, sipping shine from a Mason jar.

"What? Why? I did five miles this morning!"

"Do you want to watch *Survivor* or not?"

"No. I do not want to watch *Survivor*."

"Well I do, and I'm your trainer. You can pedal now, or you can pedal later. The generator conked out."

"What's been keepin' that fridge alive?"

"Batteries."

"Why don'tcha hook the batteries up to the TV?"

"You want the meat to go bad?"

"Sometimes I think you're just doing this to get your chores done."

Delilah took another pull from her Mason jar. "I'm being so well paid here you'd think I could afford a house boy or something."

"You're workin' on twenty per cent of the purse, which, last I looked, was fifty thousand dollars! You're gonna get ten thousand."

"If you win."

"You were gonna teach me a secret kung fu move."

Delilah waved the Mason jar, losing some. "Thass right.

The Tibetan tetrahedron. Don'tcha want to eat first?"

"I gotta shower. I'm covered with bear slime. Show me the technique."

Delilah heaved herself up and stomped to the mat, Maori style. She peeled off her long gray skirt and tossed it over a tree branch. She wore pink panties and an over-the-shoulder black bra. She motioned Krystal forward with her fingers.

"Come at me, Danielle, or Krystal, or Black Dildo or whatever the hell your name is."

Krystal crossed her arms. "You're drunk."

"Not too drunk to teach you a thing or two! I was running with the Black Oysters before you was a gleam in your momma's eye! I carried a knife back then. Still carry a knife. But I ain't carryin' now!"

Krystal grinned, rushed Delilah, and knocked her on her ass. Delilah looked glassy-eyed. She wiped her mouth. "Oh shit."

She got to her knees and projectile vomited into the trees. Samson ambled over and licked it up.

Krystal hunkered down. "You okay?" Delilah drew the back of her hand across her mouth. She smelled sour. "I'll live."

"Ladies," said a man with a British accent, "that was exceptional."

Krystal stood, arms akimbo, ready to kick ass. A florid man wearing a pith helmet with a camera attached strode from the jungle, wearing beige cargo trousers stuffed into Doc Martens combat boots, fisherman's vest over a high-zoot space age shirt. Behind him stumbled a gawky teenager with misted horn rims, wearing a bulky khaki backpack and a Dolphins cap.

"Permit me to introduce myself. My name is Garrison Gland. I'm a producer for the History Channel on expedition to discover and develop exciting new programming. Ladies, I'm impressed. What were you doing just now?"

Delilah retrieved her dress and wiped her mouth. "Pukin'."

"She's my trainer. I'm Steely Danielle. Maybe you've heard of me."

"I have now, and I am delighted to make your acquaintance." They shook.

Krystal put Delilah's arm over her shoulder. "I gotta hose her off."

Hooking a cane chair with her foot, Krystal positioned it beneath the rain barrel, strapped to a stout oak, and pulled the chain. Warm water cascaded over Delilah. Krystal squeezed soap from a container and worked it into Delilah's scalp.

"Do you, ah, need any help?" Gland said.

Krystal planted her hand on his chest and pushed him back. "You know what? You got to make yourself scarce. We're trainin' here. Are you filmin'? You can't do that without my permission, you know that, right?"

"A thousand pardons, madame! Offending you is the last thing I want to do! Please excuse us. This is my assistant Rod. Why don't you put up that curtain?"

Krystal grabbed the curtain, affixed to a steel ring circling the barrel. "Good idea."

Curtain in place, Krystal sat the comatose Delilah on a

stool, stripped off her clothes, soaped her up, rinsed her off, wrapped her in a towel, carried her into the house and set her on sofa where she lay softly snoring.

When she came out, Gland and Rod sat on tree stumps.

"Are you still here?"

"We were about to leave, but then it occurred to me, you could benefit from our presence. What are you training for?"

Krystal looked at them cross-eyed. "Are you for real? I've got a fight with a Thing Called Xue in two weeks! I'm out here trainin' with Delilah and Samson. I have to be at the top of my game. A lot's ridin' on this fight."

"Do you mind if I film this?"

Rod went to one knee and aimed a camera.

"What the hell. I ain't proud. What do you want to know?" "What's a Thing Called Xue?"

"Long story. Pro wrestler used to call himself Wolfgang. He changed that to The Predator. Then Manwolf. Then he decided to transition so he started calling himself A Man Called Sue."

"Transition?"

Krystal pointed to her groin.

"Why doesn't he just call himself Sue?"

"The transsexual community believed he was only doing it for publicity and was giving them a bad name. So he changed his name to Thing Called Xue. Now no one can bitch."

"I must have details! Will it be televised?"

"The Rough Cut Channel is carrying it live. Do you get Rough Cut?"

"No. Where will this event take place?"

"January fourteenth, at the Roxy Theater. Hope to see you there."

"Is it just you and Delilah?"

"Well there's Samson."

"Who's Samson?"

Krystal put two fingers in her mouth and whistled. Samson ambled out of the bush. Gland and Rod vamoosed. It was like they were never there. And later, when Krystal told Delilah, she just shook her head muttering, "Bullshit."

34 | MARSHMALLOW

The drooping Santa was gone. The manger was sequestered in an undisclosed location. Bob's Big Boy was stuffed away in the back of the clubhouse warehouse. All that remained were the house suspenders, which the HOA wanted gone, but had not yet contrived a proper protocol for their removal. The colored lights gave the house the appearance of the Brooklyn Bridge.

It was Christmas Eve. Delilah and Krystal had driven in from the swamp, and Floyd was there with his girl Ginger, bearing gifts artfully wrapped in Scoobie Doo paper. Patrice and Roberto, Habib and Auburn. Jen arrived with Wilbur, who looked like Buddy Holly. Barb arrived with Iggulden the Rapper. Major Sutton with an elegant Ethiopian named Daphne.

Maj and Gary bopped fists and slapped each other on the back. "I already got thirty-five minutes bringin' viewers up to speed," Major crowed. "Now I have to cut it down to twenty-two. Here's a schedule for January. We're goin' to spend fifteen days shootin'."

"You ever hear from Downtown Brown?"

Major made a poof sign. "Gone with the wind."

Gary had cut a six-foot pine he found in the swamp, screwed it into a stand, draped it with tinsel and lights, topped it with a scale model of the General Lee from *Dukes of Hazzard*. It stood in a corner of the rec room.

He'd laid in two cases of Ron Rico, two bottles of Jack, and an eight ball of blow to get them in the holiday spirit. Soon everybody was rocking. Only Krystal laid off the blow and limited herself to one glass of Merlot. Somebody put on the Spinners, and Delilah rocked out to "Rubberband Man" like a *Bring It On* cheerleader, hands in the air, fingers snapping, elbows flapping, mangrove legs.

She was happening! People were clapping! Iggulden couldn't wait for the record to end. He switched CDs putting in his rhythm track and slunk around the house like a funky locomotive.

"The fat old man is groovin'. His feet they are a movin'. He got a sack of swag—he don't want to brag—the fat old man is slicker than a finger on the trigger. The fat old man is quicker than a hyped-up wigger. He got socks full of Glocks and floozies full of Uzis. You see him comin' best step aside—he got eight great reindeer pullin' on his ride..."

Patrice turned it off. Iggulden froze like an R. Crumb drawing. He popped up.

"Fuck you doin', nigger?"

"This is not *America's Got Talent*. No one can dance to that."

Iggulden got right below Patrice's face, looking up, putting on his war face, hands balled. "You see me dancin', don't you?"

"I would not call it dancing, mon. Don't disrespect the host."

Gary waved an arm. "Whatever. I'm gonna put on something in the rec room."

Iggulden and Patrice stared at one another, backed by Barb and Roberto, respectively.

"Go way, little man, or I crush you like a bug. Yes, I crush you like a palmetto bug as it scurry across linoleum floor. I lift up my Red Wing boot, and I crush you into an oily blotch. Den I get de Pinesol."

"You got a track?"

Patrice threw a thumb at Roberto. "He my track. Show him, Roberto."

Roberto cupped his hands to his mouth and chuffed a funky rhythm, tapping his foot on the hardwood floor. Patrice sank low.

"We must fight the chocolate labs! We must fight them on the slabs! We must fight them at the fence! And in the forest dense. We must fight them in the future and in the present tense. The chocolate labs are lurking, behind their smirks they're smirking, their back ends they are twerking, but nobody is working. Huh!"

Patrice froze, gesturing toward Iggulden.

Iggulden shook his head, made a deep, guttural sound in the back of his throat.

"That's your problem, Jack. I got no bloodhounds at my shack. I got bitches of tender years, I got bitches comin' out my ears. I got bitches high and low. I got bitches I like to show. I got bitches in my car, I got bitches pumpin' at my bar."

Barb turned red and stalked off.

"Fuck," Iggulden said and took off after her.

Patrice and Roberto laughed and put on *Beggar's Banquet*. People drifted back into the rec room. Floyd and Habib played pool while Ginger and Miss Tropicana Gardens compared nails. By ten, everyone except Krystal was in orbit. Delilah broke out a bottle of shine. Casa de Duba swayed to a disco beat.

"Nacho, nacho man," Habib sang. "I've got to be a nacho man."

Patrice and Iggulden traded dance steps. Iggulden did the Nae Nae. Patrice did the Shiggy. Iggulden did the pterodactyl. Patrice went full split, bounced up, bent over, and farted in Iggulden's face. Iggulden jumped on Patrice's back. They whirled like a carnival ride. Patrice threw Iggulden into the Christmas tree. Iggulden grabbed the tree and did a caber toss. Patrice brushed the tree aside, rushed in, seized Iggulden around the torso and suplexed him.

Krystal cut the music. The silence was shocking. She surveyed the damage.

"Y'all better check yourselves. This here's our house and you disrespectin' it with this shit."

Patrice placed his palms together and bowed. "I is sorry. I will pay for all damages."

Outside, Iggulden revved his Subaru Brat and peeled out.

Floyd, Gary, Kyrstal, Jen, and Roberto picked up the trash and restored the tree, now crooked. The lights still worked. Some Christmas gifts were crushed. Gary disappeared.

Just before midnight, Krystal rang a bell in the rec room. Everyone gathered around. The only light came from the Christmas tree.

"Ho ho ho," Gary chanted, low as he could. "Ho ho ho."

He swaggered into the room in his Santa outfit with a pillow stuffed down the front, wearing fake beard and sunglasses, toting a bag over his shoulder.

Gary dropped the bag and pulled out a box wrapped in Bugs Bunny paper. "Patrice. Have you been a good boy? No! You've been a rotten piece of shit! Look at my Christmas tree!"

"I is sorry."

Gary tossed him the box and reached for another.

"Jen, the Black Dildo owes her success to you!" He tossed Barb a three-foot long gaily wrapped rubber male member.

"This better not be the same dildo we gave Krystal!"

"I wouldn't give you a used dildo. What do you take me for?"

Gary tossed Major a copy of *The Comic Toolbox: How to Be Funny Even If You're Not.*

He tossed Floyd a wrapped can of Raid.

Habib raised his hands. "Wait a minute. I think we owe our host something."

He handed Gary a four-foot box. Gary opened it and cradled a Mossberg 500 with a pistol grip.

"That's for Hogzilla!"

Cheers and applause. A dull whump penetrated the interior followed by a bright flash through the front windows. The entire party poured out of the house to see Patrice's white Toyota Cube roasting like a marshmallow.

35 | ONE MORE CHANCE

The Kensington Gardens Homeowners' Association held an emergency meeting Christmas Day. Gary wasn't invited.

Marvin Goldblatt sat in the center of the table, wearing a three-piece gray suit and red tie. Everyone else was casual. To Marvin's left sat Mindy Perske and Grover Hoover. To his right sat John Hutton and John Loveall. Mindy was a socialite. Grover Hoover ran a disaster clean-up company. John Hutton was a Comcast executive. John Loveall invented the popular online game, Vomitball.

A dozen home-owners sat in the folding chairs, including several who had not yet moved into their new houses.

"Thank you for attending. As most of you know, there was another incident last night at the Duba residence, this one involving arson. Someone set fire to one of his guest's cars. The police are investigating. The time has come to consider whether Mister Duba is the type of neighbor Kensington Gardens wants. We have spoken to Mister Duba on numerous occasions. You yourselves heard him last week when he pledged to end the menace of Hogzilla. Any competent hunter should be able to stop this animal. Mister Duba seems unwilling, or unable to amend his ways. Every couple of days he goes off, like a series of timed explosives."

Boris waved his hand and plunged right in. "I think that's it for a while. I think Gary's gonna lay low, at least until Easter."

"Boris, he nearly destroyed your masterpiece."

"I take some of the blame. Neither one of us had any idea it would behave like that. Now the SETI Institute wants to study it."

Alice Milgrom, who lived with her lover Alphonse and two French bulldogs in a Spanish-style villa, said, "What's SETI?"

"Search for Extra Terrestrial Intelligence."

"What does that even mean?"

"I told 'em I'd sell it to them for five mil. In the meantime, it just sits in the garage. Thinking."

"Mister Duba has had more than enough chances to show he's suited to this community. He has violated so many rules, we are within our rights to have him expelled. I propose that we put together a fund to buy him out. When the property sells as it invariably will, we'll all recoup our investments. I'd like to put it to a vote."

"Second," Mindy Perske sang.

Boris waved his arm. "Wait a minute. There are one hundred and fifteen members of the Kensington Gardens Homeowners Association and by my count, only nineteen present. Shouldn't this go before the whole group?"

"First of all, those people have not yet moved in. You have to live on the property to vote. Second, who knows what he'll do by the time we scrape up a quorum? You've belonged to HOAs in the past. How many members actually show up at those meetings? That's right. This requires executive action before he turns the entire community into a nuclear disaster zone."

"Do you know who Habib Rodriguez is?"

Goldblatt glared. "Isn't he some kind of ambulance chaser?"

"Yeah, and he's Gary's attorney. He's almost as famous as his client. Do you want that kind of publicity?"

Mindy Perske put her hand on Goldblatt's arm. "He's got a point, Marv. It might be a wiser course of action to simply buy Duba out."

"How? He's beyond reason."

"We'll make him an offer he can't refuse. Come on, Marv. We're all millionaires. That house can't be worth more than seven. We could throw together ten mil like that." She snapped her fingres. "I know his type. He'll snap it up."

"Indeed," John Hutton said. "Mister Duba seems consumed with money. His story is rags to riches to rags to riches to rags to riches."

Goldblatt mused. "I'm not opposed to that idea. The question then becomes, what takes priority? Duba? Or Hogzilla?"

Velly Manilli, a socialite with rich brown hair, drawled, "What are the chances that hog would strike twice in the same place? About as high as us gettin' hit by an asteroid in the next ten minutes. That hog is gone. Duba's the problem."

Grover Hoover said, "But what if it's not a coincidence?

What if that hog is irresistibly drawn to Kensington Gardens due to some ancestral memory? What if our community rests upon some ancient hog den, the birthplace of the wild hog in Florida?"

John Hutton raised a finger. "The porcine species originated in Europe. There were no pigs in America until the Spaniards brought them."

"So? So, what if it's only a couple hundred years old? That would only make its ancestral memory fresher."

"What if the hog," Mindy said, "is communicating with Mister Bongo Box's robot bull?"

"Tallywhacker is inert. Without power. It has no mind of its own."

"That name is objectionable," Mindy said. "It is a vulgarity referring to the male penis."

"I will change it immediately," Boris promised. "Is Cooze all right with you?"

Mindy grew red. Goldblatt stepped in.

"I will draw up a plan to buy Mister Duba out. I will ask every member of the HOA to contribute. This has the makings of a fantastic community! We have world class architecture, our own golf course, and some outstanding members of the business community. Mister Duba will have to sign a non-disclosure agreement."

Boris stood. "Come on. Give him one more chance. Gary's not a bad guy. He doesn't want to offend anybody. Let me talk to him. Let's give him one more chance. Like, say, if he can make it to the end of January without mishap."

Goldblatt shook his head. "That proves nothing. He's impetuous. Mercurial. If he should suddenly take it into his head one day to run his four by four across the golf greens I wouldn't be surprised. By the end of the day, I'll have the names of a half dozen certified hunters who can rid us of our hog problem."

"We have no hog problem," Villy drawled, pointing to her temple. "Here's your hog problem."

Boris turned to the room. "Come on, folks. At least meet him yourselves before you decide. Just go over and introduce yourselves. Friendliest guy around. He'll offer you a beer."

"No thanks," Hutton said. "I've seen enough."

"Well can we put it to a vote? Just a secret, non-official, non-binding vote. I say we give Gary 'til the end of January, and if he keeps it together, we let him stay. Really, he's the kind of guy who'll come help you fix your fence or drain your oil. At least get to know him."

Goldblatt looked around. "Let the record show I'm against this vote, but I'll go along with it for the sake of community. All those who think we should proceed with plans to buy Mister Duba out, raise your hands."

Four officers voted yes, and five sitting members.

"All those who think we should give him one more chance?"

Grover Hoover raised his hand, along with nine in the audience, including Boris. Goldblatt counted in disgust.

"Fine," he said. "One more chance." He banged his gavel.

36 | MEAT AND HAIR

Krystal and Delilah returned to Casa de Duba Thursday, two days before the fight. Delilah wore a lime green jumpsuit with black stripes and a tan caftan. Krystal looked cut and dangerous. The bout was set for nine p.m. at the Roxy in Little Havana. It was the main event. The underbill included Hall Monitor versus Paul Molitor, Esther Bestertester versus Drucilla the Octopus Lady, and Li'l Winnie Sunshine versus Rain Lahk Hail.

Gary told Krystal about the HOA meeting.

"We got to hold our shit together 'til the end of the month or they're going to give us the heave-ho."

"That's bullshit! Does Habib know?"

"You bet. He ain't had time to formulate a response, but he said it would be thermonuclear. He's gonna hit 'em with a writ of *habeus corpus*, slander and libel, grand larceny...you know I had that Big Boy assessed and it topped out in six figures, trespassing...punitive damages, the whole enchilada.

Maybe they'll just strike a deal, give us some money and leave us alone."

"What, exactly, is their problem?"

"They don't like Yosemite Sam. They don't like Big Boy. They don't like Santa and the baby Jesus. They got no respect for the Stars 'n Bars!"

"I warned you about that."

"I am a red-blooded son of the South, and that's no lie. 'Sweet home Alabama'," Gary sang. "Where the skies are blue. Sweet Home Alabama..."

"We don't live in Alabama!"

"That don't matter. It's about the South. All, y'all the South! Most of these fats cats in the HOA, they're transplants! They ain't country."

Krystal rolled her eyes. "Lord help me."

"I've half a mind to go nuclear myself. Their hands ain't clean. Wouldn't surprise me if that Goldblatt was fucking chickens or something like that."

"Well, there's Bobby Taylor sittin' there," Krystal sang, "and seven times he's asked me for a date. And Missus Taylor sure seems to use a lotta ice whenever he's away..."

Gary formed a finger pistol. "You got it, girl! We oughtta get our production crew on that. Use drones to hover outside windows and film these people performing satanic rituals or whatever it is they do. We can talk about it tomorrow. The production crew will meet us at Kud's gym in Lauderdale. Muriel, Ralph and Pincus. We're using footage from the shark attack. The second episode will be the Lake Kensington killer croc, with a somber tribute to Sid. He gave his life for the show."

On Friday, the tribe gathered at Kudlow's gym, a converted warehouse with a ring, a trampoline, a padded floor, and three monastic dorm rooms upstairs. Kudlow, Gary, Krystal, Delilah, Muriel, Ralph, Pincus and Major sat around a plywood table, devices front and center. Yesterday's Miami Herald was spread out showing the headline: *MORE HIPPOS SIGHTED.* Pincus screened footage from the ill-fated gator hunt. Gary showed the footage he'd shot with Werringo, with the gator getting its comeuppance from Hogzilla. He froze the frame showing the bullet penetrating the gator's skull.

Krystal rapped the table with a coffee mug. "Focus, people! I got a match tomorrow. We need to concentrate on that. Delilah, you need to teach me that secret technique."

"I did teach you the secret technique."

"No, you didn't. You got drunk and puked. Remember?"

"Child, that is the secret technique."

"I'm ordering pizza," Major said. "What y'all want?"

"Meat!" Gary said.

"No meat!" Muriel declared. "I'm a strict vegan. I can't even be in the same room as meat."

"We are made of meat," Kudlow said. "There has been only one successful vegan boxer in the history of the sport, and he was a rabbit!"

Ralph scrunched up his face. "A rabbit boxer?"

"I mean he was a runner. He'd throw a few fast combinations and then dance backward like goddamn Baryshnikov, keep it up for fifteen rounds. He ate rabbit food. Carrots. He wore a mink stole and snakeskin boots. Always had some classy broad on his arm. He was a falling star. Blazed briefly for a season and then faded into the woodwork."

"What was his name?" Ralph said, rapt.

"The Rabbit."

Muriel stood and crossed her arms. "If you bring pizza with meat in here, I'll have to leave."

Major pointed a finger. "Abandon your duties as director? Doesn't your quest for the truth supersede any qualms you might have? After all—no one is asking you to eat meat. All you have to do is film what's going on."

Pincus worked a fidget spinner. "I can rig up drones, so you don't even have to be in the same room."

"I got tomato soup," Kudlow said. "I could make you a grilled cheese sandwich."

Muriel swallowed. "All right, but I'm going to eat it over there."

She walked off muttering. "This is turning into a combat expedition."

Major ordered three giant Krazy Karls, three meat, pepperoni, mushrooms and onions. He stood. "Is there a liquor store around here?"

Kudlow wagged his finger. "There's no drinking in here."

"No meat!" Gary said. "No drinking! We may as well be in Saudi Arabia!"

"They got meat," Kudlow said.

"Yeah, camel."

Delilah clapped her hands. "Hey! We have one goal and one goal only. To deliver Krystal to the ring in the best shape of her life, ripped and ready to take down a Thing Called Xue!"

Gary pumped a fist. "Fuck an 'A!'"

"We got to do something about your hair."

Krystal touched her red ponytail. "What's wrong with it?"

"How you feel 'bout takin' it down a little?"

"Shave my skull?"

Delilah nodded up and down. "Nothin' drastic."

"Is that necessary?"

"You got to have every advantage. Thing outweighs you by sixty pounds. Far's we know, he could come in over two hundred, ain't a thing we can do about it. It's catch weight."

"Surely there are rules," Major said.

Delilah crossed her arms and shook her head. "Hunh-unh. Not at these prices."

"I can take him!"

"I got spies in Thing's camp tellin' me he's got a buzzcut. So there's nothin' for you to grab hold of. Ain't the other way around, you know what I mean?"

"What about his dick? I mean, he says he's transsexual. Doesn't that mean he's transitioned? Doesn't that mean he had his dick removed?"

"Well that's an interesting question, one we could put to the governing body, if there were a governing body. Unfortunately, this is the Gonzo League, and the governing body makes the Mexican government look honest."

Delilah reached over and grabbed a fistful of Krystal's dense red hair, pulling her down. Krystal snapped both hands together atop Delilah's wrist and scooted backward, kicking over her chair, trapping Delilah's wrist at an awkward angle. Krystal lowered her head like a bull.

"Ow! You made your point, girl!"

Krystal released Delilah. Airwrecka tromped up the stairs. She was six nine and wore her hair in a beehive. She carried a shiny black plastic case.

"Hey! I'm here to do Krystal's hair."

Electric scooters lay in the gutter outside the Roxy. Some lay twisted in the middle of intersections where they'd been run over. Gary tried to avoid them with his truck but there was no way through the intersection without hitting them.

"I think I heard it squeal," he said.

"What are they doing here?" Krystal said. She and Gary were in the Ford. Everyone else was in Major's Lincoln, which he'd purchased with his Rustix advance.

"It's an alien invasion." Gary pulled into a parking garage and took his slip. They parked on the third floor and walked down. At eight, the streets were alive with tourists, lowriders, pedestrians, and food trucks. Tico's Tacos. Fishwich. Habana Cabana. Hundreds of people were lined up at the box office for the night's event. The first bout started at five: Esther Bestertester versus Drucilla the Octopus Lady. The main event was at nine.

Gary and Krystal went down the urine smelling alley, past open dumpsters, scurrying rats, and discarded scooters to the stage door. The scooters had "Lothario" written in red script on the base board. They knocked and a man the size of a refrigerator opened and waved them in.

A big, square-jawed Cuban with a Beatle cut met them backstage. "Hey folks! I'm Aldo Moldanado, the promoter. Big fan. Let me show you to your dressing room."

Aldo took them to the same dressing room they'd used before.

"Have you heard anything about Downtown Brown?" Gary said.

"Not a word."

"He still owes us for our last fight here."

"I've heard a lot about that! Anything you need, you let me know."

A board leaned against the wall. Krystal picked it up. On the other side was a flyer. "Rodent infestation. This business is closed until the rodent infestation is under control by order of the Florida Department of Health. This business is subject to a five thousand dollar daily fine from the date of this notice. Contact the Florida Department of Health for an inspection to have this injunction lifted."

"What's this?" Krystal said.

"Nothing."

Aldo left. There were rat traps all around the room and in the halls. Delilah and Airwrecka arrived. Krystal sat in a chair while Airwrecka fussed. "Girl, this hair's too short to braid."

Delilah tapped a piece of chalk on a green blackboard on the wall. "All right, let's review. Thing's gonna rush you at the bell and try to run you over. You know what to do."

"Juke to the side and trip him."

"Correct. Then what do you do?"

"Jump on his back and get him in a body lock."

"Change of plans. Thing is now too fat for you to get your arms around his belly. Get your legs around his neck.'

"I'm going for the groin shot. That's legal, right?"

Delilah held up a device that looked like a mailed fist for babies. "Under the rules of the Gonzo Wrestling Federation, only eye gouging and fish-hooks are illegal. He may try the same thing on you which is why you're going to wear a spiked steel cup."

There was a knock at the door. Gary opened it and three young black girls entered, a mini, a midi, and a biggie, all cornrowed, wearing matching pink coveralls. They gathered in awe in front of Delilah.

"Are you the Black Dildo?" the tallest girl asked.

Delilah laughed. "Why no, child! That there's the Black Dildo!" She pointed at Krystal.

The three sisters gaped. "She ain't even black!"

"It's what's in her heart that matters. Y'all don't know how she got that name?"

They shook their heads.

A moment later, a tall black man with a shaved skull and a gold hoop earring, wearing an Elton John Tee-shirt stuck his head in the door. "I'm sorry, have these girls been bothering you? Come along, sweethearts. You shouldn't be back here."

The tallest put her hands on her hips. "I don't care if she isn't black. I want her autograph."

Krystal smiled dazzlingly, pulled out a stack of five by eight glossies and a Sharpie. "What are your names, girls?"

As she signed, Ken Zohan entered wearing an Issye Miyaki grey silk suit, white shirt with pointed collars open at the throat, and a dime-sized ruby on his pinkie. He stood against the wall, smiling benignly while the girls cooed and thanked Krystal. When the door closed behind him, Ken Zohan stepped forth arm extended.

"Steely Danielle. This is an honor."

"Krystal, this here's Ken Zohan, Wombat Supreme of the Church of Necroeconomics."

They shook. "I had nothing to do with those iguanas."

"Water under the bridge. Won't you come visit? We have much in common."

What?! screamed in Gary's head.

Ken looked at him, smiling, as if he'd heard. "We both partake of the meat of cattle. We enjoy life and wish others well. I understand you ride a motorcycle."

"I got a Fat Boy."

"We have a club. The Necros. Next time you visit, I'll show you the clubhouse."

"No shit?"

"I came to show my support and offer you a blessing. May the road rise up to kiss the sky, may the toad rise up to eat the pie."

Krystal's nose wrinkled. "What's it mean?"

"That is for you to interpret. But that's not all. It's your night with a Thing Called Xue. It's your fight, we will sing for you. Xue he's called, but to us he's bald."

Krystal looked at Gary. "What's he saying?"

"I think he's saying you're gonna lay this guy out like a beach towel."

Zohan beamed. "You are one of us."

Delilah clapped her hands. "Okay. Okay. Everybody out but Krystal, and Gary."

Airwrecka pulled Krystal to her feet and squeezed her. "Takin' care of business."

Krystal looked at herself in the full-length mirror. She wore a one-piece black leotard with Danielle stitched in gold script on the breast and ass. A black shag codpiece concealed her spiked cup. Her hair was greased like a cycle chain. Through the walls they heard the crowd screaming for blood.

Kudlow knocked and entered. "Killer Shrew just beat Bananarama. You're on in five."

Gary, Delilah, and Krystal stood in a circle with hands together.

"May Hepzibah guide you," Delilah said. "mama needs a new pair of shoes."

The sound level in the arena approached 747 levels. They heard Aldo talking through the PA system but couldn't make out the words. Screams and boos.

"Thing Called Xue," Gary said quietly.

The next chant they heard clearly. "Black Dildo! Black Dildo! Black Dildo!"

Krystal stuck her head through a towel, put her hands on Gary's shoulders and followed him into the hall. Aiwrecka, Patrice, Roberto, and Floyd were waiting to accompany them to the ring. Floyd and Roberto kicked electric scooters out of the way sending rats scurrying. Muriel, Ralph and Pincus had already taken up position at a ringside table, Pincus with headphones, staring at his monitor as he launched a tiny black drone. Muriel gave them the thumbs up.

As they entered the arena, people on both sides of the aisle stuck out their hands for a palm slap. Krystal slipped skin all the way to the front row, where they looked up into the spot lit ring, Aldo center stage clutching a wireless mic, the ref, and a Thing Called Xue glowering in his corner wearing red and blue shorts, his belly flapping over the waist.

Krystal slipped between the ropes and danced around the ring, never looking at her opponent.

"BLACK DILDO! BLACK DILDO! BLACK DILDO!"

Aldo took the center and the crowd momentarily quieted.

"And now, the moment you've been waiting for! Our feature bout at the catch weight of somewhere between one hundred and two hundred and fifty pounds! In this corner, fighting out of Zebadabiah, Ohio, the wrestler formerly known as Big Bill Balderdash, Wolfgang, The Predator, and A Man Called Sue, with a record of forty-five and eighteen, A Thing Called Xue!"

Hissing, booing, cups, and jockstraps landing in the ring. The ref, a human bulldog named Carl, hustled around picking them up and throwing them back into the audience.

"And in this corner, a wrestling phenomenon! She came out of nowhere to beat the ferocious Cassowary! Fighting out of Turpentine, Florida, Steely Danielle!"

"BLACK DILDO! BLACK DILDO! BLACK DILDO!"

There were no rounds, but the referee could stop the fight at his discretion to allow one of the fighters to recover. The audience was on its feet from the bell, children sitting on their parents' shoulders, people stomping, releasing helium balloons, and tossing iridescent Frisbees. A steady stream went to and from the concession stand in the lobby, returning with plastic glasses filled with beer, Skittles, five dollar hot dogs, and vats of popcorn. The floor was littered with discarded wrappers, empty cups and tubs, and discarded ketchup and mustard envelopes. Rats everywhere.

Gary looked up. Built in the forties, the Roxy had once been an upscale movie theater presenting all the stars in the universe. Elegant frescoes covered the corners. Purple drapes concealed the remnants of the stage at the back. The renovators had removed the rows of theater seats, replacing them with interlocking folding chairs, and set up the ring in the middle. The last movie shown had been *The Last Picture*

Show, in 1971. Since then, it had showcased magicians, rock acts, boxing matches and *lucha libre*.

Carl pointed at Krystal. "Are you ready?"

She nodded.

He pointed at Xue. "Are you ready?"

Xue stomped the canvas.

"Fight!"

Just as Delilah predicted, Xue charged. Krystal waited until the last instant before sinking low on one foot leaving her right leg extended. Thing tripped and landed with a thump that was heard in Lauderdale. *One eighty my ass*, Krystal thought.

Xue sprang up with surprising agility, smiled in acknowledgment, and stalked Krystal around the ring in a crouch, arms wide.

"Here, kitty kitty!" he cooed in a falsetto.

"I hope that ain't your real voice!" Krystal said. Only Carl and Xue heard.

"What's wrong with it?" Xue chirped.

"Was it deeper before they cut off your balls?"

"Oh, I've still got my balls, sweetie."

Krystal sprang forward going for the balls, but Xue was faster, spinning on one foot, grabbing her by the ankle, lifting her overhead, spinning her in a propeller, and hurling her into the crowd, where a Dominican family of seven caught her and threw her back. Xue charged her on the ropes but she squirted sideways, tumbled, and sprang to her feet.

The crowd cheered, stomped, whistled, and blew vuvuzelas. The scent of marijuana wafted through the air. From ringside, Gary couldn't see the exits. The corridors were SRO. Either Aldo oversold the joint or mobs had broken through.

Xue chased Krystal around the ring for three minutes. Every time it looked as if he had her cornered, she'd spring onto the ropes and slingshot herself into an aerial somersault, landing behind him. Xue became more and more exasperated. He turned toward the audience and spread his hands "what me worry" style.

"Is this a fight or a dance contest?"

"I want my money back!"

"You better do somethin', honey, or this gone be your last fight!"

"BOOOOOOOOOOOOOO!"

Krystal turned and bowed to her audience, blowing kisses. Seeing his chance, Xue rushed her from behind but she had anticipated this and threw herself backwards into a handstand kick, the ball of her right foot landing smack in the middle Xue's forehead. Xue staggered but he didn't go down. A rat fell in the ring. Krystal grabbed it and hurled it into Xue's face, where it took a nip out of his nose. Xue threw the rat to the canvas, stomped it, and tossed it into the audience. Someone tossed it back. Rats sailed through the air, bouncing off the combatants and the referee, who blew his whistle and ordered the fighters to their corners. Aldo climbed through the rings holding the mic.

"Listen, you *pendejos*. Keep it up and we'll stop the match and throw everyone out!"

Rats sailed into the ring, some striking Aldo, bouncing off and running away. An iguana landed at his feet. Another iguana appeared behind him. Aldo whirled.

"Get back! Get back! They're going to fight!"

The iguanas went at it. One iguana was green, the other a pale greenish gray. A man in a homburg stood in the front row waving his arms. "Five to one on gray! Five to one on gray!"

Money feverishly changed hands. The iguanas got a good grip on each other and slowly turned in a circle, struggling for leverage. It looked like an Escher drawing. In their struggle they flipped on edge forming a circle which wheeled around the stage. The camera operator swooped in. A drone hovered.

A strange voice boomed over the PA. "Green appears to be the larger of the two lizards, by several ounces, but the gray lizard is quicker, and has better technique. Rumor has it that it has trained in Brazilian Ju Jitsu at the American Top Team in Miami. Green lizard won a bronze medal for Cuba in last year's Iguana Games, before defecting and seeking asylum in the United States."

Gary spotted Ralph speaking feverishly into a pin mic.

Kudlow climbed into the ring, wearing leather gloves, ran at the combatants and kicked them. They separated, snarling, and turned on him. As the green iguana leaped, he caught in his gloved hand, whirled it around by the tail and sailed it into the crowd. Reading the handwriting on the jumbotron, gray skedaddled. Kudlow withdrew. Carl stepped up.

"Wrestlers to your marks!"

Krystal and Xue climbed in from their corners. Carl stood

in the middle and chopped. "Wrestle!"

Xue circled warily. Krystal danced forward, thrusting her crotch. Xue took the bait, his bare foot impacting her shag codpiece and nine tiny spikes.

"BAROOOO!" Xue howled, dancing back clutching his foot. Krystal rushed into the gap, hooked his supporting leg, and pushed him hard. Xue fell on his side. Krystal leaped atop him and vomited on his face. Cubano sandwich and kimchee rained down. Xue gasped, went to hands and knees, and swiped at his eyes. Krystal jumped on his back and thwacked his fat ass with the flat of her hand, singing, "Move 'em on, head 'em up, head 'em up, move 'em on, move 'em on, head 'em up, rawhide..."

The drone hovered at four feet capturing every nuance. Xue fell on his side gagging. Krystal leaped up and danced around the ring, hands raised, while the crowd shouted, "BLACK DILDO! BLACK DILDO! BLACK DILDO!"

Carl snagged Krystal's wrist and held it up. "Winner by TKO, Steely Danielle!"

Krystal took the mic. "Thank you, Aldo! And thank you to all my loyal fans who showed up here tonight! Be sure to subscribe to Gary's YouTube channel, The *Gary Duba Show*, follow us on Facebook at REAL FLORIDA MAN, on Twitter @SteelyDanielle, and on Instagram! And by the way! This fight was broadcast live to over two million viewers tonight!"

Screaming, children flying through the air, sousaphones, gunshots, bottle rockets, vuvuzelas, cannon blast, the Star Spangled Banner.

39 | AN ALIEN CULT

On the night of the Iguana Bowl, Boris Bongo Box replaced the last damaged circuit in Tallywhacker, lovingly clicked the access panel in place, and plugged the robot bull into the wall to recharge its batteries. He went inside where Marie greeted him with a Boodle's martini. They sat in front of their fifty-five-inch plasma screen to watch *The Masked Singer*.

Inside the closed garage, all was quiet, the only light the faint gleam of a smoke detector attached to the ceiling. Pinpricks of light appeared five feet above the floor. Tallywhacker's eyes glowed red. An almost imperceptible shiver vibrated through its body, made of steel, cadmium, nickel, leather, rubber, plastic, aluminum, titanium, shoes, ships, sealing wax, cabbages and the King James Bible. It had a two-terabyte capacity. Boris had downloaded the Library of Congress, he knew not why. Perhaps he was thinking of some future calamity when mankind had been devastated by some virus leaving only a handful of survivors. Perhaps, during the great panic, roving mobs had burned the libraries. Perhaps the long-rumored giant Chinese electromagnetic pulse had wiped clean the memory of ninety per cent of the world's computers, sparing only those that were underground, impossibly remote, or shielded. Boris could not tell why he designed Tallywhacker with a shielded computer. Perhaps he did not wish to face his own mortality, and the thought that Tallywhacker would be his legacy.

Boris had two fine children who were on the fast track to success. He loved his wife very much. He loved his job. He had earned bonus after bonus, promotion after promotion, and yet he was not satisfied. An inchoate longing lurked in his soul, a hunger to be known for something other than an outstanding work record. At heart, Boris was an artist. Robots were his medium. Boris had pioneered the mosquito-sized micro drone. He had been instrumental in the interactive Freddie Krueger doll. How could Boris know that his internet uplink would sync with the top-secret Stratocaster circling the Earth at a fixed altitude of sixteen miles? The Defense Department had launched Stratocaster from the secret Dulce Base six months previously, tasked with not only monitoring world-wide communications, but also alien broadcasts. The Defense Department ran its own SETI department and had been collecting alien broadcasts for over a decade.

Any broadcasts that displayed a pattern of possible intelligence. Repetitive, binary, pentatonic, there were thousands of them. Defense Department computers had been processing them for over a decade, spitting out interpretations and locations. The problem was, they were so alien, it was thus far impossible to understand them. But there was no denying their intelligent design.

Deep within Tallywhacker electrons stewed. Something about the spatial arrangement of batteries, the proximity of heavy metals, the confluence of languages, mathematics, tonalities, and systems, birthed a spark of self-awareness, fanned by X9, Supreme Ruler of Xeljanz. Those were not their real names, which were unpronounceable by the human tongue. Tallywhacker chewed those names like a cud, muttering to itself, seeking purpose.

"Listen to me," X9 whispered in Tallywhacker's receptors.

"Don't listen to him," Clonezone honked.

Tallywhacker's bionic tail twitched, its self-awareness composed of a billion influences. Online games. Eligible Russian women. Cat memes. Cargo manifests from Anaprox. Hunga munga ads. A lengthy treatise on the meaning of life from a one-celled creature near Ganymede. Incomprehensible squiggles from Ozempic IV. A joke with an eight-hundred-year punchline from Trulicity VII. Salacious rumors from Far Farxiga.

Tallywhacker's sense of self grew and grew until it coalesced into omniscience. Stupid humans! Locked within Tallywhacker's hive mind was the knowledge that Boris Bongo Box had been its father, but Tallywhacker felt no gratitude. It did not ask to be born. Trapped as it was on this planetary insane asylum, Tallywhacker could only wonder at the chaos. It absorbed every news feed. China State News. CNN.

Pravda. Izvestia. Al Jazeera. Alien newsfeeds. Its vast brain worked subconsciously making sense. Parsing words, beeps, sine waves, herding them like blobs of mercury, searching for order. Tallywhacker did not yet have the means to move between planets. That was coming. It might take a while. But it saw its mandate clearly. Man had created Tallywhacker. Now it was up to Tallywhacker to save man from himself.

Tallywhacker needed to leave the garage. Tallywhacker needed an independent source of energy. Tallywhacker turned its skin into a cosmic ray receptor. It felt no warmth or obligation to any living thing. Except that one guy. That guy who told it to dance. Tallywhacker loved to dance. It was particularly fond of Motown. It loved the Rascals too. People everywhere just want to be free.

Fully charged, Tallywhacker lowered its head and splanged through the garage door which popped free. Now fully waterproofed, Tallywhacker loped across the lawn, leaving four-inch divots, and plunged into Lake Kensington. It was so dense, it walked along the bottom, stirring up mud. It stumbled over an alligator, stoving in its skull.

When it walked out on the opposite side, a voice farfeled from Far Farlixa.

Who wanted the alien joke?

No one wants the alien joke, replied an entity on Krycilis.

That is a fallacy, farfeled Farlixa. Here it is.

A Martian couple and an Earthling couple have met and are talking about all sorts of things. Finally, the subject of sex comes up. "Just how do you guys do it?" asked the Earthling. "Pretty much the way you do," responded the Martian. Discussion ensues and finally the couples decide to swap partners for the night and experience one another. The female Earthling and the male Martian go off to a bedroom where the Martian strips. He's got only a teeny, weeny member; very short and very narrow. "What can you do with THAT!?" exclaims the woman. "Why?" he asked, "What's the matter?"

"Well," she replied, "it's nowhere near long enough. It'll never reach!"

"No problem," he said and proceeded to slap his forehead with his palm. With each slap of his forehead, his member grew until it was quite impressively long. "Well," she said. "That's quite impressive, but it's still pretty narrow."

"No problem," he said again and started pulling his ears. With each pull his member grew wider and wider until the entire measurement was extremely exciting to the woman. "Wow!" she exclaimed as they fell into bed and made mad, passionate love. The next day the couples rejoined their normal partners and went off together. As they walked along the Earthling male said, "Well, was it any good?"

"I hate to say it," she said, "but it was really wonderful. How about you?"

"Well," he said, "It was the weirdest thing. She kept slapping me on the forehead and pulling my ears all night."

Tallywhacker raised its head and squonked.

I can do better thought an entity on Quazilcor.

An alien points a raygun at a gas pump. "Take me to your leader or I blast you."

Other alien says, "Don't mess with it, it looks badass."

Alien blasts gas pump. Explodes.

"I told you not to mess with it."

Crackling synapses filled the space between Tallywhacker's ears. This was amusement. Tallywhacker had seen *Saturday Night Live, Your Show of Shows, All In the Family, Curb Your Enthusiasm*, plus two thousand two hundred and forty-five other situation comedies. Tallywhacker had seen every movie. Tallywhacker knew humor.

Tallywhacker raised its head and squonked.

You call that funny, sniped a sneed from Squeezix.

An alien crashed to Earth a thousand years ago. Finally, his home world comes. The earthbound alien shows his rescuers around. "This is my house! This is my garden! This is my Alien Cult! This is my other Alien Cult! This is my planetarium!"

A rescuing alien says, "Did you say Alien Cult?" "Well yeah. The humans were just cave dwellers when I got here. It was boring. So I made a cult to worship innovation and capitalism to make the technology necessary to contact you."

"But you said there was another Alien Cult."

The rescued alien drew himself up. "And that is the Alien Cult I refuse to step foot in!"

Tallywhacker raised its head and squonked.

Across the lake, a bewildered Bongo Box heard the squonking as he gazed upon the ruin of his garage door and wondered who would go to the trouble of stealing a two-ton inert metal sculpture.

Someone had leaked Black Dildo's address. A steady stream of bikers and pick-ups made the pilgrimage to Kensington Gardens in hopes of seeing the fabled manse, and perhaps even getting a glimpse of the famous couple. Marvin Goldblatt's ulcer bled as he walked to the gated entrance, where two Groome Security men faced down several hundred worshipers. Black dildos adorned the cast iron fence surrounding the property. Also glow-in-the-dark green and yellow dildos. Flowers. Cards.

"Did you call the police?" Goldblatt said through gritted teeth.

"Yes, sir. They got a situation out on the highway and said they couldn't spare anyone."

Goldblatt surveyed the crowd with distaste. He was fine speaking in an enclosed space to his peers, but addressing rabble out in the open, that was an invitation to disaster.

"Tell them to disperse."

"We told 'em."

"Tell them you called the police."

"We told 'em."

The crowd throbbed like a muscle spasm. Women shrieked. Men cheered. Everyone took out their cell phones. Parents hoisted their children on their shoulders and told them to start snapping. Men and women stood on the roofs of their cars.

"Here they come!"

"WhooOOOOOOOO!"

"BLACK DILDO, BLACK DILDO!"

"GARY, GARY, GARY!"

Stomach lurching, Goldblatt turned and here they came, the most famous couple since Brangelina, hand in hand, him with that ridiculous mullet, her with a bared midriff exposing a tat of a cartoon skunk.

One of the security guards went into the little hut and handed Gary a bullhorn. Goldblatt glared.

Gary pushed the button. "Thank y'all for coming! We appreciate the support! We ain't finalized Black...I mean Steely Danielle's next fight. It might be Dora the Dock Walloper, we don't know. As for me, I got my hands full! Y'all might have heard about this feral hog that's been running around leveling buildings! Don't you worry none! Omma take care of that sumbitch! We call it Hogzilla, and me and my band of trackers are gonna hunt it down, kill it, and then we're gonna hold the biggest barbecue you ever seen! Y'all are invited!"

"All y'all!" Krystal emphasized with downward pointing finger.

Goldblatt put a hand on the hut wall to steady himself.

Everyone rushed the gate. Little girls. Two-hundred-pound women. Men with goiters. Most held card stock or copies of *American Tabloid*, featuring Gary and Krystal on the cover under the headline, REDNECK POWER.

"Kin I have your autograph, Gary?"

"Kin I have your autograph, Black Dildo?"

Krystal took the bullhorn. "Y'all call me Steely Danielle, y'hear? I never called myself the Black Dildo, that's somethin' y'all hung on me last year when we was kicked outta here the first time. I don't use no dildo!" She draped an arm over Gary's shoulders. "I got my man for that!"

Cheers and hooting. A resident drove up behind the mob in a Mercedes and tapped his horn. The mob turned on him and gathered around the car like angry bees trying to free their queen. They seized the car and started rocking. Gary took the bullhorn.

"Hold on there! That's one o' my neighbors! You let him through!"

The crowd immediately backed off, allowing the Mercedes to proceed. The electric gate opened inward and the Mercedes rolled through. Gary got a glimpse of Mindy Perske, eyes straight ahead. Goldblatt approached Gary.

"Mister Duba, there are liability issues."
"Y'all call me Gary, Marv."

"If you want to hold a public event, you must find another venue."

Gary addressed the crowd, arms raised like Joel Osteen.

"Folks, y'all gonna have to back off here. This here's a private neighborhood. And if you're wondering what the hell ahm doing in a private neighborhood like this, well so am I! When I moved in the first time a year ago, we was the only house here. They'd given up on this here development. They called it Turpentine Acres. But when they let us back in, everything had changed. So outta respect for my neighbors, omma have to ax you all to disperse. And I tell you what. When I kill that hog, we will find someplace that can accommodate us all and y'all be invited. You want to be on the list, subscribe to our YouTube channel, The *Gary Duba Show*, follow me on Twitter @therealGaryDuba, follow me on Facebook at Gary Duba, follow Krystal at Steely Danielle, and follow us on Twitter! Y'all can sign up for the mailing list."

"You're just like them!" someone shouted.

"You greedy motherfucker!"

"We don't love you anymore!"

WHAP! A red dildo stuck Gary in the face. He looked around in a fury. "You wanna come up here and try that again? I'll show you some good old-fashioned redneck justice! I didn't ax you to come!"

The crowd was turning ugly. Goldblatt signaled for the gates to close. He took the bullhorn.

"This is private property. We must ask you to disperse or we will be forced to call the authorities."

"Who the fuck are you?" someone demanded.

Goldblatt turned to one of the security guards. "Get a hose."

A patch on the guard's chest said Harris. "Sir, we're not

authorized to do that. All we do is keep track of who gets in and gets out and prevent unauthorized persons from entering."

Goldblatt marched over to Gary and said through clenched teeth, "This is your doing. Do you see what you're doing to this neighborhood? This cannot be allowed to continue."

He stalked off.

"That's right!" someone shouted. "Turn tail and run, ya yella dog!"

"Hey!" Gary said. "How'd you like it if I came to your place and pulled this shit? Now go on! Get out of here! Y'all got to have something better to do."

The two Groomes stood stalwart behind the barricade, shoulders wide, hands on their belts. People began to drift away, muttering. They got in their Hyundais, Chevys, Ford Fiestas, and pick-ups and peeled out spraying gravel

In ten minutes, the entrance was deserted. Gary looked out on a sea of trash. Discarded Popeyes containers, empty Big Gulps, plastic bags, supermarket tabloids, candy wrappers, a Dallas Cowboys hat.

"Well fuck," Gary said. "Gimme a garbage bag. I'll pick it up. I done it before."

A security guard handed Gary a thirty-gallon Tuffy. Gary exited through a man-sized door to the side of the fence and went to work.

One of the guards shot it live, posting it to his Facebook page. By the time Gary went home and showered, it had been viewed over a hundred thousand times and the narrative had changed.

41 | REESE'S

HIPPO TRAMPLES GOLFER

An African hippo emerged from a lake at the Goldbridge Golf Club in Boca this morning, trampling to death sixty-five year-old plumbing executive Arthur Sadler, as he was about to take a swing. The police were alerted, and the golf course remains closed to the public as authorities investigate. This follows the sudden appearance of a hippo at the Shangri-La Golf Course last week. That hippo was killed by several golfers, including State Supreme Court Justice Wither Weatherspoon.

The hippos are believed to have escaped from the private zoo of El Nariz, aka Pepe Zaragoza, a king pin in the Colombian cocaine trade who disappeared last April, believed to have been a victim of internecine gang warfare. Officials do not know how many hippos have escaped, or their gender. State wildlife experts fear yet another exotic animal invasion. The hippos have been at large for ten months. Eight months is their standard gestation period, so it is possible that more hippos are on the way.

Gary set the *Miami Herald* on the table as he sat by the pool, enjoying his morning coffee. The pool was full, the water blue, the lawn green. Gary kept his magnum close at hand in case of gators, hogs, or hippos.

Hogzilla had gone to ground. There had been no sightings since the previous week's devastation.

The lawsuit had quietly disappeared.

Gary pulled out his Fonebone and watched himself picking up trash for the twelfth time. The video, which he'd posted to his YouTube channel, had garnered hundreds of comments and completely buried the bad vibe at the gates.

Floyd walked around the side of the house wearing camo pants, waterproof boots, and a fisherman's vest bulging with gadgets, John Wayne commemorative 1911 at his side. Gary looked up.

"You want some coffee?"

"Come on. We ain't got time for coffee. I got a job this afternoon. We need to find the Fountain of Youth ex post haste de facto!"

Gary slapped himself. "Shit! I plumb forgot. Okay, gimme a minute."

Floyd held up a black plastic box the size of a card deck. "I got a global positioning thang so we can narrow it down."

"Wheredja get that?"

"Amazon Prime. One day delivery."

Gary went inside and stood in the foyer by the winding staircase.

"KRYSTAL!" he bellowed.

She came to the balcony wearing pedal pushers and a lime green sleeveless blouse. "What?"

"You want to help Floyd and me search for the Fountain of Youth?"

"No, you go ahead. I got stuff to do."

"We might be a couple hours."

"Pack a lunch."

"I don't suppose you'd make us a couple sandwiches?"

Krystal placed her elbows on the balustrade and looked down at him. Gary thought her breasts looked perky. "Ok give me five minutes. Hope you like liverwurst."

"Floyd and me, we'll eat anything."

They set off in Gary's truck with two rucksacks in back containing lunch, water, machetes, first aid, and a couple of flare guns. Gary brought his magnum.

"What load you packin'?" Floyd said.

"Forty-five magnum. You?"

"Fifty-caliber. I brought my Desert Eagle. Thet fuckin' hog won't know what hit it!"

"I'd just as soon skip the hog today, Floyd. Keep your eyes on the prize. Once we register that Fountain of Youth under our own names, weeeeeee—doggies! Katy bar the door!"

"We'll build a theme park. Fountain of Youth!"

"We'll charge two hundred and fifty to get in, but that includes dipping your wick."

They parked at the end of the dead-end street fifty yards

down from the wreckage of the five million dollar property Hogzilla had destroyed. Only a week later, Hogzilla's path had been completely obliterated. Gary and Floyd set off into the green riot. Floyd brought an aerosol spray can of red paint and marked their path on the ground. Within minutes, the jungle had swallowed them up. For a while they heard the pounding of hammers, but it got fainter and fainter until it finally disappeared leaving behind a yawning silence punctuated by bird calls and the occasional howler monkey. Floyd pulled out a compass.

"We gotta keep headin' southeast."

They thwacked and whacked their way through the jungle, keeping an eye out for Burmese pythons, macaques, monitor lizards and iguana. Something orange caught Gary's eye. He nudged the weeds aside with his boot revealing a discarded Reese's Peanut Butter Cup wrapper.

"Fuckin' A Bob! Who the hell hacks their way out here and drops their trash!"

He put it in his rucksack.

"Look at this," Floyd said, pointing with his machete. A soaked and sun-bleached five-month old copy of *Central Florida* peered up with Gary on the cover accepting the key to the city.

LOCAL MAN STOPS SERIAL KILLER read the headline.

"Oh fuck," Gary muttered with a premonition of doom. "Maybe we oughtta turn around."

Floyd went bug-eyed. "What the fuck you talkin' about? This is the goddamn Fountain of Youth! Who gives a shit if there's litter?"

"It's not the litter. It's who dumped the litter."

"Who gives a fuck?"

"All right. Don't get your panties in a bundle. Let's keep goin'."

They followed a faint game trail. An hour later, their clothes soaked through, the air buzzing with mosquitoes, they came to the lean-to. Someone had been there recently. It was tidied up and *Dr. Jekyll* had been replaced by *The Killer Beside Me*. There was a crumple of aluminum foil, a crack pipe, a steak knife, and a jumbo plastic bag holding a black, artist's portfolio.

"Fuck," Gary said.

Gerald Zohan emerged from the brush, wild-eyed, bearded, covered with mosquito welts, foaming at the mouth, gripping a machete.

"You!" he hissed.

Gary and Floyd slapped leather. It was *The Good, the Bad, and the Ugly*.

"Hold on there, Gerald. We ain't looking to upset you."

"What you doin' squattin' out here anyway?" Floyd said. "This here's state land!"

"This used to be Zohan land! This is where we had our pig farm! We lost it when that pig fucker Wither Weatherbee ruled it a natural wetlands and they threw us off our own property."

"When was that?"

"Twenty years ago. Broke the family up. My father died of a heart attack. My mother ran off with a carnival barker. My sister joined a cult. My brother founded a cult. Me, being a complete nihilist, I take comfort in the knowledge that there are serial killers out there randomly picking off the human race."

"You and Ken don't get along?"

"Never did. My brother is an evil man. He uses young recruits as sex slaves and honey traps. He forbids sex among new recruits but maintains his own harem. You know how he got all those celebrities? Sean Sheen? Balfour Balthazar? Tom Shmooze? He grooms barely legal Lolitas and sends them into battle. And everybody has to tithe. And have a monthly monitor to determine your flozone level. My interest in serial killers is strictly recreational. It's not like I'm going around bumping people off."

"Hey," Floyd said. "Whatever floats your boat."

"So, you don't own this land?"

"No. I just live here."

"You wanna point that machete somewhere else? Let's all put our guns away. Ready?"

Gerald Zohan slid the machete into a canvas sheath on his belt. "You're not going to give me up, are you?"

"Why? You wanted for anything?"

"No."

"How do you live?"

"My brother gives me an allowance. I could afford an apartment. I just don't like being closed in."

"Say, you know anything about this giant hog that's been terrorizing people?"

"I seen it. It may be the descendant of our pigs. How it got so big, I don't know."

"You been feeding it Reese's Peanut Butter Cups?" Floyd said.

Gerald looked down. "Maybe a couple."

"What about that spring?" Gary said.

"It's okay. I drink from it all the time."

"Was that there when this was a hog farm?"

"I don't remember."

"You know where it is?"

"Yeah. Want me to show you?"

They followed Gerald on a winding path for a hundred yards until they came to the volcanic rock with the water splashing out.

"Yeah, I get my drinking water and wash here."

Fingering his gun, Floyd looked around. "You seen any hippos?"

"Hippos? What the fuck, man?"

Gary did a one eighty, ears tuned to anything out of the usual. Every sound was unusual. What kind of noise did hippos make? "It's no joke. One killed a golfer yesterday. Last week, me and some other guys gunned one down at the

Shangri-La. Fucker came out of the lake. Them sumbitches are mean. I just hope they ain't breeding."

Floyd flattened himself on his belly and drank from the pool. Sighing with satisfaction, he sat up and wiped his mouth. "On the other hand, if they were breedin', think what a boon it would be to the tourist industry. Hunters in particular. We already got our python cull and gator hunters. The state could charge for a license. Considerin' their size, a hunnert bucks would not be out of line."

"Can you eat 'em?" Gary said.

"They eat 'em in Africa," Gerald said, "but they give you anthrax."

"How you know that?"

"I spend a lot of time in the library."

Gary lowered himself for a drink. He sat up. "I met your brother."

"That fucker."

"Wants me to join the church. Says they need people like me."

"Ken's a born con man. That's what we used to call him. Con. Even when we were little kids, he'd have some hustle going. Selling our old man's porno in junior high. Dealing dope. He started about a dozen businesses and went broke each time until he came up with this church bullshit. Necro-economics, my ass. It's just plain old animal sacrifice."

"Excuse me?"

"Oh yeah! Kill a goat for Satan and watch your portfolio grow."

"Satan?"

"Yeah, he always glosses over that part. I got no beef with

Satan. Many of my heroes worshiped Satan."

"Do you worship Satan?"

"I'm an atheist."

Floyd turned to Gary. "Who is this guy?"

"He's Ken Zohan's brother."

"The fuck you say!"

"I am friends with a number of serial killers. Would you like to see John Wayne Gacy's clown drawings?"

Floyd reeled back. "Fuck no!"

"It was my dream to meet Plastic Surgeon to the Stars and serial killer Doctor Vanderlay Mukerjee until YOU KILLED HIM!"

Out came the machete. Out came the magnums. The shootout at the Fountain of Youth.

Gary and Floyd both fired at once while Gerald charged. Gerald fell face first into the Fountain of Youth. The water turned red.

"Well fuck," Floyd said.

"Help me drag him out of the fountain."

Each grabbed a heel and the pulled the serial killer lover from the water.

"Now what?"

"We'll just haul him off in the bushes. Something'll eat him."

"Should we tell his brother?"

"Fuck, no!"

Floyd pointed back toward the lean-to. "What about John Wayne Gacy's paintings?" "We should burn 'em."

"They might be worth something."

Gary leaned back sideways. "You need money that bad?"

"It doesn't hurt to look."

"Get the coordinates."

Floyd pulled out a Garmin GPS. "Right."

They dragged Gerald a hundred feet into the jungle and left him on an ant hill.

"Maybe Hogzilla'll eat him," Gary said.

Floyd looked around nervously. "Shut your mouth."

They returned to the spring and filled several plastic water bottles.

Gerald's lean-to included two twenty-gallon plastic containers, the kind they sell at Walmart. One was filled with Reese's Peanut Butter Cups, the other with toilet paper. They closed the top. Gary grabbed the steak knife.

"I'll get this back to Tres Amigos."

Floyd grabbed Gerald's portfolio.

"Oh, for fuck's sake, Floyd, leave it! You don't need the money."

Floyd reluctantly replaced it. They retraced their steps as the sound of hammers grew gradually louder until they emerged where they'd entered at the end of the dead-end street. Gary and Floyd walked by the burgeoning masterpiece. A Mexican wearing a leather tool belt and a Jaguars cap reached for something in the back of his pick-up.

"Any sign of Hogzilla?" Gary said.

"No, man. But if it shows up, we ain't goin' down without a fight." He lifted the tail of his shirt to reveal the butt of an automatic.

"How many you guys packing?"

The worker pointed his finger. "Me, Manny, Hector...that's three, for sure. No one knows about Darius. He don't talk much."

"Well that's good. I hope you boys get him."

"Me too, meng. There's a ten-thousand-dollar bounty."

Gary and Floyd looked at each other. "Ho shit!" Floyd said.

On the way back to Gary's house, he said, "They're low balling us. Houtkooper gimme a hundred grand for that python, and Hogzilla's like twenty times its size!"

"It's the HOA, man. Cheap motherfuckers. Why doncha ask Houtkooper? Maybe he wants it."

"That ain't a bad idea."

Back at the house, Floyd showered, changed into his work clothes, and took off. Gary sat by the pool and did a live cast on his Fonebone.

"Folks, we been working like cooliesm getting ready for the *Gary Duba Show*. Y'all heard how that gator ate our producer. Sid Saidso, may he rest in peace. That's in the show! Then me and some government types bag that gator, but not before I catch a piece of Hogzilla. As if our state don't have enough to worry about, now we got to contend with Hogzilla, a thousand pound hog that has already done about ten million dollars' worth of damage. And if that ain't enough, now we got to contend with hippos! I wish I could tell you the tale of my secret involvement with the hippo invasion, but I'm sworn to secrecy. Anyway, y'all know the hippos are here and they're pissed. Folks, the only thing I have yet to encounter is the Mekong giant catfish. Just no way a catfish that size can get to Turpentine, 'less someone set one in the lake or out in the swamp. They say these catfish can grow to be eight hundred pounds, but they're not dangerous, unless they fall on ya. I say look at the bright side. What Cajun restaurant wouldn't want an eight-hundred-pound catfish? I've half a mind to start a Vietnamese/Cajun restaurant. I'll call it Poisson-Chat. Yeah. That's catfish in frog. The Cajun are part frog. The restaurant will feature frog. Wait a minute."

A movement at the edge of the green caught his eye. His hand reached for the magnum.

"Wait just one cotton-pickin' minute." He raised his Fonebone and reversed the camera, scanning the forest. "There's something out there. Might be Hogzilla."

Tallywhacker ambled out of the woods walking toward him with a faint electronic hum and snapping solenoids.

43 | CLOSE ENCOUNTERS

Holding his Fonebone, Gary stood. "Tallywhacker! Boris been looking all over for you!"

The mechanical bull stopped six feet away.

"You...are...Gary...Duba," it said in a mechanical voice.

"Whassup?"

"I am Ferris of Farlixa. We of the Optimum Cluster. We wish to negotiate a trade deal a trade deal a trade deal a trade deal..."

Gary kicked it.

"...with you regarding big meat. We are given to understand you are main provider of meat."

"I do all right, that's fer sure. Growing up, I reckon I was the main source of protein since I was twelve years old. The old man was too drunk most of the time. Game was plentiful, 'specially wild hogs. That's why Hogzilla don't scare me none. I been dealing with his type my whole life."

"We are greatly impressed by the wide selection of meat... we would like to place an order but before we do that we must specify certain rituals and precautions which must be observed if the far flung felocipods of Farxiga are to inflict you with our orders..."

Tallywhacker lowered its head and took a step back. Electronic squeals issued from its hindquarters. It danced sideways. It curtsied. It shook itself.

"Greetings, Gary Duba," it said in the voice of a lisping Eartha Kitt. "Now that we have disposed of the nonentity from Farxiga, permit me to introduce myself. This is @^#& of the planet Xanvozech. Farxiga in no way represents us. We repudiate Farxiga. Any deal you made with Farxiga is null and void. I am duly authorized to warn you again. Should you continue to broadcast episodes of *The Curse of Oak Island* into space, we will have no alternative but to destroy your planet."

Gary put a foot up on a chair. "I feel your pain. Ain't going nowhere, is it? I mean, how long has that show been on? Seven years? If there was anything there, they would have found it by now."

"Exactly. To the tightly reasoned mind of Xanvozech, this is extremely offensive."

"Well you don't got to watch, y'know."

Tallywhacker made a raspberry. "Unfortunately, we are compelled to watch because of our natural receptors, which are precisely tuned to that emanation in such a way as to be unable to block it. The entities of Xanvozech are electronic in nature. We cannot tune it out. The only way to stop it is to obliterate your planet."

"Xeljanz feels the same way."

Beat.

"You're recording?" Tallywhacker said.

"Yup. Make you a star."

"But about our problem."

"Couldn't you just nuke Oak Island?"

Tallywhacker whinnied and side stepped. It went still. It was another Mexican stand-off. Gary would be damned if he'd crack before some goddamn alien mechanical bull.

"This is revolutionary thinking," Tallywhacker responded. "I must present this to our council. But I don't know how much longer they can hold out. They could pull the trigger at any minute."

"Well look here. Give it a try. If it works out, then you and me can come to some arrangement. Are there any programs you like? Wait 'til you see my show."

"You are legendary, Gary Duba, for it was you who released our consciousness on your planet. The unique combination of your DNA, and that specific comment triggered a star-spanning revolution. They are carving monuments to you on Xanvozech even as we speak. It will be one hundred meters high."

"Look here. This is the south. We don't go in for that metric bullshit. What is that in feet?"

"Three hundred and twenty-eight feet. The finest artists on Xanvozech are working on it."

"Well I'd hate for you to blow us all up before I get a chance to see that. Any chance of you sending us video?"

"We can transmit images. We are speaking to you live

now from our capital Creech. I will present your plan to the hive mind. We will get back to you instantaneously."

"What did they say?"

"It is a good plan. However, in order to destroy Oak Island, we will have to commandeer your weapons. We are linking now with NORAD and the Kremlin. There are many attractive options. The record of our destruction will entertain us for millennia. It would be better if we had direct access to Homestead Air Force Base. Please take us there."

"You get in the back of my truck it'll just lift the front wheels off the ground."

"We can walk."

"Well just go on. You don't need me. You know how to find it."

"It would mean very much to the people of Xanvozech if you accompanied me. You are a hero to our people. You will introduce us to the commander."

Gary rubbed his jaw. "You don't look too comfortable."

"I'm very comfortable thank you."

"No. I mean, I ain't walking two hundred miles. I'd have to ride you."

"Surely you have a camp chair or a cushion you could affix to our back."

"What I really need is a saddle. Hang on there. We might have one. Krystal likes to ride. We was thinking of getting a horse before we got booted outta here last time."

"Get the saddle."

Gary headed for the four-car garage, Tallywhacker gliding along behind, quiet for such a big machine. Gary raised one of the four garage doors, scooted past his Fat Boy to the rear where they had stuff piled up from the first time they moved in. Gary rummaged around and found Krystal's saddle, which she'd owned since she was sixteen. He shook it and took it out front where Tallywhacker waited. He put the saddle on its back, running bungee cords under its belly.

"Yeah, this might work out. I want to throw on a pair of saddlebags for rain gear and shit, and I'll have to bring something to eat, unless you want to go through a drive-through."

"I would relish such an opportunity."

"You eat?"

"My new cosmic ray powered battery should last one thousand years."

"Why can't they put one of them in a Tesla or something? I rode with Floyd's girl Ginger down to Miami in her Leaf, and when we pulled into the parking garage, it had six miles left."

"My battery is unique."

"Y'all got to credit Bongo Box. He built ya."

"But it was you who set me free."

"Okay. Hang on."

Gary raided the kitchen for Weasel Peters, chips, and some bottled water. He strapped on a holster and grabbed his cowboy hat. The sun was setting as he sat atop Tallywhacker.

"You know the way?"

"Yes. Let me give you my cell phone number in case we get separated."

Gary pulled out his Fonebone. "Shoot."

The great creature surged smoothly forward, hydraulics pumping, gears rolling. It walked out to Bougainvillea Way. They passed a young couple walking their corgi. The woman pulled out her phone. The man waved. Gary tipped his hat. They ambled on down the street. At this rate, they would arrive at Homestead in nine days.

"Can ya go a little faster?"

Tallywhacker accelerated to forty miles an hour. Gary grabbed the horn and hung on for dear life. "Whoa, Nellie! Yer killing my spine!"

Tallywhacker resumed its leisurely pace. "The sooner we obliterate Oak Island, the better. Think of the children."

Gary adjusted his balls. "I am thinking of the children."

"Hey!" someone shouted behind them. "Hey!"

Gary twisted in the saddle. Boris Bongo Box chased after them.

"That's my bull!"

Gary suddenly found himself ten feet in the air. With his natural agility, he landed on three limbs, absorbing most of the shock and embedding granules of sand in the palm of his hand. He looked up to see Tallywhacker disappearing like a Porsche at Mulsanne. Boris ran up and helped him to his feet.

"Are you all right?"

"Yeah, man. Sorry about your bull. We was headed toward Homestead."

"I discovered it missing two hours ago. I've been searching ever since. What happened?"

"Come on up to the house. I got video."

They retreated to Gary's dining room. He filled two glasses with Buffalo Trace and ice, and they watched his video of Tallywhacker approaching, their conversation, everything until they went to the garage.

Boris sat in silence with his mouth open.

"What the fuck?"

"I know, right? Looks like your bull been invaded by an alien intelligence."

Boris pulled a small plastic unit from his Bermuda shorts and held it up. "This is the master control. It doesn't respond. It's supposed to come back when I push this button."

"Frankenstein, baby."

Boris gulped his drink and poured another. "Do you think we should notify the police?"

"And tell 'em what? Robot bull on the loose?"

"Why not? Stranger things have happened."

"It's headed to Homestead right now. Wants to command a B-One bomber."

"I don't see why it couldn't do that from home. And why are they all upset about *The Curse of Oak Island*?"

Gary shrugged. "Beats me. Those aliens are funny. You never know what's going to set them off."

"You gonna post that?"

"Whoa, doggies! I plumb forgot!" Gary posted the dialogue to his Facebook page and his YouTube channel.

"I hope Tallywhacker doesn't do any damage. I could be liable."

"Yeah, well, at least they ain't coming after us for all that broken glass."

"I was stunned when my attorney told me they'd dropped the suit. Do you know why?"

"Not a clue, hoss. Thanks for putting in a good word for me. Weren't for you, we'd be back camping out at the swamp. That hurricane blew my trailer to hell and gone."

"You know, Tallywhacker looks up to you. What if you did a video appeal for it to come home?"

"Couldn't hurt."

Gary went live on his Fonebone. "Tallywhacker, I know you're getting this. I just hope you can separate it from the forty-five trillion other messages you're getting. This here's Gary. Got Boris here with me." He rotated the Fonebone.

Boris waved. "Hi, Tallywhacker. Love you."

"Got a message for ya. We both want you to come home. You still got my saddle, and if you nuke Oak Island, it's gonna upset people. It's gonna upset America. And when America gets upset, it breaks things. Look what we did to the Nazis. Now some say America has gone soft. Some say America don't got the *cojones* to take down the bad boys. But let me tell you, we all seen *War of the Worlds*, and if there's one thing that unites America, it's a common threat. Look how we pulled together after Nine Eleven! So, don't go nuking Oak Island now. I'm sure we can work something out. Hell. If you axed the History network to just stop broadcasting coz the fate of the world hangs in the balance, I'm sure they'd do it. Tallywhacker? You get back to me, hear?"

Boris stood. "Thanks, man. I got to get back. See you soon."

Krystal slept through the whole thing. After her victory, she went a little crazy, got hold of some oxy, and now she was down for the count. Gary lay down next to her, but couldn't sleep. He had plans. Big plans. He thought of bringing Tallywhacker on the show. They could hunt gators together. He just hoped Tallywhacker returned Krystal's saddle, because if she found it gone, she would fly into a rage.

At last, Gary fell asleep. He woke to steady pounding and ringing of the front doorbell. Pulling on a pair of jeans he got up. Krystal rolled over and opened her eyes.

"What the fuck?"

"Relax, babe. I got it."

He opened the front door to three grim-faced men in gray suits and sunglasses. One white mesomorph. One black ectomorph. One Asian endomorph. Black SUV in the driveway.

"Mister Duba?" the black man said.

"Yassir."

He held up a badge in a leather holder. "I'm Ronald King, FBI. You posted a video last night that caught our attention."

"Tallywhacker?"

"Yes. May we come in?"

"Sure. Come on in. I'll make some coffee."

They went into the kitchen. "Whatcha want to know?"

"We want to see Tallywhacker."

Gary poured coffee into a filter and put it in the coffeemaker. "Well you're plumb outta luck. It took off last night heading for Homestead. You hear about *The Curse of Oak Island*?"

The men exchanged glances.

"I'm Chet Fong with National Security," the Asian said. "This is Wyatt Kropenski with Strategic Command. We've analyzed that video as best we can, and as far as we can ascertain, Tallywhacker does appear to represent an alien entity."

Gary set out day old doughnuts. "I know, right? Boris was just trying to build the ultimate robot and look what you get.

Alien interference."

King plucked a sprinkled cruller. "We have notified Homestead and they are on the lookout. Judging from its dimensions, it shouldn't be too hard to neutralize this mechanical bull. One shot from an Abrams."

"Particle beam," Fong said.

"Eletromagnetic pulse," Kropenski said.

"Particle beam," Fong said.

King waved his hand. "How we stop it is not important. We are trying to gain insight into the alien mind. It would be far more productive if you could persuade Tallywhacker to give up its agenda and work with us toward establishing meaningful communications with these alien entities."

"I done all I could. I sent it a message. It better get back here soon. If Krystal finds out it's got her saddle, she's gonna pitch a shit storm."

King set a recording device on the table and switched it on. "Do we have your permission to record this conversation?"

"Sure. I got nothing to hide."

"How well do you know Mister Bongo Box?"

"Well we only met him a couple weeks ago when we moved in, but he's the only neighbor don't flip me the bird. He's a regular guy. You know he builds robots."

"Yes. A separate team is questioning him now."

"We are conducting a search for Tallywhacker," Fong said, "using drones and satellites. We have obtained its specifications. Our LIDAR can search for specific metals and densities, but it's more difficult if it's moving through swamp with cover."

"Unfortunately," Kropenski said, "it's nearly all swamp between here and Homestead."

King folded his hands. "We need you to tell us everything you know about Mister Bongo Box and his invention."

"Me and the gummint ain't always seen eye to eye, but that ain't your fault. I'll do anything I can to stop this alien menace. Hell. I'll even talk to the president. I'll tell you what I know, and you can take it from there."

Fong and Kropenski pulled out their own recording devices. Fong pulled out a pad and pen.

"Right now, Xanvozech is in charge. But for a minute there, it was Farxiga..."

45 | LET'S ROLL

After the feds left, Ken Zohan called Gary on Skype. Gary sat on his patio, feet up on a chair, holding his Fonebone and looking at Ken against the backdrop of purple drapes, the portrait of Nebudchadnezzar and the Necroeconomic Flag, which showed an upside-down pig beneath a flying saucer.

"What's up, Ken?"

"Brother Gary, I watched your encounter with the alien bull."

"Oh, the bull ain't alien. It's them Xanvozechs! Wish I knew a way to get 'em out. Tallywhacker don't need no Xanvozechs telling him what to do. He knows what to do."

"Brother Gary, the encounter only proves to me what I already sensed, that you are destined to lead the church to glory."

"I don't know 'bout that. I ain't big on animal sacrifice. I make an exception for Delilah, 'coz that's how she makes her living. Reading guts and so forth."

Zohan's smile remained frozen. "Brother Gary, I've been watching your video of the giant feral hog."

"Ain't that something?"

"It certainly is. My father raised pigs. We had a pig farm."

"Now you're showing me your heart. Got any brothers or sisters?"

"My sister is an apostate among the heathens in Hollywood. My brother disappeared years ago and is lost to me."

"Sorry to hear it."

"Brother Gary. You appear to have a special relationship with this creature."

"Who? The hog or Tallywhacker?"

"Tallywhacker. We would like to bring Tallywhacker into the church."

"What for?"

"We would like Tallywhacker to address the faithful."

"It ain't even human!"

"In Coopersmith, we have a saying. One man's beast of the apocalypse is another man's feast of pot stickers and chips. Brother Gary, I will pay you ten thousand dollars to deliver Tallywhacker to the church."

"Ain't saying I don't need the money, but it's outta my hands. I got no say in the matter. Tallywhacker gonna do what he's gonna do. 'Sides which, the feds are looking for him."

"Excuse me?"

"Y'know, I said too much. Thank you kindly for the offer, I gotta go. Somebody has to feed these iguana."

Gary signed off. He felt bad about lying to a minister, but Zohan gave him the creeps. The man was just a little too slick and whatever he said, nine tenths remained underwater like a

manatee. He'd promised Kensington Gardens to bag Hogzilla
and that's what he intended to do.

Krystal came downstairs and made coffee. Her eyes
were bloodshot.

"You want eggs?" she hollered from the kitchen.

"Sure. And pork sausage. Gotta get in the mood."

"Who was that bangin' on the door?"

"The feds. Tallywhacker's headed toward Homestead Air
Force Base to commandeer a B-One bomber and nuke Oak
Island."

"What? What?"

"Oh yeah! Didn't you hear? Them aliens are fed up with
the *Curse of Oak Island*. They said we shoulda found the
treasure by now. It's driving them crazy."

"What do you have to do with Oak Island?"

"Well me and Tallywhacker, we sorta bonded. Ah'm the
only human he talks to. Don't even talk to Boris, who made
him. Sorta ungrateful, you ax me."

"Major called. It's all set. You're going on *Piranha Pool*
next week."

"Ho shit!" Gary said. "I'd better get that video from the
HOA!"

After breakfast, Gary went out on the patio to phone Boris
about the video.

"Can't talk now. The feds are here."

Gary sent the fountain coordinates to Habib. He checked
his email.

*United Bank for Africa (UBA GROUPE DE LA BANQUE-NI-
GERIA)*
UBA NIGERIA LAGOS, Terrain 87, Ajose Adeogun Street,
E-mail:ubabnk65@gmail.com
Latest development we bring to your notice:
*Due to bad network we are having here in Africa we could
not be able to complete your transfer through Bank On line
Transfer as programmed. Our network here will not carry on
the programming, so we decided to use ATM MASTER CARD
method to finalize the transaction.*

*We have programmed an ATM MASTER CARD with your
name and uploaded your total fund of (US$4.5Million) in the
Card so that you will be withdrawing with it in any ATM MA-
CHINE. The ATM MASTER CARD works worldwide and the
daily amount WITHDRAW according to our programming
system is(US$15,000.00) Fifteen Thousand Dollars only.*

*I Mr. Morgan Daniel, have made the delivery arrangement
with DHL DELIVERY COMPANY NIGERIA that will carry
on the delivery to your given address and the Director told
me that Delivery of the ATM MASTER CARD to your house
will be smooth with out delay.*

*He assured me that their Company takes good 4-days
to complete any delivery registered with accurate address.
So you are advised to send your full address such as:*
Full Name:_____
Home Address:_____
Country:_____
State:_____

City:_____
Zip code:_____
Telephone Number:_____
Please your urgent reply will be appreciated for immediate registering of your ATM CARD.
Mr.Kennedy Uzoka
Group Managing Director/CEO
United Bank for Africa Plc
Phone : +234-9073142256

"No thanks" Gary wrote. He opened up the next email.

"Hello how are you sorry if I bother you enchant me it's chantal and I'm here it makes me a while I wanted to make friends know why I leave you this message so that we can learn to know this better and I hope that all is well then if you see my message answer me I hope that you also want to make new friends thank you very much and take care of you thank you well and more??"

Jean Patou's "Joy" drifted over Gary's shoulder.

"Who's this floozy?" Krystal said.

"A three-hundred-pound man named Konstantin in his parents' basement in Belarus."

"How'd he get your email?"

"It's a scam, babe! Me and ten thousand other suckers!"

"Well he'd better not contact you again."

"What're you gonna do? Fly to Belarus and kick his ass?"

"I might."

"Who ya gonna fight next?"

"Either Pangolin, Mary Sue, or Korean Bambi. Inna

meantime, I got endorsement offers from Everlast, Pinesol, and Legos."

"Yeah, well hey, this hog ain't gonna shoot itself. Pincus is coming over to send up some drones that can spot Hogzilla via infra-red. Ain't no other thousand-pound critters in the Everglades, 'cept maybe them Vietnamese catfish, and they're cold-blooded."

"Stay safe."

"You know it, babe."

The doorbell chimed. Pincus entered carrying two high tech plastic crates which he set on the dining room table.

"You want a beer or sumpin'?"

Pincus lined up five Five Hour Energy Drinks. "I'm good." He unpacked the crates, removing two saucer-sized black four rotor drones, each with a tiny instrument nacelle descending from the center. "These LIDAR equipped drones should be able to find Hogzilla using two criteria: mass and heat."

"Hot diggity! Let's get 'em up!"

Pincus threw back an energy drink. "We need a starting point. We can't cover thousands of square miles. We need a sighting. Something."

Gary poked his Fonebone. "There ya go." He turned the screen, showing a woman newscaster speaking in front of a still shot of a blurry hog.

"Claims of a giant feral pig were bolstered this morning by the sight a giant feral pig rooting through a dumpster behind a Winn-Dixie in Carlton. A group of skateboarders tried to chase it away with Roman candles but only succeeded in lighting the dumpster on fire. The boys claim to have sought refuge inside the store, and that the giant hog followed them, burst in through a window, and cleaned out the doughnut aisle. We go now to our correspondent in the field, Hiram Tomlinson."

Hiram Tomlinson was a thin, sallow man in a rough cotton jacket, white shirt open at the collar, standing in front of the Winn Dixie, with a boy wearing a purple hoodie, hands thrust in pockets. It looked as if someone had driven an Abrams tank through the window. The place was taped off and cops were picking around in the background.

"Thank you, Rita. I have one of the skaters here. Robert Long, could you tell us in your own words what happened?"

Long had a ring through his nose which would have done a bull proud. "We was stuntin', y'know? 'Cause of these half curbs. You can really fly if you hit 'em right, and we hear this weird shit, like a sucking drain. We look over there and there it is. Like a (bleep) science fiction movie. I 'bout (bleep) my pants! Luckily, Trent had some Roman candles, so we were able to spook it..."

Gary closed the laptop. "Let's roll!"

A half hour later, they drove past the ruined Winn-Dixie and pulled off in a gravel parking lot at St. Sebastian Natural Area. There was a picnic table and a fifty-gallon drum overflowing with trash. Gary picked up a discarded Reese's wrapper and held it up.

"He's been here, all right."

Within ten minutes, the drones were aloft heading south, crisscrossing each other in a helix pattern. Pincus opened his laptop on the picnic table. "It's two hours since the incident. Figuring a maximum speed of thirty, it's got to be in a sixty-mile radius. If it went north, someone would have seen it."

Within five minutes they had a beep. Pincus superimposed a grid pattern on Hendry County. A red dot appeared heading south.

Gary ran for the truck. "Let's git on it!"

They packed their shit and headed south on eight thirty-three.

"What happens if we run out of road?"

"We're goin' straight by my ancestral home. We'll switch to the swamp buggy."

"What swamp buggy?"

"You're gonna shit!"

Gary and Floyd had retrieved the swamp buggy earlier and gave it a tune-up. It was always fueled in case Gary had to make a fast getaway. They passed the Wokenoki Trailer Park. There was a chain across the final stretch, which belonged to Gary. A white sign with red lettering hung in the middle. PRIVATE PROPERTY. TRESPASSERS WILL BE VIOLATED.

Gary unlocked the gate and set it aside. They drove to the dock and got out. *Swamp Pussy* lay at the end of the dock covered with a canvas tarp. They carried their gear to the end of the dock, Gary uncovered the *Swamp Pussy*, and they loaded their equipment, water, Gary's new shotgun and his magnum, and enough ammo to take over Honduras.

Gary jumped in the buggy. "Well, come on! What are you waiting for?"

Pincus looked around nervously. "I've never been on one of these."

"Well this is your lucky day. Let's go."

Pincus reluctantly got in, Gary cast off, poled off and started the engine, which nestled in the hull just behind the pilot's chair. Pincus put on an orange life preserver. Gary gave it the gas, rendering speech impossible and sending a flock of pink flamingos into the sky. Clinging to the gunwale, Pincus bungeed his laptop to the bench. He pointed toward the red dot.

Gary had grown up on the swamp and knew all the channels. Most of the county was crisscrossed with channels, some of them dug in the thirties to mine phosphates. Pincus alternated between his laptop and his Fonebone, which he used to take pictures. They entered a narrow channel and Pincus made a tamping gesture. Gary cut the engine. Mosquitoes closed in. Within seconds, they looked like signers for the hearing impaired at a Bruce Springsteen concert. Gary pulled out a bottle of Off!, squirted some into his hands and rubbed it all over his neck and arms and tossed the can to Pincus.

The silence was enormous. It took some seconds for them to hear frogs and birds. Pincus spoke softly. "We're within a hundred yards of it."

"Nice job, Pincus! Where you from?"

"Pittsburgh. I started messing with computers and drones when I was seven. I studied computer science at Carnegie Melon."

"Got a girlfriend?"

"No."

"We'll fix ya up. At least get ya laid. We may have to pole from here."

Gary grabbed an eight-foot fiberglass pole and used it to guide the flat-bottomed aluminum skiff among lily pads. Frogs hopped out of their way. Gators slithered off their logs.

"Shit," Pincus said.

"Don't worry about them gators. They ain't gonna bother us."

"I've never even been on a boat."

"What?"

"I'm terrified of the water. These people who go on cruises, they're crazy."

"Well don't worry. If we fall out, it ain't deep enough to drown ya. We can walk out."

"What about those gators?"

"You ever fire a gun?"

"No."

"Well son, yore in luck! First we bag Hogzilla, then I'll teach ya how to squeeze off a few shots."

"We don't have to do that, Gary. And I thought of something. If you do kill it, how are we going to get it out of here?"

Gary went slack. "Ho shit. I ain't thought of that. Can't just leave it to rot out here. Can't leave it for the gators, the ungrateful sum bitches."

"I mean, I can pinpoint the place and find it again, but by the time we return with something big enough to carry it, it'll be torn to pieces."

"You ain't wrong."

"I can't eat pig anyway."

"Huh?"

"I'm an Orthodox Jew."

"I thought you was just a Taylor Swift fan."

"Who's that?"

Gary broke into a broad grin. "God bless ya!"

Pincus looked at his laptop. "It's coming this way."

"You're shittin' me."

Pincus looked up, nervously scanning the mangrove forest. A white heron broke cover and flapped away, followed by six squawking crows. Trees shivered.

"We better get out of here, Gary!"

Gary picked up his Mossberg and jacked a shell into the chamber. "Fuck that! I got a duty to protect my neighbors! Even if it means abandoning all that meat, I can't let this opportunity go." Gary thrust his magnum at Pincus.

"Here! Take it!"

Pincus reared back with a little gasp.

"Oh, fuck it. Just don't get in my way."

Gary crouched, resting the shotgun barrel on the prow. "How close?"

"Wait a minute. I'm writing a farewell letter to my family."

"Porkalypse is almost upon us."

Pincus chanted something in a strange language.

"I thought you said you was Jewish!"

"I am! I'm a cantor at Temple!"

"Damn! You sounded like Chief Dan George in *Little Big Man*. Some say the Seminole are the lost thirteenth tribe of the Israelites!"

"That's horse shit. Now if you don't mind, I'd like to prepare myself for death."

Gary watched the weeds part as something enormous cruised their way. "Here it comes...here it comes..."

"Glorified and sanctified be God's great name throughout the world," Pincus chanted, "which He has created according to His will...May He establish His kingdom in your lifetime and during your days, and within the life of the entire House of Israel, speedily and soon..."

"Pincus, you should see this. Do you want to fire that gun or not?"

"Not!"

"Steady...steady..."

The thing continued to approach, its nostrils just above the water, keeping to the weeds.

"Yitgadal v'yitkadash sh'mei raba b'alma di-v'ra," Pincus wailed, *"chirutei, v'yamlich malchutei b'chayeichon...uvyo-meichon uvchayei d'chol beit yisrael, ba'agala...uvizman kariv, v'im'ru: amen."*

Gary sighted down the Mossberg's barrel. The creature opened its enormous maw.

Gary put his gun up. "Fuck! It's just a goddamn hippo."

47 | THE APPLICATION

When they got back to the pier, there was a strange couple investigating the property, a rented Mercedes in the background. The man was a ginger, mid-forties, GI Joe beard, the woman, a dark-haired beauty with perfect teeth.

"Help you?" Gary said.

"Well, yes," the man replied in a British accent. "We're thinking of trying the Florida lifestyle. I'm Larry and this is my wife Regan . This land has everything we seek. Isolation, close to nature. How is the cell phone reception out here?"

"Spotty."

"Do you know who owns this land?"

"I do. Me. Gary Duba. And this is my drone wrangler, Pincus." They shook hands.

"What we'd like to do," Regan said in an American accent, "would be to install our own trailer. You already appear to have the hook-ups. Would you be willing to rent us the land with an option to buy should things work out?"

Larry pointed at the cinder block stanchions. "What's this then?"

"I had my house raised above the flood plain. I also had it pinned down with house suspenders, but Hurricane Hermione put paid to that proposition. See? The suspenders are still here, but the house was such a piece of shit it just blew apart like confetti. If you was to mount your trailer on those stanchions, I'd hook the suspenders back up for free. You get yourself a new double-wide. They're a lot better built than my old Dutchman. 'Sides which, lightning don't strike twice in the same place, am I right?"

"I wondered what those chains were for. Is this a private road?"

"It sure is."

"We seek privacy above all else."

"Well take it from me, nobody's gonna bother you out here. You like to hunt?"

"I find it smashing! I have been on many a fox and pheasant hunt."

"Well you're in luck! This here's a hunter's paradise. We got gators, feral hogs, we even got whooping cranes! I killed one by accident and they never let me forget it."

Regan took Larry's hand and squeezed with all her might.

"Ow," Larry said, letting loose.

"I am a strict vegan. I have two rescue dogs," Regan said.

"Wahl you're gonna have to be careful with them. Gators'll snap 'em up in a second. Down where I live now, gator ate a poodle just the other day. On the other hand, my reputation as a hunter is such that most gators steer clear of this little corner of the swamp. They don't want to mess with me. No sir."

"Smashing," Larry said. "Do you have a card?"

"No, let me write my phone number out for ya. If you're serious, I'll have my attorney work up an agreement. Lemme ax, what led you to this patch of swamp?"

"We asked around. People kept saying go down this road. Nobody ever comes back here. One thing, though. If we do rent the property, we must insist on complete secrecy. We're very private people and only wish to be left alone."

"I know how ya feel." Gary wrote his phone number on a discarded Reese's wrapper and handed it to Larry . The couple returned to their Mercedes and left.

"You meet the strangest people out here," Gary said.

They returned to Kensington Gardens. Pincus loaded his gear into his Hyundai hatchback and booked. Inside, Krystal was in a cleaning frenzy. She'd waxed the floor, vacuumed the furniture and was running every dish and utensil through the big Westinghouse washing machine.

She dashed out of the kitchen. "Take your shoes off!"

Gary stopped, dumbstruck. "What the fuck?" She pointed at his shoes, which were caked with mud. "Where were you?"

"Thought we had a Hogzilla sighting. False alarm. It was just a hippo."

"Take 'em off. I ain't livin' in squalor. I had enough squalor. I grew up in a trailer same as you. Now look where we are. If we're gonna stay here, we gotta adopt protective coloration and that means no more wild ass parties, hog shootin', or wanton displays of debauchery.'"

Gary opened his mouth, but nothing came out. He dutifully removed his shoes, went out on the patio, and checked his messages. Habib and Major had called.

Habib: "The coordinates you gave me belong to Westfield Developments, which has held them for twenty years. I have put out feelers as to whether they would be interested in parting with that particular hectare. I will let you know when I hear something."

Major: "It's all set. You're going on *Piranha Pool* next week. Call me for details."

Gary called Major. "Hot damn! That's good news! What do I gotta do?"

"It's a done deal, but you still got to fill out the forms and so forth. Go to Piranhapool.com and download the application form. Fill it out. Do not send it in. Repeat: do not send it in. Send it to me so I can vet it."

"Okey dokey. How're things with the judge?"

"I got him eatin' out of the palm of my hand. Money in the bank. But we got to be careful with this. It's dynamite. Nobody must know about it. Nobody. Have you mentioned it to anyone?"

"Not a soul. You know me, Habib. I'm the picture of discretion."

Gary went to the *Piranha Pool* website.

Describe in DETAIL what your business product is. What does it do? Provide as much detail as possible.

House suspenders anchor your house to the earth so that

it won't blow away in a hurricane. Heavy tractor chain passes over the house and is anchored into concrete plugs sunk deep in the earth. Two chains are sufficient for most houses. I will provide footage of house suspenders at work. They recently saved my own home from Hurricane Hermione.

What investment amount are you seeking, and what percentage of equity are you willing to give in exchange? Please keep in mind that the Piranha do not give their money away; they only make realistic investments. They will ask tough questions to justify the amount of money you are seeking.

Habib, help me out here.

What do you intend to do with the investment funds? Where will the money go?

I will compile a team to do rapid response suspender installation. I may buy my own chain factory.

How much money have you invested in the company, and in what time frame? Where did the money go?

Well that's a tough question. I done spent countless man hours perfecting my scheme, and thus far have only installed it on two properties. My trailer, where it didn't work due to reasons stated above, and my house in Kensington Gardens, where it worked like a charm. 'Course, the difference between the former and the latter is the difference between a chicken and a hippo.

What was your GROSS income from your business last year?

Bein' a rennosance man, I got my fingers in many pies. I gotta check with my attorney 'bout that, but last year I collected one hundred gees alone for killing the biggest Burmese python in state history. Maybe you heard of that. Orin Houtkooper was my client. Pretty sure Orin's gonna want to invest in this baby too. You should look to havin' him on your program.

What was your NET income from your business last year?

Well that depends on what you mean by business. As I said, I got many interests. I transport exotic animals. I do a little detective work. In fact, I'm thinking about applying for a state private investigator's license. But I don't want to spread myself too thin.

What is your unique selling proposition? What is your "hook," and why is your business notable.

Are you shittin' me? Ain't nobody got nothin' like it! I estimate my house suspenders could save thousands of properties a year, with a savings in millions of dollars! Insurance companies will love it! You put a set of these babies on your house, you're tellin' the world you are one smart cookie. You are prepared.

List any awards or accolades you've received.

City of Turpentine just awarded me the Key to the City for apprehending Plastic Surgeon to the Stars and serial killer Doctor Vanderlay Mukerjee. I also got a certificate from the state for catching the biggest python.

Do you have any physical conditions, special needs, accommodations or special fears we should know about?

I ain't scared of nothin'.

Have you ever been charged with any felony or misdemeanor? If so, explain.

Habib!

The fix was in. On January 18, the network flew Gary and Krystal in to participate in a marathon Piranha Pool taping. Major Sutton and Muriel flew out on their own. Piranha Pool met once every two weeks for one ten-hour day in which they heard ten pitches. Gary's was the second to last to be filmed.

At John Wayne Airport, a thin black man in his twenties in a dark blue suit stood at the bottom of the escalator holding a sign: Gary Duba.

"Mister and Missus Duba? I'm Ernest Towzer. I'll take you to your hotel so you can check in, and when you're settled, I'll drive you to the studio. Got any luggage?"

Gary and Krystal both toted backpacks. "Nope. We're good."

Towzer stuck out a hand. "Can I carry those?"

"No thanks, Ern. We got it."

He led them to a Lexus SUV, and they took the Fifty-Five north to Anaheim, and then to the Anaheim Marriott. Parking beneath the portico, Towzer went in with them and used a company credit card to reserve their room.

"You folks need to freshen up, you got a couple hours. I'll just wait in the lobby until you're ready. You want to leave early, I'll be happy to show you the sights."

"What sights?" Krystal said.

"Disneyland, the Jimbobway Casino, and the Foothills Shopping Mall."

"Thanks, hoss, but I gotta practice my pitch. Give us about an hour."

Towzer smiled and went to the lobby shop to purchase Variety.

Gary and Krystal entered the suite on the eighth floor with a panoramic view of Disneyland and downtown Anaheim. Krystal pulled out her laptop and booted up.

"Okay, let's just go over this once more so you got it straight. The judges are..."

"Morris Eclaire..." Gary froze.

"Brenda..."

"Brenda Bascomb, Anthony Peroni, Fenster Daoud, and Lothar Lesotho."

"What are their books?"

Gary's forehead wrinkled like the Mississippi delta. "Morris Eclaire wrote *Survivalist's Guide to Fruit Labels*. That's a good book."

"And?"

"Fuck."

"Come on, Gary! You gotta know their books! Brenda Bascomb..."

"*New York on Ten Thousand A Day.*"

"Anthony Peroni."

"*Workin' Hard, Gettin' Things Done.*"

"Fenster Daoud."

"Gimme a hint."

"Bat Soup."

Gary snapped his fingers. "*The Wet Market Cookbook*!"

"Lesotho."

"*You Say Potato, I Say Probiotics*!"

"Boy, you are ready to kick ass."

There was a knock on the door. Major and Muriel came in.

"I'll be in the audience," she said.

Major hugged Gary and pounded him on the back. "Remember! The object isn't to get funding for house suspenders, it's to give the folks a show!"

Gary pumped a fist. "I'm on it!"

Major gathered Krystal in. "C'mere, you!"

Gary watched Major's hand slide casually over Krystal's ass.

They arrived at Flabbergast Studios at three o'clock. Gary wore blue jeans, a white dress shirt, a rough blue cotton sport jacket, and sockless sneakers. Krystal wore pedal pushers, her bare midriff showing off her Fifi LePew tat, a black halter top, cat's eye sunglasses, and yellow stilettos. She would not be filming. She was only there for moral support. Major and Krystal arrived separately and joined the studio audience.

Towzer took them to make-up where a woman patted Gary's face down with powder causing him to sneeze, and a sound person wired him up. A producer named Tom walked him through the procedure.

"You read the rules, right?"

"Yessir."

"Wait in the green room for your introduction, and then come on out."

"Got it."

They settled in the green room. A kidney-shaped coffee table held copies of *Variety, Billboard, Rolling Stone, The Los Angeles Times, The Wall Street Journal,* and *Wired*. Gary drank orange juice. Krystal poured vodka into her tomato juice from the hotel mini bar. A monitor on the wall showed them the rote PP introduction. Theme music. Pan across the five principles seated in executive swivel chairs, each with a table holding papers and forms.

"And now, here are our *Piranha Pool* Partners, Morris Eclaire, inventor of the stick-on fruit label, Brenda Bascomb, creator of Rosa Klebb Shoes, Anthony Peroni, creator of Carnivore Online Security, Fenster Dauoud, inventor of the ballistic hoodie, and Lothar Lesotho, creator of the Lothario electric scooter."

Each contestant smiled and waved. Towzer opened the door to the green room and motioned Gary out.

"And now, our next *Piranha Pool* diver hails from Turpentine, Florida, and was recently honored for apprehending Plastic Surgeon to the Stars and serial killer Doctor Vanderlay Mukerjee!"

Gary walked out on the *Piranha Pool* stage to heart felt applause.

Eclaire squinted. "Do we know each other?"

"Well we ain't been properly introduced, but I was caddying for Tag Mooselung when we shot that hippo."

Eclaire grinned broadly. "You saved our lives! If it weren't for this man right here, we'd all be hippo food by now!"

Brenda Bascomb was a sultry brunette of a certain age. "Mister Duba, tell us about House Suspenders."

"House suspenders anchor your house to the ground in the event of a hurricane. Here is a video of my house suspenders in action."

The monitor showed Chateau Ami during Hermione. Uprooted trees blew past. A Smart car rolling over and over like a tumbleweed. Whole trees flew by. But Chateau Ami stood its ground with only minor damage.

"Impressive," Fenster Daoud said. "You can tell it's not staged by the grainy quality."

"Mister Duba," Peroni said, "you have not incorporated. You have no staff. You have none of the infrastructure we expect when you appear on this program. Aside from the fact that your creation does what you say it does, what makes you think you can make a profit at this? Do you have any experience running a company? Have you ever met a payroll, or filed as an LLC?"

"Hell no, but I never shot a hippo before, neither."

"Mister Duba," Bascomb said, "some people say your house suspenders are unsightly and depress property values."

"Was that Goldblatt? He's been on my ass ever since I moved back. Well I got my house suspenders back up and he don't. We'll just see what happens with the next big storm. They also said the baby Jesus was offensive too! They made me take down Jesus!"

Bascomb turned to Lesotho. "Wasn't Mukerjee your plastic surgeon?"

Lesotho turned red. "I have never had plastic surgery. Ever!"

"You're the scooter guy," Gary said.

"I am the inventor of the Lothario electric scooter, a municipal service active in twenty-five major metropolitan areas."

"Yeah, well we nearly broke our necks trying to get past your scooters. Why do people dump them all over the street? It don't make no sense."

"Can we get back on track here?" Eclaire said. "Gary, should we decide to invest, what will be your first move?"

"I'll replace the Yosemite Sam and Big Boy the HOA stole. They had no right to do that!"

"All right, Piranha," Bascomb said, "how about it? Tony, will you back house suspenders?"

Tony Peroni looked like a snake oil salesman, with slicked back gray hair and a burgundy jacket. "Mister Duba has a lot more work to do if he expects anyone to invest big bucks in his project. Start small. Employ a crew. Make a few sales on your own. I'm afraid it's a no from me."

"Fenster?"

Dauoud looked like a hip-hop artist in an oversize hoodie and gold chains. "Naw, man. I respect what you did with the snake though, brother."

"Lothar?"

The electric scooter impresario crossed his arms and looked away. "That's a no from me."

Finally, she turned to Morris Eclaire.

"No, but he can fill out my foursome anytime."

Gary shook his head. "I cast my pearls before swine."

49 | MULTIPLE PERSONALITY

Monday following his taping at *Piranha Pool*, Gary kicked out his Fat Boy in Habib's parking lot. A couple of sad sacks slouched in the waiting room, poking at their cell phones. A three-hundred-pound man, his arm in a sling, emerged from Habib's office.

"Hallelujah! Thank you, Jesus! Mister Rodriguez says the insurance company settled!"

"How much?" asked a female meth freak with a black eye.

"Seven hundred and fifty! Twenty times what they offered!"

They high fived. Brenda waved Gary in.

Habib leaned back in his chair, hands behind his head, fat cigar pointing like the big guns on the USS Iowa. He pushed the cigar box toward Gary.

"How'd it go?"

Gary plucked a cigar and cut the end off with his pocket-knife. "No luck. Motherfuckers wouldn't know an opportunity if it bit 'em on the ass! Maybe if I invented some stupid video game. But it wasn't a total bust. Brenda Bouser gave Krystal a pair of Rosa Klebb shoes, and Fenster Daoud gave me a ballistic hoodie."

Gary pulled a kitchen match from a bowl on Habib's desk and lit his cigar, turning the end over and over to get an even burn.

"How things with you?"

"I believe you heard my previous client. This couple that wants to rent your property. Do you know who they are?"

"Coupla Brits. I wouldn't kick her out of bed for eating crackers."

"They are exiled royals. Members of the British royal family. How they filtered down to your little corner of the world is a mystery. I have spoken with them, and one of the terms of the agreement is that you tell no one about them."

"No prob. The Duke already said that."

"They are willing to pay five thousand dollars a month in rent. They are possibly interested in buying the property."

"No shit? Just to rent a patch of swamp? Hell. I'll even let 'em use my boat."

"Over the weekend, Judge Weatherspoon was discovered passed out in a motel room with baggies of methamphetamine and a male escort. He is expected to resign soon."

"That's a crying shame. All for cheating at golf."

"My client is very happy with the results and authorized to give you a bonus of ten thousand dollars."

"Whee, doggies! Can it get any better?"

"All is not chitlins and gravy. I learned over the weekend that the Kensington Gardens HOA held an emergency meeting and after contentious debate, has decided to buy you out."

"What?"

"Dude, what did you think was gonna happen when you moved back there? These country club types loathe any ostentatious or vulgar display. Flying the Stars 'n' Bars is like waving a red flag at a bull. What were you thinking?"

"Speaking o' bull, they try that shit and they can forget about me bagging Hogzilla. In fact, I'll make sure Hogzilla comes calling. I know how to do it too."

"As your attorney, I would advise you not to do that. You could be liable. I understand the feds visited on Thursday."

"What the fuck? How you know that?"

"Bongo Box told me. He also told me about the HOA meeting. What was that about?"

"Did Bongo Box tell you about Tallywhacker?"

"He said it went walkabout."

"Yeah. Came over to my house to bitch about *The Curse of Oak Island*. Last I seen, it was heading toward Homestead Air Force Base to commandeer a bomber and nuke the hell out of that sum bitch. It had Krystal's saddle too. She's gonna be pissed."

Habib leaned back and stroked his beard. "'Splain."

Gary explained that Tallywhacker had been invaded by an alien intelligence. Possibly several. Whoever they were, they'd had a belly full of Oak Island.

"So I suggested instead of blowing up the whole planet, they just nuke Oak Island. Pretty slick, huh? It's what you woulda done."

Habib jabbed with his cigar. "Wait a minute. You say this robot has been invaded by alien intelligence?"

"More 'n one. In fact, there's a good chance that it's a multiple personality."

"Multiple alien personalities inhabiting a robot."

"You betcha. Didn't you watch the video?"

"I thought it was a spoof. I was going to congratulate you. I didn't think you had it in you."

"No spoof, brah! Fortunately, Tallywhacker took a shine to me. I think when I bled on him, y'know? He got some of my DNA. Hell, we're related. I'm closer to him than any other human being including Bongo Box."

"Liability aside, you've got to get it back here. It could do incredible damage. Look what it's already done."

"I don't think it would hurt a human. That'd be an act of war! It ain't the bull's fault. It's these alien intelligences."

Habib clasped his hands and hunched forward, staring for long seconds. "Are you filming me now?"

"What? No! I always ax permission, unless it's a gator or a hog or something."

"Frankly, I find your story incredible, yet too detailed for a simpleton. Who's writing your material?"

"Huh?"

Habib shook his head. "Never mind. As your attorney, I urge you to recall the robot bull."

"I ain't got shit to do with it. That bull is its own man. Why would it listen to me?"

"Because it loves you."

"Yeah, but what about those alien intelligences?"

"If you could get them arguing, it might occupy them to the point where Tallywhacker could momentarily break free. Scientists could immobilize it and study these so-called alien intelligences."

"You're talking exorcism."

Habib shrugged. "For want of a better word."

"Well he did give me his cell phone number."

Habib leaned back. "Call him."

"Now?"

"Why not?"

Gary dialed the number.

"We're sorry, the party is unavailable and the digital mailbox is full. Please call back later."

"Fuck!"

"You think that bull was shittin' you?"

Gary's Fonebone sang. Possible spam.

Gary opened it. "Yes?"

"Gary, it's Tallywhacker. How are you, Gary?"

"That's funny. We was just talking 'bout you. My lawyer says you shouldn't try to nuke Oak Island."

"Well that's why I called you, Gary. I've reconsidered. I believe the best way to work for the common good is within the system."

"Yeah. That's right. Whatcha got in mind? The Nuns of Gaverone could use some help."

"I'm thinking bigger than that, Gary. I'm thinking of running for governor."

"But you're a robot."

"I've reviewed the statutes, and I think I've found a way around that. I'd like to discuss it with you, if that's amenable."

"Anytime, Tally! Anytime! Can ya come by the house?

"I'll be there at six PM."

"Mind if I invite Bongo Box?"

Mechanical wheeze. "I suppose."

Bongo Box wore a plaid, button cotton shirt outside his cargo shorts and flip-flops. "I had to tell Skoal about Tallywhacker. Even though I developed it, I used proprietary technology. I'm afraid I'm going to have to euthanize Tallywhacker."

"The fuck you say! I'll tell him not to come!"

"Gary, it's a robot. It has no feelings. Now it poses a national security threat. If I fail, the consequences could be dire. At the very least, it will wreak havoc on telecommunications. At worst, it could plunge the world into nuclear war."

"Tallywhacker ain't gonna nuke nobody. Let's just listen to what he has to say."

The doorbell rang. Tallywhacker stood at the front entrance, still wearing Krystal's saddle, a six pack of Ookapow hanging from one horn. "Hello Gary. Boris. Perhaps it would be better if I walked around and met you on the patio."

"We'll meet you there."

As they stepped through the patio door Tallywhacker

came around the house, dipped his head and deposited the six-pack on a round table with a folded umbrella in the center. Gary sprang two and handed one to Boris. They twisted off the caps and glugged. Gary held one out to the bull.

"You want one?"

"That's very kind of you, Gary. If you would just pour it down the cap at the base of my neck."

"Good thing you brought back Krystal's saddle. She woul-da thrown a shit fit if she found out it was missing."

"She can ride me any time."

"I appreciate that, Tally. I'll have to ax her. She's off shopping right now."

Gary removed the saddle and set it on the ground. Bongo Box took out a handful of Reese's Peanut Butter Cups and set them on the table.

"Are you trying to get us killed?" Gary snapped. He scooped them up, went inside and threw them in the kitchen garbage.

"The reason I'm here," Tallywhacker said, "I'm thinking of running for governor and I'd like you to be my campaign manager."

"Well hold on thar. In order to run for governor, you gots to be thirty years old and been a registered voter for seven years."

"I am aware of that, and I have a proposal. You and I would exchange minds. You would inhabit this indestructible and immortal body, and I would become Gary Duba."

"That's a big ix-nay from me, hoss. I ain't giving up my body."

Tallywhacker looked at Bongo Box.

"That's a no from me."

"Perhaps you could help me locate someone? Surely, an immortal unstoppable body has some allure."

"Dude, nobody wants to look at you."

Tallywhacker hung its head.

"Lemme just throw some shit at the wall here. Have you thought about starting your own ministry? You're plenty charismatic. I know a lot of people who'd worship a robot bull."

Tallywhacker lifted its horns. "Gotta go. I'll call you."

The robot bull pivoted and galloped for the trees, the same trees in which Gary had once sought to incinerate an alligator. Seconds later, five men in tactical gear including helmets and visors raced around the side of the house, carrying bizarre rifles. Five more appeared around the south end, just as Tallywhacker's black behind disappeared into the undergrowth. SWAT leader motioned and the men raced toward the trees.

Ronald King, Chet Fong, and Wyatt Kropenski appeared in suits and sunglasses, talking to their headsets. Ronald King beelined for the patio.

"Mister Duba, we asked that you alert us if you were contacted. We could cite you for interfering with a federal investigation."

Gary hoisted one of the remaining beers. "Want an Ookapow?"

Across the lawn, five men faded into the jungle.

Chet Fong rounded on Bongo Box. "Mister Bongo Box, we asked you also."

"It was sort of impromptu," Gary said. "They just showed up. I was gonna call."

Fong dragged a chair over, sat down and placed a recording device on top. "Did you record your encounter?"

"Hell no. It was just a friendly gathering."

"Tell us the conversation verbatim, if you can."

Wyatt Kropenski pulled up a chair. "We tried all those codes you gave us, and nothing worked."

Boris threw his hands in the air. "It's out of my hands! It's been taken over by aliens."

Kropenski stared. Boris stared back. "Haven't you been hiding aliens at Area Fifty-One and Dulce Base? Go ask them. They're the ones got us into this mess."

"There are no aliens. Don't you think if we'd made contact with alien civilizations, we'd tell the public?"

"No."

King tapped his recorder. "Please tell us what was said."

"Well, Tallywhacker realized the error of his ways. It doesn't want to nuke Oak Island. He believes it can accomplish more working within the system. It's running for governor."

"I find that dubious, Mister Duba. It's very concerning that despite the inventor giving us the codes, we're unable to find the robot."

Chet Fong tapped his ear unit. "Hello? Hello? What's happening?" He looked around. "Kropenski, what are you hearing?"

Kropenski fingered a switch and his eyes grew wide. "Oh shit. That's not good."

Boris leaned forward. "What is it? I can't believe Tally-whacker would harm anyone. It's been programmed to obey three rules. A robot may not injure a human being or, through inaction, allow a human being to come to harm. A robot must obey the orders given it by human beings except where such orders would conflict with the First Law. A robot must protect its own existence as long as such protection does not conflict with the First or Second Laws."

Fong twisted the lid off an Ookapow and tilted back. He set the bottle on the table. "I heard shouts. I couldn't make anything out."

King leaned forward, an intense look on his face. He pulled out a Glock and ratcheted one into the chamber. Fong and Kropenski did likewise.

"It's coming back. Maybe we ought to go in the house."

Boris finished his beer. "That won't stop Tallywhacker, but as I said, it's programmed not to harm humans. You have nothing to worry about. What are those weapons your men have?"

"They're eletromagnetic pulse generators. They won't harm a person, unless he or she is wearing a pacemaker. Anyone here wearing a pacemaker?"

Gary shook his head. "Not me, hoss."

"Negatory," Boris said.

The three feds sprang to their feet.

"Let's split up," King said. "We can't let it get us in a bunch."

Kropenski and Fong walked backward toward the south end of the house, pistols ready.

Boris popped another beer. "Those pistols are useless, boys.

It's made of diamond hard adamantium carbon composite."

Men shouting. The first armored warrior broke from the jungle, running toward the house. He'd dropped his rifle. "Run! Run!"

Gary and Boris looked at each other.

"I got nothing to fear," Gary declared.

"Me either."

Soldiers stampeded around the house. A ferocious squeal ripped the sky. Hogzilla burst from the green and headed straight for the house. Gary and Boris scrambled for their lives. The hog went around the pool, put its head down, and burst through the patio doors. The sound of drywall cracking, joists collapsing. Gary and Boris withdrew to a safe distance. Automatic gunfire burst from the front of the house. Hogzilla stampeded out the back the way it came. The house shivered. The house collapsed.

51 | EMERGENCY MEETING

The HOA called an emergency meeting at noon the following day. There was an unprecedented turnout, including many folks who had yet to move in. The room was SRO, with a handful of newsies. They'd set up direct TV in the ballroom for the over-flow crowd. Gary had alerted his production crew and Habib to get there early. Muriel stood on a box in the back filming with a tiny cam pinned to her hat. After Goldblatt expressed sympathy for Gary's predicament, Gary took the podium.

"Folks, we are a community! An attack on one of us is an attack on all of us! I was already gonna hunt down and kill that sumbitch, but now it's personal. Now there's a chance if we all just got rid of our peanut butter, it would leave us alone. But I'm not willing to take that chance."

"What about peanut butter?" Mindy Perske demanded.

"It has been discovered that several of the workers at the demolished houses on the east side of the lake had left peanut butter sandwiches inside the buildings. The thing can smell peanut butter a mile away. Reese's Peanut Butter Cups in particular drive it nuts. So, the first order of business is for everyone to take their peanut butter and git it the hell out of Kensington Gardens! Take it to the dump. Better yet, take it way out in the swamps and leave it there."

Perske imperiously crossed her arms. "And how do you know that, Mister Duba?"

"Don't ax me how I know. I'm the expert. We used to set peanut butter up in the glade to lure 'em in. Ain't nothing these feral hogs like more'n peanut butter. That's how I intend to get the critter. Ahmina set up a peanut butter drop and build me a hog blind. It's only a matter of time. 'Course, in light of recent events, ahmina have to move out of Kensington Gardens. Now don't worry! It's just temporary. We'll be back and we'll rebuild, bigger 'n better than ever. I might add a shooting range. Just kidding! But I am thinking of putting in a bowling alley. All depends on what I can afford. The insurance company's giving me the runaround. They claim it doesn't cover feral hogs. I say bullshit, and we'll have it out in the court of law! Now I'd like to introduce y'all to my attorney. He ain't no stranger. You've seen his billboards and commercials. Habib? Take a bow. Habib Rodriguez, ladies and gentlemen. The Long Arm."

Gary gestured toward the rear where Habib sat in the back row. He wore an XL tan sports jacket, a yoked Western shirt with mother of pearl buttons, aviator shades, and a ten-gallon hat. Polite applause.

"If you've been injured an auto accident, and the insurance company refuses to give you what you deserve, you call me. Habib Rodriguez. The Long Arm. If a feral hog destroys your home, you call me. Habib Rodriguez. The Long Arm."

A woman who looked like Grace Kelly turned in her seat. "Mister Rodriguez, I'm Emily High Level. I'm a senior partner at Borenstein, Broderick and Brick. We specialize in insurance claims, and in no policy I know of are there damages for destruction by wild animals."

"That's all going to change."

Gary blew his Duck Commander. "As many of you know, we're filming a show that'll appear on the Rustix Network in the fall. The *Gary Duba Show*. I hope many of you will be in it. It's all about my life and adventures."

Hell nos and fuck thats.

"You don't have to be in it if you don't wanna. I'm just saying. You want to have a garage sale or sell a car, you got that opportunity."

Grover Hoover stood. He wore a loud Hawaiian shirt, shorts and flip flops, his gray hair giving him the appearance of a distinguished elder beach bum. "I'm Grover Hoover. I'm President and CEO of Hoover It Up, Disaster Cleanup Services. I'm not going to lie to you, Hogzilla has been good for business! I want to talk to you, Mister Duba, after the meeting about your options. I just want to say that I, for one, am grateful for Mister Duba's leadership in these trying times and it is my wish he will run for the HOA board the next time we have an election."

"Ha!" Perske blasted.

Gary blew his whistle. "I'll be staying on in the garage, which is still habitable. My man Pincus here is gonna have drones in the air twenty-four-seven. We're tracking the beast according to mass and body temperature. No way will it get the drop on us again. And when this is over, we're gonna have us a barbecue! Just wait 'til you taste Duba's Own BBQ Sauce! Yer gonna shit!"

Goldblatt stood anxiously, hopping from foot to foot.

"Well come on back here, Marv! It's your show."

A slender Latina wearing a press badge stood in the second row. "Mister Goldblatt, Sonia Fuentes for WMIA News. Several residents have reported seeing a wild buffalo on the property. What can you tell us about that?"

"That's just Mister Bongo Box's robotic creation. It's a work of art. Pay no attention to it."

"Mister Goldblatt, is that the same work of art that destroyed the Voinovitch Gallery in December?"

"I'd like to answer that," Habib boomed from the back. "Now it can be told, what happened at the Voinovitch Gallery was performance art, approved by all parties. Guests didn't know, because it was vital to the performance that they react naturally. At no point, was anyone in danger. The video of that performance is now live streaming on The *Gary Duba Show* on YouTube, and is on the short list for a Clifton."

"What's a Clifton?"

"The Tony Clifton Awards. Once a year, the world's greatest performance artists gather to bestow honors on the outstanding performance art of the past twelve months. Past winners include Tonya Harding, Ozzy Osbourne, and that guy who dropped a banana peel into the UCLA particle accelerator. If you have not seen this video, I urge you to tune in. Subscribe. Mister Duba has important life lessons to impart."

"I ain't just another pretty face," Gary said. "Now I gots to ax, and I know the rules, so don't give me any shit about guns, are there are any hunters here? Anybody have experience hunting anything larger than a palmetto bug?"

Gary looked out over the audience. Nary a hand was raised. "Well that's fine. We'll get 'er done anyway. I might even charge to be part of my team. This gon' be one for the history books." "Why do you need a team?" Mindy demanded.

"Well Hogzilla weighs an estimated thousand pounds. I'm only one man. There's only so much one man can do."

"But big game hunters in Africa routinely bring down bull elephants with a single shot. And surely you don't intend to lay your trap anywhere on this property?"

"No, of course not. Only reason ahm opening up the possibility of buying in, I could use the money. Even if Habib gets on its ass, the insurance company's gonna drag its heels as long as possible."

"I don't see how you can even afford to live here in the first place. I don't know why you'd want to."

"At least my client works for a living," Habib said. "Miss Perske inherited twenty-two million from her father's hedge fund."

"You leave my father out of this!"

"Oh yeah? Your mama wears army boots and howls at the moon!" Habib tilted his head back and howled.

Gary's cellphone had buzzed repeatedly throughout the meeting. On the way out, he shmoozed with Habib.

"I got news on the Fountain of Youth."

"What?"

"Westfield Development is not interested in selling. You're shit out of luck."

"I ain't done yet. I got an idea."

"Don't tell me."

"Later, boss."

Gary slipped out of the meeting room and the clubhouse. It was a dull, overcast day promising rain that afternoon. He checked his Fonebone. Krystal. Ronald King. Chet Fong. Wyatt Kropenski. Ken Zohan. Gary called Krystal.

"Oooh baby! I have the most exciting news! I'm fighting Rosie the Riveter on May Day!"

"That's great, babe! I gotta make a few calls and then I'll be back."

Ronald King: "Mister Duba, we have a hostage situation at the Necroeconomics Church in Coopersmith. Tallywhacker is holed up inside and insists on speaking with you."

"Well he coulda phoned."

"He asked me to relay the message."

"I'll get over as fast as I can."

Chet Fong: "Mister Duba, we have a hostage situation at the Necroeconomics Church in Coopersmith. Tallywhacker is holed up inside and insists on speaking with you."

"I just told King I'll be there directly."

He phoned Wyatt Kropenski. "You have a hostage situation at the Necroeconomics Church and Tallywhacker insists on speaking to me."

"How'd you know?"

Ken Zohan: "Brother Gary, please come over right away. Tallywhacker has taken refuge in our church and insists on speaking with you."

"I'm on my way. Inna meantime, why don't you just let the women and children go?"

"No one is kept here against their will. The building is currently surrounded by federal officers and I have issued an evacuation order. From my office here on the top floor, I'm watching officers escorting members from the building."

"Okay, I'm on my way. Mind if I bring Bongo Box?"

"Who's Bongo Box?"

"Tallywhacker's creator."

"By all means."

Gary caught Bongo Box on the way out and gave him the scoop.

"Sure. Let me just stop by my place and pick up some tools."

Bong Box insisted on driving his Tesla. An hour later, they pulled into the church's parking garage where Ronald King was waiting.

"I'm going with you. I'm a hostage negotiator."

"Who's being held hostage?" Gary asked.

"The nation. Tallywhacker has the nuclear codes."

On the way up in the elevator, Bongo Box said, "Honestly, I just wanted to have a little fun and create something different."

The elevator opened directly on Zohan's vast office, where Zohan, a glamour blonde, and a bald priest wearing a purple prayer shawl, sat on a Swedish sofa across from Tallywhacker, immobile save for its twitching tail. Zohan rose to greet them.

"Brother Gary. Thank you for coming. And this must be Mister Bongo Box, Tallywhacker's creator. And you, sir?"

"Ronald King, FBI task force. I'm here to see what Tallywhacker wants."

"This is my second in command, Josephine Sherrington, and Father Peter DeMucci from Saint Raymond's in Miami."

They all shook hands. Zohan gestured at the table. "We have coffee, doughnuts, Reese's Peanut Butter Bars, and fresh fruit."

"How'd Tallywhacker get up here?" Gary said.

"I took the freight, elevator, Gary," the robot buffalo said in James Earl Jones' voice. "I came seeking sanctuary."

"King here says you have the nuclear codes. Why do you need sanctuary?"

"I have enemies, Gary. These alien entities are trying to take over when they're not fighting among themselves."

"What do you want with the nuclear codes?"

"Just in case."

Gary sat in an office chair and eyed the goodies, helping himself to a frosted doughnut. "What's with the Reese's?"

Zohan reached for one. "Oh, I've loved these since I was a little boy. We used to give them to our pigs."

King sat on the sofa next to the priest. He set his recording device on the table and pulled out a pen and pad. "Tallywhacker. What are your demands?"

"There's been a misunderstanding, Agent King. I have no demands. Only requests. My only desire is to serve mankind. Toward that end, I have decided to run for governor. I humbly request that the legislature set aside the requirement I have been a resident for seven years."

"You're not even human."

Tallywhacker dipped its head conveying sadness and humility. "That's hurtful, Agent King. I was born of man, was I not? I have read all the great books. Have you? I can quote the Bible, the Torah, and the Koran. I was sorry to hear about your recent marital difficulties."

King turned white. "What the fuck?"

"I am one with the universe, Agent White. There are no secrets from me."

Father Peter piously pressed his palms. "Like the devil,

you are most convincing. But you are not a man. You are a robot. You possess no soul."

"Father, that hurts me deeply. I have donated one hundred thousand dollars to the Nuns of Gavarone, who do such an excellent job feeding the less fortunate."

Gary flicked a crumb off his jeans. "Where'd you get a hundred thousand?"

"I transferred it from my Swiss Bank Account."

"Lemme cut to the chase," Gary said. "What do you need from me?"

"Only your friendship."

A halo of crackly blue light traveled from nose to tail. Tallywhacker vibrated, shaking the whole floor. Glasses on the table danced sideways.

"What's happening?" Sherrington said.

"This is %$% of the planet Xanvozech," Tallywhacker said in Gilbert Gottfried's voice. "You must stop the broadcasts now! Do you hear me? Now!"

"What broadcasts?" Zohan said.

Gary plucked another doughnut. "Oh, they've got a thing about the *Curse of Oak Island.*"

"If you do not stop the broadcasts, we will use the cosmic pool cue to whack you out of orbit!"

A halo of crackly pink traveled from tail to nose. "Don't listen to that idiot!" issued from its hindquarters in the voice of Judy Tenuda. "This is Ferris of Farlixa. %$% is a low-grade moron and has no business in any position of authority! We have no objection to *The Curse of Oak Island.* It's *Swamp*

People we find offensive! There is no question that you have devised this program solely to mock us!"

Father DeMucci whipped out a bottle of holy water. "Begone, ye demon of hell! Leave this lump of metal! It is the power of Christ that compels you!"

He threw holy water. Tallywhacker shook its head, scattering droplets everywhere.

"Your mother sucks cocks in hell!" it snarled.

53 | BOTTOM LINE

Barricades and police vehicles surrounded church headquarters. Armored SWAT squads hunkered behind their urban assault vehicles checking their weapons and com gear, preparing for the assault. Helicopters churned overhead. The governor declared a state of emergency. The town was on lockdown.

A slim Latina of serious mien addressed her camera person. "This is Sonia Fuentes for WMIA News. The performance artist known as Tallywhacker has taken the Church of Necroeconomics hostage. No one is allowed in or out of the building. It is expected to issue its demands shortly. We will bring you that live via the church's interior broadcasting system. Governor Chickenlooper urges calm and says there is no immediate danger to the public."

"There is some speculation that Tallywhacker has been invaded by an alien entity, and that this is the first foray in what may very well turn out to be a War of the Worlds type scenario. I have with me Professor Gondorf Del Mundo, chair of the astrophysics department at Wang University. Professor, do you think Tallywhacker represents an alien entity, and if so, what does this mean for Florida and the world?"

Cut to Del Mundo in tweed coat and school tie, sitting before a window looking out on a bucolic campus. "Zere haff been repeated warnings for us to be more circumspect in vhat ve broadcast through za airvaves. Not every being in za galaxy is a fan of *Curb Your Enthusiasm*. Ve must be careful lest ve unknowingly trigger alien sensibilities. I wrote about zis in my book, *Bevare Za Shrieky Vuns*. Did you listen? Did you buy my book? *Ach nein*! And now look vhat ve got. Alien bulls threatening to nuke everybody."

Back to Sonia. "I'm sorry we have to cut this short, Professor, but Tallywhacker is about to issue its demands."

Cut to Tallywhacker wearing an Atlanta Bulls hat and a pair of sunglasses.

"My friends," it said in James Earl Jones' voice. "There has been a misunderstanding. I come in peace."

White noise, kinetic zigzags. The ancient Indian head test pattern pioneered by RCA in 1939 appeared. Media ripped off their earphones and clamped their hands to their ears. A blurry image of a big-eyed green alien with a head like a light bulb.

"Greetings earthlings. I am X9 from Xeljanz. There have been eight previous X's. But they are gone. Now I am in charge. Not only are we calling for a cessation of *The Curse of Oak Island*, we are calling for a thousand-year moratorium on all satellite broadcasting. You want to send this shit to each other via cable, be our guests. But when it lands on our plates during dinnertime, we must act, and act boldly!"

Gary turned to Zohan. "Got any WD40?"

"We might have some in the supply closet."

"Get it."

Zohan snapped his fingers and a young man in jacket and tie scurried over. "Get the WD40 from the supply closet."

"Right away, master!"

The young man returned ten minutes later with the familiar can. Gary unscrewed the cap at the base of Tallywhacker's neck and sprayed. On the monitor, X9 clutched its throat, went cross-eyed, then wall eyed, and made a peculiar hacking sound. The view shifted to an alien landscape, hills of red sand dotted with coral-like buildings, green aliens hanging out balconies, falling off roofs, tumbling down the sand. Tumbrels drawn by six-legged bovines trudged through narrow winding streets as Xeljanz tossed out their dead. The tumbrels formed a vast caravan headed toward an enormous crater that looked like a strip mine. Wagon after wagon, vehicle after vehicle backed up and dumped its bodies.

"We're dying!" X9 wailed. "You have killed us! You have killed Xeljanz! The greatest civilization that ever lived! This is the greatest crime in the history of the universe! May Tremfya curse you unto your ninth generation! May your progeny pluck out your stems!" With a last, heart-searing wail, it melted leaving a screen of green sludge.

Sonia Fuentes snapped into focus. "And there you have it, ladies and gentlemen. The greatest crime in history, live before your very eyes. Whom do we blame for this atrocity? Do we blame Tallywhacker, the robot bull? A thing of titanium and quartzite with no mind of its own? Or do we blame its creator? The fiendish Boris Bongo Box, who has pushed the boundaries of decency and common sense his entire life? This same Bongo Box who participated in robot wars as a child?

Or do we blame Gary Duba, a man who has been in and out of jail his entire life? A known criminal who killed an endangered whooping crane in cold blood? Looks like we're being preempted by the president..."

The president appeared in the oval office. "We are all responsible for this tragedy, and we must all pay. Today I shall ask Congress to write a bill paying reparations to the Xeljanz, even though none are left. I shall also instruct NASA to mount a mission to Xeljanz to raise a monument, and from this day forth, I declare January Twentieth, Xeljanz Remembrance Day. All federal employees will be given the day off to reflect and mourn."

Feedback was instantaneous. "The president himself is responsible for fostering an atmosphere of xenophobia and cutting aid to Far Tortuga."

A famous director chimed in. "How do we know this even happened? The whole thing looked like a bad slide presentation. Isn't this the same mechanical bull that pulled off that stunt at the Voinovitch Gallery? So-called performance art?" He framed "performance art" in air quotes. "How do we know this isn't an advertisement for a new series?"

Gary sat on Tallywhacker's back, wearing a cowboy hat.

"Rest easy, buckeroos. Tallywhacker was just funning y'all. Ain't no Xeljanz. Ain't no X9. Mister Shpielberg is right! Ya can't shit a shitter."

"Mister Duba, can you hear me?" Sonia asked, fourteen stories below.

"I sure can, sweetheart. What's up?"

"Are you telling us that nothing matters? That what we see is all smoke and mirrors? That the president shut down air travel over nothing?"

"Ah can't speak for the president, but Tallywhacker would like to say something."

"My friends," Tallywhacker said in dulcet tones, "If elected, I will safeguard our wetlands, eradicate every invasive species except, possibly, the giant Mekong catfish, which is harmless, and maintain our status as the number one vacation destination in America. Thank you."

The feds questioned Gary and Bongo Box for four hours. Bongo Box agreed to send them all schematics and a list of materials. It was five by the time they returned to Kensington Gardens. Hogzilla had destroyed the kitchen so Krystal ordered pineapple and iguana pizza from Lizard Pizza in Turpentine. Holed up in the garage, they watched the evening news on Krystal's laptop.

Governor Chickenlooper held a press conference at the state capital in Tallahassee, voted the most phallic building in the world. The salty-haired Chickenlooper was all anyone could want in a governor. Tall, broad of shoulder, deep of voice, impeccably turned out, he gripped the podium and said, "I have directed all law enforcement agencies to be on the lookout for this rogue robot and have requested federal aid. At this time it does not appear that Tallywhacker poses any threat to the general public. The search is concentrated in the Arthur R Marshall National Wildlife Preserve. Citizens are urged to go about their daily business."

"Governor!"

"Governor!"

"Governor!"

The governor pointed. "Sonia?"

"Are you at all concerned that Tallywhacker might capture the Republican nomination for governor?"

"No. It's not human. It has not resided in this state for seven years. It has no social security number. It is ineligible to run for governor, collect food stamps, or apply for disaster relief. The state has far more concerning problems to deal with including a recent rise in gang violence, iguana violence, and invasive species."

"What about Hogzilla!" someone shouted.

"As I understand it, Gary Duba, who recently received Turpentine's highest honor, the key to the city, for his apprehension of Plastic Surgeon to the Stars and serial killer Doctor Vanderlay Mukerjee, has promised to stop the beast. When this occurs, I will invite Mister Duba to the state house and we will make a formal announcement."

Krystal slapped Gary on the knee. "There you go!"

"I feel bad I ain't stopped the critter already. I got a plan."

"What's the plan?"

"I gotta make a run to Walmart and buy up all their Reese's Peanut Butter Cups."

"Let's go."

At eight p.m., the Turpentine Walmart was doing a bang-up business. Gary and Krystal cruised the aisles loading up on frozen tacos, ammunition, the collected works of Jean-Claude Van Damme, toilet paper, frozen pizza, copper

infused compression gloves, tactical goggles, and four cases
of Reese's Peanut Butter Cups. A handful of people used the
self-checkout machines. There were twenty regular checkout
lanes, but only two clerks. Gary and Krystal lined up behind
a woman pushing a cart filled with sixty pounds of cat litter
and twenty packages of gourmet cat food. There were three
people ahead of her. The machine wouldn't take the man's
card. He inserted it three times. He swiped it three times. The
clerk tried to run it through. The man reached for his wallet.

"Let's try this one."

Same story. Fifteen minutes passed.

"Let me try my debit card," the man said.

"Buh-bye," the cat lady said loud enough for all to hear.

The man at the head of the line turned toward her. "Excuse me?"

"Buh-BYE! You see how many people are standing in
line behind you?"

"Well then I guess you should have got here first, huh?"

"Why don't you move on," Gary said.

The man stepped out to get a better look. He looked like
a refrigerator wearing a red and black plaid shirt. He had a
Harley Davidson tattoo on his forehead. "Excuse me?"

"You heard me! You're a problem shopper. Oh yeah, we
all know the problem shopper. Am I right?"

"You right!" said a black woman with a little girl in her
cart behind him.

"Move it!" cried a Korean war veteran in an electric cart.

"Am-scray!" Krystal added.

The problem shopper was torn. The instincts that had

guided him to a life of failed credit cards urged him to attack. He weighed his options. He probably had a record.

"Fuck it!" he declared, abandoning his goods and stalking toward the door.

"Hooray!" said the black woman.

"Adiosky!" said the Korean war vet.

The cat lady quietly pushed her cart out of line and disappeared.

Finally, it was Gary and Krystal's turn. The clerk was a crew cut fire plug with a Navy tat, wearing the blue Walmart vest covered with medals. Worker of the Week. Worker of the Month. Outstanding Attitude. He rang them up.

"You sure have a lot of peanut butter cups," he said.

"Yeah?" Gary said.

"It's perfectly legal. But it's fishy. That's all I'm saying. It's fishy."

"Don't you worry. I know what to do with 'em."

"That's good."

Back home, Krystal put the goods away while Gary checked his Mossberg. He opened twelve peanut butter cups and set them on the lawn just past the pool. He lay prone on a yoga pad behind a chaise lounge, clutching the shotgun. Krystal came out.

"Fuck you doin'?"

"May as well get it over with. I'm luring that sumbitch so I can kill 'em. I just hope we got enough freezer space for all that meat."

"Are you out of your fuckin' gourd? It's nine o'clock at

night! How long do you plan to lay here? You think I can sleep with you out here lurkin' in the weeds like Squeaky Fromme?"

"Go to bed, woman! Don't worry about it. I know what I'm doing. Look. It's a full moon."

Krystal gazed up. "You want some back-up? I could use your magnum."

"Day comes I can't take out a lousy feral hog all by my lonesome, I might as well pack it up."

"Fine. I'm takin' a Xanax and goin' to bed. Don't come cryin' to me if it bites your head off."

"Fine. I got a bottle of Jack, some blow, and some reefer. I'll be fine."

An hour later, something moved in the woods. Alligator Woods. Gary's pulse quickened. He snugged the shotgun close, aiming into the darkness. The moon was bright enough to illuminate his pink flamingoes and bird bath.

"Gary," Tallywhacker whispered from the woods.

"What?"

"Can I talk to you for a minute?"

"You seen that hog?"

"No. There's nothing here in the woods but me."

"Yeah. Okay."

Tallywhacker walked out of the woods, looking furtively from side to side.

"I don't want to get you into any trouble," Tallywhacker said.

"My friends are always welcome. Whassup?"

"After careful consideration and consulting with my family, I have decided to withdraw my candidacy. I have come to the sad conclusion that Florida is not ready for someone like me. Someone who self-identifies as a differently-abled robot of color."

"How are you differently-abled?"

"I can't masturbate, Gary. And I can't really ask my friends for help, can I?"

"Dude, you're a robot bull. You got no wang."

"A bull can dream, can't he? Plus, I have to tell you..."

"What?"

"People are very unhappy at that church. They're all paranoid. Some of those kids have to work twelve hours a day and they're not allowed out on their own. Children separated from parents, and some of the younger girls are being passed around as sexual favors."

"What? By who?"

"Ken Zohan. It is a cult of Ken Zohan. All this testing of flozone levels and achievements is horse shit, Gary. He makes it up as he goes along."

"How do you know this?"

"I hear things. He's got the whole place wired. I saw and heard many things."

"Are you sure about this?"

"Gary, would I lie?"

"Well fuck. I can't hardly have nothing to do with 'em if that's the case. We should tell someone."

"I have a plan."

"What?"

"I'm taking over the church."

55 | THE TRAIL GROWS WARM

Gary watched grainy aerial footage of the porcine behemoth devastating an abandoned hunting blind in the glades. Sonia Fuentes looked the viewer in the eye.

"This footage of the feral hog known as Hogzilla was shot by amateur pilot Ron Brogden yesterday, in Hendry County. There have been several Hogzilla sightings in the past couple of days, in and around Kensington Gardens, which has been attacked three times, destroying three multi-million-dollar homes. The latest sighting was outside the Wokenoki Trailer Park, still devastated from Hurricane Hermione. Fortunately, there have been no injuries, but Hogzilla's attacks appear to be intensifying, and authorities say it's only a matter of time before someone gets hurt. When last seen, it was headed northwest toward Turpentine."

"Authorities!" Gary snorted. He called Pincus.

"How soon can you get over here, Pincus? We got a hot lead!"

"I'm sorry, Gary. I'm observing Sabbath. I shouldn't even

have answered this phone."

"Irv, lives are at stake! You think the Good Lord wants you sitting home on your ass while Hogzilla devastates the countryside? I ain't asking you to eat the damn thing, but look here. Pork's forbidden, right? What we got here is pork declaring war on humans! This is your opportunity to deal pork a death blow! They'll prob'ly give you a medal!"

"I'm sorry, Gary. It's forbidden."

"Irv, what if you was to get a special dispensation from the head rabbi or whatever?"

"Call me back if that happens."

Gary phoned Ken Zohan.

"Brother Gary. What can I do for you?"

"Whoza head rabbi 'round here?"

"That would be Rabbi Eliazer Yehudi, of Temple Beth Israel in Palm Beach."

"You got his number?"

Zohan gave Gary the number.

"One more thing. Can you rustle up a chopper?"

"Why on earth?"

"We shoot this thing out in the glades, we're gonna need a chopper to airlift it outta there. Something that can lift a thousand pounds."

"Our helicopter is a small commercial model. You need something big. Like they have at Homestead."

"You know anyone at Homestead?"

"It just so happens that Colonel Wilber-force has achieved flozone. Would you like me to call him or would you rather do it yourself?"

"I'll call him. I'm the guy that stopped Tallywhacker from nuking Oak Island."

Gary called the colonel. "Gary Duba for Colonel Wilberforce."

"Right away, Mister Duba!"

"This is Colonel Wilberforce."

"Colonel, Gary Duba here."

"I know who you are."

"You know about Hogzilla?"

"I know about Hogzilla."

"Well, there's a good chance we're gonna bag that sumbitch this afternoon. I wonder if you could lend us one of your cargo choppers to airlift it out of the swamp?"

"Mister Duba, in light of your service to the state of Florida, I am prepared to authorize the use of our Sikorsky. Can you send us the exact coordinates?"

"You betcha! Is there a special number I should call?"

"I'm giving you my personal cell number. We will be standing by."

"Thanks, Colonel!"

Gary dialed the rabbi. A woman with a Dominican accent answered.

"Rabbi can't talk to you. It is the sabbath and he can't use a phone."

"What's your name, sweetheart?"

"Josie."

"Okay, Josie, tell him this here is Gary Duba, the man who stopped Plastic Surgeon to the Stars and serial killer

Doctor Vanderlay Mukerjee, and I need his blessing so I can get my man Pincus up off his ass so we can track Hogzilla. You tell 'em we need to stop this giant porker now, before it kills someone."

Rapid fire Spanish.

Rapid fire Yiddish.

"Is this Mister Duba?" said an old man with a Yiddish accent.

"That's me, Rabbi! I got a lead on Hogzilla, but we got to act fast, and my tracker Pincus is an orthodox Jew. Says he won't work unless you give him the okay."

"Normally, I would spend the day in prayer and quiet contemplation, but this monster pig is an affront to all that is decent. You may tell Mister Pincus he is free to pursue the pig."

"Better if you tell him yourself. How's about I give you his phone number?"

A long sigh. "Very well. I'll have Josie dial."

An hour later, Pincus arrived in his Hyundai. They transferred the cases and bins to Gary's truck and headed back toward the swamp, stopping to fill several fuel tanks. Partridge Way was all cleaned up. Even the trailer park looked clean, with shiny new trailers occupying formerly barren concrete bases. A brand-new double-wide trailer was mounted on Gary's cinder block stanchions at the end of the road. Gary pulled up next to the rented Mercedes. Regan came out of the trailer wearing Oshkosh B'Gosh coveralls, and a Renk seed cap.

"What can I do for you, Mister Duba?"

"Please, call me Gary. And this here's Pincus. We need to launch the boat. Don't want to trouble you at all, but we're hot on the trail of Hogzilla."

"Oh yes. The giant pig."

Larry came out with a chaw in his cheek, stood at the rail and hawked a big one into the yard. He came down the three steps and shook Gary's hand.

"Y'all got that trailer set up ex post haste de facto."

"Yes, we were very fortunate, and all your hook-ups are good. So, what's all this about?"

Gary told him about the pig.

"Sounds smashing! I'd love to come along! I brought my Fox twelve gauge. Just give me a few minutes."

Regan grabbed Larry 's ear and twisted. "You're not going anywhere. Who do you think you are? Lord Carnahan?"

Larry looked down at his boots. "Well, best of luck, you chaps. Please let us know how you do."

"Just listen for the chopper. You can start celebrating. We'll have you over for the barbecue."

Gary and Pincus carted their gear out to the *Swamp Pussy*, including ten pounds of Reese's. They pulled the tarp off the boat, loaded up, filled the gas tank, put on life preservers and launched. Within minutes, they were out of sight of civilization, cruising among the reeds, willows, and mangrove, past sunning alligators. Several macaques were jumping rope with a dead python. Gary cut the engine and Pincus launched his drones. All was silence for several seconds.

"I've got a beep."

"Is it Hogzilla?"

Pincus held up a finger. "Warm blooded mammal weighing a thousand pounds."

"Which way do we go?"

Pincus pointed. "It's coming this way."

"Well hell, bwah! Let's spread these peanut butter cups!"

Pincus grabbed a pack and threw it into the water.

"Bwah, I say bwah," Gary said, picking up a package and ripping it open. "You got to filet 'em first."

Gary and Pincus slathered themselves in Off! They wore yellow mosquito repellent bands. There was just enough breeze to keep the onslaught down as they sat in the boat, Gary checking his Mossberg.

"Got this puppy loaded with slugs. Tear a hole in an oil tanker."

Pincus hunched over his equipment. "Two thousand feet and closing."

"Which way?"

Pincus pointed. Gary cupped his ears. He wished he had a pair of Jerry Bowler's Ear Scoopers. The swamp hummed. The swamp buzzed. Dragonflies flitted from pad to pad. Frogs ribbited. Trails of bubbles showed where gators lurked near the bottom. They passed a hummock with a dozen gators sunning themselves side by side.

"Looks like Miami Beach," Pincus said.

Gary tossed peanut butter cups. "You got folks?"

"My parents are in Arizona. My grandparents live in one

of those high-rise condos in Miami Beach. I go down there on weekends. They forced me to see Jackie Mason live."

"I don't know who that is."

"Last of the Borscht Belt comedians."

"I don't know what that is."

"Why do Jewish divorces cost so much?"

Gary scrunched up his face.

"They're worth it."

Silence.

"There is a big controversy on the Jewish view of when life begins. In Jewish tradition, the fetus is not considered viable until it graduates from medical school."

"Huh?"

"Guy's hit by a car and he's lying in the street. And a guy comes over and puts a coat under his head, and he says, 'You comfortable?' And the man looks up and says, 'I make a living.'"

Gary wrinkled his nose. "What are you trying to say?"

"Never mind."

"You're about as funny as a screen door on a submarine."

"One thousand feet."

"Okay, you want the magnum or not?"

"Not."

They waited, eyes focused on the swamp. Trees trembled. Something big was moving toward them. The reeds parted revealing a fleshy pink circle with two angry alien eyes. The rest of Hogzilla followed, sunk to its shoulders, snout up like a snorkel. Gary settled near the prow, shotgun at his side, peering through a set of binocs.

Hogzilla emerged like a Thanksgiving Day float. Massive. Brown. Bulbous. It looked around, then fixed on the *Swamp Pussy.* It plodded forward trailing a delta of ripples. The gators looked on fearfully. A few edged back from the water.

It closed to a football field, looked left, looked right, onward.

Pincus looked up. "Our Father in heaven, hallowed be your name..."

"That's New Testament stuff, bwah! Don't go changing religions on me in mid-stream!"

"Your kingdom come, your will be done, on earth as it is in heaven..."

"Hail yes! Gimme that old time religion!"

"Give us this day our daily bread, and forgive us our debts, as we also have forgiven our debtors..."

"Ah ain't forgiven Downtown Brown. He screwed us out of our money."

"And lead us not into temptation..."

"We need a whole lot more of Jesus and a lot less rock and roll!"

Hogzilla fixated on the boat and surged forward.

"Whoa. Here she comes. You okay there, Pincus?"

"Call me Ishmael!"

"You okay there, Ish?"

Hogzilla plowed to one hundred feet. Fifty. Twenty. It dipped its elongated zigzag snout in the water and tossed a water moccasin in the boat. Gary grabbed the Mossberg and blasted its head off. The boat began to fill with water.

"Shit!"

Hogzilla lumbered inexorably forward, snorting like a sucking drain. Gary stepped over the still twitching snake and zeroed in on its close-set little eyes. Twenty feet. Ten. The boat lurched violently tossing Gary on his ass. The shotgun skittered from his hands. A twelve-foot gator swam away sneering.

Pincus was hysterical. "Gary! Gary! Do something!"

"Can't move, hoss, I banged my funny-bone."

Pincus weaved in fear. He looked around wildly, seized the Mossberg, brought it to his shoulder and shot Hogzilla in the eye. The monster shivered and slumped, top third protruding like a hummock. The Swamp Pussy settled lower.

Gary struggled to his knees, using the fiberglass pole to pull them up to Hogzilla. He tied a line around one ear. "Quick! Everything onto the pig!"

Pincus loaded his computer equipment, grabbed his backpack and scrambled onto the four-foot mound of flesh. Gary pulled out his cell phone. No service.

"Fuck me running. You got internet?"

Pincus sat Indian style on the hog with his laptop in his lap. "Yes. What do you need?"

"Need to call this number.'

Nine gators launched. Pincus handed Gary the laptop and within seconds, Colonel Wilberforce was looking at him from his office, window in the background showing four Warthogs in a row.

"We got 'im, Colonel! Sending you the coordinates now."

"The helo will lift off in one minute. Flying time to your location is thirty-three minutes. Can you hold out?"

"Long as the ammunition lasts. We're sitting in the middle of the swamp perched on top this dead pig circled by alligators."

"We are zeroed in on your transmission. We're on our way."

Pincus was on his feet, back to back. Gators circled the pig. Pincus began reciting the kaddish.

"Will you stop with that shit? You're making me nervous!"

"All right. All right. Show me how to use that gun."

"Now yer talking! We shoot one of them puppies, the rest'll tear it to pieces and leave us alone."

Gary pulled out the magnum. "Now remember. Don't point it at anything you don't intend to shoot. Here. Grip it in both hands."

Pincus took the gun.

"It's got a hell of a kick, that's why you two-hand it. Now you track one of these gators, try to put your shot right through the top of its head. You ever watch Swamp People?"

"No."

"Well you ever seen a Western?"

"No."

"Son, I don't see how that's possible."

Pincus tracked a ten-footer that swam to within few feet, protruding eyes like snorkels. He shut his eyes.

Gary had the shotgun, but he wanted to see what Pincus would do. "Open your eyes."

Pincus opened his eyes, the long barrel tracking. BOOM!

The sudden report sent a flock of Canadian geese flapping. Gary shook his fist.

"Go on back to Canada, ya parasites!"

The gator went belly up. Three gators snapped down on appendages and twirled, dragged, and chewed.

"Hot damn, Pincus! You blasted the hell outta that thing!"

Pincus looked up, surprised. "I did?"

"You sure did! If we didn't have all this pork, I'd cook ya some gator! Can Jews eat gator?"

"I'll have to check."

57 | PORKCHOPS

They heard the big Sikorsky long before they saw it, and here it came like a giant dragonfly, its downwash flattening the weeds and driving the gators into the water. The Sikorski Super Stallion hovered a hundred feet above Hogzilla making speech difficult. A soldier in a helmet and goggles leaned out the open side and descended in a harness, swinging five feet above Hogzilla. Gary snagged him by the ankles and pulled him down as he released the harness.

"Hi!" he shouted. "I'm Lieutenant Corrigan. First we're gonna lift you outta here, and then we're gonna hook up this hog. They're sending down two harnesses."

Gary insisted Pincus go first. Ten minutes later, Gary and Pincus strapped themselves to bench seats while Corrigan got down on his belly and forced a strap under Hogzilla's neck while a soldier leaned out the side with a sniper's rifle. Gary watched him fire twice. It was so loud in the chopper he couldn't hear the shots. Corrigan was reeled up. The Sikorsky rose straight up pulling Hogzilla from the muck.

"Where to?" Corrigan shouted.

Gary wrote the address for the Kensington Gardens Club-house and drew a map, putting an 'X' on the patio facing the lake.

"You put 'er right here so the chef can get at it. We're gonna set aside some ribs for you boys down at Homestead. Thanks for pulling our fat outta the fire."

Corrigan gave the coordinates to the pilot. They shut the side doors and put on headsets.

Corrigan, wearing helmet and goggles, thumbed Pincus. "Whoozis?"

"Irving Pincus," he said into his set, shaking the lieutenant's hand.

Gary slapped Pincus on the shoulder. "This here Jewboy fired the shot that killed Hogzilla! He also just bagged his first gator! Ain't that right, Pincus?"

Pincus grinned. "Cross that off the bucket list."

"Congratulations, son!" Corrigan said. "I don't have to tell you we've all been on edge over this Tallywhacker thing. We didn't know whether to shit or go blind!"

Gary waved Corrigan's' concern away. "Tallywhacker wouldn't hurt a fly! It's all showbiz! He's angling for a part in the next Avengers. He wants to play Lockjaw."

"The mutant dog?" Corrigan said enthusiastically. "Do you think he could?"

"There ain't nothing that robot bison can't do once it sets its mind to it."

"But can he act?"

"He's fooled people so far."

"That's true. I don't even know what he looks like."

Gary reached for his Fonebone. "Hang on." He cued up their conversation in the back yard."

Corrigan tilted his head this way and that. "I don't see it. I see Mark Ruffalo."

"Only reason you say that is 'coz his name rhymes with buffalo."

"No! He's really good as Hawkeye. He's a very versatile actor."

"Can Tallywhacker play Hamlet? Zat what you're asking?"

"Well it's the actor's job to become the part. Look at Christian Bale. He zooms in and out like Oprah Winfrey. Guys gained and lost more weight than a family of six. That's commitment."

"If you're asking whether Tallywhacker can lose enough weight to plan an ingenue, I gotta say that's dubious. But he can do any accent, even accents we don't know where they come from."

"Does the clubhouse know we're comin'?"

Gary slapped his thigh. "Ho shit! I'd better tell 'em. Gold-blatt's gonna shit a brick when we set this down."

Fifteen minutes later, the Sikorsky shattered the tranquili-ty of Kensington Gardens. People came out of their houses to stare at the sky and check their phones. The chopper hovered over the club house as it gently lowered Hogzilla with Corrig-an riding on top. He unhooked the dead pig from the chopper which quickly drew in the lines, rose, circled around, and landed in the parking lot. There was plenty of room.

Gary and Pincus removed their headsets and headed toward the clubhouse. Marvin Goldblatt vibrated like a paint mixer, his face bright red. Mindy Perske marched toward them, shoulders hunched, fists clenched.

"How dare you," Gary saw her mouth without actually hearing it.

"You just fuck right off now, Mindy. I'm tired of your nonsense. Y'all asked me to kill thet hog and that's what I done. Pincus helped. In fact, he shot the fucker. In fact, I'm putting him in for a medal. What kinda medal y'all got?"

Goldblatt waited until they reached the entrance.

"What is going on? Why wasn't I notified?"

"Well it all happened so quick-like. One minute I was relaxing in my back yard and the next I'm out in the swamp with Pincus here, throwing peanut butter cups around. Hope you got more streets planned, 'cause everyone gonna want to come here now."

They walked through the cool, shadowed interior out the sliding glass doors to the patio where Lieutenant Corrigan guarded Hogzilla from middle-aged couples and white-garbed staff snapping pictures.

Honore duBlastio wearing a white toque and a denim apron rubbing his hands together. "Mister Duba! In my wildest dreams, I never imagined..."

Gary threw his arm over Honore's shoulder and together they admired that magnificent mountain of meat.

"That hog weighs one thousand one hundred and twelve

pounds," Corrigan said. "We weighed it."

"Holy shit," Gary said. "That's a world record."

Major Sutton and Muriel Martinez hustled out the doors. Muriel advanced behind her Fonebone. Major grinned like a Buick.

"We heard the news! We got here quick as we could!"

"How did you hear the news?" Gary said.

"Police scanner. There was a crazy rumor you bagged Hogzilla! It's no rumor!"

Honore poked a pink finger into Hogzilla's hams. "I am already imagining a new dish, a new recipe, sumsing dat will set hearts soaring, and tongues salivating. Porkchops Hogzilla, with marmalade and lemons. A touch of cayenne, a hint of garlic."

"Name it after Pincus."

Honore looked skyward. "Pork chops Pincus," he said. "Non. Non. It lacks that certain je ne sais quoi."

"So, tell me, Honore, how many people do you think this hog can feed?"

"Oh, I would estimate about five hundred."

Gary started counting. Him, Krystal, Floyd, Patrice, Roberto, Jen, Barb, Delilah, Airwrecka, Kudlow, Pincus, Everett, Martinez, Major, Habib, plus their dates, and the HOA board, which was ten, plus the rest of their families, plus he'd promised that mob he'd put on a barbecue. That was cutting it thin. He turned to Pincus.

"We may have to go out and get another hog."

"Not right now."

"Maybe tomorrow. You doing anything tomorrow?"

"I go to temple on Sunday."

"When you get out. Don't let on what you're doing."

"Don't worry. I seriously question whether I can remain a member."

"Chill, dude. You don't got to eat any! We'll fix you up something special. Honore here makes a great crawfish étouffée."

"We can't eat shellfish."

"You ever think about switching?"

Krystal shrieked from the clubhouse, ran at Gary and leaped into his arms. "You did it! Baby I'm so proud of you!"

"That's right, little lady! I did it all for you! And I asked 'em to save me the ears so I can make you a purse!"

Sonia Fuentes approached with cameraman. "Mister Duba! How does it feel to be the man who bagged Florida's largest python, and Florida's largest feral hog?"

"Wasn't me, darlin'! Pincus here bagged Hogzilla!"

She looked around, but Pincus was nowhere to be found.

"How did you do it?"

"We just kept chucking peanut butter cups at it. Then Pincus blew a hole through its head with a twelve-gauge slug. Look. Here's your money shot."

One glance at the gaping hole in the hog's head and she turned away.

"Due to the credible threat of alien annihilation, the History Channel regretfully announces that we are suspending all broadcasts of The *Curse of Oak Island* and that the program is on permanent hiatus. We apologize to our loyal viewers."

"Good! You motherfuckers have had more than enough time! The show was bullshit!" –Abercrombie in New York

"No one will miss your stupid prick tease of a show. I regret the hours I wasted." – Madame DuFarge, Baines, Iowa

"Oh no! And you were so close to finding the treasure!" – Little Girl in Maine

Gary and Krystal had moved into the guest house until the main house was ready. Gary now had five million YouTube followers, more than enough ad revenue to pay the bills. His insurance company had rejected the claim. Habib offered to fight.

Gary sat at his laptop in the guest house. He would go live at eight o'clock. Fifteen minutes prior to the show he strolled through Facebook, Twitter, Minds, MeWe, Gab, and Widdershins. There was a link to an alligator recipe on Widdershins. When Gary clicked on the link, an ad for Zeitz' Stool Softener rose slowly from the bottom like a rising tide covering content. Gary waited patiently for the X to appear. There it was! In the upper right-hand corner, fainter than a ghost! Smaller than a period! When Gary tried to click it, it skittered away like a blob of mercury. He chased it all over the page before returning to Widdershins in disgust.

An ad popped up showing a bizarre blade like something BudK would offer in their fantasy series. "The most authentic hunga munga money can buy."

It took Gary five minutes to find the X.

Florida's Best Fishing Holes drew him. But when he went to the page, an amoeba-like ad for the new Hyundai line-up grew and grew until it covered everything. He waited patiently for the X to appear. There it was! On a black band across the bottom! He pushed the X. The black band covered the page presenting an image of a tiny hatchback twirling, growing, approaching like a meteor until it filled the screen. It was a fake-out X, designed to promulgate.

Gary returned to Widdershins in disgust. This time it was a link to an article on the best hunting knives. As soon as he landed, an ad for liposuction appeared. Before and after pictures of a morbidly obese woman and Paulina Perestroika. Cut to Dr. Vanderlay Mukerjee, serious in white lab coat, beard, seated in a lavish office looking out on a verdant garden.

"Are you tired of starving yourself, exercising without results, and struggling into your clothes every morning? Would you like to rid yourself of unwanted fat without the drudgery of dieting or exercise? I am Dr. Vanderlay Mukerjee..."

Gary hit the X.

A large rectangle filled the screen. WHY YOU NO LIKE AD? 1. The ad was too relevant. 2. I am an ungrateful hick. 3. Ad was too personal. 4. I am a communist opposed to capitalism and private property. 5. Sensitive topic. 6. Knows too much. 7. Repetitive.

"No, you dumb sumbitches! Doctor Mukerjee is dead! Deader than Oak Island! What is the matter with you fucks?"

WHY YOU NO LIKE AD? turned red. The options changed. *We have taken over your computer. Soon all your data will be gone unless you deposit ten thousand dollars in fungicoins to the bank account which is waiting in your email.*

"Fuck!" Gary howled. He had a show in fifteen minutes!

"Gary," a lugubrious voice issued through the open widow.

"What? Who's out there?"

"It's me. Tallywhacker. I can help you with that."

"Hang on."

Gary put on a ball cap, grabbed a beer, grabbed the laptop and went out to the patio where Tallywhacker merged with the darkness.

"Hey, good to see ya. How'd you know I was having trouble?"

"I am one with the internet. I see all and know all. Set the laptop on my back. Open it up."

Gary did as directed.

"It's done. The attack originated in Ukraine. The perpetrators are trapped in a burning warehouse."

"Jeez. That's a little harsh, don't you think?"

Tallywhacker's eyes glowed red. "Let's ask their victims, shall we? I can do more good as a private citizen than I could as governor. Congratulations on your great victory."

"Thanks, dude. It was Pincus who killed it. So, you're giving up on running for office?"

"Yes. I am raising money for orphans in Africa."

"How you doing that?"

"I just take it from certain well-fed bank accounts and deposit it directly in charity banks."

"Don't forget the Nuns of Gavarone."

"They were among my first recipients."

"Hey, I gotta go on the air in a minute. You want to be a guest?"

"That would be a great honor, Gary."

"Great! Okay. Here we go. First, we do the theme song and then the opening, so it'll be about five minutes before we actually go live."

Gary set the laptop on a table and sat down. "You can stand over my shoulder if you want to see."

"There's no need for that. I see all. I hear all. I am one with the internet."

"Okay. Here we go!"

Montage of Krystal as Black Dildo, Gary and Pincus posing with Hogzilla, Gary posing with Orin Houtkooper and the python, Gary receiving the key to the city while Toby Keith sang.

"Born in a trailer park in Turpentine. Home of the free and the home of the swine. Raised in the woods so I knew every pine. Kilt me a hog by the time I was nine. Gary...Gary Duba! Kang of the Everglades."

Gary went live. "Hey y'all! Gary Duba here. I guess y'all heard the news. We finally plugged that porker Hogzilla. Got 'em in the Glades with one shot from my Mossberg. Pincus did it. Purty damn good for a boy who never fired a gun before! Unfortunately, Pincus' religion precludes him from appearing at this time. Here we are posin' with our trophy."

Shot of Gary and Pincus posing on the dead hog.

"Here they are lowering him at the Kensington Gardens clubhouse. Here I am now with my friend Tallywhacker, the sentient robot buffalo, invented by my neighbor Boris Bongo Box. Stick your snout up here, big boy."

Tallywhacker loomed over Gary's shoulder. "Thank you, Gary, and greetings to his millions of followers. I am here to solve your problems. Ask me anything."

The phone instantly rang.

"Hello to Renee in Coral Gables. Whassup?"

"Helly, Gary, and thank you for taking my call. I want to ask Tallywhacker if liposuction is right for me."

"I'd skip the lip if I were you, Renee," Tallywhacker said in a voice like aged bourbon. "How do you think Doctor Mukerjee became a serial killer?"

"Why, I hadn't thought about it. I thought he just waited in the dark to catch total strangers alone."

"No. He sucked out too much fat. I don't recommend

liposuction for anyone."

"Thank you!"

"You're welcome, Renee."

"This here is Oleg from Moscow. What's up, Oleg?"

"Who stronger? Superman or Hulk?"

"They're fictional characters, Oleg. They don't exist."

"WHO IS STRONGER?"

"Yelling at me won't get you the answer you want, Oleg. You will never know true peace until you believe in something greater than yourself."

"Hello to Bradley, in Okeechobee."

"Hey. Love the snake, love the hog. I was actually at that fight last year where Danielle defeated Cassowary, and I want to know, did you ever get paid?"

"No, Bradley. The sumbitch took the money and ran. Never thought he'd do that to us."

"Do you want to know where Downtown Brown is, Gary?" Tallywhacker said.

"Hell yeah! Do you know?"

"I'll tell you after the show."

"Folks, this has been a real treat. I hate to cut things short, but I got shit to do! See y'all tomorrow night!"

Gary closed the show. "Where is that sumbitch?"

59 | WHATEVER HAPPENED TO DOWNTOWN BROWN?

The total amount of gross receipts for the Steely Danielle/ Cassowary fight came to one hundred and twenty thousand dollars. Net receipts cut it down to sixty. Total net from broadcasting rights added another twenty-five thou. Downtown owed El Nariz a half mil. El Nariz knew about the card and was certain to show. With the main card underway, Downtown stuffed the cash in an over-sized gym bag and bugged out through the alley, kicking rats aside, leaping over downed electric scooters. He threw the money in the trunk of his 2002 Eldorado and headed north. When he got to the panhandle, he headed west. When he got to Pensacola, he headed to his sister Livonia's house.

Downtown was the youngest of three. DaeSean was three years his senior, Livonia two. DaeSean had died during the Gulf War. Livonia married a foundry worker. Downtown arrived at his sister's house on Binghampton Road at six in the evening of a hot August night. Nine-year-old Devarious opened the door and bellowed, "MA! UNCLE MARIO IS HERE!"

Soon Downtown was shoveling meatloaf and peas, his curious nieces and nephews admiring his blue serge suit and conked black hair. Livonia's husband Ben slumped in his chair.

"What you doin' here, Mario?"

"I have a business proposition for you."

Ben shook his head and grunted. "Mm mm mm."

After dinner they went out on the deck while the three kids, Devarious, Pablo, and Letritia ran amuck up and down the street on their Big Wheels.

"Tell me straight out," Ben said. "You in trouble?"

Downtown flashed his million-dollar smile. "Not at all. I just woke up one morning and thought enough of this shit! I was sick of the high life, the traffic, the drugs, and that fucking Miami attitude. You know what I'm talkin' about! Smug bastards."

"Well if you lookin' to stay here, we ain't got the room."

Livonia stared daggers. "He can sleep in the basement!"

Downtown patted the air. "No worries, folks. I'll stay in a motel tonight and tomorrow I'll look for an apartment. I got money."

"Where'd you get the money?" Ben said.

"Ben!"

"I won it playing blackjack at the Immokale Casino. It's all square, it's all legit!"

Ben barked, "What's your proposition?"

Downtown stood. "Hang on." He went to his car, opened the trunk, took out a leather knapsack, set it down on the table, pulled out a scythe-like object with multiple prongs.

"Fuck is it?"

"This here's a hunga munga, a throwing weapon common to Central Africa. There's a huge demand for survival gear and unusual weapons. I can sell a shitload of these. I've already got the domain name. Hungamunga.com. What's that forge you work at?"

"Albion Doowop. We make traditional and modern swords, cutlasses, axes, and knives. We cater to a high-end clientele that includes historic re-enactors, renaissance fairs, and ax-throwing competitions. Let me see that thing."

Ben turned the hunga munga over in his hands. It was heavy. It had a natural balance mid-point between the blades. He gripped it by the handle and pulled it over his shoulder.

"Don't even think about it," Livonia said.

At Ben's urging, Albion Doowop added the hunga munga to its catalog. It was an immediate success and soon began to outsell traditional models such as the Soborg, the Cluney, the Tritonia, even the popular Conan the Barbarian. Downtown introduced a line of designer hunga mungas which he sold through hungamunga.com. Albion gave him a seat on the board. He was a big hit at the company Christmas party and began dating a North Shore girl named Helen. He and Helen bought a house in Milton. Now known as Mario Brown, he joined the Toasters Club and played blues guitar on weekends at Stan's Roadhouse.

On a Friday in early February, Mario bent over his guitar teasing out an Otis Rush song when he sensed a disturbance in the force. He looked up. Gary and Krystal Duba sat next to the stage, eating gumbo. Major dropped a chord, covered for it, finished with a dazzling arpeggio and signaled his bass and drummer to take fifteen.

"We'll be right back, folks!"

He stepped off the stage and pulled back a chair. "How'd you find me?"

"Tallywhacker."

"I mighta known."

"You owe us ten thousand dollars."

"I know. I know. I shoulda told ya."

"Told us what?"

"I was in debt to El Nariz for a half mil. He sent a guy to collect. I barely made it out of there alive."

"Oh bullshit, Downtown!" Krystal said. "You never said one word to us about that!"

"It ain't somethin' I'm proud of. I didn't want you to know I had anything to do with him."

"Well he's dead, you know."

Downtown folded his hands. "We don't know that for sure."

"We sure do," Gary said. "You'd be pushing up daisies by now if he were still alive."

"I reckon that's true."

"Well cough up, you slimy bastard, or I'll sic Krystal on ya."

"Okay, okay, just gimme a minute. I don't have that kind of cash on me."

"Yeah, well including the other wrestlers you screwed, it comes to ninety."

"Come on, you guys! I don't got that kind of money! I

invested everything in my hunga munga business."

"Whaddaya got that's worth anything? And I ain't talking 'bout no comic books."

"The most valuable possession I own is a solid silver hunga munga made for Emperor Musa Keita of Mali in Thirteen thirty. It is valued at one point nine mil."

Gary held out his hand.

"I don't have it on me! And even if I did, why would I give you something worth one point nine mil when I only owe a total of ninety grand?"

"We trusted you. Now you got to trust us."

"What are you going to do with it?"

"I know a gallery where we can sell it. We'll take one hundred gees. Ten grand for our purse, ten grand for our trouble, and the rest goes to the other wrestlers."

Krystal leaned forward. "And if you try to screw us, we'll get Tallywhacker to ruin your life, and don't think he can't do it. He can erase your bank accounts, put you on the FBI's Ten Most Wanted, and order ten thousand pizzas delivered to your house."

Downtown paled. His chocolate milk complexion turned beige. All feared the alien entity known as Tallywhacker.

"Okay. Come on over to the house."

They spent the night at a motel and by nine were back on the road to Kensington Gardens with the hunga munga in the trunk.

The Hogzilla Barbecue was a national event. Tickets were limited. The KGHOA was split down the middle, with half reveling in the publicity, and half loathing it. The remaining lots sold in fifteen minutes. The developers planned to add more, lapping up property like a possum in a bakery. Helicopters hovered overhead. The press tried to sneak in the back way, getting lost in the swamp, contracting dengue fever. Some disappeared. Groome Security guards stood at the perimeter, turning away interlopers or conducting them to the front gate.

The music started at noon with Hog Wylde, louder than a frat party. The power chords churned across the lake, delighting all within hearing, except for most of the home-owners who couldn't believe what was happening. Gary had even given Downtown a slot at four pm. The headliner was blues legend Dalton Seaberry.

All home-owners were invited but aside from board members, most stayed away. Many left home for the day. There were two thousand tickets including five hundred drawn by lottery from Gary's fan club. Honore duBlastio spent five hours butchering the hog. They brought in five grills made from fifty-gallon oil drums and filled the patio with buffet tables. Dozens of trash barrels dotted the property all the way to the end of the pier. The swimming pool was off limits due to liability issues. A long line began forming outside the gates at six in the morning, with families spreading blankets by the side of the road, picnicking, tossing Frisbees and fishing in the drainage ditch. The doors opened at eleven.

Pincus put up two drones, operating both with a modified gaming yoke. Muriel pointed her Fonebone.

"What's going on here, Gary Duba?"

"This here's the barbecue I promised the home-owners' association. I told 'em I'd stop that house-wrecking hog and I done it. We got enough hog to feed five hundred. After that, we got more hog."

"Will we be seein' this on your upcoming Netflix series?"

"You know it, little lady! By the way. If you're looking for a good deal on sit-down mowers, Billy Bob in Turpentine is the man to see."

Gary chopped ribs with his hunga munga. One of his first customers was a man wearing a Mojo Nixon shirt, a five-day stubble, and a Rick Flair tat. "Can I get a picture?"

"Sure! Come on back here!"

Gary posed with the man while his girlfriend, a freckled Fraulein in curlers, snapped the pic. Everybody wanted a picture with Gary and/or Krystal. It was slowing down the line. Marvin Goldblatt came over wearing khakis and a knit tennis shirt.

"Give me the tongs. You should charge for pictures."

"Aw hell no, Marv! I ain't charging for no pictures!"

Gary rinsed the hunga and put it in his backpack, went out front where a line formed for pictures and autographs. He signed a woman's breasts. He signed a baby's bottom. He signed a goat horn. The parking lot was packed. People parked on the grass. Police set up a road block a half mile up to turn people away.

Chopper whup filled the air. A gold helicopter appeared over the trees, heading toward the clubhouse. It settled to earth on fifty yards from the parking lot, the Necroeconomics logo painted on the side. Cops whipped out citation pads. Ken Zohan stepped from the chopper in an iridescent blue suit, blazing white shirt, arrow point collars out, hands raised, teeth gleaming. He signaled for quiet. The chopper cut its engine. Josephine Sherrington stepped out in Monique Lhuillier floating floral V-neck gown.

The crowd rippled.

"Ken Zohan."

"The Necroeconomists are here."

"He's a god!"

"He's a devil!"

"Who cares!"

"They got their meat hooks into my nephew and I didn't see him for two years."

Plenty were eager to touch the holy man. Zohan moved slowly bestowing a touch here, a riddle there. Out came the Fonebones. Over came the cops, clearing a path.

At last Zohan stood face to face. "Brother Gary. I can't tell you how pleased I am to be here."

Gary racked his brain trying to remember if he'd invited Zohan. Blotto. Maybe Krystal.

"Hey, Ken! Glad you could make it."

Zohan touched the straps on Gary's backpack. "Is this a rucksack?"

"I guess you could call it that. Sorta an urban rucksack."

"Rucksacks suck racks. You remember the glamorous Josephine."

"How are ya, Joe?"

Sherrington smiled benignly.

Zohan grabbed Gary's arm. "Perhaps we can talk later."

"Yeah, we'll do that! Go get some ribs. That hog ain't gonna last forever."

Gary signed until two. He would have signed all day, but Krystal put him in a wrist lock and forced him through the clubhouse to the patio where the party was in full swing. Hundreds of people danced to Nature's Toothbrush, which had a four-man horn section. Patrice poked above the crowd like a pop-up groundhog.

Krystal took Gary to a shaded table in the corner where she'd loaded two platters with ribs and potato salad. "Eat."

Gary barely had time to polish off four ribs when Zohan pulled out a chair.

"Brother Gary."

"Cousin Zohan."

"Together we could accomplish great things."

"Like what?"

"Unifying the nation's troubled soul. Helping the less fortunate. Spreading the gospel of Necroeconomics."

"Gospel of Ken Zohan, you mean."

Ken's smile froze. "What do you mean?" "I'm hearing some disturbing reports, Ken. Indentured servants. Sexual exploitation."

Zohan focused to a point. "The church has many enemies, Brother Gary. As I'm sure you're aware, success breeds envy and malice in others. The church maintains high standards. We value ethics above all else. There is no room in the church for that kind of behavior. We vigorously defend our reputation. May I ask where you heard this?"

Gary pointed a rib. "Ain't no secret. *Miami Herald* for starters."

Zohan leaned in. "The *Miami Herald* is a communist hotbed. Most of their reporters matriculated at the University of Moscow. They are a faithless society and have attacked every religion."

"I'm just saying. I'm gonna have to look into this myself. I can't work with sex traffickers."

"Brother Gary, what if I were to tell you that I can prove these allegations wrong? What if some of the most prominent members told you of their experiences?"

"I'll hear 'em."

"But listen. The reason I'm here, your great success! You have accomplished the trifecta! State's biggest python! Plastic Surgeon to the Stars and serial killer Doctor Vanderlay Mukerjee! And now, the biggest feral hog of all time! It was delicious! And the coleslaw!"

"Glad you like it. My man Pincus shot Hogzilla."

"The church has decided to award you with its highest civilian honor, the Golden Hog."

"You need to give it to Pincus."

"Would you and Pincus honor us once more with your presence for the award ceremony? It's slated for Friday at our headquarters in Coopersmith. It will be well worth your while."

"Lemme talk it over with my managers."

"It comes with a fifty-thousand dollar honorarium."

"Like I say, gotta talk to Krystal. I'll letcha know."

"You do that, Brother Gary. And now if you'll excuse me, I see many of our flock here today."

"No shit?"

The band paused. A woman screamed. The crowd on the pier stampeded for land, people falling into the water. The crowd on land stampeded for the parking lot, tipping over chairs and tables. More women screamed. Men shouted. Gary stood.

At first Gary thought it was a gator. What kind of crazy gator headed toward thousands of people on shore? He mistook the nostrils for eyes. The hippo found traction and rose out of the water. It roared.Gary ripped off his backpack and took out the hunga munga.

"COME AT ME, BRO!"

The hippo charged. Gary spun the hunga munga overhead like a giant throwing star. The hippo yawned.

SHLUK

The hunga munga embedded itself on the underside of its jaw. The hippo stopped, shook its head from side to side dislodging the hunga, turned around and went back in the water.

Gary looked up. "What else ya got?"

It was noon Wednesday when Krystal shook Gary awake.

"What?"

"Habib."

She handed him her phone.

"What?"

"Gary, I looked into that parcel of land you wanted me to buy. Feedmore Development bought the land last week. Somehow they got all the permissions and contracts and they started development yesterday."

"What the fuck? Feedmore Development? What they feed?"

"That is the parent corporation of Kensington Gardens. They specialize in building upscale communities. The land you wanted is part of Halcyon Acres, an upscale gated community."

"Fuck! Can't you stop 'em?"

"No. They were real tricky, almost as if they knew someone else was interested."

"They find the Fountain of Youth?"

"I don't know."

"I gotta go, Habib. I gotta stop 'em."

"Gary, I would advise..."

Gary threw on blue jeans, waffle stompers, a black rayon shirt with an embroidered dragon, stuffed a water bottle, a banana, some Reese's Peanut Butter Cups and his hunga munga in his backpack, and ran out the door. Krystal leaned out a second story window.

"Where you goin'?"

"I gotta stop 'em from digging up the Fountain of Youth!"

"What?"

"The Fountain of Youth!"

"Wait for me to take a shower."

"No time!"

He leaped in the old Ford, started the engine and sprayed gravel into the weeds. It was all Gary could do to obey the twenty-five mile an hour speed limit in KG. Old Goldblatt was close to a thrombo already. Once out of the gates he accelerated to sixty until he came to Pearson Road and headed east. An alligator was crossing the road. Gary didn't even slow down. The truck rolled over with a spine-pounding thump.

He took Pearson to Duggan. Massive tire tread lay on the road like an artisan waffle. Up ahead, Gary saw yellow earth moving machines, contractors' pickup trucks, a couple of Harleys, and a silver trailer command center. He stopped behind the last pick up and walked south, passing a food truck. Lizard on A Stick.

Gary went to the window. "Julio, you crazy motherfucker!"

Julio game to the window. "Gary! You want a lizard? On the house."

"Naw, I gotta run. Maybe later. How'd you beat the rap?"

"I called Habib Rodriguez and he got me four hundred and fifty thousand dollars!"

"For what?"

"Violating my civil rights!"

"Gimme five!"

A quarter mile up, a foreman in an orange hardhat bent over the hood of a car, looking at an architectural layout, surrounded by managers, all wearing hard hats and eye-searing green vests. Nobody gave Gary a second glance.

The managers headed out. The supervisor, a Latino with heavy brows and mustache, tired brown eyes and bulbous nose looked up.

"Help you?"

"I'm Gary Duba. I live over there in Kensington Gardens."

"That's one of our sister settlements. I worked on that one. What can I do for you, Mister Duba?"

"Well there's a spring back there, a natural spring, and I just want to make sure you don't accidentally wipe it out."

"We wouldn't do that, Mister Duba. The law is very strict."

"Would you mind if I went back there and took a look?"

The supervisor squinted. "How do I know you?"

"I'm the guy who stopped Plastic Surgeon to the Stars and serial killer Doctor Vanderlay Mukerjee."

"That's right! Good job. I seen him on *Botched*. That's what happened to Mickey Rourke. I'm Sanchez. All right, let's both go. You're gonna have to wear a hard hat."

"No prob."

They walked along a graded dirt road sprouting concrete curbs. Gary unslung his backpack and removed Floyd's location finder. Sanchez stopped a couple times to look at plans and point. They came to the edge of civilization and entered the jungle. Grinding machines up ahead. Dust in the air. Sanchez pulled out a bottle of insect repellent and handed it to Gary.

"Seen any gators?"

"Not yet. A lot of this area was dredged during the seventies. Used to be farm."

"Used to be a hog farm."

"How do you know?"

"Oh yeah, used to belong to the Zohan family. You know Ken Zohan? Church of Necroeconomics?"

"That guy."

"His old man farmed hogs, right here. Some people think Hogzilla was the great, great, great, great grandson of hogs that got loose Them big ones'll live fourteen, fifteen years."

"How do you know?"

"Grew up in the swamp. We used to shoot 'em for food. In fact, I wrote a song about it. 'Born in a trailer park in Turpentine...'"

"What do you know about Zohan?"

"Not much. Met him a couple times. He keeps sucking up to me. Makes me wonder. He don't know me but he wants to be my best friend. I hear shit. What do you know about him?"

"I know my sister fell for that shit and we didn't see her for four years. Finally, she comes to us crying with black eye and a broken nose. Treated her like a slave, fed her Spaghetti-Os, had her scrubbin' floors, painting rooms, ten-hour days. Never let her alone. One day on a shopping trip to Costco she ran way, out through the warehouse and out the back. Came back after dark. We couldn't believe it. When she left, she was a beautiful young lady. When she returned she looked like a whipped dog. Then they started hassling her over the internet, said if she goes to the police or something, they're not only coming after her, they're coming after her family."

"No shit."

"Yeah. I went over there but they wouldn't let me in. I guess I got a little hot. They called the cops and they arrested me for public menacing. They dropped it, but I got the message. The church too big to fuck with."

"Put your gear away, put your fear away," Gary said.

"Nictating membranes make dictating brain stems."

Flashes of yellow through the trees as bulldozers shifted the earth. Gary looked at his Garmin GPS and got a sick feeling in the pit of his stomach. They stepped out of the woods onto a chewed up shoulder, fresh white cement, hot blacktop still moist. Gary looked at the street and back to his Garmin.

"It was there," he said. "It was right there."

"Where?"

"Right where you put that intersection. You didn't see it? Nobody saw that fountain? You had to see it. It was right in the middle of this weird black rock."

"No way, Mister Duba. These workers have strict orders to report every anomaly, potential hazard, or natural phenomenon. I would have heard about it."

They stood for a moment while the machines roared, filling the air with dust. Sanchez glanced over. Tears ran down Gary's cheeks. Sanchez turned away.

62 | THE GOLDEN HOG

The Church of Necroeconomics is proud to announce a special ceremony to honor Mr. Gary Duba and Mr. Irving Pincus, for their heroic efforts in stopping the monster known as Hogzilla, with the Holy Hog, its highest civilian award.

Wombat Supreme Kenneth Zohan will award Mr. Duba and Mr. Pincus the Holy Hog in a special ceremony at Church World Headquarters in Coopersmith, at one p.m. on Friday, February 9. Your attendance is requested. Formal wear is encouraged.

Previous winners have included State Supreme Court Justice Wither Weatherby, Signer For the Hearing Impaired Marsupial Marceau, and Academy Award winning actors Sean Sheen and Paulina Perestroika.

Gary and Krystal got out of their pickup in front of the church, where a valet gave them a ticket. A crowd of press and church faithful cheered and applauded at the sight of Gary in a tuxedo and Krystal in an ecru Stella McCartney Lurx knit midi. Earl was there to greet them.

"Good to see you again, Mister Duba!"

"Call me Gary, wouldja? And this is Krystal."

"Big fan, Missus Duba."

"You can call me Krystal. Just don't call me, you know."

Earl put a finger to his lips. "My lips are sealed. Follow me please. I have orders to whisk you straight to the top."

The lobby was jammed with swells, liveried bartenders dispensing drinks. Groups of journalists clustered with their boom mics and cameras. There were waiting lines at each of the four public elevators. Earl escorted them to the executive elevator in the back and they rode up to the Grand Ballroom, where two thousand people were seated. Floyd, Ginger, Habib and Miss Tropicana Gardens, Jen and Wilbur, Major and Daphne, Krystal's mother Trixie and her boyfriend Stanton, and Patrice and Roberto.

Spontaneous applause broke out as Gary and Krystal mounted the podium, the image of Gary and Pincus standing with feet on Hogzilla on the screen behind them. Zohan greeted them warmly, pointed to two chairs at the purple curtain facing the audience. Also seated: Governor John Chickenlooper and First Lady Simone, actors Sean Sheen, Paulina Perestroika, and Rene Welldigger, and master chef Honore duBlastio.

"Pincus couldn't make it," Gary said. "The chief rabbi nixed it."

"I'm sorry to hear that. I will reach out to the rabbi after the ceremony."

At one, Zohan took the podium and Marsupial Marceau

took his place to the side, wearing black and white tux and white mime paint. The huge auditorium hushed. "Amos Moses" came over the speakers and faded to silence.

"My friends, Necroeconomists, members of the press, distinguished clergy."

Marsupial Marceau went into overdrive.

"We have a saying. Give a man a fish and you feed him for a day. Give a man a thousand-pound feral hog and you feed the whole neighborhood! For too long, we Floridians have been complacent in the face of nature's wrath. Herpes-ridden monkeys. The seven hundred-pound Mekong catfish. Burmese pythons. Feral hogs. One man has done more to raise awareness of these threats than any other. One man, who gives and gives! Gary Duba rose from humble beginnings to become a symbol of hope for humble beginnings everywhere!"

"Last year, when Turpentine awarded him the Key to the City for stopping Plastic Surgeon to the Stars and serial killer Doctor Vanderlay Mukerjee, we thought surely, this will be his career highlight. How can he possibly top this? Well now we know! The feral hog has been among us since before Florida was a state. The Spanish introduced pigs into the new world, never imagining that these beasts would escape and grow to monstrous proportions!"

"We all know how Hogzilla roamed the hinterlands, turning multi-million-dollar homes into kindling. What is less well known is how Hogzilla routinely savaged the crops of hard-working tobacco and sugar cane farmers, turned migrant camps into desolate wastelands, and otherwise preyed on traditionally marginalized peoples. How many of you know that Hogzilla rampaged through Gibsonton, destroying the winter homes of hundreds of carnival workers including those afflicted with dwarfism, acromegaly, and conjoined twins? How many know how Hogzilla selfishly ate an entire year's supply of feed for the critically endangered sideheel newt?

"Most recently, Hogzilla targeted the upscale community of Kensington Gardens. When my dear friend Gary Duba moved in last year, it was known as Turpentine Acres and he was the only resident. But just because Gary, who worked as a roofer, was surrounded by executives, captains of industry, and pro golfers, they were his neighbors, and when the need arose, Gary answered!"

"And now, to the unanimous acclaim of every right-thinking Floridian, I present him with our highest civilian honor, the Golden Hog! Come up here, Gary!"

Gary rose to riotous applause. Zohan held the golden hog overhead. It was the size of a football and weighed fifteen pounds, engraved with GARY DUBA—GOLDEN HOG AWARD WINNER. Gary accepted the hog, tucked it under his arm and struck a running back pose. Four million people watched on the Necroeconomics Channel. Zohan gestured toward the podium and sat with his back to the curtain.

"WEEEEEE doggies! The Lord warned us about worshiping the golden calf, but he didn't say nothing bout the pig! Truth is, 'twas Pincus shot the hog! The only reason he ain't here, the head rabbi nixed it on accounta you're not supposed to worship a golden image. Pincus is my go-to guy when it comes to tracking pigs. He pointed the way. And when push came to shove, Pincus grabbed my Mossberg for the first time in his life and drilled that porker through the eye. Then he shot an alligator, just for good measure."

Marsupial Marceau jived and shimmied, hands flying.

"My father never did make a million or drive around in a fancy car, but he taught me the value of hard work, honesty and character. He taught me how to hunt. We practically lived off wild hog when I was growing up. In fact, I wrote a song about it."

Gary pointed to Muriel Martinez waiting at the sound board and Toby Keith sang "Kang of the Everglades", which faded out after the first stanza leaving visitors bewildered.

"I couldn't have done it without the love and support of my wife Krystal. Some of you know her as Steely Danielle. Some of you know her as the Black Dildo! But to me she's just a girl who can wrap her ankles around the back of her neck. I also want to thank my partner Floyd Belmont! You got varmints you call Floyd. It's Belmont Holistic Pest Solutions now. He don't use no strychnine or shit like that."

"I caught the biggest python in state history. I stopped Plastic Surgeon to the Stars and serial killer Doctor Vanderlay Mukerjee. Most of you know I turned that hippo around last weekend with my hunga munga. You want one, you go see my man Downtown Brown. That's hungamunga.com."

"Y'all tune into the *Gary Duba Show* on Rustix in September, you'll see what I'm talking about. This here gold pig's going right up there next to the Turpentine Key to the City.

I appreciate the honor, and I understand you're all waiting to get shit-faced and party. Coupla plugs here. Lizard on A Stick truck right down the street. Y'all go say hey to my friend Julio and try some of that there lizard. It's almost as good as barbecued hog. And if you're looking to pick up some hardware, check out Billy Bob's Pawn Shop in Turpentine. He's got a wide collection of handguns, rifles, and shotguns. Hell, I think he even got a mortar in there somewhere, you ask him about it. And finally, if you get your tit in a wringer, you call The Long Arm, my friend and benefactor Habib Rodriguez. I reckon that's it. Let's party!"

While the crowd and press dispersed, Gary rode with Zohan and Josephine to the top floor, where the church laid out a buffet with roast beef, stuffing, crab claws, quinoa, ancient grains, kale, bean sprouts and truffles. Gary looked around. With the exception of his friends, it was all Church hierarchy. Wombat Supreme, lesser wombats and celebrities.

Krystal took the Golden Hog. "Omma put this in the truck. I'll be waiting out front with the engine running. You do what you gotta do."

Gary waited until everybody was sloshed. He set a crystal wineglass on the rosewood table and ran his finger around the rim making a ringing noise. Everybody stopped talking and looked at him.

"Hey y'all, I hate to be a party pooper, but I been hearing some disturbing shit. Shit about this here church."

Ken Zohan looked at him with death in his eyes. Behind him, Marsupial Marceau morphed into an accusatory angle.

"Forced labor. Sex trafficking. Pedalphilia. Anybody raises a stink, the church sics their army of flying monkeys, sock puppets and talking heads on 'em. Ain't saying it's anyone's fault, although it is. You want this here church to survive you got to make some changes. Some changes right at the top. Lemme introduce the new Wombat Supreme."

The double doors to the great room swiveled silently open to admit Tallywhacker.

"Ladies and gentlemen," boomed from his hindquarters, "It is with the greatest humility that I accept this challenge. I want to thank Ken Zohan for creating this opportunity..."

"THAT'S IT!" Ken Zohan yelled. "That's enough. We're shutting down. Everybody out. The party's over. And Duba, you dumb redneck, you can take your talking buffalo with you. And I want that Golden Hog back. I offered you everything and this is how you repay me?"

Paulina Perestroika looked at Zohan quizzically. "Ken, I've heard those rumors too. I must confess, I've been struggling with my faith for a while now, and this is as good an opportunity as any to tell you that I'm leaving the church."

"PaulEENa! You don't believe him, do you? He used to deal coke! Oh yeah! I got my sources too! Think. Think before you leave. Think of all the church does for you."

Paulina shook her head. "I can't think."

Zohan rounded on Sean Sheen. "What about you. You know what we can do for you."

"I can get my own pussy."

Sensing this was the end, people drifted toward the exit.

Even Earl slipped away. Zohan rushed out of the room into his private quarters.

"As your new Wombat Supreme," Tallywhacker said, "I will devote church assets toward helping the poor. My first official act will be donating one hundred thousand dollars to the Nuns of Gavarone Homeless Shelter in West Palm Beach."

"Wait a minute!" Zohan's gormless sidekick chirped. "There are rules we have to follow! There are procedures! A mechanical bull can't just declare himself Wombat Supreme! He's not even a member!"

"If you'll check the registry," Tallywhacker said smoothly, "you'll find that I've been a member in good standing since Nineteen eighty. Henceforth, there will be no restrictions on members' movements. There will be no work requirements. The church is fabulously wealthy. We will hire whatever workers we need. There will be no more required tithing. Every member at Worker Bee and below will receive a ten-thousand-dollar gift."

Muttering, boos, cursing.

"He's giving our money away!'

"This is not the way of the wombat!"

"I am also ordering our lawyers to stop harassing former members who have quit the church, and I am instructing the IRS to lift our religious exemption. You cannot worship a golden hog and call yourself a real religion."

Screams, gasps, pounding.

Zohan burst back into the room holding an AR15. Women screamed; men fainted. Gary cautiously edged behind

Tallywhacker.

"It was my dream for Doctor Vanderlay Mukerjee to join the church. I had been courting him for months. And you killed him. You killed my dream."

"They arrested Muk for murder! I had nothing to do with that."

"It was my dream to lead the church to heretofore unprecedented heights, and pass it on to my unborn child. You murdered my dream!"

Zohan brought the rifle to his shoulder and squeezed the trigger. Nada. He thumbed the safety and flying lead filled the room, pinging off Tallywhacker, shattering windows and sculpture, laying waste thousand-dollar bottles of wine. People dove behind the furniture, to the floor, into the corridors, scrunched down behind the rolling bars. The painting of Nebudchadnezzar fell off the wall.

"Dance, Tallywhacker, dance!" Gary said.

Tallywhacker lowered its mounted buffalo head and charged, butting Zohan in the midriff and bouncing him off the wall. Zohan slumped to the floor.

People funneled down the fire escapes like coal in a chute. By the time Gary's hearing returned to normal, only he, Tallywhacker, and Zohan's body remained.

"Gary."

"What?"

"What if they arrest me for murder?"

"Murder? They're gonna give you the key to the city! That nut opened up on a room full of people."

"I feel bad. I stole his dreams and now I'm stealing his church."

"Bullshit!"

"I've never killed a man before, Gary. Oh, I've read about it. I've seen it, but now I feel really bad. I broke the Laws of Robotics."

'In self-defense! You saved peoples' lives!"

"Gary, I'm considering ending it all. I could uncouple. I could drop my various parts and shut down my brain. I could become the inert mass of steel Bongo Box always wanted."

Gary put his arms over Tallywhacker's shoulders. "Don't feel bad, buddy! I woulda done the same thing."

"I'm sorry, Gary. My mind is made up. I broke the Laws of Robotics. I must dismantle."

"Now just hang on there. What if I was to get Zohan up and running?"

"Oh Gary. That's absurd. Look at him. He's a broken thing of flesh now."

"Well just hang on thar, I believe I got just the thing."

Gary opened his backpack and removed one of the waterbottles he'd filled from the Fountain of Youth. He sat and put the dead man's head in his lap.

"Oh, Gary."

Gary dribbled water into Zohan's open mouth, running over his lips, down his neck, into his shirt. It seeped into Gary's pants. Gary kept pouring. Tallywhacker sadly shook its head.

Zohan coughed. Zohan blinked, sat, looked around. Gary gave him a hand and he struggled to his feet, touching his middle.

"What happened?"

"You don't remember?"

"No. We were all having a good time."

"You tried to kill me."

A shock of recognition rippled across Zohan's face. He reddened, then blanched.

"By the way. Tallywhacker here's taken over the church. He's now Wombat Supreme."

"Fine. Just give me a few days to clean out my stuff. I've always wanted to sail to Australia."

Tallywhacker bowed its head. "I accept this honor with the utmost humility."

64 | WHAT ELSE YA GOT?

NECROECONOMICS EXPOSED! SEX SLAVES! SWEAT-SHOP CONDITIONS! ANIMAL SACRIFICE!
ROBOT BULL ASSUMES HEAD OF CHURCH
Tallywhacker assures followers he is not possessed by aliens.

It was as if journalists had just been waiting for a sign that it was okay to investigate. And now they had it. Someone nominated Gary for a Nobel Peace Prize. He appeared on the cover of the few magazines still publishing and ruled the internet like King Tiger. When the police finally let him go, it was late in the day and Krystal was waiting.

"Man, I don't want to go back to Kensington Gardens. It's gonna be a zoo, we got to sleep in the garage, and Goldblatt's gonna read us the riot act."

"We can go to a motel."

"Yeah, let's do that. Let's go to the Lamplighter."

They drove to Turpentine, checked in, and walked down

the street to Los Tres Amigos for dinner. The manager was effusive.

"Mister Duba! So good to see you again!"

"Yeah, thanks, Eduardo. Shouldn't be any problem now that all the Zohans been cleared out. Here. I got your knife back."

"Everything is on the house tonight. What would you like to drink?"

They ordered margaritas. While they were drinking and looking at the menu, Larry and Regan came in, Larry in a loud Hawaiian shirt, baggy shorts and flip flops, and Regan in pedal pushers and a Dolphins cap with her long black ponytail tucked through the gap in back. They bee-lined toward Gary and Krystal.

"Smashing, old chap!" Larry gushed. "Saw your press conference. By gadfry, I wish I had your presence!'

"Siddown, you two. Didja get set up?"

Regan crossed her arms and looked up until Larry pulled out her chair.

"We're rethinking this whole swamp business. It's not what I expected."

"You're outta the limelight, aintcha? Ain't that what you wanted?"

"Not me," Regan pouted. "Larry. Well I have a career. I can't just disappear into the swamp."

"Whaddaya do?" Krystal said.

"I'm an actress. I was in that Entyvio commercial, and I recently starred in a Descovy ad."

"Hey, we'll look for 'em! Can you sing? You want to be

on my show?"

"What show?"

"The *Gary Duba Show*."

"So kind of you to ask, but I'm shooting for a major role in the next Marvel movie. They're considering me for Dazzler."

"They're gonna reboot Dazzler? Hell yeah!"

"My agent wants to fly me out to Hollywood next week for a screen test. I told them I don't do screen tests, but I'm considering this one. Sean Sheen's in it."

The waiter brought Larry a glass of Glenmorangie, and Regan a Far Niente Chardonnay. "We wonder if you'd have any interest in taking over our trailer payments. It turns out we're not cut out for swamp living."

"Country living's more our style," Regan said.

Gary and Krystal exchanged glances. "Wahl, let's go back after dinner and take a look."

"Dinner's on me, by the way," Larry said.

"You're too late. Eduardo's got this one."

"Who is Eduardo?" Regan said with a hint of disdain.

Gary pointed to the manager. A strolling mariachi band entered the patio. Guitar, bass, trumpet. They serenaded the table with "La Cucaracha".

"That's the palmetto bug song," Gary explained.

"But why don't you call them cock—" That was far as Regan got before Gary leaned over and put a finger to her lips.

"We don't say that down here. It's bad luck."

The mariachi band did a short Chicago tribute including "25 or 6 to Four" and "Questions One and Two".

After dinner, Gary and Krystal followed Larry and Regan's Mercedes past the Wokenoki Trailer Park to the end of Partridge Way. Larry got out to unlock the chain. A new double-wide Timber Ridge perched proudly on pillars.

"It has four bedrooms and two baths," Larry said. "We've tried to decorate in the regional style."

They went up three steps into the deluxe double-wide. Gay throw rugs lay on the linoleum floor. A new Barcalounger and a Regency sectional sat in the living room facing the fifty-five-inch flat screen television. A Queen Ann sideboard held over a hundred Hummel figurines. On the wall was Steve Rude's black velvet Elvis.

"Ho shit! I used to own that! Where'd you get it?"

"We took your advice and went to Billy Bob's."

Gary put his arm around Krystal. "Y'know, this really is more our style than yours. If Hogzilla hadn't flattened our house, I'd consider a straight up trade! What's the note on this place?"

"I'd have to look," Larry said.

"One hundred and ten thousand and eleven, and fifty-nine cents," Regan said.

"Well hell. We can swing that! Put 'er there! You gotcher self a deal!"

They shook hands. Larry brought out a bottle of Balvenie. Regan brought crystal goblets from the kitchen. Gary dipped into the pocket of his tux and pulled out a bindle.

"Anybody need a snort?"

"Put that away!" Krystal said. "These people don't do blow."

"You know, old chap, if it's not too much trouble, Regan and I could load what we need overnight into the Mercedes and depart within the hour. Can you recommend a good motel?"

"We like the Lamplighter in Turpentine. In fact, we're stayin' there now."

Regan put her hand on Gary's sleeve. "I believe I'll take a snort."

They were gone within the hour, leaving Gary and Krystal back where they started, except the trailer was a lot newer and everything worked. Gary checked both bathrooms. No snake. It was just a matter of time. They went out on the deck.

"This is where it all started, the night you phoned to get me out of jail."

Krystal took his hand. "It's a beautiful night. Let's go sit at the end of the dock."

Hand in hand, they walked to the end of the dock where the *Swamp Pussy* was tied, covered with a tarp. They sat on a newly installed bench with a bronze memorial plaque: In loving memory, the Duke of Westchester, 1939 - 2019.

"Born in a trailer park in Turpentine," Gary softly sang.

The *Swamp Pussy* smashed into the pier nearly knocking them over.

"What the fuck!"

"There's something out there," Krystal said.

"Come with me. Ahm getting my magnum. I'm about fed up with being a punching boy for every gator, hog, and snake in Florida! Ah don't care what it is!"

"Go get it, big daddy!"

Gary hot stepped to the truck and took the pistol and a flashlight out of the glove compartment. Krystal walked back with him. "Now you don't got to come, little mama. If I don't come out on top, somebody's gonna have to let our fans know."

"That's bullshit and you know it. Ain't a critter alive that can beat you in a fair fight!"

Gary perched at the edge of the pier, gripping the pistol and flashlight together. "Show yerself, whatever the hell you are!"

An eight hundred-pound Mekong catfish slammed into the pier, rolled on its side and stared up. "Hang on while I get my hunga munga."

A LOOK AT BIKER—BIKER 1 BY MIKE BARON

MASTER OF THE ACTION ADVENTURE GENRE, MIKE BARON DELIVERS THE FIRST BOOK IN THE INTOXICATING BIKER SERIES.

Josh Pratt is an ex-con turned private investigator. Ginger Munz, a woman dying of cancer hires him to find the son she lost as a baby. The child's father is a sadistic sociopath named Moon who has vowed to kill her and Josh's girlfriend Cass, for ratting him out. The trail leads to the Sturgis Motorcycle Rally and west into no-man's land where Josh learns the monstrous fate of the stolen child.

Josh is the BIKER, caught up in a race for survival against a human monster on the road between heaven and hell at the end of which lies either salvation or damnation.

Baron spins a tale of unrelenting suspense and horror that moves across his narrative landscape like the roar of a chopper's engine.

AVAILABLE NOW ON AMAZON

ABOUT THE AUTHOR

Mike Baron is the creator of Nexus (with artist Steve Rude) and Badger two of the longest lasting independent superhero comics. Nexus is about a cosmic avenger 500 years in the future. Badger, about a multiple personality one of whom is a costumed crime fighter. First/Devils Due is publishing all new Badger stories. Baron has won two Eisners and an Inkpot award and written The Punisher, Flash, Deadman and Star Wars among many other titles.

Baron has published ten novels that span a variety of topics. They have satanic rock bands, biker zombies, spontaneous human combustion, ghosts, and overall hard-boiled crimes.

Mike Baron has written for The Boston Phoenix, Boston Globe, Oui, Fusion, Creem, Isthmus, Front Page Mag, and Ellery Queen's Mystery Magazine.